MR. BRITLING SEES IT THROUGH

MR. BRITLING
SEES IT THROUGH

by
H. G. Wells

CASEMATE
uk
Oxford & Philadelphia

Published in Great Britain and
the United States of America in 2016 by
CASEMATE PUBLISHERS
10 Hythe Bridge Street, Oxford OX1 2EW, UK

and

1950 Lawrence Road, Havertown, PA 19083, USA

© Casemate Publishers 2016

Paperback Edition: ISBN 978-1-61200-415-0
Digital Edition: ISBN 978-1-61200-416-7 (epub)

A CIP record for this book is available from the British Library

Printed in the Czech Republic by FINIDR

For a complete list of Casemate titles, please contact:

CASEMATE PUBLISHERS (UK)
Telephone (01865) 241249
Fax (01865) 794449
Email: casemate-uk@casematepublishers.co.uk
www.casematepublishers.co.uk

CASEMATE PUBLISHERS (US)
Telephone (610) 853-9131
Fax (610) 853-9146
Email: casemate@casematepublishing.com
www.casematepublishing.com

CONTENTS

BOOK I

MATCHING'S EASY AT EASE

BOOK II

MATCHING'S EASY AT WAR

BOOK III

THE TESTAMENT OF MATCHING'S EASY

BOOK I

MATCHING'S EASY AT EASE

CHAPTER THE FIRST

MR. DIRECK VISITS MR. BRITLING

§ 1

I⊤ was the sixth day of Mr. Direck's first visit to England, and he was at his acutest perception of differences. He found England in every way gratifying and satisfactory, and more of a contrast with things American than he had ever dared to hope.

He had promised himself this visit for many years, but being of a sunny rather than energetic temperament—though he firmly believed himself to be a reservoir of clear-sighted American energy—he had allowed all sorts of things, and more particularly the uncertainties of Miss Mamie Nelson, to keep him back. But now there were no more uncertainties about Miss Mamie Nelson, and Mr. Direck had come over to England just to convince himself and everybody else that there were other interests in life for him than Mamie. . . .

And also, he wanted to see the old country from which his maternal grandmother had sprung. Wasn't there even now in his bedroom in New York a water-colour of Market Saffron church, where the dear old lady had been confirmed? And generally he wanted to see Europe. As an interesting side-show to the excursion he hoped, in his capacity of the rather underworked and rather oversalaried secretary of the Massachusetts Society for the Study of Contemporary Thought, to discuss certain agreeable possibilities with Mr. Britling, who lived at Matching's Easy.

Mr. Direck was a type of man not uncommon in America. He was very much after the fashion of that clean and pleasant-looking person one sees in the advertisements in American magazines, that agreeable person who smiles and says, "Good, it's the Fizgig Brand," or "Yes, it's a Wilkins, and that's the Best," or "My shirt-front never rucks; it's a Chesson." But now he was saying, still with the same firm smile, "Good. It's English." He was pleased by every unlikeness to things American, by every item he could hail as characteristic; in the train to London he had laughed aloud with pleasure at the checker-board of little fields upon the hills of Cheshire, he had chuckled to find himself in a compartment without a corridor; he had tipped the polite yet kindly guard magnificently, after doubting for a moment whether he ought to tip him at all, and he had gone about his hotel in London saying "Lordy! Lordy! My *word!*" in a kind of ecstasy, verifying the delightful absence of telephone, of steam-heat, of any dependent bathroom. At breakfast the waiter (out of Dickens, it seemed) had refused to know what "cereals" were, and had given him his egg in a china egg-cup such as you see in the pictures in *Punch*. The Thames, when he sallied out to see it, had been too good to be true, the smallest thing in rivers he had ever seen, and he had had to restrain himself from affecting a marked accent and accosting some passer-by with the question, "Say! But is this little wet ditch here the Historical River Thames?"

In America, it must be explained, Mr. Direck spoke a very good and careful English indeed, but he now found the utmost difficulty in controlling his impulse to use a high-pitched nasal drone and indulge in dry "Americanisms" and poker metaphors upon all occasions. When people asked him questions he wanted to say "Yep" or "Sure," words he would no more have used in America than he could have used a bowie-knife. But he had a sense of *rôle*. He wanted to be visibly and audibly America eye-witnessing. He wanted to be just exactly what he supposed an Englishman would expect him to be. At any rate, his clothes had been made by a strongly American New York tailor, and upon the strength of them a taxi-man had assumed politely but firmly that the shillings on his taximeter were dollars, an incident that helped greatly to sustain the effect of Mr. Direck, in Mr. Direck's mind, as something standing out with an almost representative clearness against the English scene. . . . So much so that the taxi-man got the dollars. . . .

Because all the time he had been coming over he had dreaded that it wasn't true, that England was a legend, that London would turn out to be just another thundering great New York, and the English exactly like New Englanders. . . .

§ 2

And now here he was on the branch line of the little old Great Eastern Railway, on his way to Matching's Easy in Essex, and he was suddenly in the heart of Washington Irving's England.

Washington Irving's England! Indeed it was. He couldn't sit still and just peep at it, he had to stand up in the little compartment and stick his large firm-featured, kindly countenance out of the window as if he greeted it. The country under the June sunshine was neat and bright as an old-world garden, with little fields of corn surrounded by dogrose hedges, and woods and small rushy pastures of an infinite tidiness. He had seen a real deer park, it had rather tumble-down iron gates between its shield-surmounted pillars, and in the distance, beyond all question, was Bracebridge Hall nestling among great trees. He had seen thatched and timbered cottages, and half-a-dozen inns with creaking signs. He had seen a fat vicar driving himself along

11

a grassy lane in a governess cart drawn by a fat grey pony. It wasn't like any reality he had ever known. It was like travelling in literature.

Mr. Britling's address was the Dower House, and it was, Mr. Britling's note had explained, on the farther edge of the park at Claverings. Claverings! The very name for some stately home of England. . . .

And yet this was only forty-two miles from London. Surely it brought things within the suburban range. If Matching's Easy were in America, commuters would live there. But in supposing that, Mr. Direck displayed his ignorance of a fact of the greatest importance to all who would understand England. There is a gap in the suburbs of London. The suburbs of London stretch west and south and even west by north, but to the northeastward there are no suburbs; instead there is Essex. Essex is not a suburban county; it is a characteristic and individualised county which wins the heart. Between dear Essex and the centre of things lie two great barriers, the East End of London and Epping Forest. Before a train could get to any villadom with a cargo of season-ticket holders it would have to circle about this rescued woodland and travel for twenty unprofitable miles, and so once you are away from the main Great Eastern lines Essex still lives in the peace of the eighteenth century, and London, the modern Babylon, is, like the stars, just a light in the noctural sky. In Matching's Easy, as Mr. Britling presently explained to Mr. Direck, there are half-a-dozen old people who have never set eyes on London in their lives—and do not want to.

"Aye-ya!"

"Fussin' about thea."

"Mr. Robinson, 'e went to Lon', 'e did. That's 'ow 'e 'urt 'is fut."

Mr. Direck had learned at the main-line junction that he had to tell the guard to stop the train for Matching's Easy; it stopped only "by request"; the thing was getting better and better; and when Mr. Direck seized his grip and got out of the train there was just one little old Essex station-master and porter and signalman and everything, holding a red flag in his hand and talking to Mr. Britling about the cultivation of the sweet peas which glorified the station. And there was the Mr. Britling who was the only item of business and the greatest expectation in Mr. Direck's European journey, and he was quite unlike the portraits Mr. Direck had seen and quite unmistakably Mr. Britling all the same, since there was nobody else upon the platform, and he was advancing with a gesture of welcome.

"Did you ever see such peas, Mr. Dick?" said Mr. Britling by way of introduction.

"My *word!*" said Mr. Direck in a good old Farmer Hayseed kind of voice.

"Aye-ya!" said the station-master in singularly strident tones. "It be a rare year for sweet peas," and then he slammed the door of the carriage in a leisurely manner and did dismissive things with his flag, while the two gentlemen took stock, as people say, of one another.

§ 3

Except in the doubtful instance of Miss Mamie Nelson, Mr. Direck's habit was good fortune. Pleasant things came to him. Such was his position as the salaried secretary of this society of thoughtful Massachusetts business men to which allusion has been made. Its purpose was to bring itself expeditiously into touch with the best thought of the age.

Too busily occupied with practical realities to follow the thought of the age through all its divagations and into all its recesses, these Massachusetts business men had had to consider methods of access more quintessential and nuclear. And they had decided not to hunt out the best thought in its merely germinating stages, but to wait until it had emerged and flowered to some trustworthy recognition, and then, rather than toil through recondite and possibly already reconsidered books and writings generally, to offer an impressive fee to the emerged new thinker, and to invite him to come to them and to lecture to them and to have a conference with them, and to tell them simply, competently and completely at first-hand just all that he was about. To come, in fact, and be himself—in a highly concentrated form. In this way a number of interesting Europeans had been given very pleasant excursions to America, and the society had been able to form very definite opinions upon their teaching. And Mr. Britling was one of the representative thinkers upon which this society had decided to inform itself. It was to broach this invitation and to offer him the impressive honorarium by which the society honoured not only its guests but itself, that Mr. Direck had now come to Matching's Easy. He had already sent Mr. Britling a letter of introduction, not indeed intimating his precise purpose, but mentioning merely a desire to know him, and the letter had been so happily phrased and its writer had left such a memory of pleasant hospitality on Mr. Britling's mind during Mr. Britling's former visit to New York, that it had immediately produced for Mr. Direck an invitation not merely to come and see him but to come and stay over the weekend.

And here they were shaking hands.

Mr. Britling did not look at all as Mr. Direck had expected him to look. He had expected an Englishman in a country costume of golfing tweeds, like the Englishman in country costume one sees in American illustrated stories. Drooping out of the country costume of golfing tweeds, he had expected to see the mildly unhappy face, pensive even to its downcast moustache, with which Mr. Britling's publisher had for some faulty and unfortunate reason familiarised the American public. Instead of this, Mr. Britling was in a miscellaneous costume, and mildness was the last quality one could attribute to him. His moustache, his hair, his eyebrows, bristled; his flaming freckled face seemed about to bristle too. His little hazel eyes came out with a "ping" and looked at Mr. Direck. Mr. Britling was one of a large but still remarkable class of people who seem at the mere approach of photography to change their hair, their clothes, their moral natures. No photographer had ever caught a hint of his essential Britlingness and bristlingness. Only the camera could ever induce Mr. Britling to brush his hair, and for the camera alone did he reserve that expression of submissive martyrdom Mr. Direck knew. And Mr. Direck was altogether unprepared for a certain casualness of costume that sometimes overtook Mr. Britling. He was wearing now a very old blue flannel blazer, no hat, and a pair of knickerbockers, not tweed breeches but tweed knickerbockers of a remarkable bagginess, and made of one of those virtuous socialistic homespun tweeds that drag out into woolly knots and strings wherever there is attrition. His stockings were worsted and wrinkled, and on his feet were those extraordinary slippers of bright-coloured bastlike interwoven material one buys in the north of France. These were purple with a touch of green. He had, in fact, thought of the necessity of meeting Mr. Direck at the station at the very last moment, and had come away from his study in the clothes that had happened to him when he got up. His face wore the amiable expression of a wire-haired terrier disposed to be friendly, and it struck Mr. Direck that for a man of his real intellectual distinction Mr. Britling was unusually short.

For there can be no denying that Mr. Britling was, in a sense, distinguished. The hero and subject of this novel was at its very beginning a distinguished man. He was in the *Who's Who* of two continents. In the last few years he had grown with some rapidity into a writer recognised and welcomed by the more cultivated sections of the American public and even known to a select circle of British readers. To his American discoverers he had first appeared as an essayist, a serious essayist who wrote about æsthetics and Oriental thought and national character and poets and painting. He had come through America some years ago as one of those Kahn scholars, those promising writers and intelligent men endowed by Albert Kahn of Paris, who go about the world nowadays in comfort and consideration as the travelling guests of that original philanthropist—to acquire the international spirit. Previously he had been a critic of art and literature and a writer of thoughtful third leaders in the London *Times*. He had begun with a Pembroke fellowship and a prize poem. He had returned from his world tour to his reflective yet original corner of *The Times*, and to the production of books about national relationships and social psychology that had brought him rapidly into prominence.

His was a naturally irritable mind; this gave him point and passion; and moreover he had a certain obstinate originality and a generous disposition. So that he was always lively, sometimes spacious, and never vile. He loved to write and talk. He talked about everything, he had ideas about everything; he could no more help having ideas about everything than a dog can resist smelling at your heels. He sniffed at the heels of reality. Lots of people found him interesting and stimulating, a few found him seriously exasperating. He had ideas in the utmost profusion about races and empires and social order and political institutions and gardens and automobiles and the future of India and China and æsthetics and America and the education of mankind in general. . . . And all that sort of thing. . . .

Mr. Direck had read a very great deal of all this expressed opiniativeness of Mr. Britling: he found it entertaining and stimulating stuff, and it was with genuine enthusiasm that he had come over to encounter the man himself. On his way across the Atlantic and during the intervening days, he had rehearsed this meeting in varying keys, but always on the supposition that Mr. Britling was a large, quiet, thoughtful sort of man, a man who would, as it were, sit in attentive rows like a public meeting and listen. So Mr. Direck had prepared quite a number of pleasant and attractive openings, and now he felt was the moment for some one of these various simple, memorable utterances. But in none of these forecasts had he reckoned with either the spontaneous activities of Mr. Britling or with the station-master of Matching's Easy. Oblivious of any conversational necessities between Mr. Direck and Mr. Britling, this official now took charge of Mr. Direck's gripsack, and, falling into line with the two gentlemen as they walked towards the exit gate, resumed what was evidently an interrupted discourse upon sweet peas, originally addressed to Mr. Britling.

He was a small, elderly man with a determined-looking face and a sea voice, and it was clear he over-estimated the distance of his hearers.

"Mr. Darling what's head gardener up at Claverings, 'e can't get sweet peas like that, try 'ow 'e will. Tried everything 'e 'as.

Sand ballast, 'e's tried. Seeds same as me. 'E came along 'ere only the other day, 'e did, and 'e says to me, 'e says, 'darned 'f I can see why a station-master should beat a professional gardener at 'is own game,' 'e says, 'but you do. And in your orf time, too, so's to speak,' 'e says. 'I've tried sile,' 'e says——"

"Your first visit to England?" asked Mr. Britling of his guest.

"Absolutely," said Mr. Direck.

"I says to 'im, 'there's one thing you 'aven't tried,' I says," the station-master continued, raising his voice by a Herculean feat still higher.

"I've got a little car outside here," said Mr. Britling. I'm a couple of miles from the station."

"I says to 'im, I says, ''ave you tried the vibration of the trains?' I says. 'That's what you 'aven't tried, Mr. Darling. That's what you *can't* try,' I says. 'But you rest assured that that's the secret of my sweet peas,' I says, 'nothing less and nothing more than the vibration of the trains.'"

Mr. Direck's mind was a little confused by the double nature of the conversation and by the fact that Mr. Britling spoke of a car when he meant an automobile. He handed his ticket mechanically to the station-master, who continued to repeat and endorse his anecdote at the top of his voice as Mr. Britling disposed himself and his guest in the automobile.

"You know you 'aven't 'urt that mud-guard, sir, not the slightest bit that matters," shouted the station-master. "I've been a looking at it—er. It's my fence that's suffered most. And that's only strained the post a lil' bit. Shall I put your bag in behind, sir?"

Mr. Direck assented, and then, after a momentary hesitation, rewarded the station-master's services.

"Ready?" asked Mr. Britling.

"That's all right, sir," the station-master reverberated.

With a rather wide curve Mr. Britling steered his way out of the station into the highroad.

§ 4

And now it seemed was the time for Mr. Direck to make his meditated speeches. But an unexpected complication was to defeat this intention. Mr. Direck perceived almost at once that Mr. Britling was probably driving an automobile for the first or second or at the extremest the third time in his life.

The thing became evident when he struggled to get into the high gear—an attempt that stopped the engine, and it was even more startlingly so when Mr. Britling narrowly missed a collision with a baker's cart at a corner. "I pressed the accelerator," he explained afterwards, "instead of the brake. One does at first. I missed him by less than a foot." The estimate was a generous one. And after that Mr. Direck became too anxious not to distract his host's thoughts to persist with his conversational openings. An attentive silence came upon both gentlemen that was broken presently by a sudden outcry from Mr. Britling and a great noise of tormented gears. "Damn!" cried Mr. Britling, and "How the *devil?*"

Mr. Direck perceived that his host was trying to turn the car into a very beautiful gateway, with gate-houses on either side. Then it was manifest that Mr. Britling had abandoned this idea, and then they came to a stop a dozen yards or so along the main road. "Missed it," said Mr. Britling, and took his hands off the steering-wheel and blew stormily, and then whispered some bars of a fretful air and became still.

"Do we go through those ancient gates?" asked Mr. Direck after a little pause.

Mr. Britling looked over his right shoulder and considered problems of curvature and distance. "I think," he said, "I will go round outside the park. It will take us a little longer, but it will be simpler than backing and manœuvring here now. . . . These electric starters are remarkably convenient things. Otherwise now I should have to get down and wind up the engine."

After that came a corner, the rounding of which seemed to present few difficulties until suddenly Mr. Britling cried out, "Eh! *eh!* EH! Oh, *damn!*"

Then the two gentlemen were sitting side by side in a rather sloping car that had ascended the bank and buried its nose in a hedge of dog-rose and honeysuckle, from which two missel-thrushes, a blackbird and a number of sparrows had made a hurried escape. . . .

§ 5

"Perhaps," said Mr. Britling without assurance, and after a little peaceful pause, "I can reverse out of this."

He seemed to feel some explanation was due to Mr. Direck. "You see, at first—it's perfectly simple—one steers *round* a corner and then one doesn't put the wheels straight again, and so one keeps on going round—more than one meant to. It's the bicycle habit; the bicycle rights itself. One expects a car to do the same thing. It was my fault. The book explains all this question clearly, but just at the moment I forgot."

He reflected and experimented in a way that made the engine scold and fuss. . . .

"You see, she won't budge for the reverse. . . . She's—embedded. . . . Do you mind getting out and turning the wheel back? Then if I reverse, perhaps we'll get a move on. . . ."

Mr. Direck descended, and there were considerable efforts.

"If you'd just grip the spokes. Yes, so. . . . One, Two, Three! . . . No! Well, let's just sit here until somebody comes along to help us. Oh! Somebody will come all right. Won't you get up again?"

And after a reflective moment Mr. Direck resumed his seat beside Mr. Britling. . . .

§ 6

The two gentlemen smiled at each other to dispel any suspicion of discontent.

"My driving leaves something to be desired," said Mr. Britling with an air of frank impartiality. "But I have only just got this car for myself—after some years of hired cars—the sort of lazy arrangement where people supply car, driver, petrol, tires, insurance and everything at so much a month. It bored me abominably. I can't imagine now how I stood it for so long. They sent me down a succession of compact, scornful boys who used to go fast when I wanted to go slow, and slow when I wanted to go fast, and who used to take every corner on the wrong side at top speed, and charge dogs and hens for the sport of it, and all sorts of things like that. They would not even let me choose my roads. I should have got myself a car long ago, and driven it, if it wasn't for that infernal business with a handle one had to do when the engine stopped. But here, you see, is a reasonably cheap car with an electric starter—American, I need scarcely say. And here I am—going at my own pace."

Mr. Direck glanced for a moment at the pretty disorder of the hedge in which they were embedded, and smiled and admitted that it was certainly much more agreeable.

Before he had finished saying as much, Mr. Britling was talking again.

He had a quick and rather jerky way of speaking; he seemed to fire out a thought directly it came into his mind, and he seemed to have a loaded magazine of thoughts in his head. He spoke almost exactly twice as fast as Mr. Direck, clipping his words much more, using much compacter sentences, and generally cutting his corners, and this put Mr. Direck off his game.

That rapid attack while the transatlantic interlocutor is deploying is indeed a not infrequent defect of conversations between Englishmen and Americans. It is a source of many misunderstandings. The two conceptions of conversation differ fundamentally. The English are much less disposed to listen than the Americans; they have not quite the same sense of conversational give and take, and at first they are apt to reduce their visitors to the rôle of auditors wondering when their turn will begin. Their turn never does begin. Mr. Direck, realising this only very gradually, sat deeply in his slanting seat with a half face to his celebrated host and said "Yep" and "Sure" and "That *is* so," in the dry grave tones that he believed an Englishman would naturally expect him to use.

Mr. Britling, from his praise of the enterprise that has at last brought a car he could drive within his reach, went on to that favourite topic of all intelligent Englishmen, the adverse criticism of things British. He pointed out that the central position of the brake and gear levers in his automobile made it extremely easy for the American manufacturer to turn it out either as a left-handed or a right-handed car, and so adapt it either to the Continental or to the British rule of the road. No English cars were so adaptable. We British suffered much from our insular rule of the road, just as we suffered much from our insular weights and measures. But we took a perverse pride in such disadvantages. The irruption of American cars into England was a recent phenomenon, it was another triumph for the tremendous organising ability of the American mind. They were doing with the automobiles what they had done with clocks and watches and rifles, they had standardised and machined wholesale, while the British were still making the things one by one. It was an extraordinary thing that England, which was the originator of the industrial system and the original developer of the division of labour, should have so fallen away from systematised manufacturing. He believed this was largely due to the influence of Oxford and the Established Church. . . .

At this point Mr. Direck was moved by an anecdote. "It will help to illustrate what you are saying, Mr. Britling, about systematic organisation if I tell you a little incident that happened to a friend of mine in Toledo, where they are setting up a big plant with a view to capturing the entire American and European market in the class of the thousand-dollar car——"

"There's no end of such little incidents," said Mr. Britling, cutting in without apparent effort. "You see, we get it on both sides. Our manufacturer class was, of course, originally an insurgent class. It was a class of distended craftsmen. It had the craftsman's natural enterprise and natural radicalism. As soon as it prospered and sent its boys to Oxford it was lost. Our manufacturing class was assimilated in no time to the conservative classes, whose education has always had a mandarin quality—very, very little of it, and very old and choice. In America you have so far had no real conservative class at all. Fortunate continent! You cast out your Tories, and you were left with nothing but Whigs and Radicals. But our peculiar bad luck has been to get a sort of revolutionary who is a Tory mandarin too. Ruskin and Morris, for example, were as reactionary and antiscientific as the dukes and the bishops. Machine haters. Science haters. Rule of Thumbites to the bone. So are our current Socialists. They've filled this country with the idea that the ideal automobile ought to be made entirely by the hand labour of traditional craftsmen, quite individually, out of beaten copper, wrought iron and seasoned oak. All this electric-starter business and this electric-lighting outfit I have here is perfectly hateful to the English mind. . . . It isn't that we are simply backward in these things, we are antagonistic. The British mind has never really tolerated electricity; at least, not that sort of electricity that runs through wires. Too slippery and glib for it. Associates it with Italians and fluency generally, with Volta, Galvani, Marconi and so on. The proper British electricity is that high-grade useless long-sparking stuff you get by turning round a glass machine; stuff we used to call frictional electricity. Keep it in Leyden jars. . . . At Claverings here they still refuse to have electric bells. There was a row when the Solomonsons, who were tenants here for a time, tried to put them in. . . ."

Mr. Direck had followed this cascade of remarks with a patient smile and a slowly nodding head. "What you say," he said, "forms a very marked contrast indeed with the sort of thing that goes on in America. This friend of mine I was speaking of, the one who is connected with an automobile factory in Toledo——"

"Of course," Mr. Britling burst out again, "even conservatism isn't an ultimate thing. After all, we and your enterprising friend at Toledo are very much the same blood. The conservatism, I mean, isn't racial. And our earlier energy shows it isn't in the air or in the soil. England has become unenterprising and sluggish because England has been so prosperous and comfortable. . . ."

"Exactly," said Mr. Direck. "My friend of whom I was telling you was a man named Robinson, which indicates pretty clearly that he was of genuine English stock, and, if I may say so, quite of your build and complexion; racially, I should say, he was, well—very much what you are. . . ."

§ 7

This rally of Mr. Direck's mind was suddenly interrupted.

Mr. Britling stood up, and putting both hands to the sides of his mouth, shouted "Yi-ah! Aye-ya! Thea!" at unseen hearers.

After shouting again several times, it became manifest that he had attracted the attention of two willing but deliberate labouring men. They emerged slowly, first as attentive heads, from the landscape. With their assistance the car was restored to the road again. Mr. Direck assisted manfully, and noted the respect that was given to Mr. Britling, and the shillings that fell to the men, with an intelligent detachment. They touched their hats, they called Mr. Britling "Sir." They examined the car distantly but kindly. "Aint 'urt 'e, not a bit 'e ain't, not reely," said one encouragingly. And indeed except for a slight crumpling of the mud-guard and the detachment of the wire of one of the headlights the automobile was uninjured. Mr. Britling resumed his seat; Mr. Direck gravely and in silence got up beside him. They started with the usual convulsion, as though something had pricked the vehicle unexpectedly and shamefully behind. And from this point Mr. Britling, driving with meticulous care, got home without further mishap, excepting only that he scraped off some of the metal edge of his foot-board against the gate-post of his very agreeable garden.

His family welcomed his safe return, visitor and all, with undisguised relief and admiration. A small boy appeared at the corner of the house, and then disappeared hastily again.

"Daddy's got back all right at last," they heard him shouting to unseen hearers.

§ 8

Mr. Direck, though he was a little incommoded by the suppression of his story about Robinson—for when he had begun a thing he liked to finish it—found Mr. Britling's household at once thoroughly British, quite un-American and a little difficult to follow. It had a quality that at first he could not define at all. Compared with anything he had ever seen in his life before it struck him as being—he found the word at last—sketchy. For instance, he was introduced to nobody except his hostess, and she was indicated to him by a mere wave of Mr. Britling's hand. "That's Edith," he said, and returned at once to his car to put it away. Mrs. Britling was a tall, freckled woman with pretty bright brown hair and preoccupied brown eyes. She welcomed him with a handshake, and then a wonderful English parlour-maid—she at least was according to expectations—took his gripsack and guided him to his room. "Lunch, sir," she said, "is outside," and closed the door and left him to that and a towel-covered can of hot water.

It was a square-looking old red-brick house he had come to, very handsome in a simple Georgian fashion, with a broad lawn before it and great blue cedar-trees, and a drive that came frankly up to the front door and then went off with Mr. Britling and the car round to unknown regions at the back. The centre of the house was a big airy hall, oak-panelled, warmed in winter only by one large fireplace and abounding in doors which he knew opened into the square separate rooms that England favours. Book-shelves and stuffed birds comforted the landing outside his bedroom. He descended to find the hall occupied by a small bright bristling boy in white flannel shirt and knickerbockers and bare legs and feet. He stood before the vacant open fireplace in an attitude that Mr. Direck knew instantly was also Mr. Britling's. "Lunch is in the garden," the Britling scion proclaimed, "and I've got to fetch you. And, I say! is it true? Are you American?"

"Why surely," said Mr. Direck.

"Well, I know some American," said the boy. "I learned it."

"Tell me some," said Mr. Direck, smiling still more amiably.

"Oh! Well—Gol darn you! Ouch. Gee-whizz! Soak him Maud! It's up to you, Duke. . . ."

"Now where did you learn all that?" asked Mr. Direck recovering.

"Out of the Sunday Supplement," said the youthful Britling.

"Why! Then you know all about Buster Brown," said Mr. Direck. "He's Fine—eh?"

The Britling child hated Buster Brown. He regarded Buster Brown as a totally unnecessary infant. He detested the way he wore his hair and the peculiar cut of his knickerbockers and—him. He thought Buster Brown the one drop of paraffin in the otherwise delicious feast of the Sunday Supplement. But he was a diplomatic child.

"I think I like Happy Hooligan better," he said. "And dat ole Maud."

He reflected with joyful eyes, Buster clean forgotten. "Every week," he said, "she kicks some one."

It came to Mr. Direck as a very pleasant discovery that a British infant could find a common ground with the small people at home in these characteristically American jests. He had never dreamt that the fine wine of Maud and Buster could travel.

"Maud's a treat," said the youthful Britling, relapsing into his native tongue.

Mr. Britling appeared coming to meet them. He was now in a grey flannel suit—he must have jumped into it—and altogether very much tidier. . . .

§ 9

The long narrow table under the big sycamores between the house and the adapted barn that Mr. Direck learned was used for "dancing and all that sort of thing" was covered with a blue linen diaper cloth, and that too surprised him. This was his first meal in a private household, and for obscure reasons he had expected something very stiff and formal with "spotless napery." He had also expected a very stiff and capable service by implacable parlour-maids, and the whole thing indeed highly genteel. But two cheerful women servants appeared from what was presumably the kitchen direction, wheeling a curious wicker erection, which his small guide informed him was called Aunt Clatter—manifestly deservedly—and which bore on its shelves the substance of the meal. And while the maids at this migratory sideboard carved and opened bottles and so forth, the small boy and a slightly larger brother, assisted a little by two young men of no very defined position and relationship, served the company. Mrs. Britling sat at the head of the table, and conversed with Mr. Direck by means of hostess questions and imperfectly accepted answers while she kept a watchful eye on the proceedings.

The composition of the company was a matter for some perplexity to Mr. Direck. Mr. and Mrs. Britling were at either end of the table, that was plain enough. It was also fairly plain that the two bare-footed boys were little Britlings. But beyond this was a cloud of uncertainty. There was a youth perhaps seventeen, much darker than Britling, but with nose and freckles rather like his, who might be an early son or a stepson; he was shock-headed and with that look about his arms and legs that suggests overnight growth; and there was an unmistakable young German, very pink, with close-cropped fair hair, glasses and a panama hat, who was probably the tutor of the younger boys. (Mr. Direck also was wearing his hat, his mind had been filled with an exaggerated idea of the treacheries of the English climate before he left New York. Every one else was hatless.) Finally, before one reached the limits of the explicable there was a pleasant young man with a lot of dark hair and very fine dark blue eyes, whom everybody called "Teddy." For him, Mr. Direck hazarded "secretary."

But in addition to these normal and understandable presences, there was an entirely mysterious pretty young woman in blue linen who sat and smiled next to Mr. Britling, and there was a rather kindred-looking girl with darker hair on the right of Mr. Direck who impressed him at the very outset as being still prettier, and—he didn't quite place her at first—somehow familiar to him; there was a large irrelevant middle-aged lady in black with a gold chain and a tall middle-aged man with an intelligent face, who might be a casual guest; there was an Indian young gentleman faultlessly dressed up to his brown soft linen collar and cuffs, and thereafter an uncontrolled outbreak of fine bronze modelling and abundant fuzzy hair; and there was a very erect and attentive baby of a year or less, sitting up in a perambulator and gesticulating cheerfully to everybody. This baby it was that most troubled the orderly mind of Mr. Direck. The research for its paternity made his conversation with Mrs. Britling almost as disconnected and absent-minded as her conversation with him. It almost certainly wasn't Mrs. Britling's. The girl next to him or the girl next to Mr. Britling or the lady in black might any of them be married, but if so where was the spouse? It seemed improbable that they would wheel out a foundling to lunch. . . .

Realising at last that the problem of relationship must be left to solve itself if he did not want to dissipate and consume his mind entirely, Mr. Direck turned to his hostess, who was enjoying a brief lull in her administrative duties, and told her what a memorable thing the meeting of Mr. Britling in his own home would be in his life, and how very highly America was coming to esteem Mr. Britling and his essays. He found that with a slight change of person, one of his premeditated openings was entirely serviceable here. And he went on to observe that it was novel and entertaining to find Mr. Britling driving his own automobile and to note that it was an automobile of American manufacture. In America they had standardised and systematised the making of such things as automobiles to an extent that would, he thought, be almost startling to Europeans. It was certainly startling to the European manufacturers. In illustration of that he might tell a little story of a friend of his called Robinson—a man who curiously enough in general build and appearance was very reminiscent indeed of Mr. Britling. He had been telling Mr. Britling as much on his way here from the station. His friend was concerned with several others in one of the biggest attacks that had ever been made upon what one might describe in general terms as the thousand-dollar light automobile market. What they said practically was this: This market is a jig-saw puzzle waiting to be put together and made one. We are going to do it. But that was easier to figure out than to do. At the very outset of this attack he and his associates found themselves up against an expected and very difficult proposition. . . .

At first Mrs. Britling had listened to Mr. Direck with an almost undivided attention, but as he had developed his opening the feast upon the blue linen table had passed on to a fresh phrase that demanded more and more of her directive intelligence. The two little boys appeared suddenly at her elbows.

"Shall we take the plates and get the strawberries, Mummy?" they asked simultaneously. Then one of the neat maids in the background had to be called up and instructed in undertones, and Mr. Direck saw that for the present Robinson's illuminating experience was not for her ears. A little baffled, but quite understanding how things were, he turned to his neighbour on his left.

The girl really had an extraordinarily pretty smile, and there was something in her soft bright brown eye—like the movement of some quick little bird. And—she was like somebody he knew! Indeed she was. She was quite ready to be spoken to.

"I was telling Mrs. Britling," said Mr. Direck, "what a very great privilege I esteem it to meet Mr. Britling in this highly familiar way."

"You've not met him before?"

"I missed him by twenty-four hours when he came through Boston on the last occasion. Just twenty-four hours. It was a matter of very great regret to me."

"I wish I'd been paid to travel round the world."

31

"You must write things like Mr. Britling and then Mr. Kahn will send you."

"Don't you think if I promised well?"

"You'd have to write some promissory notes, I think—just to convince him it was all right."

The young lady reflected on Mr. Britling's good fortune.

"He saw India. He saw Japan. He had weeks in Egypt. And he went right across America."

Mr. Direck had already begun on the liner to adapt himself to the hopping inconsecutiveness of English conversation. He made now what he felt was quite a good hop, and he dropped his voice to a confidential undertone. (It was probably Adam in his first conversation with Eve who discovered the pleasantness of dropping into a confidential undertone beside a pretty ear with a pretty wave of hair above it.)

"It was in India, I presume," murmured Mr. Direck, "that Mr. Britling made the acquaintance of the coloured gentleman?"

"Coloured gentleman!" She gave a swift glance down the table as though she expected to see something purple with yellow spots. "Oh, that is one of Mr. Lawrence Carmine's young men!" she explained even more confidentially and with an air of discussing the silver bowl of roses before him. He's a great authority on Indian literature, he belongs to a society for making things pleasant for Indian students in London, and he has them down."

"And Mr. Lawrence Carmine?" he pursued.

Even more intimately and confidentially she indicated Mr. Carmine, as it seemed by a motion of her eyelash.

Mr. Direck prepared to be even more *sotto voce* and to plumb a much profounder mystery. His eye rested on the perambulator; he leaned a little nearer to the ear. . . . But the strawberries interrupted him.

"Strawberries!" said the young lady, and directed his regard to his left shoulder by a movement of her head.

He found one of the boys with a high-piled plate ready to serve him.

And then Mrs. Britling resumed her conversation with him. She was so ignorant, she said, of things American that she did not even know if they had strawberries there. At any rate, here they were at the crest of the season, and in a very good year. And in the rose season too. It was one of the dearest vanities of English people to think their apples and their roses and their strawberries the best in the world.

"And their complexions," said Mr. Direck, over the pyramid of fruit, quite manifestly intending a compliment. So that was all right. . . . But the girl on the left of him was speaking across the table to the German tutor, and did not hear what he had said. So that even if it wasn't very neat it didn't matter. . . .

Then he remembered that she was like that old daguerreotype of a cousin of his grandmother's that he had fallen in love with when he was a boy. It was her smile. Of course! Of course! . . . And he'd sort of adored that portrait. . . . He felt a curious disposition to tell her as much. . . .

"What makes this visit even more interesting if possible to me," he said to Mrs. Britling, "than it would otherwise be is that this Essex country is the country in which my maternal grandmother was raised, and also long way back my mother's father's people. My mother's father's people were very early New England people indeed. . . . Well, no. If I said *Mayflower* it wouldn't be true. But it would approximate. They were Essex Hinkinsons. That's what they were. I must be a good third of me at least Essex. My grandmother was an Essex Corner. I must confess I've some thought——"

"Corner?" said the young lady at his elbow sharply.

"I was telling Mrs. Britling I had some thought——"

"But about those Essex relatives of yours?"

"Well, of finding if they were still about in these parts.... Say! I haven't dropped a brick, have I?"

He looked from one face to another.

"*She's* a Corner," said Mrs. Britling.

"Well," said Mr. Direck, and hesitated for a moment. It was so delightful that one couldn't go on being just discreet. The atmosphere was free and friendly. His intonation disarmed offence. And he gave the young lady the full benefit of a quite expressive eye. "I'm very pleased to meet you, Cousin Corner. How are the old folks at home?"

§ 10

The bright interest of this cousinship helped Mr. Direck more than anything to get the better of his Robinson-anecdote crave, and when presently he found his dialogue with Mr. Britling resumed, he turned at once to this remarkable discovery of his long-lost and indeed hitherto unsuspected relative. "It's an American sort of thing to do, I suppose," he said apologetically, "but I almost thought of going on, on Monday, to Market Saffron, which was the locality of the Hinkinsons, and just looking about at the tombstones in the churchyard for a day or so."

"Very probably," said Mr. Britling, "you'd find something about them in the parish registers. Lots of our registers go back three hundred years or more. I'll drive you over in my lil' old car."

"Oh! I wouldn't put you to that trouble," said Mr. Direck hastily.

34

"It's no trouble. I like the driving. What I have had of it. And while we're at it, we'll come back by Harborough High Oak and look up the Corner pedigree. They're all over that district still. And the road's not really difficult; it's only a bit up and down and roundabout."

"I couldn't think, Mr. Britling, of putting you to that much trouble."

"It's no trouble. I want a day off, and I'm dying to take Gladys——"

"Gladys?" said Mr. Direck with sudden hope.

"That's my name for the lil' car. I'm dying to take her for something like a decent run. I've only had her out four times altogether, and I've not got her up yet to forty miles. Which I'm told she ought to do easily. We'll consider that settled."

For the moment Mr. Direck couldn't think of any further excuse. But it was very clear in his mind that something must happen; he wished he knew of somebody who could send a recall telegram from London, to prevent him committing himself to the casual destinies of Mr. Britling's car again. And then another interest became uppermost in his mind.

"You'd hardly believe me," he said, "if I told you that that Miss Corner of yours has a quite extraordinary resemblance to a miniature I've got away there in America of a cousin of my maternal grandmother's. She seems a very pleasant young lady."

But Mr. Britling supplied no further information about Miss Corner.

"It must be very interesting," he said, "to come over here and pick up these American families of yours on the monuments and tombstones. You know, of course, that district south of Evesham where every church monument bears the stars and stripes, the arms of departed Washingtons. I doubt though if you'd still find the name about there. Nor will you find many Hinkinsons in Market Saffron. But lots of this country here has five or six hundred-year-old families still flourishing. That's why Essex is so much more genuinely Old England than Surrey, say, or Kent. Round here you'll find Corners and Fairlies, and then you get Capels, and then away down towards Dunmow and Braintree Maynards and Byngs. And there are oaks and hornbeams in the park about Claverings that have echoed to the howling of wolves and the clank of men in armour. All the old farms here are moated—because of the wolves. Claverings itself is Tudor, and rather fine too. And the cottages still wear thatch. . . ."

He reflected. "Now if you went south of London instead of northward it's all different. You're in a different period, a different society. You're in London suburbs right down to the sea. You'll find no genuine estates left, not of our deep-rooted familiar sort. You'll find millionaires and that sort of people, sitting in the old places. Surrey is full of rich stockbrokers, company-promoters, bookies, judges, newspaper proprietors. Sort of people who fence the paths across their parks. They do something to the old places—I don't know what they do—but instantly the countryside becomes a villadom. And little sub-estates and red-brick villas and art cottages spring up. And a kind of new, hard neatness. And pneumatic tire and automobile spirit advertisements, great glaring boards by the roadside. And all the poor people are inspected and rushed about until they forget who their grandfathers were. They become villa parasites and odd-job men, and grow basely rich and buy gramophones. This Essex and yonder Surrey are as different as Russia and Germany. But for one American who comes to look at Essex, twenty go to Godalming and Guildford and Dorking and Lewes and Canterbury. Those Surrey people are not properly English at all. They are strenuous. You have to get on or get out. They drill their gardeners, lecture very fast on agricultural efficiency, and have miniature rifle-ranges in every village. It's a county of new notice-boards and barbed-wire fences; there's always a policeman round the corner. They dress for dinner. They dress for everything. If a man gets up in the night to look for a burglar he puts on the correct costume—or doesn't go. They've got a special scientific system for urging on their tramps. And they lock up their churches on a week-day. Half their soil is hard chalk or a rationalistic sand, only suitable for bunkers and villa foundations. And they play golf in a large, expensive, thorough way because it's the thing to do. . . . Now here in Essex we're as lax as the eighteenth century. We hunt in any old clothes. Our soil is a rich succulent clay; it becomes semifluid in winter—when we go about in waders shooting duck. All our finger-posts have been twisted round by facetious men years ago. And we pool our breeds of hens and pigs. Our roses and oaks are wonderful; that alone shows that this is the real England. If I wanted to play golf—which I don't, being a decent Essex man—I should have to motor ten miles into Hertfordshire. And for rheumatics and longevity Surrey can't touch us. I want you to be clear on these points, because they really will affect your impressions of this place. . . . This country is a part of the real England—England outside London and outside manufacturers. It's one with Wessex and Mercia or old Yorkshire—or for the matter of that with Meath or Lothian. And it's the essential England still. . . ."

§ 11

It detracted a little from Mr. Direck's appreciation of this flow of information that it was taking them away from the rest of the company. He wanted to see more of his new-found cousin, and what the baby and the Bengali gentleman—whom manifestly one mustn't call "coloured"—and the large-nosed lady and all the other inexplicables would get up to. Instead of which Mr. Britling was leading him off alone with an air of showing him round the premises, and talking too rapidly and variously for a question to be got in edgeways, much less any broaching of the matter that Mr. Direck had come over to settle.

There was quite a lot of rose-garden, it made the air delicious, and it was full of great tumbling bushes of roses and of neglected standards, and it had a long pergola of creepers and trailers and a great arbour, and underneath over the beds everywhere, contrary to all the rules, the blossom of a multitude of pansies and stock and little trailing plants swarmed and crowded and scrimmaged and drilled and fought great massed attacks. And then Mr. Britling talked their way round a red-walled vegetable-garden with an abundance of fruit-trees, and through a door into a terraced square that had once been a farmyard, outside the converted barn. The barn doors had been replaced by a door-pierced window of glass, and in the middle of the square space a deep tank had been made, full of rain-water, in which Mr. Britling remarked casually that "everybody" bathed when the weather was hot. Thyme and rosemary and such-like sweet-scented things grew on the terrace about the tank, and ten trimmed little trees of *arbor vitae* stood sentinel. Mr. Direck was tantalisingly aware that beyond some lilac-bushes were his new-found cousin and the kindred young woman in blue playing tennis with the Indian and another young man, while whenever it was necessary the large-nosed lady crossed the stage and brooded soothingly over the perambulator. And Mr. Britling, choosing a seat from which Mr. Direck just couldn't look comfortably through the green branches at the flying glimpses of pink and blue and white and brown, continued to talk about England and America in relation to each other and everything else under the sun.

Presently through a distant gate the two small boys were momentarily visible wheeling small but serviceable bicycles, followed after a little interval by the German tutor. Then an enormous grey cat came slowly across the garden court, and sat down to listen respectfully to Mr. Britling. The afternoon sky was an intense blue, with little puff-balls of cloud lined out across it.

Occasionally, from chance remarks of Mr. Britling's, Mr. Direck was led to infer that his first impressions as an American visitor were being related to his host, but as a matter of fact he was permitted to relate nothing; Mr. Britling did all the talking. He sat beside his guest and spirted and played ideas and reflections like a happy fountain in the sunshine.

Mr. Direck sat comfortably, and smoked with quiet appreciation the one after-lunch cigar he allowed himself. At any rate, if he himself felt rather word-bound, the fountain was nimble and entertaining. He listened in a general sort of way to the talk, it was quite impossible to follow it thoughtfully throughout all its chinks and turnings, while his eyes wandered about the garden and went ever and again to the flitting tennis-players beyond the green. It was all very gay and comfortable and complete; it was various and delightful without being in the least *opulent;* that was one of the little secrets America had to learn. It didn't look as though it had been made or bought or cost anything, it looked as though it had happened rather luckily. . . .

Mr. Britling's talk became like a wide stream flowing through Mr. Direck's mind, bearing along momentary impressions and observations, drifting memories of all the crowded English sights and sounds of the last five days, filmy imaginations about ancestral names and pretty cousins, scraps of those prepared conversational openings on Mr. Britling's standing in America, the explanation about the lecture club, the still incompletely forgotten purport of the Robinson anecdote. . . .

"Nobody planned the British estate system, nobody planned the British aristocratic system, nobody planned the confounded constitution, it came about, it was like layer after layer wrapping round an agate, but you see it came about so happily in a way, it so suited the climate and the temperament of our people and our island, it was on the whole so cosy, that our people settled down into it, you can't help settling down into it, they had already settled down by the days of Queen Anne, and Heaven knows if we shall ever really get away again. We're like that little shell the *Lingula*, that is found in the oldest rocks and lives today: it fitted its easy conditions, and it has never modified since. Why should it? It excretes all its disturbing forces. Our younger sons go away and found colonial empires. Our surplus cottage children emigrate to Australia and Canada or migrate into the towns. It doesn't alter *this*. . . ."

§ 12

Mr. Direck's eye had come to rest upon the barn, and its expression changed slowly from lazy appreciation to a brightening intelligence. Suddenly he resolved to say something. He resolved to say it so firmly that he determined to say it even if Mr. Britling went on talking all the time.

"I suppose, Mr. Britling," he said, "this barn here dates from the days of Queen Anne."

"The walls of the yard here are probably earlier: probably monastic. That grey patch in the corner, for example. The barn itself is Georgian."

"And here it is still. And this farmyard, here it is still."

Mr. Britling was for flying off again, but Mr. Direck would not listen; he held on like a man who keeps his grip on a lasso.

"There's one thing I would like to remark about your barn, Mr. Britling, and I might, while I am at it, say the same thing about your farmyard."

Mr. Britling was held. "What's that?" he asked.

"Well," said Mr. Direck, "the point that strikes me most about all this is that that barn isn't a barn any longer, and that this farmyard isn't a farmyard. There isn't any wheat or chaff or anything of that sort in the barn, and there never will be again: there's just a pianola and a dancing floor, and if a cow came into this farmyard everybody in the place would be shooing it out again. They'd regard it as a most unnatural object."

He had a pleasant sense of talking at last. He kept right on. He was moved to a sweeping generalisation.

"You were so good as to ask me, Mr. Britling, a little while ago, what my first impression of England was. Well, Mr. Britling, my first impression of England that seems to me to matter in the least is this: that it looks and feels more like the traditional Old England than any one could possibly have believed, and that in reality it is less like the traditional Old England than any one would ever possibly have imagined."

He was carried on even further. He made a tremendous literary epigram. "I thought," he said, "when I looked out of the train this morning that I had come to the England of Washington Irving. I find it is not even the England of Mrs. Humphry Ward."

CHAPTER THE SECOND

MR. BRITLING CONTINUES HIS EXPOSITION

§ 1

MR. DIRECK found little reason to revise his dictum in the subsequent experiences of the afternoon. Indeed the afternoon and the next day were steadily consistent in confirming what a very good dictum it had been. The scenery was the traditional scenery of England, and all the people seemed quicker, more irresponsible, more chaotic, than any one could have anticipated, and entirely inexplicable by any recognised code of English relationships. . . .

"You think that John Bull is dead and a strange generation is wearing his clothes," said Mr. Britling. "I think you'll find very soon it's the old John Bull. Perhaps not Mrs. Humphry Ward's John Bull, or Mrs. Henry Wood's John Bull, but true essentially to Shakespeare, Fielding, Dickens, Meredith. . . .

"I suppose," he added, "there are changes. There's a new generation grown up. . . ."

He looked at his barn and the swimming-pool. "It's a good point of yours about the barn," he said. "What you say reminds me of that very jolly thing of Kipling's about the old mill-wheel that began by grinding corn and ended by driving dynamos. . . .

"Only I admit that barn doesn't exactly drive a dynamo. . . .

"To be frank, it's just a pleasure barn. . . .

"The country can afford it. . . ."

42

§ 2

He left it at that for the time, but throughout the afternoon Mr. Direck had the gratification of seeing his thought floating round and round in the back-waters of Mr. Britling's mental current. If it didn't itself get into the stream again its reflection at any rate appeared and reappeared. He was taken about with great assiduity throughout the afternoon, and he got no more than occasional glimpses of the rest of the Dower House circle until six o'clock in the evening.

Meanwhile the fountains of Mr. Britling's active and encyclopædic mind played steadily.

He was inordinately proud of England, and had abused her incessantly. He wanted to state England to Mr. Direck as the amiable summation of a grotesque assembly of faults. That was the view into which the comforts and prosperities of his middle age had brought him from a radicalism that had in its earlier stages been angry and bitter. And for Mr. Britling England was "here." Essex was the county he knew. He took Mr. Direck out from his walled garden by a little door into a trim paddock with two white goals. "We play hockey here on Sundays," he said, in a way that gave Mr. Direck no hint of the practically compulsory participation of every visitor to Matching's Easy in this violent and dangerous exercise, and thence they passed by a rich deep lane into a highroad that ran along the edge of the deer park of Claverings. "We will call in on Claverings later," said Mr. Britling. "Lady Homartyn has some people there for the weekend, and you ought to see the sort of thing it is and the sort of people they are. She wanted us to lunch there tomorrow, but I didn't accept that because of our afternoon hockey."

Mr. Direck received this reason uncritically.

The village reminded him of Abbey's pictures. There was an inn with a sign standing out in the road, a painted sign of the Clavering Arms; it had a water-trough (such as Mr. Weller senior ducked the dissenter in) and a green painted table outside its inviting door. There were also a general shop and a number of very pleasant cottages, each marked with the Mainstay crest. All this was grouped about a green with real geese drilling thereon. Mr. Britling conducted his visitor (through a lych-gate) into the churchyard, and there they found mossy, tumble-down tombstones, one with a skull and cross-bones upon it, that went back to the later seventeenth century. In the aisle of the church were three huge hatchments, and there was a side chapel devoted to the Mainstay family and the Barons Homartyn, with a series of monuments that began with painted Tudor effigies and came down to a vast stained-glass window of the vilest commercial Victorian. There were also mediæval brasses of parish priests, and a marble crusader and his lady of some extinguished family which had ruled Matching's Easy before the Mainstays came. And as the two gentlemen emerged from the church they ran against the perfect vicar, Mr. Dimple, ample and genial, with an embracing laugh and an enveloping voice. "Come to see the old country," he said to Mr. Direck. "So Good of you Americans to do that! So Good of you. . . ."

There was some amiable sparring between the worthy man and Mr. Britling about bringing Mr. Direck to church on Sunday morning. "He's terribly Lax," said Mr. Dimple to Mr. Direck, smiling radiantly. "Terribly Lax. But then nowadays Everybody *is* so Lax. And he's very Good to my Coal Club; I don't know what we should do without him. So I just admonish him. And if he doesn't go to church, well, anyhow he doesn't go anywhere else. He may be a poor churchman, but anyhow he's not a dissenter. . . ."

"In England, you see," Mr. Britling remarked, after they had parted from the reverend gentleman, "we have domesticated everything. We have even domesticated God."

For a while Mr. Britling showed Mr. Direck English lanes and then came back along narrow white paths across small fields of rising wheat, to the village and a little gate that led into the park.

"Well," said Mr. Direck, "what you say about domestication does seem to me to be very true indeed. Why! even those clouds up there look as though they had a shepherd and were grazing."

"Ready for shearing almost," said Mr. Britling.

"Indeed," said Mr. Direck, raising his voice a little. "I've seen scarcely anything in England that wasn't domesticated, unless it was some of your back streets in London."

Mr. Britling seemed to reflect for a moment. "They're an excrescence," he said. . . .

§ 3

The park had a trim wildness like nature in an old Italian picture; dappled fallow deer grouped close at hand and looked at the two men fearlessly; the path dropped through oak-trees and some stunted bracken to a little loitering stream, that paused ever and again to play at ponds and waterfalls and bear a fleet of water-lily leaves, and then their way curved round in an indolent sweep towards the cedars and shrubberies of the great house. The house looked low and extensive to an American eye, and its red-brick chimneys rose like infantry in open order along its extended line. There was a glimpse of flower-bright garden and terraces to the right as they came round the corner to the front of the house through a path cut in the laurel bushes.

Mr. Britling had a moment of exposition as they approached the entrance.

"I expect we shall find Philbert from the Home Office—or is it the Local Government Board?—and Sir Thomas Loot, the Treasury man. There may be some other people of that sort, the people we call the Governing Class. Wives also. And I rather fancy the Countess of Frensham is coming, she's strong on the Irish question, and Lady Venetia Trumpington, who they say is a beauty—I've never seen her. It's Lady Homartyn's way to expect me to come in—not that I'm an important item at these weekend social feasts—but she likes to see me on the table—to be nibbled at if any one wants to do so—like the olives and the salted almonds. And she always asks me to lunch on Sunday and I always refuse—because of the hockey. So you see I put in an appearance on the Saturday afternoon. . . ."

They had reached the big doorway.

It opened into a large cool hall adorned with the heads of hippopotami and rhinoceroses and a stuffed lion, and furnished chiefly with a vast table on which hats and sticks and newspapers were littered. A man servant with a subdued, semiconfidential manner conveyed to Mr. Brtiling that her ladyship was on the terrace, and took the hats and sticks that were handed to him and led the way through the house. They emerged upon a broad terrace looking out under great cedar trees upon flower-beds and stone urns and tennis lawns and yew hedges that dipped to give a view of distant hills. On the terrace were grouped perhaps a dozen people for the most part holding teacups, they sat in deck chairs and folding seats about a little table that bore the tea-things. Lady Homartyn came forward to welcome the newcomers.

Mr. Direck was introduced as a travelling American gratified to see a typical English country house, and Lady Homartyn in an habituated way ran over the points of her Tudor specimen. Mr. Direck was not accustomed to titled people, and was suddenly in doubt whether you called a baroness "My Lady" or "Your Ladyship," so he wisely avoided any form of address until he had a lead from Mr. Britling. Mr. Britling presently called her "Lady Homartyn." She took Mr. Direck and sat him down beside a lady whose name he didn't catch, but who had had a lot to do with the British Embassy at Washington, and then she handed Mr. Britling over to the Right Honourable George Philbert, who was anxious to discuss certain points in the latest book of essays. The conversation of the lady from Washington was intelligent but not exacting, and Mr. Direck was able to give some of his attention to the general effect of the scene.

He was a little disappointed to find that the servants didn't wear livery. In American magazine pictures and in American cinematograph films of English stories and in the houses of very rich Americans living in England, they do so. And the Mansion House is misleading; he had met a compatriot who had recently dined at the Mansion House, and who had described "flunkies" in hair-powder and cloth of gold—like Thackeray's Jeames Yellowplush. But here the only servants were two slim, discreet and attentive young gentlemen in black coats and with a gentle piety of manner instead of pride. And he was a little disappointed too by a notable lack of splendour in the company. The ladies affected him as being ill-dressed; there was none of the hard snap, the "*There!* and what do you say to it?" about them of the well-dressed American woman, and the men too were not so much tailored as unobtrusively and yet grammatically clothed.

§ 4

He was still only in the fragmentary stage of conversation when everything was thrown into commotion by the important arrival of Lady Frensham, and there was a general reshuffling of places. Lady Frensham had arrived from London by automobile; she appeared in veils and swathings and a tremendous dust-cloak, with a sort of nephew in her train who had driven the car. She was manifestly a constitutionally triumphant woman. A certain afternoon lassitude vanished in the swirl of her arrival. Mr. Philbert removed wrappings and handed them to the man servant.

"I lunched with Sir Edward Carson today, my dear," she told Lady Homartyn, and rolled a belligerent eye at Philbert.

"And is he as obdurate as ever?" asked Sir Thomas.

"Obdurate! It's Redmond who's obdurate," cried Lady Frensham. "What do you say, Mr. Britling?"

"A plague on both your parties," said Mr. Britling.

"You can't keep out of things like that," said Lady Frensham with the utmost gusto, "when the country's on the very verge of civil war. . . . You people who try to pretend there isn't a grave crisis when there is one, will be more accountable than any one—when the civil war does come. It won't spare you. Mark my words!"

The party became a circle.

Mr. Direck found himself the interested auditor of a real English country-house weekend political conversation. This at any rate was like the England of which Mrs. Humphry Ward's novels had informed him, but yet not exactly like it. Perhaps that was due to the fact that for the most part these novels dealt with the England of the nineties, and things had lost a little in dignity since those days. But at any rate here were political figures and titled people, and they were talking about the "country." . . .

Was it possible that people of this sort did "run" the country, after all? . . . When he had read Mrs. Humphry Ward in America he had always accepted this theory of the story quite easily, but now that he saw and heard them——!

But all governments and rulers and ruling classes when you look at them closely are incredible. . . .

"I don't believe the country is on the verge of civil war," cried Mr. Britling.

"Facts!" cried Lady Frensham, and seemed to wipe away delusions with a rapid gesture of her hands.

"You're interested in Ireland, Mr. Dirks?" asked Lady Homartyn.

"We see it first when we come over," said Mr. Direck rather neatly, and after that he was free to attend to the general discussion.

Lady Frensham, it was manifest, was one of that energetic body of aristocratic ladies who were at that time taking up an irreconcilable attitude against Home Rule "in any shape or form." They were rapidly turning British politics into a system of bitter personal feuds in which all sense of imperial welfare was lost. A wild ambition to emulate the extremest suffragettes seemed to have seized upon them. They insulted, they denounced, they refused every invitation lest they should meet that "traitor" the Prime Minister, they imitated the party hatreds of a fiercer age, and even now the moderate and politic Philbert found himself treated as an invisible object. They were supported by the extremer section of the Tory press, and the most extraordinary writers were set up to froth like lunatics against the government as "traitors," as men who "insulted the King"; *The Morning Post* and the lighter-witted side of the Unionist press generally poured out a torrent of partisan nonsense it is now almost incredible to recall. Lady Frensham, bridling over Lady Homartyn's party, and for a time leaving Mr. Britling, hurried on to tell of the newest developments of the great feud. She had a wonderful description of Lady Londonderry sitting opposite "that old rascal," the Prime Minister, at a performance of Mozart's "Zauberflöte."

"If looks could kill!" cried Lady Frensham with tremendous gusto.

"Sir Edward is quite firm that Ulster means to fight. They have machine-guns—ammunition. And I am sure the army is with us. . . ."

"Where did they get those machine-guns and ammunition?" asked Mr. Britling suddenly.

"Ah! that's a secret," cried Lady Frensham.

"Um," said Mr. Britling.

"You see," said Lady Frensham; "it *will* be civil war! And yet you writing people who have influence do nothing to prevent it!"

"What are we to do, Lady Frensham?"

"Tell people how serious it is."

"You mean, tell the Irish Nationalists to lie down and be walked over. They won't be. . . ."

"We'll see about that," cried Lady Frensham, "we'll see about that!"

She was a large and dignified person with a kind of figurehead nobility of carriage, but Mr. Direck was suddenly reminded of a girl cousin of his who had been expelled from college for some particularly elaborate and aimless rioting. . . .

"May I say something to you, Lady Frensham," said Mr. Britling, "that you have just said to me? Do you realise that this Carsonite campaign is dragging these islands within a measurable distance of civil war?"

"It's the fault of your Lloyd George and his government. It's the fault of your Socialists and sentimentalists. You've made the mischief and you have to deal with it."

"Yes. But do you really figure to yourself what a civil war may mean for the empire? Surely there are other things in the world besides this quarrel between the 'loyalists' of Ulster and the Liberal government; there are other interests in this big empire than party advantages? You think you are going to frighten this Home Rule government into some ridiculous sort of collapse that will bring in the Tories at the next election. Well, suppose you don't manage that. Suppose instead that you do really contrive to bring about a civil war. Very few people here or in Ireland want it—I was over there not a month ago—but when men have loaded guns in their hands they sometimes go off. And then people see red. Few people realise what an incurable sore opens when fighting begins. Suppose part of the army revolts and we get some extraordinary and demoralising fighting over there. India watches these things. Bengal may imitate Ireland. At that distance rebellion and treason are rebellion and treason whether they are coloured orange or green. And then suppose the Germans see fit to attack us!"

Lady Frensham had a woman's elusiveness. "Your Redmondites would welcome them with open arms."

"It isn't the Redmondites who invite them now, any-how," said Mr. Britling, springing his mine. "The other day one of your 'loyalists,' Andrews, was talking in *The Morning Post* of preferring conquest by Germany to Home Rule; Craig has been at the same game; Major Crawford, the man who ran the German Mausers last April, boasted that he would transfer his allegiance to the German Emperor rather than see Redmond in power."

"Rhetoric!" said Lady Frensham. "Rhetoric!"

"But one of your Ulster papers has openly boasted that arrangements have been made for a 'powerful Continental monarch' to help an Ulster rebellion."

"Which paper?" snatched Lady Frensham.

Mr. Britling hesitated.

Mr. Philbert supplied the name. "I saw it. It was *The Irish Churchman*."

"You two have got your case up very well," said Lady Frensham. "I didn't know Mr. Britling was a party man."

"The Nationalists have been circulating copies," said Philbert. "Naturally."

"They make it look worse than mere newspaper talk and speeches," Mr. Britling pressed. "Carson, it seems, was lunching with the German Emperor last autumn. A fine fuss you'd make if Redmond did that. All this gun-running, too, is German gun-running."

"What does it matter if it is?" said Lady Frensham, allowing a belligerent eye to rest for the first time on Philbert. "You drove us to it. One thing we are resolved upon at any cost. Johnny Redmond may rule England if he likes; he shan't rule Ireland. . . ."

Mr. Britling shrugged his shoulders, and his face betrayed despair.

"My one consolation," he said, "in this storm is a talk I had last month with a young Irishwoman in Meath. She was a young person of twelve, and she took a fancy to me—I think because I went with her in an alleged dangerous canoe she was forbidden to navigate alone. All day the eternal Irish Question had banged over her observant head. When we were out on the water she suddenly decided to set me right upon a disregarded essential. 'You English,' she said, 'are just a bit disposed to take all this trouble seriously. Don't you fret yourself about it . . . Half the time we're just laffing at you. You'd best leave us all alone. . . .' "

And then he went off at a tangent from his own anecdote.

"But look at this miserable spectacle!" he cried. "Here is a chance of getting something like a reconciliation of the old feud of English and Irish, and something like a settlement of these ancient distresses, and there seems no power, no conscience, no sanity in any of us, sufficient to save it from this cantankerous bitterness, this sheer wicked mischief of mutual exasperation. . . . Just when Ireland is getting a gleam of prosperity. . . . A murrain on both your parties!"

"I see, Mr. Britling, you'd hand us all over to Jim Larkin!"

"I'd hand you all over to Sir Horace Plunkett——"

"That doctrinaire dairyman!" cried Lady Frensham, with an air of quite conclusive repartee. "You're hopeless, Mr. Britling. You're hopeless."

And Lady Homartyn, seeing that the phase of mere personal verdicts drew near, created a diversion by giving Lady Frensham a second cup of tea, and fluttering like a cooling fan about the heated brows of the disputants. She suggested tennis. . . .

§ 5

Mr. Britling was still flushed and ruffled as he and his guest returned towards the Dower House. He criticised England himself unmercifully, but he hated to think that in any respect she fell short of perfection; even her defects he liked to imagine were just a subtler kind of power and wisdom. And Lady Frensham had stuck her voice and her gestures through all these amiable illusions. He was like a lover who calls his lady a foolish rogue, and is startled to find that facts and strangers do literally agree with him.

But it was so difficult to resolve Lady Frensham and the Irish squabble generally into anything better than idiotic mischief, that for a time he was unusually silent—wrestling with the problem, and Mr. Direck got the conversational initiative.

"To an American mind it's a little—startling," said Mr. Direck, "to hear ladies expressing such vigorous political opinions."

"I don't mind that," said Mr. Britling. "Women over here go into politics and into public houses—I don't see why they shouldn't. If such things are good enough for men they are good enough for women; we haven't your sort of chivalry. But it's the peculiar malignant silliness of this sort of Toryism that's so discreditable. It's discreditable. There's no good in denying it. Those people you have heard and seen are a not unfair sample of our governing class—of a certain section of our governing class—as it is today. Not at all unfair. And you see how amazingly they haven't got hold of anything. There was a time when they could be politic. . . . Hidden away they have politic instincts even how. . . . But it makes me sick to think of this Irish business. Because, you know, it's true—we *are* drifting towards civil war there."

"You are of that opinion?" said Mr. Direck.

"Well, isn't it so? Here's all this Ulster gun-running—you heard how she talked of it? Isn't it enough to drive the south into open revolt? . . ."

"Is there very much, do you think, in the suggestion that some of this Ulster trouble is a German intrigue? You and Mr. Philbert were saying things——"

"I don't know," said Mr. Britling shortly.

"I don't know," he repeated. "But it isn't because I don't think our Unionists and their opponents aren't foolish enough for anything of the sort. It's only because I don't believe that the Germans are so stupid as to do such things. . . . Why should they? . . .

"It makes me—expressionless with anger," said Mr. Britling after a pause, reverting to his main annoyance. "They won't consider any compromise. It's sheer love of quarrelling. . . . Those people there think that nothing can possibly happen. They are like children in a nursery playing at rebellion. Unscathed and heedless. Until there is death at their feet they will never realise they are playing with loaded guns. . . ."

For a time he said no more; and listened perfunctorily while Mr. Direck tried to indicate the feeling in New England towards the Irish Question and the many difficult propositions an American politician has to face in that respect. And when Mr. Britling took up the thread of speech again it had little or no relation to Mr. Direck's observations.

"The psychology of all this recent insubordination and violence is—curious. Exasperating too. . . . I don't quite grasp it. . . . It's the same thing whether you look at the suffrage business or the labour people or at this Irish muddle. People may be too safe. You see we live at the end of a series of secure generations in which none of the great things of life have changed materially. We've grown up with no sense of danger—that is to say, with no sense of responsibility. None of us, none of us—for though I talk my actions belie me—really believe that life can change very fundamentally any more for ever. All this"—Mr. Britling waved his arm comprehensively— "looks as though it was bound to go on steadily for ever. It seems incredible that the system could be smashed. It seems incredible that anything we can do will ever smash the system. Lady Homartyn, for example, is incapable of believing that she won't always be able to have weekend parties at Claverings, and that the letters and the tea won't come to her bedside in the morning. Or if her imagination goes to the point of supposing that some day *she* won't be there to receive the tea, it means merely that she supposes somebody else will be. Her pleasant butler may fear to lose his 'situation,' but nothing on earth could make him imagine a time when there will not be a 'situation' for him to lose. Old Asquith thinks that we always have got along, and that we always shall get along by being quietly artful and saying, 'Wait and see.' And it's just because we are all convinced that we are so safe against a general breakdown that we are able to be so recklessly violent in our special cases. Why shouldn't women have the vote? they argue. What does it matter? And bang goes a bomb in Westminister Abbey. Why shouldn't Ulster create an impossible position? And off trots some demented Carsonite to Germany to play at treason on some half word of the German Emperor's and buy half a million rifles. . . .

"Exactly like children being very, very naughty. . . .

"And," said Mr. Britling with a gesture to round off his discourse, "we do go on. We shall go on—until there is a spark right into the magazine. We have lost any belief we ever had that fundamental things happen. We English are everlasting children in an everlasting nursery. . . ."

And immediately he broke out again.

"The truth of the matter is that hardly any one has ever yet mastered the fact that the world is round. The world is round—like an orange. The thing is told us—like any old scandal—at school. For all practical purposes we forget it.—Practically we all live in a world as flat as a pancake. Where time never ends and nothing changes. Who really believes in any world outside the circle of the horizon? Here we are and visibly nothing is changing. And so we go on to—nothing will ever change. It just goes on—in space, in time. If we could realise that round world beyond, then indeed we should go circumspectly. . . . If the world were like a whispering gallery, what whispers might we not hear now—from India, from Africa, from Germany, warnings from the past, intimations of the future. . . .

"We shouldn't heed them. . . ."

§ 6

And indeed at the very moment when Mr. Britling was saying these words, in Sarajevo in Bosnia, where the hour was somewhat later, men whispered together, and one held nervously to a black parcel that had been given him and nodded as they repeated his instructions, a black parcel with certain unstable chemicals and a curious arrangement of detonators therein, a black parcel destined ultimately to shatter nearly every landmark of Mr. Britling's and Lady Frensham's cosmogony. . . .

§ 7

When Mr. Direck and Mr. Britling returned to the Dower House the guest was handed over to Mrs. Britling and Mr. Britling vanished, to reappear at supper-time, for the Britlings had a supper in the evening instead of dinner. When Mr. Britling did reappear every trace of his vexation with the levities of British politics and the British ruling class had vanished altogether, and he was no longer thinking of all that might be happening in Germany or India. . . .

While he was out of the way Mr. Direck extended his acquaintance with the Britling household. He was taken round the garden and shown the roses by Mrs. Britling, and beyond the rose-garden in a little arbour they came upon Miss Corner reading a book. She looked very grave and pretty reading a book. Mr. Direck came to a pause in front of her, and Mrs. Britling stopped beside him. The young lady looked up and smiled.

"The last new novel?" asked Mr. Direck pleasantly.

"Campanella's 'City of the Sun.' "

"My word! but isn't that stiff reading?"

"You haven't read it," said Miss Corner.

"It's a dry old book anyhow."

"It's no good pretending you have," she said, and there Mr. Direck felt the conversation had to end.

"That's a very pleasant young lady to have around," he said to Mrs. Britling as they went on towards the barn court.

"She's all at loose ends," said Mrs. Britling. "And she reads like a——Whatever does read? One drinks like a fish. One eats like a wolf."

They found the German tutor in a little court playing Badminton with the two younger boys. He was a plump young man with glasses and compact gestures; the game progressed chiefly by misses and the score was counted in German. He won thoughtfully and chiefly through the ardour of the younger brother, whose enthusiastic returns invariably went out. Instantly the boys attacked Mrs. Britling with a concerted enthusiasm. "Mummy! Is it to be dressing-up supper?"

Mrs. Britling considered, and it was manifest that Mr. Direck was material to her answer.

"We wrap ourselves up in curtains and bright things instead of dressing," she explained. "We have a sort of wardrobe of fancy dresses. Do you mind?"

Mr. Direck was delighted.

And this being settled, the two small boys went off with their mother upon some special decorative project they had conceived and Mr. Direck was left for a time to Herr Heinrich.

Herr Heinrich suggested a stroll in the rose-garden, and as Mr. Direck had not hitherto been shown the rose-garden by Herr Heinrich, he agreed. Sooner or later everybody, it was evident, had got to show him that rose-garden.

"And how do you like living in an English household?" said Mr. Direck, getting to business at once. "It's interesting to an American to see this English establishment, and it must be still more interesting to a German."

"I find it very different from Pomerania," said Herr Heinrich. "In some respects it is more agreeable, in others less so. It is a pleasant life, but it is not a serious life.

"At any time," continued Herr Heinrich, "some one may say, 'Let us do this thing,' or 'Let us do that thing,' and then everything is disarranged.

"People walk into the house without ceremony. There is much kindness but no politeness. Mr. Britling will go away for three or four days, and when he returns and I come forward to greet him and bow, he will walk right past me, or he will say just like this, 'How do, Heinrich?' "

"Are you interested in Mr. Britling's writings?" Mr. Direck asked.

"There again I am puzzled. His work is known even in Germany. His articles are reprinted in German and Austrian reviews. You would expect him to have a certain authority of

59

manner. You would expect there to be discussion at the table upon questions of philosophy and æsthetics. . . . It is not so. When I ask him questions it is often that they are not seriously answered. Sometimes it is as if he did not like the questions I asked of him. Yesterday I asked of him did he agree or did he not agree with Mr. Bernard Shaw. He just said—I wrote it down in my memoranda—he said: 'Oh! Mixed Pickles.' What can one understand of that?—Mixed Pickles!" . . .

The young man's sedulous blue eyes looked out of his pink face through his glasses at Mr. Direck, anxious for any light he could offer upon the atmospheric vagueness of this England.

He was, he explained, a student of philology preparing for his doctorate. He had not yet done his year of military service. He was studying the dialects of East Anglia——

"You go about among the people?" Mr. Direck inquired.

"No, I do not do that. But I ask Mr. Carmine and Mrs. Britling and the boys many questions. And sometimes I talk to the gardener."

He explained how he would prepare his thesis and how it would be accepted, and the nature of his army service and the various stages by which he would subsequently ascend in the orderly professorial life to which he was destined. He confessed a certain lack of interest in philology, but, he said, "it is what I have to do." And so he was going to do it all his life through. For his own part he was interested in ideas of universal citizenship, in Esperanto and Ido and universal languages and suchlike attacks upon the barriers between man and man. But the authorities at home did not favour cosmopolitan ideas, and so he was relinquishing them. "Here, it is as if there were no authorities," he said with a touch of envy.

Mr. Direck induced him to expand that idea.

Herr Heinrich made Mr. Britling his instance. If Mr. Britling were a German he would certainly have some sort of title, a definite position, responsibility. Here he was not even called Herr Doktor. He said what he liked. Nobody rewarded him; nobody reprimanded him. When Herr Heinrich asked him of his position, whether he was above or below Mr. Bernard Shaw or Mr. Arnold White or Mr. Garvin or any other publicist, he made jokes. Nobody here seemed to have a title and nobody seemed to have a definite place. There was Mr. Lawrence Carmine; he was a student of Oriental questions; he had to do with some public institution in London that welcomed Indian students; he was a Geheimrath——

"Eh?" said Mr. Direck.

"It is—what do you call it?—the Essex County Council." But nobody took any notice of that. And when Mr. Philbert, who was a minister in the government, came to lunch he was just like any one else. It was only after he had gone that Herr Heinrich had learned by chance that he was a minister and "Right Honourable." . . .

"In Germany everything is definite. Every man knows his place, has his papers, is instructed what to do. . . ."

"Yet," said Mr. Direck, with his eyes on the glowing roses, the neat arbour, the long line of the red wall of the vegetable-garden and a distant gleam of corn-field, "it all looks orderly enough."

"It is as if it had been put in order ages ago," said Herr Heinrich.

"And was just going on by habit," said Mr. Direck, taking up the idea.

Their comparisons were interrupted by the appearance of "Teddy," the secretary, and the Indian young gentleman, damp

61

and genial, as they explained, "from the boats," It seemed that "down below" somewhere was a pond with a punt and an island and a toy dinghy. And while they discussed swimming and boating, Mr. Carmine appeared from the direction of the park conversing gravely with the elder son. They had been for a walk and a talk together. There were proposals for a Badminton foursome. Mr. Direck emerged from the general interchange with Mr. Lawrence Carmine, and then strolled through the rose-garden to see the sunset from the end. Mr. Direck took the opportunity to verify his impression that the elder son was the present Mrs. Britling's stepson, and he also contrived by a sudden admiration for a distant row of evening primroses to deflect their path past the arbour in which the evening light must now be getting a little too soft for Miss Corner's book.

Miss Corner was drawn into the sunset party. She talked to Mr. Carmine and displayed, Mr. Direck thought, great originality of mind. She said "The City of the Sun" was like the cities the boys sometimes made on the playroom floor. She said it was the dearest little city, and gave some amusing particulars. She described the painted walls that made the tour of the Civitas Solis a liberal education. She asked Mr. Carmine, who was an authority on Oriental literature, why there were no Indian nor Chinese Utopias.

Now it had never occurred to Mr. Direck to ask why there were no Indian nor Chinese Utopias, and even Mr. Carmine seemed surprised to discover this deficiency.

"The primitive patriarchal village *is* Utopia to India and China," said Mr. Carmine, when they had a little digested the inquiry. "Or at any rate it is their social ideal. They want no Utopias.

"Utopias came with cities," he said, considering the question. "And the first cities, as distinguished from courts and autocratic capitals, came with ships. India and China belong to an earlier age. Ships, trade, disorder, strange relationships, unofficial literature, criticism—and then this idea of some novel remaking of society. . . ."

§ 8

Then Mr. Direck fell into the hands of Hugh, the eldest son, and anticipating the inevitable, said that he liked to walk in the rose-garden. So they walked in the rose-garden.

"Do you read Utopias?" said Mr. Direck, cutting any preface, in the English manner.

"Oh, *rather!*" said Hugh, and became at once friendly and confidential.

"We all do," he explained. "In England everybody talks of change and nothing ever changes."

"I found Miss Corner reading—what was it? the Sun People?—some old classical Italian work."

"Campanella," said Hugh, without betraying the slightest interest in Miss Corner. "Nothing changes in England, because the people who want to change things change their minds before they change anything else. I've been in London talking for the last half-year. Studying art they call it. Before that I was a science student, and I want to be one again. Don't you think, sir, there's something about science—it's steadier than anything else in the world?"

Mr. Direck thought that the moral truths of human nature were steadier than science, and they had one of those little discussions of real life that begin about a difference inadequately apprehended, and do not so much end as are abandoned. Hugh struck him as being more speculative and detached than any American college youth of his age that he knew—but that might not be a national difference but only the Britling strain. He seemed to have read more, and more independently, and to be doing less. And he was rather more restrained and self-possessed.

Before Mr. Direck could begin a proper inquiry into the young man's work and outlook, he had got the conversation upon America. He wanted tremendously to see America. "The dad says in one of his books that over here we are being and that over there you are beginning. It must be tremendously stimulating to think that your country is still being made. . . ."

Mr. Direck thought that an interesting point of view. "Unless something tumbles down here, we never think of altering it," the young man remarked. "And even then we just shore it up."

His remarks had the effect of floating off from some busy mill of thought within him. Hitherto Mr. Direck had been inclined to think this silent observant youth with his hands in his pockets and his shoulders a little humped, as probably shy and adolescently ineffective. But the head was manifestly quite busy. . . .

"Miss Corner," he began, taking the first thing that came into his head, and then he remembered that he had already made the remark he was going to make not five minutes ago.

"What form of art," he asked, "are you contemplating in your studies at the present time in London? . . ."

Before this question could be dealt with at all adequately, the two small boys became active in the garden beating in everybody to "dress up" before supper. The secretary, Teddy, came in a fatherly way to look after Mr. Direck and see to his draperies.

§ 9

Mr. Direck gave his very best attention to this business of draping himself, for he had not the slightest intention of appearing ridiculous in the eyes of Miss Corner. Teddy came with an armful of stuff that he thought "might do."

"What'll I come as?" asked Mr. Direck.

"We don't wear costumes," said Teddy. "We just put on all the brightest things we fancy. If it's any costume at all, its Futurist."

"And surely why shouldn't one?" asked Mr. Direck, greatly struck by this idea. "Why should we always be tied by the fashions and periods of the past?"

He rejected a rather Mephistopheles-like costume of crimson and a scheme for a brigand-like ensemble based upon what was evidently an old bolero of Mrs. Britling's, and after some reflection he accepted some black silk tights. His legs were not legs to be ashamed of. Over this he tried various brilliant wrappings from the Dower House *armoire*, and chose at last, after some hesitation in the direction of a piece of gold and purple brocade, a big square of green silk curtain stuff adorned with golden pheasants and other large and dignified ornaments; this he wore toga fashion over his light silken undervest—Teddy had insisted on the abandonment of his shirt "if you want to dance at all"—and fastened with a large green glass-jewelled brooch. From this his head and neck projected, he felt, with a tolerable dignity. Teddy suggested a fillet of green ribbon, and this Mr. Direck tried, but after prolonged reflection before the glass rejected. He was still weighing the effect of this fillet upon the mind of Miss Corner when Teddy left him to make his own modest preparations. Teddy's departure gave him a chance for profile studies by means of an arrangement of the long mirror and the table looking-glass that he had been too shy to attempt in the presence of the secretary. The general effect was quite satisfactory.

"Wa-a-a-l," he said with a quiver of laughter, "now who'd have thought it?" and smiled a consciously American smile at himself before going down.

The company was assembling in the panelled hall, and made a brilliant show in the light of the acetylene candles against a dark background. Mr. Britling in a black velvet cloak and black silk tights was a deeper shade among shadows; the high lights were Miss Corner and her sister, in glittering garments of peacock green and silver that gave a snakelike quality to their lithe bodies. They were talking to the German tutor, who had become a sort of cotton Cossack, a spectacled Cossack in buff and bright green. Mrs. Britling was dignified and beautiful in a purple djibbêh, and her stepson had become a handsome still figure of black and crimson. Teddy had contrived something elaborate and effective in the Egyptian style, with a fish-basket and a cuirass of that thin matting one finds behind wash-stands; the small boys were brigands, with immensely baggy breeches and cummerbunds in which they had stuck a selection of paper-knives and toy pistols and similar weapons. Mr. Carmine and his young man had come provided with real Indian costumes; the feeling of the company was that Mr. Carmine was a mullah. The aunt-like lady with the noble nose stood out amidst these levities in a black silk costume with a gold chain. She refused, it seemed, to make herself absurd, though she encouraged the others to extravagance by nods and enigmatical smiles. Nevertheless she had put pink ribbons in her cap. A family of father, golden-haired mother, and two young daughters, sympathically attired, had just arrived, and were discarding their outer wrappings with the assistance of host and hostess.

It was all just exactly what Mr. Direck had never expected in England, and equally unexpected was the supper on a long candle-lit table without a cloth. No servants were present, but on a sideboard stood a cold salmon and cold joints and kalter aufschnitt and kartoffel salat, and a variety of other comestibles, and many bottles of beer and wine and whisky. One helped oneself and anybody else one could, and Mr. Direck did his best to be very attentive to Mrs. Britling and Miss Corner, and was greatly assisted by the latter.

Everybody seemed extremely gay and bright-eyed. Mr. Direck found something exhilarating and oddly exciting in all this unusual bright costume and in this easy mutual service; it made everybody seem franker and simpler. Even Mr. Britling had revealed a sturdy handsomeness that had not been apparent to Mr. Direck before, and young Britling left no doubts now about his good looks. Mr. Direck forgot his mission and his position and indeed things generally, in an irrational satisfaction that his golden pheasants harmonised with the glitter of the warm and smiling girl beside him. And he sat down beside her—"You sit anywhere," said Mrs. Britling—with far less compunction than in his ordinary costume he would have felt for so direct a confession of preference. And there was something in her eyes, it was quite indefinable and yet very satisfying, that told him that now he had escaped from the stern square imperatives of his patriotic tailor in New York she had made a discovery of him.

Everybody chattered gaily, though Mr. Direck would have found it difficult to recall afterwards what it was they chattered about, except that somehow he acquired the valuable knowledge that Miss Corner was called Cecily and her sister Letty, and then—so far old Essex custom held—the masculine section was left for a few minutes for some imaginary drinking and a lighting of cigars and cigarettes, after which everybody went through interwoven moonlight and afterglow to the barn. Mr. Britling sat down to a pianola in the corner and began the familiar cadences of "Whistling Rufus."

"You dance?" said Miss Cecily Corner.

"I've never been much of a dancing man," said Mr. Direck. "What sort of dance is this?"

"Just anything. A two-step."

Mr. Direck hesitated and regretted a well-spent youth, and then Hugh came prancing forward with outstretched hands and swept her away.

Just for an instant Mr. Direck felt that this young man was a trifle superflous. . . .

But it was very amusing dancing.

It wasn't any sort of taught formal dancing. It was a spontaneous retort to the leaping American music that Mr. Britling footed out. You kept time, and for the rest you did as your nature prompted. If you had a partner you joined hands, you fluttered to and from one another, you paced down the long floor together, you involved yourselves in romantic pursuits and repulsions with other couples. There was no objection to your dancing alone. Teddy, for example, danced alone in order to develop certain Egyptian gestures that were germinating in his brain. There was no objection to your joining hands in a cheerful serpent. . . .

Mr. Direck's gaze hung on to Cissie and her partner. They danced very well together; they seemed to like and understand each other. It was natural of course for two young people like that, thrown very much together, to develop an affection for one another. . . . Still, she was old by three or four years.

It seemed unreasonable that the boy anyhow shouldn't be in love with her. . . .

It seemed unreasonable that any one shouldn't be in love with her. . . .

Then Mr. Direck remarked that Cissie was watching Teddy's manœuvres over her partner's shoulder. With real affection and admiration. . . .

But then most refreshingly she picked up Mr. Direck's gaze and gave him the slightest of smiles. She hadn't forgotten him.

The music stopped with an effect of shock, and all the bobbing, whirling figures became walking glories.

"Now that's not difficult, is it?" said Miss Corner, glowing happily.

"Not when you do it," said Mr. Direck.

"I can't imagine an American not dancing a two-step. You must do the next with me. Listen! It's ' 'Way Down Indiana' . . . ah! I knew you could."

Mr. Direck, too, understood now that he could, and they went off holding hands rather after the fashion of two skaters.

"My word!" said Mr. Direck. "To think I'd be dancing."

But he said no more because he needed his breath.

He liked it, and he had another attempt with one of the visitor daughters, who danced rather more formally, and then Teddy took the pianola and Mr. Direck was astonished by the spectacle of an eminent British thinker in a whirl of black velvet and extremely active black legs engaged in a kind of Apache dance in pursuit of the visitor wife. In which Mr. Lawrence Carmine suddenly mingled.

"In Germany," said Herr Heinrich, "we do not dance like this. It could not be considered seemly. But it is very pleasant."

And then there was a waltz, and Herr Heinrich bowed to and took the visitor wife round three times, and returned her very punctually and exactly to the point whence he had taken her, and the Indian young gentleman (who must not be called "coloured") waltzed very well with Cecily. Mr. Direck tried to take a tolerant European view of this brown and white combination. But he secured her as soon as possible from this Asiatic entanglement, and danced with her again, and then he danced with her again.

"Come and look at the moonlight," cried Mrs. Britling.

And presently Mr. Direck found himself strolling through the rose-garden with Cecily. She had the sweetest moonlight face, her white shining robe made her altogether a thing of moonlight. If Mr. Direck had not been in love with her before he was now altogether in love. Mamie Nelson, whose freakish unkindness had been rankling like a poisoned thorn in his heart all the way from Massachusetts, suddenly became Ancient History.

A tremendous desire for eloquence arose in Mr. Direck's soul, a desire so tremendous that no conceivable phrase he could imagine satisfied it. So he remained tongue-tied. And Cecily was tongue-tied, too. The scent of the roses just tinted the clear sweetness of the air they breathed.

Mr. Direck's mood was an immense solemnity, like a dark ocean beneath the vast dome of the sky, and something quivered in every fibre of his being, like moonlit ripples on the sea. He felt at the same time a portentous stillness and an immense enterprise. . . .

Then suddenly the pianola, pounding a cake-walk, burst out into ribald invitation. . . .

"Come back to dance!" cried Cecily, like one from whom a spell has just been broken. And Mr. Direck, snatching at a vanishing scrap of everything he had not said, remarked, "I shall never forget this evening."

She did not seem to hear that.

They danced together again. And then Mr. Direck danced with the visitor lady, whose name he had never heard. And then he danced with Mrs. Britling, and then he danced with Letty. And then it seemed time for him to look for Miss Cecily again.

And so the cheerful evening passed until they were within a quarter of an hour of Sunday morning. Mrs. Britling went to exert a restraining influence upon the pianola.

"Oh! one dance more!" cried Cissie Corner.

"Oh! one dance more!" cried Letty.

"One dance more," Mr. Direck supported, and then things really *had* to end.

There was a rapid putting out of candles, and a stowing away of things by Teddy and the sons, two chauffeurs appeared from the region of the kitchen and brought Mr. Lawrence Carmine's car and the visitor family's car to the front door, and everybody drifted gaily through the moonlight and the big trees to the front of the house. And Mr. Direck saw the perambulator waiting— the mysterious perambulator—a little in the dark beyond the front door.

The visitor family and Mr. Carmine and his young Indian departed. "Come to hockey!" shouted Mr. Britling to each departing car-load, and Mr. Carmine receding answered: "I'll bring three!"

Then Mr. Direck, in accordance with a habit that had been growing on him throughout the evening, looked round for Miss Cissie Corner and failed to find her. And then behold she was descending the staircase with the mysterious baby in her arms. She held up a warning finger, and then glanced at her sleeping burden. She looked like a silvery Madonna. And Mr. Direck remembered that he was still in doubt about that baby. . . .

Teddy, who was back in his flannels, seized upon the perambulator. There was much careful baby stowing on the part of Cecily; she displayed an infinitely maternal solicitude. Letty was away changing; she reappeared jauntily taking leave, disregarding the baby absolutely, and Teddy departed bigamously, wheeling the perambulator between the two sisters into the hazes of the moonlight. There was much crying of good nights. Mr. Direck's curiosities narrowed down to a point of great intensity. . . .

Of course, Mr. Britling's circle must be a very "Advanced" circle. . . .

§ 10

Mr. Direck found he had taken leave of the rest of the company, and drifted into a little parlour with Mr. Britling and certain glasses and siphons and a whisky decanter on a tray. . . .

"It is a very curious thing," said Mr. Direck, "that in England I find myself more disposed to take stimulants and that I no longer have the need for iced water that one feels at home. I ascribe it to a greater humidity in the air. One is less dried and one is less braced. One is no longer pursued by a thirst, but one needs something to buck one up a little. Thank you. That is enough."

Mr. Direck took his glass of whisky and soda from Mr. Britling's hand.

Mr. Britling seated himself in an arm-chair by the fireplace and threw one leg carelessly over the arm. In his black velvet cloak and cap, and his black silk tights, he was very like a minor character, a court chamberlain, for example, in some cloak and rapier drama. "I find this weekend dancing and kicking about wonderfully wholesome," he said. "That and our Sunday hockey. One starts the new week clear and bright about the mind. Friday is always my worst working day."

Mr. Direck leaned against the table, wrapped in his golden pheasants, and appreciated the point.

"Your young people dance very cheerfully," he said.

"We all dance very cheerfully," said Mr. Britling.

"Then this Miss Corner," said Mr. Direck, "she is the sister, I presume, is she? of that pleasant young lady who is married—she is married, isn't she?—to the young man you call Teddy."

"I should have explained these young people. They're the sort of young people we are producing over here now in quite enormous quantity. They are the sort of equivalent of the Russian Intelligentsia, an irresponsible middle-class with ideas. Teddy, you know, is my secretary. He's the son, I believe, of a Kilburn solicitor. He was recommended to me by Datcher of *The Times*. He came down here and lived in lodgings for a time. Then suddenly appeared the young lady."

"Miss Corner's sister?"

"Exactly. The village was a little startled. The cottager who had let rooms came to me privately. Teddy is rather touchy on the point of his personal independence, he considers any demand for explanations as an insult, and probably all he had said to the old lady was, 'This is Letty—come to share my rooms.' I put the matter to him very gently. 'Oh, yes,' he said, rather in the manner of some one who has overlooked a trifle. 'I got married to her in the Christmas holidays. May I bring her along to see Mrs. Britling?' We induced him to go into a little cottage I rent. The wife was the daughter of a Colchester journalist and printer. I don't know if you talked to her."

"I've talked to the sister rather."

"Well, they're both idea'd. They're highly educated in the sense that they do really think for themselves. Almost fiercely. So does Teddy. If he thinks he hasn't thought anything he thinks for himself, he goes off and thinks it different. The sister is a teacher who wants to take the B.A. degree in London University. Meanwhile she pays the penalty of her sex."

"Meaning——?" asked Mr. Direck startled.

"Oh! that she puts in a great deal too much of her time upon housework and minding her sister's baby."

"She's a very interesting and charming young lady indeed," said Mr. Direck. "With a sort of Western college freedom of mind—and something about her that isn't American at all."

Mr. Britling was following the train of his own thoughts.

"My household has some amusing contrasts," he said. "I don't know if you have talked to that German?

"He's always asking questions. And you tell him any old thing and he goes and writes it down in his room upstairs, and afterwards asks you another like it in order to perplex himself by the variety of your answers. He regards the whole world with a methodical distrust. He wants to document it and pin it down. He suspects it only too justly of disorderly impulses, and a capacity for self-contradiction. He is the most extraordinary contrast to Teddy, whose confidence in the universe amounts almost to effrontery. Teddy carries our national laxness to a foolhardy extent. He is capable of leaving his watch in the middle of Claverings Park and expecting to find it a month later—being carefully taken care of by a squirrel, I suppose—when he happens to want it. He's rather like a squirrel himself—without the habit of hoarding. He is incapable of asking a question about anything; he would be quite sure it was all right anyhow. He would feel that asking questions betrayed a want of confidence—was a sort of incivility. But my German, if you notice—his normal expression is one of grave solicitude. He is like a conscientious ticket-collector among his impressions. And did you notice how beautifully my pianola rolls are all numbered and catalogued? He did that. He set to work and did it as soon as he got here, just as a good cat when you bring it into a house sets to work and catches mice. Previously the pianola music was chaos. You took what God sent you.

"And he *looks* like a German," said Mr. Britling.

"He certainly does that," said Mr. Direck.

"He has the fair type of complexion, the rather full habit of body, the temperamental disposition, but in addition that close-cropped head—it is almost as if it were shaved—the plumpness, the glasses—those are things that are made. And the way he carries himself. And the way he thinks. His meticulousness. When he arrived he was delightful, he was wearing a student's corps cap and a rucksack, he carried a violin; he seemed to have come out of a book. No one would ever dare to invent so German a German for a book. Now a young Frenchman or a young Italian or a young Russian coming here might look like a foreigner, but he wouldn't have the distinctive national stamp a German has. He wouldn't be plainly French or Italian or Russian. Other peoples are not made; they are neither made nor created but proceeding—out of a thousand indefinable causes. The Germans are a triumph of directive will. I had to remark the other day that when my boys talked German they shouted. 'But when one talks German one *must* shout,' said Herr Heinrich. 'It is taught so in the schools.' And it is. They teach them to shout and to throw out their chests. Just as they teach them to read notice-boards and not think about politics. Their very ribs are not their own. My Herr Heinrich is comparatively a liberal thinker. He asked me the other day, 'But why should I give myself up to philology? But then,' he considered, 'it is what I have to do.' "

Mr. Britling seemed to have finished, and then just as Mr. Direck was planning a way of getting the talk back by way of Teddy to Miss Corner, he snuggled more deeply into his chair, reflected and broke out again.

"This contrast between Heinrich's carefulness and Teddy's easygoingness, come to look at it, is I suppose one of the most fundamental in the world. It reaches to everything. It mixes up with education, statecraft, morals. Will you make or will you take? Those are the two extreme courses in all such things. I suppose the answer of wisdom to that is, like all wise answers, a compromise. I suppose one must accept and then make all one can of it. . . . Have you talked at all to my eldest son?"

"He's a very interesting young man indeed," said Mr. Direck. "I should venture to say there's a very great deal in him. I was most impressed by the few words I had with him."

"There, for example, is one of my perplexities," said Mr. Britling.

Mr. Direck waited for some further light on this sudden transition.

"Ah! your troubles in life haven't begun yet. Wait till you're a father. That cuts to the bone. You have the most delicate thing in the world in hand, a young kindred mind. You feel responsible for it, you know you are responsible for it; and you lose touch with it. You can't get at it. Nowadays we've lost the old tradition of fatherhood by divine right—and we haven't got a new one. I've tried not to be a cramping ruler, a director, a domestic tyrant to that lad—and in effect it's meant his going his own way. . . . I don't dominate. I hoped to advise. But you see he loves my respect and good opinion. Too much. When things go well I know of them. When the world goes dark for him, then he keeps his trouble from Just when I would so eagerly go into it with him. . . . There's something the matter now, something—it may be grave. I feel he wants to tell me. And there it is!—it seems I am the last person to whom he can humiliate himself by a confession of blundering, or weakness. . . . Something I should just laugh at and say, 'That's in the blood of all of us, dear Spit of myself. Let's see what's to be done.' . . ."

He paused and then went on, finding in the unfamiliarity and transitoriness of his visitor a freedom he might have failed to find with a close friend.

"I am frightened at times at all I don't know about in that boy's mind. I know nothing of his religiosities. He's my son and he must have religiosities. I know nothing of his ideas or of his knowledge about sex and all that side of life. I do not know of the things he finds beautiful. I can guess at times, that's all; when he betrays himself. . . . You see, you don't know really what love is until you have children. One doesn't love women. Indeed you don't! One gives and gets; it's a trade. One may have tremendous excitements and expectations and overwhelming desires. That's all very well in its way. But the love of children is an exquisite tenderness: it rends the heart. It's a thing of God. And I lie awake at nights and stretch out my hands in the darkness to this lad—who will never know—until his sons come in their time. . . ."

He made one of his quick turns again.

"And that's where our English way makes for distresses. Mr. Prussian respects and fears his father; respects authorities, attends, obeys and—*his father has a hold upon him*. But I said to myself at the outset, 'No, whatever happens, I will not usurp the place of God. I will not be the Priest-Patriarch of my children. They shall grow and I will grow beside them, helping but not cramping or overshadowing.' They grow more. But they blunder more. Life ceases to be a discipline and becomes an experiment. . . ."

"That's very true," said Mr. Direck, to whom it seemed the time was ripe to say something. "This is the problem of America perhaps even more than of England. Though I have not had the parental experience you have undergone. . . . I can see very clearly that a son is a very serious proposition."

"The old system of life was organisation. That is where Germany is still the most ancient of European states. It's a reversion to a tribal cult. It's atavistic. . . . To organise or discipline, or mould characters or press authority, is to assume that you have reached finality in your general philosophy. It implies an assured end. Heinrich has his assured end, his philological professorship or thereabouts as a part of the Germanic machine. And that too has its assured end in German national assertion. Here, we have none of those convictions. We know we haven't finality, and so we are open and apologetic and receptive, rather than wilful. . . . You see all organisation, with its implication of finality, is death. We feel that. The Germans don't. What you organise you kill. Organised morals or organised religion or organised thought are dead morals and dead religion and dead thought. Yet some organisation you must have. Organisation is like killing cattle. If you do not kill some the herd is just waste. But you mustn't kill all or you kill the herd. The unkilled cattle are the herd, the continuation; the unorganised side of life is the real life. The reality of life is adventure, not performance. What isn't adventure isn't life. What can be ruled about can be machined. But priests and schoolmasters and bureaucrats get hold of life and try to make it *all* rules, *all* etiquette and regulation and correctitude. . . . And parents and the love of parents make for the same thing. It is all very well to experiment for oneself, but when one sees these dear things of one's own, so young and inexperienced and so capable of every sort of gallant foolishness, walking along the narrow plank, going down into dark jungles, ah! then it makes one want to wrap them in laws and foresight and fence them about with 'Verboten' boards in all the conceivable aspects. . . ."

"In America of course we do set a certain store upon youthful self-reliance," said Mr. Direck.

"As we do here. It's in your blood and our blood. It's the instinct of the English and the Irish anyhow to suspect government and take the risks of the chancy way. . . . And manifestly the Russians, if you read their novelists, have the same twist in them. . . . When we get this young Prussian here, he's a marvel to us. He really believes in Law. He *likes* to obey. That seems a sort of joke to us. It's curious how foreign these Germans are—to all the rest of the world. Because of their docility. Scratch the Russian and you get the Tartar. Educate the Russian or the American or the Englishman or the Irishman or Frenchman or any real northern European except the German, and you get the Anarchist, that is to say the man who dreams of order without organisation—of something beyond organisation. . . .

"It's one o'clock," said Mr. Britling abruptly, perceiving a shade of fatigue upon the face of his hearer and realising that his thoughts had taken him too far, "and Sunday. Let's go to bed."

§ 11

For a time Mr. Direck could not sleep. His mind had been too excited by this incessant day with all its novelties and all its provocations to comparison. The whole complicated spectacle grouped itself, with a naturalness and a complete want of logic that all who have been young will understand, about Cecily Corner.

She had to be in the picture, and so she came in as though she were the central figure, as though she were the quintessential England. There she was, the type, the blood, the likeness, of no end of Massachusetts families, the very same stuff indeed, and yet she was different. . . .

For a time his thoughts hovered ineffectively about certain details of her ear and cheek, and one may doubt if his interest in these things was entirely international.

Then he found himself under way with an exposition of certain points to Mr. Britling. In the security of his bed he could imagine that he was talking very slowly and carefully while Mr. Britling listened; already he was more than half-way to dreamland or he could not have supposed anything so incredible.

"There's a curious sort of difference," he was saying. "It is difficult to define, but on the whole I might express it by saying that such a gathering as this if it was in America would be drawn with harder lines, would show its bones more and have everything more emphatic. And just to take one illustrative point: in America in such a gathering as this there would be bound to be several jokes going on as it were, running jokes and running criticisms, from day to day and from week to week. . . . There would be jokes about your writing and your influence and jokes about Miss Corner's advanced reading. . . . You see, in America we pay much more attention to personal character. Here people, I notice, are not talked to about their personal characters at all, and many of them do not seem to be aware and do not seem to mind what personal characters they have. . . .

"And another thing I find noteworthy is the way in which what I might call mature people seem to go on having a good time instead of standing by and applauding the young people having a good time. . . . And the young people do not seem to have set out to have a good time at all. . . . Now in America, a charming girl like Miss Corner would be distinctly more aware of herself and her vitality than she is here, distinctly more. Her peculiarly charming side-long look, if I might make so free with her—would have been called attention to. It's a perfectly beautiful look, the sort of look some great artist would have loved to make immortal. It's a look I shall find it hard to forget. . . . But she doesn't seem to be aware in the least of it. In America she would be aware of it. She would be distinctly aware of it. She would have been *made* aware of it. She would have been advised of it. It would be looked for and she would know it was looked for. She would *give* it as a singer gives her most popular song. Mamie Nelson, for example, used to give a peculiar little throw back of the chin and a laugh. . . . It was talked about. People came to see it. . . .

"Of course Mamie Nelson was a very brilliant girl indeed. I suppose in England you would say we spoiled her. I suppose we did spoil her. . . ."

It came into Mr. Direck's head that for a whole day he had scarcely given a thought to Mamie Nelson. And now he was thinking of her—calmly. Why shouldn't one think of Mamie Nelson calmly?

She was a proud imperious thing. There was something Southern in her. Very dark blue eyes she had, much darker than Miss Corner's. . . .

But how tortuous she had been behind that outward pride of hers! For four years she had let him think he was the only man who really mattered in the world, and all the time quite clearly and definitely she had deceived him. She had made a fool of him and she had made a fool of the others perhaps—just to have her retinue and play the queen in her world. And at last humiliation, bitter humiliation, and Mamie with her chin in the air and her bright triumphant smile looking down on him.

Hadn't he, she asked, had the privilege of loving her?

She took herself at the value they had set upon her.

Well—somehow—that wasn't right. . . .

All the way across the Atlantic Mr. Direck had been trying to forget her downward glance with the chin up, during that last encounter—and other aspects of the same humiliation. The years he had spent upon her! The time! Always relying upon her assurance of a special preference for him. He tried to think he was suffering from the pangs of unrequited love, and to conceal from himself just how bitterly his pride and vanity had been rent by her ultimate rejection. There had been a time when she had given him reason to laugh in his sleeve at Booth Wilmington.

Perhaps Booth Wilmington had also had reason for laughing in his sleeve. . . .

Had she even loved Booth Wilmington? Or had she just snatched at him? . . .

Wasn't he, Direck, as good a man as Booth Wilmington anyhow? . . .

For some moments the old sting of jealousy rankled again. He recalled the flaring rivalry that had ended in his defeat, the competition of gifts and treats. . . . A thing so open that all Carrierville knew of it, discussed it, took sides. . . . And over it all Mamie with her flashing smile had sailed like a processional goddess. . . .

Why, they had made jokes about him in the newspapers!

One couldn't imagine such a contest in Matching's Easy. Yet surely even in Matching's Easy there are lovers.

Is it something in the air, something in the climate that makes things harder and clearer in America? . . .

Cissie—why shouldn't one call her Cissie in one's private thoughts anyhow?—would never be as hard and clear as Mamie. She had English eyes—merciful eyes. . . .

That was the word—*merciful!*

The English light, the English air, are merciful. . . .

Merciful. . . .

They tolerate old things and slow things and imperfect apprehensions. They aren't always getting at you. . . .

They don't laugh at you. . . . At least—they laugh differently. . . .

Was England the tolerant country? With its kind eyes and its wary sidelong look. Toleration. In which everything mellowed and nothing was destroyed. A soft country. A country with a passion for imperfection. A padded country. . . .

England—all stuffed with soft feathers . . . under one's ear. A pillow—with soft, kind Corners. . . . Beautiful rounded Corners. . . . Dear, dear Corners. Cissie Corners. Corners. Could there be a better family?

Massachusetts—but in heaven. . . .

Harps playing two-steps, and kind angels wrapped in moonlight.

Very softly I and you,

One tum, two tum, three tum, too.

Off—we—go! . . .

CHAPTER THE THIRD

THE ENTERTAINMENT OF MR. DIRECK REACHES A CLIMAX

§ 1

BREAKFAST was in the open air, and a sunny, easy-going feast. Then the small boys laid hands on Mr. Direck and showed him the pond and the boats, while Mr. Britling strolled about the lawn with Hugh, talking rather intently. And when Mr. Direck returned from the boats in a state of greatly enhanced popularity he found Mr. Britling conversing over his garden railings with what was altogether a new type of Britisher in Mr. Direck's experience. It was a tall, lean sun-bitten youngish man of forty perhaps, in brown tweeds, looking more like the Englishman of the American illustrations than anything Mr. Direck had met hitherto. Indeed he came very near to a complete realisation of that ideal except that there was a sort of intensity about him, and that his clipped moustache had the restrained stiffness of a wiry-haired terrier. This gentleman Mr. Direck learned was Colonel Rendezvous. He spoke in clear short sentences, they had an effect of being punched out, and he was refusing to come into the garden and talk.

"Have to do my fourteen miles before lunch," he said. "You haven't seen Manning about, have you?"

"He isn't here," said Mr. Britling, and it seemed to Mr. Direck that there was the faintest ambiguity in this reply.

"Have to go alone, then," said Colonel Rendezvous. "They told me that he had started to come here."

"I shall motor over to Bramley High Oak for your Boy Scout festival," said Mr. Britling.

"Going to have three thousand of 'em," said the Colonel. "Good show."

His steely eyes seemed to search the cover of Mr. Britling's garden for the missing Manning, and then he decided to give him up. "I must be going," he said. "So long. Come up!"

A well-disciplined dog came to heel, and the lean figure had given Mr. Direck a semi-military salutation and gone upon its way. It marched with a long elastic stride; it never looked back.

"Manning," said Mr. Britling, "is probably hiding up in my rose-garden."

"Curiously enough, I guessed from your manner that that might be the case," said Mr. Direck.

"Yes. Manning is a London journalist. He has a little cottage about a mile over there"—Mr. Britling pointed vaguely—"and he comes down for the weekends. And Rendezvous has found out he isn't fit. And everybody ought to be fit. That is the beginning and end of life for Rendezvous. Fitness. An almost mineral quality, an insatiable activity of body, great mental simplicity. So he takes possession of poor old Manning and trots

85

him for that fourteen miles—at four miles an hour. Manning goes through all the agonies of death and damnation, he half dissolves, he pants and drags for the first eight or ten miles, and then I must admit he rather justifies Rendezvous' theory. He is to be found in the afternoon in a hammock suffering from blistered feet, but otherwise unusually well. But if he can escape it, he does. He hides."

"But if he doesn't want to go with Colonel Rendezvous, why does he?" said Mr. Direck.

"Well, Rendezvous is accustomed to the command of men. And Manning's only way of refusing things is on printed forms. Which he doesn't bring down to Matching's Easy. Ah! behold!"

Far away across the lawn between two blue cedars there appeared a leisurely form in grey flannels and a loose tie, advancing with manifest circumspection.

"He's gone," cried Britling.

The leisurely form, obviously amiable, obviously a little out of condition, became more confident, drew nearer.

"I'm sorry to have missed him," he said cheerfully. "I thought he might come this way. It's going to be a very warm day indeed. Let us sit about somewhere and talk.

"Of course," he said, turning to Direck, "Rendezvous is the life and soul of the country."

They strolled towards a place of seats and hammocks between the big trees and the rose-garden and the talk turned for a time upon Rendezvous. "They have the tidiest garden in Essex," said Manning. "It's not Mrs. Rendezvous' fault that it is so. Mrs. Rendezvous, as a matter of fact, has a taste for the picturesque. She just puts the things about in groups in the beds. She wants them, she says, to grow anyhow. She desires a romantic disorder. But she never gets it. When he walks down the path all the plants dress instinctively. . . . And there's a tree near their gate; it used to be a willow. You can ask any old man in the village. But ever since Rendezvous took the place it's been trying to present arms. With the most extraordinary results. I was passing the other day with old Windershin. 'You see that there old poplar,' he said. 'It's a willow,' said I. 'No,' he said, 'it did used to be a willow before Colonel Rendezvous he came. But now it's a poplar,' . . . And by Jove, it *is* a poplar!" . . .

The conversation thus opened by Manning centred for a time upon Colonel Rendezvous. He was presented as a monster of energy and self-discipline; as the determined foe of every form of looseness, slackness, and easygoingness.

"He's done wonderful work for the local Boy Scout movement," said Manning

"It's Kitchenerism," said Britling.

"It's the army side of the efficiency stunt," said Manning.

There followed a digression upon the Boy Scout movement, and Mr. Direck made comparisons with the propaganda of Seton Thompson in America. "Teddy Rooseveltism," said Manning. "It's a sort of reaction against everything being too easy and too safe."

"It's got its anti-decadent side," said Mr. Direck.

"If there is such a thing as decadence," said Mr. Britling.

"If there wasn't such a thing as decadence," said Manning, "we journalists would have had to invent it.". . . .

"There is something tragic in all this—what shall I call it?—Kitchenerism," Mr. Britling reflected. "Here you have it rushing about and keeping itself—screwed up, and trying desperately to keep the country screwed up. And all because there may be a war some day somehow with Germany. Provided Germany *is* insane. It's that war, like some sort of bee in Rendezvous' brains, that is driving him along the road now to Market Saffron—he always keeps to the roads because they are severer—through all the dust and sunshine. When he might be here gossiping. . . .

"And you know, I don't see that war coming," said Mr. Britling. "I believe Rendezvous sweats in vain. I can't believe in that war. It has held off for forty years. It may hold off for ever."

He nodded his head towards the German tutor, who had come into view across the lawn, talking profoundly with Mr. Britling's eldest son.

"Look at that pleasant person. There he is—*echt Deutsch*—if anything ever was. Look at my son there! Do you see the two of them engaged in mortal combat? The thing's too ridiculous. The world grows sane. They may fight in the Balkans still; in many ways the Balkan States are in the very rear of civilisation; but to imagine decent countries like this or Germany going back to bloodshed! No. . . . When I see Rendezvous keeping it up and keeping it up, I begin to see just how poor Germany must be keeping it up. I begin to realise how sick Germany must be getting of the highroad and the dust and heat and the everlasting drill and restraint. . . . My heart goes out to the South Germans. Old Manning here always reminds me of Austria. Think of Germany coming like Rendezvous on a Sunday morning, and looking stiffly over Austria's fence. 'Come for a good hard walk, man. Keep fit.' . . ."

"But suppose this Balkan trouble becomes acute," said Manning.

"It hasn't; it won't. Even if it did we should keep out of it."

"But suppose Russia grappled Austria and Germany flung herself suddenly upon France—perhaps taking Belgium on the way."

"Oh!—we should fight. Of course we should fight. Could anyone but a congenital idiot suppose we shouldn't fight? They know we should fight. They aren't altogether idiots in Germany. But the thing's absurd. Why *should* Germany attack France? It's as if Manning here took a hatchet suddenly and assailed Edith. . . . It's just the dream of their military journalists. It's such schoolboy nonsense. Isn't that a beautiful pillar rose? Edith only put it in last year. . . . I hate all this talk of wars and rumours of wars. . . . It's worried all my life. And it gets worse and it gets emptier every year. . . ."

§ 2

Now just at that moment there was a loud report. . . .

But neither Mr. Britling nor Mr. Manning nor Mr. Direck was interrupted or incommoded in the slightest degree by that report. Because it was too far off over the curve of this round world to be either heard or seen at Matching's Easy. Nevertheless it was a very loud report. It occurred at an open space by a river that ran through a cramped Oriental city, a city spiked with white minarets and girt about by bare hills under a blazing afternoon sky. It came from a black parcel that the Archduke Francis Ferdinand of Austria, with great presence of mind, had just flung out from the open hood of his automobile, where, tossed from the side of the quay, it had descended a few seconds before. It exploded as it touched the cobbled road just under the front of the second vehicle in the procession, and it blew to pieces the front of the automobile and injured the aide-de-camp who was in it and several of the spectators. Its thrower was immediately gripped by the bystanders. The procession stopped. There was a tremendous commotion amongst that

89

brightly costumed crowd, a hot excitement in vivid contrast to the Sabbath calm of Matching's Easy. . . .

Mr. Britling, to whom the explosion was altogether inaudible, continued his dissertation upon the common sense of the world and the practical security of our Western peace.

§ 3

Lunch was an open-air feast again. Three visitors had dropped in; they had motored down from London piled up on a motor-cycle and a side-car; a brother and two sisters they seemed to be, and they had apparently reduced hilariousness to a principle. The rumours of coming hockey, that had been floating on the outskirts of Mr. Direck's consciousness ever since his arrival thickened and multiplied. . . . It crept into his mind that he was expected to play. . . .

He decided he would not play. He took various people into his confidence. He told Mr. Britling, and Mr. Britling said, "We'll make you full-back, where you'll get a hit now and then and not have very much to do. All you have to remember is to hit with the flat side of your stick and not raise it above your shoulders." He told Teddy, and Teddy said, "I strongly advise you to dress as thinly as you can consistently with decency, and put your collar and tie in your pocket before the game begins. Hockey is properly a winter game." He told the maiden aunt-like lady with the prominent nose, and she said almost enviously, "Every one here is asked to play except me. I assuage the perambulator. I suppose one mustn't be envious. I don't see why I shouldn't play. I'm not so old as all that." He told Hugh, and Hugh warned him to be careful not to get hold of one of the sprung sticks. He considered whether it wouldn't be wiser to go to his own room and lock himself in, or stroll off for a walk through Claverings Park. But then he would miss Miss Corner, who was certain, it seemed, to come up for hockey. On the other hand, if he did not miss her he might make himself ridiculous in her eyes, and efface the effect of the green silk stuff with the golden pheasants.

He determined to stay behind until she arrived, and explain to her that he was not going to play. He didn't somehow want her to think he wasn't perfectly fit to play.

Mr. Carmine arrived in an automobile with two Indians and a gentleman who had been a prospector in Alaska, the family who had danced overnight at the Dower House reappeared, and then Mrs. Teddy, very detached with a special hockey-stick, and Miss Corner wheeling the perambulator. Then came further arrivals. At the earliest opportunity Mr. Direck secured the attention of Miss Corner, and lost his interest in any one else.

"I can't play this hockey," said Mr. Direck. "I feel strange about it. It isn't an American game. Now if it were baseball——!"

He left her to suppose him uncommonly hot stuff at baseball.

"If you're on my side," said Cecily, "mind you pass to me."

It became evident to Mr. Direck that he was going to play this hockey after all.

"Well," he said, "if I've got to play hockey, I guess I've got to play hockey. But can't I just get a bit of practice somewhere before the game begins?"

So Miss Corner went off to get two sticks and a ball and came back to instruct Mr. Direck. She said he had a good eye. The two small boys scenting play in the air got sticks and joined them. The overnight visitor's wife appeared from the house in abbreviated skirts, and wearing formidable shin-guards. With her abundant fair hair, which was already breaking loose, so to speak, to join the fray, she looked like a short stout dismounted Valkyr. Her gaze was clear and firm.

§ 4

Hockey as it was played at the Dower House at Matching's Easy before the war was a game combining danger, physical exercise and kindliness in a very high degree. Except for the infant in the perambulator and the outwardly calm but inwardly resentful aunt, who wheeled the child up and down in a position of maximum danger just behind the unnetted goal, every one was involved. Quite able-bodied people acquainted with the game played forward, the less well-informed played a defensive game behind the forward line, elderly, infirm, and bulky persons were used chiefly as obstacles in goal. Several players wore padded leg-guards, and all players were assumed to have them and expected to behave accordingly.

Proceedings began with an invidious ceremony called picking up. This was heralded by Mr. Britling, clad in the diaphanous flannels and bearing a hockey-stick, advancing with loud shouts to the centre of the hockey-field. "Pick up! Pick up!" echoed the young Britlings.

Mr. Direck became aware of a tall, drooping man with long hair and long digressive legs in still longer white flannel trousers, and a face that was somehow familiar. He was talking with affectionate intimacy to Manning, and suddenly Mr. Direck remembered that it was in Manning's weekly paper, *The Sectarian*, in which a bitter caricaturist enlivened a biting text, that he had become familiar with the features of Manning's companion. It was Raeburn, Raeburn the insidious, Raeburn the completest product of the party system. . . . Well, that was the

English way. "Come for the pick up!" cried the youngest Britling, seizing upon Mr. Direck's elbow. It appeared that Mr. Britling and the overnight dinner-guest—Mr. Direck never learned his name—were picking up.

Names were shouted. "I'll take Cecily!" Mr. Direck heard Mr. Britling say quite early. The opposing sides as they were picked fell into two groups. There seemed to be difficulties about some of the names. Mr. Britling, pointing to the more powerful-looking of the Indian gentlemen, said, "*You*, sir."

"I'm going to speculate on Mr. Dinks," said Mr. Britling's opponent. Mr. Direck gathered that Mr. Dinks was to be his hockey name.

"You're on *our* side," said Mrs. Teddy. "I think you'll have to play forward, outer right, and keep a sharp eye on Cissie."

"I'll do what I can," said Mr. Direck.

His captain presently confirmed this appointment.

His stick was really a sort of club and the ball was a firm hard cricket-ball. . . . He resolved to be very gentle with Cecily, and see that she didn't get hurt.

The sides took their places for the game, and a kind of order became apparent to Mr. Direck. In the centre stood Mr. Britling and the opposing captain, and the ball lay between them. They were preparing to "bully-off" and start the game. In a line with each of them were four other forwards. They all looked spirited and intent young people, and Mr. Direck wished he had had more exercise to justify his own alert appearance. Behind each centre forward hovered one of the Britling boys. Then on each side came a vaguer row of three backs, persons of gentler disposition or maturer years. They included Mr. Raeburn, who was considered to have great natural abilities for hockey but little experience. Mr. Raeburn was behind Mr. Direck. Mrs. Britling was the centre back. Then in a corner of Mr. Direck's side was a small girl of six or seven, and in the half-circle about the goal a lady in a motoring dust-coat and a very short little man whom Mr. Direck had not previously remarked. Mr. Lawrence Carmine, stripped to the braces, which were richly ornamented with Oriental embroidery, kept goal for our team.

The centre forwards went through a rapid little ceremony. They smote their sticks on the ground, and then hit the sticks together. "One," said Mr. Britling. The operation was repeated. "Two," . . . "Three."

Smack, Mr. Britling had got it and the ball had gone to the shorter and sturdier of the younger Britlings, who had been standing behind Mr. Direck's captain. Crack, and it was away to Teddy; smack, and it was coming right at Direck.

"Lordy!" he said and prepared to smite it.

Then something swift and blue had flashed before him, intercepted the ball and shot it past him. This was Cecily Corner, and she and Teddy were running abreast like the wind towards Mr. Raeburn.

"Hey!" cried Mr. Raeburn, "stop!" and advanced, as it seemed to Mr. Direck, with unseemly and threatening gestures towards Cissie.

But before Mr. Direck could adjust his mind to this new phase of affairs, Cecily had passed the right honourable gentleman with the same mysterious ease with which she had flashed by Mr. Direck, and was bearing down upon the miscellaneous Landwehr which formed the "backs" of Mr. Direck's side.

"*You* rabbit!" cried Mr. Raeburn, and became extraordinarily active in pursuit, administering great lengths of arm and leg with a centralised efficiency he had not hitherto displayed.

Running hard to the help of Mr. Raeburn was the youngest Britling boy, a beautiful contrast. It was like a puffball supporting and assisting a conger-eel. In front of Mr. Direck the little stout man was being alert. Teddy was supporting the attack near the middle of the field, crying "Centre!" while Mr. Britling, very round and resolute, was bouncing straight towards the threatened goal. But Mrs. Teddy, running as swiftly as her sister, was between Teddy and the ball. Whack! the little short man's stick had clashed with Cecily's. Confused things happened with sticks and feet, and the little short man appeared to be trying to cut down Cecily as one cuts down a tree, she tried to pass the ball to her centre forward—too late, and then Mrs. Teddy had intercepted it, and was flickering back towards Mr. Britling's goal in a rush in which Mr. Direck perceived it was his duty to join.

Yes, he had to follow up Mrs. Teddy and pick up the ball if he had a chance and send it in to her or the captain or across to the left forwards, as circumstances might decide. It was perfectly clear.

Then came his moment. The little formidably padded lady who had dined at the Dower House overnight made a gallant attack upon Mrs. Teddy. Out of the confusion of this clash the ball spun into Mr. Direck's radius. Where should he smite and how? A moment of reflection was natural.

But now the easy-fitting discipline of the Dower House style of hockey became apparent. Mr. Direck had last observed the tall young Indian gentleman, full of vitality and anxious for destruction, far away in the distance on the opposing right wing. Regardless of the more formal methods of the game, this young man had resolved, without further delay and at any cost, to hit the ball hard, and he was travelling like some Asiatic typhoon with an extreme velocity across the remonstrances of Mr. Britling and the general order of his side. Mr. Direck became aware of him just before his impact. There was a sort of collision from which Mr. Direck emerged with a feeling that one side of his face was permanently flattened, but still gallantly resolved to hit the comparatively lethargic ball. He and the staggered but resolute Indian clashed sticks again. And Mr. Direck had the best of it. Years of experience couldn't have produced a better pass to the captain. . . .

"Good pass!"

Apparently from one of the London visitors.

But this was *some* game!

The ball executed some rapid movements to and fro across the field. Our side was pressing hard. There was a violent convergence of miscellaneous backs and such-like irregulars upon the threatened goal. Mr. Britling's dozen was rapidly losing its disciplined order. One of the side-car ladies and the gallant Indian had shifted their activities to the defensive back, and with them was a spectacled gentleman waving his stick, high above all recognised rules. Mr. Direck's captain and both Britling boys hurried to join the fray. Mr. Britling, who seemed to Mr. Direck to be for a captain rather too demagogic, also ran back to rally his forces by loud cries. "Pass outwardly!" was the burthen of his contribution.

The struggle about the Britling goal ceased to be a game and became something between a fight and a social gathering. Mr. Britling's goal-keeper could be heard shouting, "I can't *see* the ball! *Lift your feet!*" The crowded conflict lurched towards the goal-posts. "My shin!" cried Mr. Manning. "No, you *don't!*"

Whack, but again whack!

Whack! "Ah! *would* you?" Whack.

"Goal!" cried the side-car gentleman.

"Goal!" cried the Britling boys. . . .

Mr. Manning, as goal-keeper, went to recover the ball, but one of the Britling boys politely anticipated him.

The crowd became inactive, and then began to drift back to loosely conceived positions.

"It's no good swarming into goal like that," Mr. Britling, with a faint asperity in his voice, explained to his followers. "We've got to keep open and not *crowd* each other."

Then he went confidentially to the energetic young Indian to make some restrictive explanation of his activities.

Mr. Direck strolled back towards Cecily. He was very warm and a little blown, but not, he felt, disgraced. He was winning.

"You'll have to take your coat off," she said.

It was a good idea.

It had occurred to several people, and the boundary-line was already dotted with hastily discarded jackets and wraps and so forth. But the lady in the motoring dust-coat was buttoning it to the chin.

"One goal love," said the minor Britling boy.

"We haven't begun yet, Sunny," said Cecily.

"Sonny! That's American," said Mr. Direck.

"No. We call him Sunny Jim," said Cecily. "They're bullying off again."

"Sunny Jim's American too," said Mr. Direck, returning to his place. . . .

The struggle was resumed. And soon it became clear that the first goal was no earnest of the quality of the struggle. Teddy and Cecily formed a terribly efficient combination. Against their brilliant rushes, supported in a vehement but effective manner by the Indian to their right and guided by loud shoutings from Mr. Britling (centre), Mr. Direck and the side-car lady and Mr. Raeburn struggled in vain. One swift advance was only checked by the dust-coat, its folds held the ball until help arrived; another was countered by a tremendous swipe of Mr. Raeburn's that sent the ball within an inch of the youngest Britling's head and right across the field; the third resulted in a swift pass from Cecily to the elder Britling son away on her right, and he shot the goal neatly through the lattice of Mr. Lawrence Carmine's defensive movements. And after that very rapidly came another goal for Mr. Britling's side and then another.

Then Mr. Britling cried out that it was "Half Time," and explained to Mr. Direck that whenever one side got to three goals they considered it was half time and had five minutes' rest and changed sides. Everybody was very hot and happy, except the lady in the dust-coat, who was perfectly cool. In everybody's eyes shone the light of battle, and not a shadow disturbed the brightness of the afternoon for Mr. Direck except a certain unspoken anxiety about Mr. Raeburn's trousers.

You see Mr. Direck had never seen Mr. Raeburn before, and knew nothing about his trousers.

They appeared to be coming down.

To begin with they had been rather loose over the feet and turned up, and as the game progressed, fold after fold of concertina-ed flannel gathered about his ankles. Every now and then Mr. Raeburn would seize the opportunity of some respite from the game to turn up a fresh six inches or so of this accumulation. Naturally Mr. Direck expected this policy to end unhappily. He did not know that the flannel trousers of Mr. Raeburn were like a river, that they could come down for ever and still remain inexhaustible. . . .

He had visions of this scene of happy innocence being suddenly blasted by a monstrous disaster. . . .

Apart from this worry Mr. Direck was as happy as any one there!

Perhaps these apprehensions affected his game. At any rate he did nothing that pleased him in the second half, Cecily danced all over him and round and about him, and in the course of ten minutes her side had won the two remaining goals with a score of Five-One; and five goals is "game" by the standards of Matching's Easy.

And then with the very slightest of delays these insatiable people picked up again. Mr. Direck slipped away and returned in a white silk shirt, tennis trousers and a belt. This time he and Cecily were on the same side, the Cecily-Teddy combination was broken, and he it seemed was to take the place of the redoubtable Teddy on the left wing with her.

This time the sides were better chosen and played a long, obstinate, even game. One-One. One-Two. One-Three. (Half Time.) Two-Three. Three all. Four-Three. Four all. . . .

By this time Mr. Direck was beginning to master the simple strategy of the sport. He was also beginning to master the fact that Cecily was the quickest, nimblest, most indefatigable player on the field. He scouted for her and passed to her. He developed tacit understandings with her. Ideas of protecting her had gone to the four winds of heaven. Against them Teddy and a side-car girl with Raeburn in support made a memorable struggle. Teddy was as quick as a cat. "Four-Three" looked like winning, but then Teddy and the tall Indian and Mrs. Teddy pulled square. They almost repeated this feat and won, but Mr. Manning saved the situation with an immense oblique hit that sent the ball to Mr. Direck. He ran with the ball up to Raeburn and then dodged and passed to Cecily. There was a lively struggle to the left; the ball was hit out by Mr. Raeburn and thrown in by a young Britling; lost by the forwards and rescued by the padded lady. Forward again! This time will do it!

Cecily away to the left had worked round Mr. Raeburn once more. Teddy, realising that things were serious, was tearing back to attack her.

Mr. Direck supported with silent intentness. "Centre!" cried Mr. Britling. "Cen-tre!"

"Mr. Direck!" came her voice, full of confidence. (Of such moments is the heroic life.) The ball shot behind the hurtling Teddy. Mr. Direck stopped it with his foot, a trick he had just learned from the eldest Britling son. He was neither slow nor hasty. He was in the half-circle, and the way to the goal was barred only by the dust-coat lady and Mr. Lawrence Carmine. He made as if to shoot to Mr. Carmine's left and then smacked the ball, with the swiftness of a serpent's stroke, to his right.

He'd done it! Mr. Carmine's stick and feet were a yard away.

Then hard on this wild triumph came a flash of horror. One can't see everything. His eye followed the ball's trajectory. . . .

Directly in its line of flight was a perambulator.

The ball missed the legs of the lady with the noble nose by a kind of miracle, hit and glanced off the wheel of the perambulator, and went spinning into a border of antirrhinums.

"Good!" cried Cecily. "Splendid shot!"

He'd shot a goal. He'd done it well. The perambulator it seemed didn't matter. Though apparently the impact had awakened the baby. In the margin of his consciousness was the figure of Mr. Britling remarking: "Aunty. You really mustn't wheel the perambulator *just* there."

"I thought," said the aunt, indicating the goal-posts by a facial movement, "that those two sticks would be a sort of protection. . . . Aah! *Did* they then?"

Never mind that.

"That's *game!*" said one of the junior Britlings to Mr. Direck with a note of high appreciation, and the whole party, relaxing and crumpling like a lowered flag, moved towards the house and tea.

§ 5

"We'll play some more after tea," said Cecily. "It will be cooler then."

"My word, I'm beginning to like it," said Mr. Direck.

"You're going to play very well," she said.

And such is the magic of a game that Mr. Direck was humbly proud and grateful for her praise, and trotted along by the side of this creature who had revealed herself so swift and resolute and decisive, full to overflowing of the mere pleasure of just trotting along by her side. And after tea, which was a large confused affair, enlivened by wonderful and entirely untruthful reminiscences of the afternoon by Mr. Raeburn, they played again, with fewer inefficients and greater skill and swiftness, and Mr. Direck did such quick and intelligent things that everybody declared that he was a hockey-player straight from heaven. The dusk, which at last made the position of the ball too speculative for play, came all too soon for him. He had played in six games, and he knew he would be as stiff as a Dutch doll in the morning. But he was very, very happy.

The rest of the Sunday evening was essentially a sequel to the hockey.

Mr. Direck changed again, and after using some embrocation, that Mrs. Britling recommended very strongly, came down in a black jacket and a cheerfully ample black tie. He had a sense of physical well-being such as he had not experienced since he came aboard the liner at New York. The curious thing was that it was not quite the same sense of physical well-being that one had in America. That is bright and clear and a little dry, this was—humid. His mind quivered contentedly, like sunset midges over a lake—it had no hard bright flashes—and his body wanted to sit about. His sense of intimacy with Cecily increased each time he looked at her. When she met his eyes she smiled. He'd caught her style now, he felt; he attempted no more compliments, and was frankly her pupil at hockey and Badminton. After supper Mr. Britling renewed his suggestion of an automobile excursion on the Monday.

"There's nothing to take you back to London," said Mr. Britling, "and we could just hunt about the district with the little old car and see everything you want to see. . . ."

Mr. Direck did not hesitate three seconds. He thought of Gladys; he thought of Miss Cecily Corner.

"Well, indeed," he said, "if it isn't burthening you, if I'm not being any sort of inconvenience here for another night, I'd be really very glad indeed of the opportunity of going around and seeing all these ancient places. . . ."

§ 6

The newspapers came next morning at nine, and were full of the Sarajevo Murders. Mr. Direck got *The Daily Chronicle* and found headlines quite animated for a British paper.

"Who's this Archduke," he asked, "anyhow? And where is this Bosnia? I thought it was a part of Turkey."

"It's in Austria," said Teddy.

"It's in the middle ages," said Mr. Britling. "What an odd, pertinacious business it seems to have been. First one bomb, then another; then finally the man with the pistol. While we were strolling about the rose-garden. It's like something out of 'The Prisoner of Zenda.'"

"Please," said Herr Heinrich.

Mr. Britling assumed an attentive expression.

"Will not this generally affect European politics?"

"I don't know. Perhaps it will."

"It says in the paper that Serbia has sent those bombs to Sarajevo."

"It's like another world," said Mr. Britling, over his paper. "Assassination as a political method. Can you imagine anything of the sort happening nowadays west of the Adriatic? Imagine some one assassinating the American Vice-President, and the bombs being at once ascribed to the arsenal at Toronto! . . . We take our politics more sadly in the West. . . . Won't you have another egg, Direck?"

"Please! Might this not lead to a war?"

"I don't think so. Austria may threaten Serbia, but she doesn't want to provoke a conflict with Russia. It would be going too near the powder-magazine. But it's all an extraordinary business."

"But if she did?" Herr Heinrich persisted.

"She won't. . . . Some years ago I used to believe in the inevitable European war," Mr. Britling explained to Mr. Direck, "but it's been threatened so long that at last I've lost all belief in it. The Powers wrangle and threaten. They're far too cautious and civilised to let the guns go off. If there was going to be a war it would have happened two years ago when the Balkan League fell upon Turkey. Or when Bulgaria attacked Serbia. . . ."

Herr Heinrich reflected, and received these conclusions with an expression of respectful edification.

"I am naturally anxious," he said, "because I am taking tickets for my holidays at an Esperanto Conference at Boulogne."

§ 7

"There is only one way to master such a thing as driving an automobile," said Mr. Britling outside his front door, as he took his place in the driver's seat, "and that is to resolve that from the first you will take no risks. Be slow if you like. Stop and think when you are in doubt. But do nothing rashly, permit no mistakes."

It seemed to Mr. Direck as he took his seat beside his host that this was admirable doctrine.

They started out of the gates with an extreme deliberation. Indeed twice they stopped dead in the act of turning into the road, and the engine had to be restarted.

"You will laugh at me," said Mr. Britling: "but I'm resolved to have no blunders this time."

"I don't laugh at you. It's excellent," said Mr. Direck.

"It's the right way," said Mr. Britling. "Care—oh, damn! I've stopped the engine again. Ugh!—ah!—*so!*—Care, I was saying—and calm."

"Don't think I want to hurry you," said Mr. Direck. "I don't."

They passed through the village at a slow, agreeable pace, tooting loudly at every corner, and whenever a pedestrian was approached. Mr. Direck was reminded that he had still to broach the lecture project to Mr. Britling. So much had happened——

The car halted abruptly and the engine stopped.

"I thought that confounded hen was thinking of crossing the road," said Mr. Britling. "Instead of which she's gone through the hedge. She certainly *looked* this way. . . . Perhaps I'm a little fussy this morning. . . . I'll warm up to the work presently."

"I'm convinced you can't be too careful," said Mr. Direck. "And this sort of thing enables one to see the country better. . . ."

Beyond the village Mr. Britling seemed to gather confidence. The pace quickened. But whenever other traffic or any indication of a side way appeared discretion returned. Mr. Britling stalked his sign-posts, crawling towards them on the belly of the lowest gear; he drove all the morning like a man who is flushing ambuscades. And yet accident overtook him. For God demands more from us that mere righteousness.

He cut through the hills to Market Saffron along a lane-road with which he was unfamiliar. It began to go up-hill. He explained to Mr. Direck how admirably his engine would climb hills on the top gear.

They took a curve and the hill grew steeper, and Mr. Direck opened the throttle.

They rounded another corner, and still more steeply the hill rose before them.

The engine began to make a chinking sound, and the car lost pace. And then Mr. Britling saw a pleading little white board with the inscription "Concealed Turning." For the moment he thought a turning might be concealed anywhere. He threw out his clutch and clapped on his brake. Then he repented of what he had done. But the engine, after three Herculean throbs, ceased to work. Mr. Britling with a convulsive clutch at his steering-wheel set the electric hooter snarling, while one foot released the clutch again and the other, on the accelerator, sought in vain for help. Mr. Direck felt they were going back, back, in spite of all this vocalisation. He clutched at the emergency brake. But he was too late to avoid misfortune. With a feeling like sitting gently in butter, the car sank down sideways and stopped with two wheels in the ditch.

Mr. Britling said they were in the ditch—said it with quite unnecessary violence. . . .

This time two cart-horses and a retinue of five men were necessary to restore Gladys to her self-respect. . . .

After that they drove on to Market Saffron, and got there in time for lunch, and after lunch Mr. Direck explored the church and the churchyard and the parish register. . . .

After lunch Mr. Britling became more cheerful about his driving. The road from Market Saffron to Blandish, whence one turns off to Matching's Easy, is the London and Norwich highroad; it is an old Roman Stane Street and very straightforward and honest in its stretches. You can see the crossroads half a mile away, and the low hedges give you no chance of a surprise. Everybody is cheered by such a road, and everybody drives more confidently and quickly, and Mr. Britling particularly was heartened by it and gradually let out Gladys from the almost excessive restriction that had hitherto marked the day. "On a road like this nothing can happen," said Mr. Britling.

"Unless you broke an axle or burst a tire," said Mr. Direck.

"My man at Matching's Easy is most careful in his inspection," said Mr. Britling, putting the accelerator well down and watching the speed indicator creep from forty to forty-five. "He went over the car not a week ago. And it's not one month old—in use that is."

Yet something did happen.

It was as they swept by the picturesque walls under the big old trees that encircle Brandismead Park. It was nothing but a slight miscalculation of distances. Ahead of them and well to the left rode a postman on a bicycle; towards them, with that curious effect of implacable fury peculiar to motor-cycles, came a motor-cyclist. First Mr. Britling thought that he would not pass between these two, then he decided that he would hurry up and do so, then he reverted to his former decision, and then it seemed to him that he was going so fast that he must inevitably run down the postman. His instinct not to do that pulled the car sharply across the path of the motor-cyclist. "Oh, my God!" cried Mr. Britling; "My God!" twisted his wheel over and distributed his feet among his levers dementedly.

He had an imperfectly formed idea of getting across right in front of the motor-cyclist, and then they were going down the brief grassy slope between the road and the wall, straight at the wall, and still at a good speed. The motor-cyclist smacked against something and vanished from the problem. The wall seemed to rush up at them and then—collapse. There was a tremendous concussion. Mr. Direck gripped at his friend the emergency brake, but had only time to touch it before his head hit against the frame of the glass wind-screen, and a curtain fell upon everything. . . .

He opened his eyes upon a broken wall, a crumpled motor-car, and an undamaged motor-cyclist in the aviator's cap and thin oilskin overalls dear to motor-cyclists. Mr. Direck stared and then, still stunned and puzzled, tried to raise himself. He became aware of acute pain.

"Don't move for a bit," said the motor-cyclist. "Your arm and side are rather hurt, I think. . . ."

§ 8

In the course of the next twelve hours Mr. Direck was to make a discovery that was less common in the days before the war than it has been since. He discovered that even pain and injury may be vividly interesting and gratifying.

If any one had told him he was going to be stunned for five or six minutes, cut about the brow and face and have a bone in his wrist put out, and that as a consequence he would find himself pleased and exhilarated, he would have treated the prophecy with ridicule; but here he was lying stiffly on his back with his wrist bandaged to his side and smiling into the darkness even more brightly than he had smiled at the Essex landscape two days before. The fact is pain hurts or irritates, but in itself it does not make a healthily constituted man miserable. The expectation of pain, the certainty of injury may make one hopeless enough, the reality rouses our resistance. Nobody wants a broken bone or a delicate wrist, but very few people are very much depressed by getting one. People can be much more depressed by smoking a hundred cigarettes in three days or losing one per cent. of their capital.

And everybody had been most delightful to Mr. Direck.

He had had the monopoly of damage. Mr. Britling, holding on to the steering-wheel, had not even been thrown out. "Unless I'm internally injured," he said, "I'm not hurt at all. My liver perhaps—bruised a little. . . ."

Gladys had been abandoned in the ditch, and they had been very kindly brought home by a passing automobile. Cecily had been at the Dower House at the moment of the rueful arrival. She had seen how an American can carry injuries.

She had made sympathy and helpfulness more delightful by expressed admiration.

"She's a natural born nurse," said Mr. Direck, and then rather in the tone of one who addressed a public meeting: "But this sort of thing brings out all the good there is in a woman."

He had been quite explicit to them and more particularly to her, when they told him he must stay at the Dower House until his arm was cured. He had looked the application straight into her pretty eyes.

"If I'm to stay right here just as a consequence of that little shake up, maybe for a couple of weeks, maybe three, and if you're coming to do a bit of a talk to me ever and again, then I tell you I don't call this a misfortune. It isn't a misfortune. It's right down sheer good luck. . . ."

And now he lay as straight as a mummy, with his soul filled with radiance of complete mental peace. After months of distress and confusion, he'd got straight again. He was in the middle of a real good story, bright and clean. He knew just exactly what he wanted.

"After all," he said, "it's true. There's ideals. *She's* an ideal. Why, I loved her before ever I set eyes on Mamie. I loved her before I was put into pants. That old portrait, there it was pointing my destiny. . . . It's affinity. . . . It's natural selection. . . .

"Well, I don't know what she thinks of me yet, but I do know very well what she's *got* to think of me. She's got to think all the world of me—if I break every limb of my body making her do it.

"I'd a sort of feeling it was right to go in that old automobile.

"Say what you like, there's a Guidance. . . ."

He smiled confidentially at the darkness as if they shared a secret.

CHAPTER THE FOURTH

MR. BRITLING IN SOLILOQUY

§ 1

VERY different from the painful contentment of the bruised and broken Mr. Direck was the state of mind of his unwounded host. He too was sleepless, but sleepless without exaltation. The day had been too much for him altogether; his head, to borrow an admirable American expression, was "busy."

How busy it was, a whole chapter will be needed to describe. . . .

The impression Mr. Britling had made upon Mr. Direck was one of indefatigable happiness. But there were times when Mr. Britling was called upon to pay for his general cheerful activity in lump sums of bitter sorrow. There were nights— and especially after seasons of exceptional excitement and nervous activity—when the reckoning would be presented and Mr. Britling would welter prostrate and groaning under a stormy sky of unhappiness—active insatiable unhappiness—a beating with rods.

The sorrows of the sanguine temperament are brief but furious; the world knows little of them. The world has no need to reckon with them. They cause no suicides and few crimes. They hurry past, smiting at their victim as they go. None the less they are misery. Mr. Britling in these moods did not perhaps experience the grey and hopeless desolations of the melancholic nor the red damnation of the choleric, but he saw a world that bristled with misfortune and error, with poisonous thorns and traps and swampy places and incurable blunderings. An almost insupportable remorse for being Mr. Britling would pursue him—justifying itself upon a hundred counts. . . .

And for being such a Britling! . . .

Why—he revived again that bitter question of a thousand and one unhappy nights—why was he such a fool? Such a hasty fool? Why couldn't he look before he leaped? Why did he take risks? Why was he always so ready to act upon the supposition that all was bound to go well? (He might as well have asked why he had quick brown eyes.)

Why, for instance, hadn't he adhered to the resolution of the early morning? He had begun with an extremity of caution. . . .

It was a characteristic of these moods of Mr. Britling that they produced a physical restlessness. He kept on turning over and then turning over again, and sitting up and lying back, like a martyr on a gridiron. . . .

This was just the latest instance of a lifelong trouble. Will there ever be a sort of man whose thoughts are quick and his acts slow? Then indeed we shall have a formidable being. Mr. Britling's thoughts were quick and sanguine and his actions even more eager than his thoughts. Already while he was a young man Mr. Britling had found his acts elbow their way through the hurry of his ideas and precipitate humiliations. Long before his reasons were marshalled, his resolutions were formed. He had attempted a thousand remonstrances with himself; he had sought to remedy the defects in his own character by written inscriptions in his bedroom and memoranda inside his watch-case. "Keep steady!" was one of them. "Keep the End in View." And, "Go steadfastly, coherently, continuously; only so can you go where you will." In distrusting all impulse, scrutinising all imagination, he was persuaded lay his one prospect of escape from the surprise of countless miseries. Otherwise he danced among glass bombs and barbed wire.

There had been a time when he could exhort himself to such fundamental charge and go through phases of the severest discipline. Always at last to be taken by surprise from some unexpected quarter. At last he had ceased to hope for any triumph so radical. He had been content to believe that in recent years age and a gathering habit of wisdom had somewhat slowed his leaping purpose. That if he hadn't overcome he had at least to a certain extent minimised it. But this last folly was surely the worst. To hurl through this patient world with—how much did the car weigh? A ton certainly and perhaps more—reckless of every risk. Not only to himself but others. At this thought, he clutched the steering-wheel again. Once more he saw the bent back of the endangered cyclist, once more he felt rather than saw the seething approach of the motor-bicycle, and then through a long instant he drove helplessly at the wall. . . .

Hell perhaps is only one such incident, indefinitely prolonged. . . .

Anything might have been there in front of him. And indeed now, out of the dreamland to which he could not escape something had come, something that screamed sharply. . . .

"Good God!" he cried, "if I had hit a child! I might have hit a child!" The hypothesis flashed into being with the thought, tried to escape and was caught. It was characteristic of Mr. Britling's nocturnal imagination that he should individualise this child quite clearly as rather plain and slender, with reddish hair, staring eyes, and its ribs crushed in vivid and dreadful manner, pinned against the wall, mixed up with some bricks, only to be extracted, oh! *horribly*.

But this was not fair! He had hurt no child! He had merely pitched out Mr. Direck and damaged his wrist. . . .

It wasn't his merit that the child hadn't been there!

The child might have been there!

Mere luck.

He lay staring in despair—as an involuntary God might stare at many a thing in this amazing universe—staring at the little victim his imagination had called into being only to destroy. . . .

§ 2

If he had not crushed a child other people had. Such things happened. Vicariously at any rate he had crushed many children. . . .

Why are children ever crushed?

And suddenly all the pain and destruction and remorse of all the accidents in the world descended upon Mr. Britling.

No longer did he ask why am I such a fool, but why are we all such fools? He became Man on the automobile of civilisation, crushing his thousands daily in his headlong and yet aimless career. . . .

That was a trick of Mr. Britling's mind. It had this tendency to spread outward from himself to generalised issues. Many minds are like that nowadays. He was not so completely individualised as people are supposed to be individualised—in our law, in our stories, in our moral judgments. He had a vicarious factor. He could slip from concentrated reproaches to the liveliest remorse for himself as The Automobilist in General, or for himself as England, or for himself as Man. From remorse for smashing his guest and his automobile he could pass by what was for him the most imperceptible of transitions to remorse for every accident that has ever happened through the error of an automobilist since automobiles began. All that long succession of blunderers became Mr. Britling. Or rather Mr. Britling became all that vast succession of blunderers.

These fluctuating lapses from individuation made Mr. Britling a perplexity to many who judged only by the old personal standards. At times he seemed a monster of cantankerous self-righteousness, whom nobody could please or satisfy, but indeed when he was most pitiless about the faults of his race or nation he was really reproaching himself, and when he seemed more egotistical and introspective and self-centred he was really ransacking himself for a clue to that same confusion of purposes that waste the hope and strength of humanity. And now through the busy distresses of the night it would have perplexed a watching angel to have drawn the line and shown when Mr. Britling was grieving for his own loss and humiliation and when he was grieving for these common human weaknesses of which he had so large a share.

And this double refraction of his mind by which a concentrated and individualised Britling did not present a larger impersonal Britling beneath, carried with it a duplication of his conscience and sense of responsibility. To his personal conscience he was answerable for his private honour and his debts and the Dower House he had made and so on, but to his impersonal conscience he was answerable for the whole world. The world from the latter point of view was his egg. He had a sub-conscious delusion that he had laid it. He had a sub-conscious suspicion that he had let it cool and that it was addled. He had an urgency to incubate it. The variety and interest of his talk was largely due to that persuasion, it was a perpetual attempt to spread his mental feathers over the task before him. . . .

§ 3

After this much of explanation it is possible to go on to the task which originally brought Mr. Direck to Matching's Easy, the task that Massachusetts society had sent him upon, the task of organising the mental unveiling of Mr. Britling. Mr. Direck saw Mr. Britling only in the daylight, and with an increasing distraction of the attention towards Miss Cecily Corner. We may see him rather more clearly in the darkness, without any distraction except his own.

Now the smashing of Gladys was not only the source of a series of reproaches and remorses directly arising out of the disaster; it had also a wide system of collateral consequences, which were also banging and blundering their way through the Britling mind. It was extraordinarily inconvenient in quite another respect that the automobile should be destroyed. It upset certain plans of Mr. Britling's in a direction growing right out from all the Dower House world in which Mr. Direck supposed him to be completely set and rooted. There were certain matters from which Mr. Britling had been averting his mind most strenuously throughout the weekend. Now, there was no averting his mind any more.

Mr. Britling was entangled in a love-affair. It was, to be exact, and disregarding minor affinities, his eighth love-affair. And the new automobile, so soon as he could drive it efficiently, was to have played quite a solvent and conclusive part in certain entangled complications of this relationship.

A man of lively imagination and quick impulses naturally has love-affairs as he drives himself through life, just as he naturally has accidents if he drives an automobile.

And the peculiar relations that existed between Mr. Britling and Mrs. Britling tended inevitably to make these love-affairs troublesome, undignified and futile. Especially when they were viewed from the point of view of insomnia.

Mr. Britling's first marriage had been a passionately happy one. His second was by comparison a marriage in neutral tint. There is much to be said for that extreme Catholic theory which would make marriage not merely lifelong but eternal. Certainly Mr. Britling would have been a finer if not a happier creature if his sentimental existence could have died with his first wife or continued only in his love for their son. He had married in the glow of youth, he had had two years of clean and simple loving, helping, quarrelling and the happy ending of quarrels. Something went out of him into all that which could not be renewed again. In his first extremity of grief he knew this perfectly well—and then afterwards he forgot it. While there is life there is imagination, which makes and forgets and goes on.

He met Edith under circumstances that did not in any way recall his lost Mary. He met her, as people say, "socially"; Mary, on the other hand, had been a girl at Newnham while he was a fellow of Pembroke, and there had been something of accident and something of furtiveness in their lucky discovery of each other. There had been a flush in it; there was dash in it. But Edith he saw and chose and had to woo. There was no rushing together; there was solicitation and assent. Edith was a Bachelor of Science of London University and several things like that, and she looked upon the universe under her broad forehead and broad-waving brown hair with quiet watchful eyes that had nothing whatever to hide, a thing so incredible to Mr. Britling that he had loved and married her very largely for the serenity of her mystery. And for a time after their marriage he sailed over those brown depths plumbing furiously.

Of course he did not make his former passion for Mary at all clear to her. Indeed, while he was winning Edith it was by no means clear to himself. He was making a new emotional drama, and consciously and subconsciously he dismissed a hundred reminiscences which sought to invade the new experience, and would have been out of key with it. And without any deliberate intention to that effect he created an atmosphere between himself and Edith in which any discussion of Mary was reduced to a minimum, and in which Hugh was accepted rather than explained. He contrived to believe that she understood all sorts of unsayable things; he invented miracles of quite uncongenial mute mutuality. . . .

It was over the chess-board that they first began to discover their extensive difficulties of sympathy. Mr. Britling's play was characterised by a superficial brilliance, much generosity and extreme unsoundness; he always moved directly his opponent had done so—and then reflected on the situation. His reflection was commonly much wiser than his moves. Mrs. Britling was, as it were, a natural antagonist to her husband; she was as calm as he was irritable. She was never in a hurry to move, and never disposed to make a concession. Quietly, steadfastly, by caution and deliberation, without splendour, without error, she had beaten him at chess until it led to such dreadful fits of anger that he had to renounce the game altogether. After every such occasion he would be at great pains to explain that he had merely been angry with himself. Nevertheless he felt, and would not let himself think (what she concluded from incidental heated phrases), that that was not the complete truth about the outbreak.

Slowly they got through the concealments of that specious explanation. Temperamentally they were incompatible.

They were profoundly incompatible. In all things she was defensive. She never came out; never once had she surprised him half-way upon the road to her. He had to go all the way to her and knock and ring, and then she answered faithfully. She never surprised him even by unkindness. If he had a cut finger she would bind it up very skilfully and healingly, but unless he told her she never discovered he had a cut finger. He was amazed she did not know of it before it happened. He piped and she did not dance. That became the formula of his grievance. For several unhappy years she thwarted him and disappointed him, while he filled her with dumb inexplicable distresses. He had been at first so gay an activity, and then he was shattered; fragments of him were still as gay and attractive as ever, but between were outbreaks of anger, of hostility, of something very like malignity. Only very slowly did they realise the truth of their relationship and admit to themselves that the fine bud of love between them had failed to flower, and only after long years were they able to delimit boundaries where they had imagined union, and to become—allies. If it had been reasonably possible for them to part without mutual injury and recrimination they would have done so, but two children presently held them, and gradually they had to work out the broad mutual toleration of their later relations. If there was no love and delight between them there was a real habitual affection and much mutual help. She was proud of his steady progress to distinction, proud of each intimation of respect he won; she admired and respected his work; she recognised that he had some magic of liveliness and unexpectedness that was precious and enviable. So far as she could help him she did. And even when he knew that there was nothing behind it, that it was indeed little more than an imaginative inertness, he could still admire and respect her steady dignity and her consistent honourableness. Her practical capacity was for him a matter for continual self-congratulation. He marked the bright order of her household, her flowering borders, the prosperous high-born roses of her garden with a wondering appreciation. He had never been able to keep anything in order. He relied more and more upon her. He showed his respect for her by a scrupulous attention to her dignity, and his confidence by a franker and franker emotional neglect. Because she expressed so little he succeeded in supposing she felt little, and since nothing had come out of the brown depths of her eyes he saw fit at last to suppose no plumb-line would ever find anything there. He pursued his interests; he reached out to this and that; he travelled; she made it a matter of conscience to let him go unhampered; she felt, she thought—unrecorded; he did, and he expressed and re-expressed and over-expressed, and started this and that with quick irrepressible activity, and so there had accumulated about them the various items of the life to whose more ostensible accidents Mr. Direck was now for an indefinite period joined.

It was in the nature of Mr. Britling to incur things; it was in the nature of Mrs. Britling to establish them. Mr. Britling had taken the Dower House on impulse, and she had made it a delightful home. He had discovered the disorderly delights of mixed Sunday hockey one weekend at Pontings that had promised to be dull, and she had made it an institution. . . . He had come to her with his orphan boy and a memory of a passionate first loss that sometimes, and more particularly at first, he seemed to have forgotten altogether, and at other times was only too evidently lamenting with every fibre of his being. She had taken the utmost care of the relics of her duskily pretty predecessor that she found in unexpected abundance in Mr. Britling's possession, and she had done her duty by her sometimes rather incomprehensible stepson. She never allowed herself to examine the state of her heart towards this youngster; it is possible that she did not perceive the necessity for any such examination. . . .

So she went through life, outwardly serene and dignified, one of a great company of rather fastidious, rather unenterprising women who have turned for their happiness to secondary things, to those fair inanimate things of household and garden which do not turn again and rend one, to æstheticisms and delicacies, to order and seemliness. Moreover she found great satisfaction in the health and welfare, the growth and animation of her own two little boys. And no one knew, and perhaps even she had contrived to forget, the phases of astonishment and disillusionment, of doubt and bitterness and secret tears, that spread out through the years in which she had slowly realised that this strange, fitful, animated man who had come to her, vowing himself hers, asking for her so urgently and persuasively, was ceasing, had ceased, to love her, that his heart had escaped her, that she had missed it; she never dreamt that she had hurt it, and that after its first urgent, tumultuous, incomprehensible search for her it had hidden itself bitterly away. . . .

§ 4

The mysterious processes of nature that had produced Mr. Britling had implanted in him an obstinate persuasion that somewhere in the world, from some human being, it was still possible to find the utmost satisfaction for every need and craving. He could imagine as existing, as waiting for him, he knew not where, a completeness of understanding, a perfection of response, that would reach all the gamut of his feelings and sensations from the most poetical to the most entirely physical, a beauty of relationship so transfiguring that not only would she—it went without saying that this completion was a woman—be perfectly beautiful in its light but, what was manifestly more incredible, that he too would be perfectly beautiful and quite at his ease. . . . In her presence there could be no self-reproaches, no lapses, no limitations, nothing but happiness and the happiest activities. . . . To such a persuasion half the imaginative people in the world succumb as readily and naturally as ducklings take to water. They do not doubt its truth any more than a thirsty camel doubts that presently it will come to a spring.

This persuasion is as foolish as though a camel hoped that some day it would drink from such a spring that it would never thirst again. For the most part Mr. Britling ignored its presence in his mind, and resisted the impulses it started. But at odd times, and more particularly in the afternoon and while travelling and in between books, Mr. Britling so far succumbed to this strange expectation of a wonder round the corner that he slipped the anchors of his humour and self-contempt and joined the great cruising brotherhood of the Pilgrims of Love. . . .

In fact—though he himself had never made a reckoning of it—he had been upon eight separate cruises. He was now upon the eighth. . . .

Between these various excursions—they took him round and about the world, so to speak, they cast him away on tropical beaches, they left him dismasted on desolate seas, they involved the most startling interventions and the most inconvenient consequences—there were interludes of penetrating philosophy. For some years the suspicion had been grwoing up in Mr. Britling's mind that in planting this persuasion in his being, the mysterious processes of Nature had been, perhaps for some purely biological purpose, pulling, as people say, his leg, that there were not these perfect responses, that loving a woman is a thing one does thoroughly once for all—or so—and afterwards recalls regrettably in a series of vain repetitions, and that the career of the Pilgrim of Love, so soon as you strip off its credulous glamour, is either the most pitiful or the most vulgar and vile of perversions from the proper conduct of life. But this suspicion had not as yet grown to prohibitive dimensions with him, it was not sufficient to resist the seasons of high tide, the sudden promise of the salt-edged breeze, the invitation of the hovering sea-bird; and he was now concealing beneath the lively surface of activities with which Mr. Direck had grown familiar a very extensive system of distresses arising out of the latest, the eighth of these digressional adventures. . . .

Mr. Britling had got into it very much as he had got into the ditch on the morning before his smash. He hadn't thought the affair out and he hadn't looked carefully enough. And it kept on developing in just the ways he would rather that it didn't.

The seventh affair had been very disconcerting. He had made a fool of himself with quite a young girl; he blushed to think how young; it hadn't gone very far, but it had made his nocturnal reflections so disagreeable that he had—by no means for the first time—definitely and for ever given up these foolish dreams of love. And when Mrs. Harrowdean swam into his circle, she seemed just exactly what was wanted to keep his imagination out of mischief. She came bearing flattery to the pitch of adoration. She was the brightest and cleverest of young widows. She wrote quite admirably criticism in *The Scrutator* and *The Sectarian*, and occasional poetry in *The Right Review*— when she felt disposed to do so. She had an intermittent vein of high spirits that was almost better than humour and made her quickly popular with most of the people she met, and she was only twenty miles away in her pretty house and her absurd little jolly park.

There was something, she said, in his thought and work that was like walking in mountains. She came to him because she wanted to clamber about the peaks and glens of his mind.

It was natural to reply that he wasn't by any means the serene mountain elevation she thought him, except perhaps for a kind of loneliness. . . .

She was a great reader of eighteenth-century memoirs, and some she conveyed to him. Her mental quality was all in the vein of the friendships of Rousseau and Voltaire, and pleasantly and trippingly she led him along the primrose path of an intellectual liaison. She came first to Matching's Easy, where she was sweet and bright and vividly interested and a great contrast to Mrs. Britling, and then he and she met in London, and went off together with a fine sense of adventure for a day at Richmond, and then he took some work with him to her house and stayed there. . . .

Then she went away into Scotland for a time and he wanted her again tremendously and clamoured for her elobuently, and then it was apparent and admitted between them that they were admirably in love, oh! immensely in love.

The transitions from emotional mountaineering to ardent intimacies were so rapid and impulsive that each phase obliterated its predecessor, and it was only with a vague perplexity that Mr. Britling found himself transferred from the rôle of a mountainous objective for pretty little pilgrims to that of a sedulous lover in pursuit of the happiness of one of the most uncertain, intricate, and entrancing of feminine personalities. This was not at all his idea of the proper relations between men and women, but Mrs. Harrowdean had a way of challenging his gallantry. She made him run about for her; she did not demand but she commanded presents and treats and surprises; she even developed a certain jealousy in him. His work began to suffer from interruptions. Yet they had glowing and entertaining moments together that could temper his rebellious thoughts with the threat of irreparable loss. "One must love, and all things in life are imperfect," was how Mr. Britling expressed his reasons for submission. And she had a hold upon him too in a certain facile pitifulness. She was little; she could be stung sometimes by the slightest touch and then her blue eyes would be bright with tears.

Those possible tears could weigh at times even more than those possible lost embraces.

And there was Oliver.

Oliver was a person Mr. Britling had never seen. He grew into the scheme of things by insensible gradations. He was a government official in London; he was, she said, extraordinarily dull, he was lacking altogether in Mr. Britling's charm and interest, but he was faithful and tender and true. And considerably younger than Mr. Britling. He asked nothing but to love. He offered honourable marriage. And when one's heart was swelling unendurably one could weep in safety on his patient shoulder. This patient shoulder of Oliver's ultimately became Mr. Britling's most exasperating rival.

She liked to vex him with Oliver. She liked to vex him generally. Indeed in this by no means abnormal love-affair there was a very strong antagonism. She seemed to resent the attraction Mr. Britling had for her and the emotions and pleasure she had with him. She seemed under the sway of an instinctive desire to make him pay heavily for her, in time, in emotion, in self-respect. It was intolerable to her that he could take her easily and happily. That would be taking her cheaply. She valued his gifts by the bother they cost him, and was determined that the path of true love should not, if she could help it, run smooth. Mr. Britling on the other hand was of the school of polite and happy lovers. He thought it outrageous to dispute and contradict, and he thought that making love was a cheerful comfortable thing to be done in a state of high good humour and intense mutual appreciation. This levity offended the lady's pride. She drew unfavourable contrasts with Oliver. If Oliver lacked charm he certainly did not lack emotion. He desired sacrifice, it seemed, almost more than satisfactions. Oliver was a person of the most exemplary miserableness; he would weep copiously and frequently. She could always make him weep when she wanted to do so. By holding out hopes and then dashing them, if by no other expedient. Why did Mr. Brittling never weep? She wept.

Some base streak of competitiveness in Mr. Britling's nature made it seem impossible that he should relinquish the lady to Oliver. Besides, then, what would he do with his dull days, his afternoons, his need for a properly demonstrated affection?

So Mr. Britling trod the path of his eighth digression, rather overworked in the matter of flowers and the selection of small jewellery, stalked by the invisible and indefatigable Oliver, haunted into an unwilling industry of attentions—attentions on the model of the professional lover of the French novels—by the memory and expectation of tearful scenes. "Then you don't love me! And it's all spoiled. I've risked talk and my reputation. . . . I was a fool ever to dream of making love beautifully. . . ."

Exactly like running your car into a soft wet ditch when you cannot get out and you cannot get on. And your work and your interests waiting and waiting for you! . . .

The car itself was an outcome of the affair. It was Mrs. Harrowdean's idea; she thought chiefly of agreeable expeditions to friendly inns in remote parts of the country, inns with a flavour of tacit complicity, but it fell in very pleasantly with Mr. Britling's private resentment at the extraordinary inconvenience of the railway communications between Matching's Easy and her station at Pyecrafts, which involved a journey to Liverpool Street and a long wait at a junction. And now the car was smashed up—just when he had acquired skill enough to take it over to Pyecrafts without shame, and on Tuesday or Wednesday at latest he would have to depart in the old way by the London train. . . .

Only the most superficial mind would assert nowadays that man is a reasonable creature. Man is an unreasonable creature, and it was entirely unreasonable and human for Mr. Britling during his nocturnal self-reproaches to mix up his secret resentment at his infatuation for Mrs. Harrowdean with his ill-advised attack upon the wall of Brandismead Park. He ought never to have bought that car; he ought never to have been so ready to meet Mrs. Harrowdean more than half-way.

What exacerbated his feeling about Mrs. Harrowdean was a new line she had recently taken with regard to Mrs. Britling. From her first rash assumption that Mr. Britling was indifferent to his wife, she had come to realise that on the contrary he was in some ways extremely tender about his wife. This struck her as an outrageous disloyalty. Instead of appreciating a paradox she resented an infidelity. She smouldered with perplexed resentment for some days, and then astonished her lover by a series of dissertations of a hostile and devastating nature upon the lady of the Dower House.

He tried to imagine he hadn't heard all that he had heard, but Mrs. Harrowdean had a nimble pen and nimbler afterthoughts, and once her mind had got to work upon the topic she developed her offensive in half-a-dozen brilliant letters. . . . On the other hand, she professed a steadily increasing passion for Mr. Britling. And to profess passion for Mr. Britling was to put him under a sense of profound obligation—because indeed he was a modest man. He found himself in an emotional quandary.

You see, if Mrs. Harrowdean had left Mrs. Britling alone everything would have been quite tolerable. He considered Mrs. Harrowdean a charming human being, and altogether better than he deserved. Ever so much better. She was all initiative and response and that sort of thing. And she was so discreet. She had her own reputation to think about, and one or two of her predecessors—God rest the ashes of those fires!—had not been so discreet. Yet one could not have this sort of thing going on behind Edith's back. All sorts of things one might have going on behind Edith's back, but not this writing and saying of perfectly beastly things about Edith. Nothing could alter the fact that Edith was his honour. . . .

§ 5

Throughout the weekend Mr. Britling had kept this trouble well battened down. He had written to Mrs. Harrowdean a brief ambiguous note saying, "I am thinking over all that you have said," and after that he had scarcely thought about her at all. Or at least he had always contrived to be much more vividly thinking about something else. But now in these night silences the suppressed trouble burst hatches and rose about him.

What a mess he had made of the whole scheme of his emotional life! There had been a time when he had started out as gaily with his passions and his honour as he had started out with Gladys to go to Market Saffron. He had as little taste for complications as he had for ditches. And now his passions and his honour were in a worse case even than poor muddy smashed-up Gladys as the cart-horses towed her off, for she at any rate might be repaired. But he—he was a terribly patched fabric of explanations now. Not indeed that he had ever stooped to explanations. But there he was! Far away, like a star seen down the length of a tunnel, was that first sad story of a love as clean as starlight. It had been all over by eight-and-twenty and he could find it in his heart to grieve that he had ever given a thought to love again. He should have lived a decent widower. . . . Then Edith had come into his life, Edith that honest and unconscious defaulter. And there again he should have stuck to his disappointment. He had stuck to it—nine days out of every ten. It's the tenth day, it's the odd seductive moment, it's the instant of confident pride—and there is your sanguine temperament in the ditch.

He began to recapitulate items in the catalogue of his escapades, and the details of his automobile misadventures mixed themselves up with the story of his heart-steering. For example there was that tremendous Siddons affair. He had been taking the corner off a girlish friendship and he had taken it altogether too far. What a frightful mess that had been. When once one is off the road anything may happen, from a crumpled mud-guard to the car on the top of you. And there was his forty miles an hour spurt with the great and gifted Delphine Marquise—for whom he was to have written a play and been a perfect d'Annunzio. Until Willersley appeared—very like the motor-cyclist—buzzing in the opposite direction. And then had ensued angers, humiliations. . . .

Had every man this sort of crowded catalogue? Was every forty-five-year-old memory a dark tunnel receding from the star of youth? It is surely a pity that life cannot end at thirty. It comes to one clean and in perfect order. . . .

Is experience worth having?

What a clean, straight thing the spirit of youth is! It is like a bright new spear. It is like a finely tempered sword. The figure of his boy took possession of his mind, his boy who looked out on the world with his mother's dark eyes, the slender son of that whole-hearted first love. He was a being at once fine and simple, an intimate mystery. Must he in his turn get dented and wrinkled and tarnished?

The boy was in trouble.—What was the trouble?

Was it some form of the same trouble that had so tangled and tainted and scarred the private pride of his father? And how was it possible for Mr. Britling, disfigured by heedless misadventures, embarrassed by complications and concealments, to help this honest youngster out of his perplexities? He imagined possible forms of these perplexities. Graceless forms. Ugly forms. Such forms as only the nocturnal imagination would have dared present. . . .

Oh, why had he been such a Britling? Why was he still such a Britling?

Mr. Britling sat up in his bed and beat at the bedclothes with his fists. He uttered uncompleted vows. "From this hour forth . . . from this hour forth. . . ."

He must do something, he felt. At any rate he had his experiences. He could warn. He could explain away. Perhaps he might help to extricate, if things had got to that pitch.

Should he write to his son? For a time he revolved a long, tactful letter in his mind. But that was impossible. Suppose the trouble was something quite different? It would have to be a letter in the most general terms. . . .

§ 6

It was in the doubly refracting nature of Mr. Britling's mind that while he was deploring his inefficiency in regard to his son, he was also deploring the ineffectiveness of all his generation of parents. Quite insensibly his mind passed over to the generalised point of view.

In his talks with Mr. Direck, Mr. Britling could present England as a great and amiable spectacle of carelessness and relaxation, but was it indeed an amiable spectacle? The point that Mr. Direck had made about the barn rankled in his thoughts. His barn was a barn no longer, his farmyard held no cattle; he was just living laxly in the buildings that ancient needs had made, he was living on the accumulated prosperity of former times, the spendthrift heir of toiling generations. Not only was he a pampered, undisciplined sort of human being; he was living in a pampered, undisciplined sort of community. The two things went together. . . . This confounded Irish business, one could laugh at it in the daylight, but was it indeed a thing to laugh at? We were drifting lazily towards a real disaster. We had a government that seemed guided by the principles of Mr. Micawber, and adopted for its watchword "Wait and See." For months now this trouble had grown more threatening.

Suppose presently that civil war broke out in Ireland! Suppose presently that these irritated, mishandled suffragettes did some desperate irreconcilable thing, assassinated for example! That bomb in Westminster Abbey the other day might have killed a dozen people. . . . Suppose the smouldering criticism of British rule in India and Egypt were fanned by administrative indiscretions into a flame. . . .

And then suppose Germany made trouble. . . .

Usually Mr. Britling kept his mind off Germany. In the daytime he pretended Germany meant nothing to England. He hated alarmists. He hated disagreeable possibilities. He declared the idea of a whole vast nation waiting to strike at us incredible. Why should they? You cannot have seventy million lunatics. . . . But in the darkness of the night one cannot dismiss things in this way. Suppose, after all, their army was more than a parade, their navy more than a protest?

We might be caught—— It was only in the vast melancholia of such occasions that Mr. Britling would admit such possibilities, but we might be caught by some sudden declaration of war. . . . And how should we face it?

He recalled the afternoon's talk at Claverings and such samples of our governmental machinery as he chanced to number among his personal acquaintance. Suppose suddenly the enemy struck! With Raeburn and his friends to defend us! Or if the shock tumbled them out of power, then with these vituperative Tories, these spiteful advocates of weak tyrannies and privileged pretences, in the place of them. There was no leadership in England. In the lucid darkness he knew that with a terrible certitude. He had a horrible vision of things disastrously muffed; of Lady Frensham and her *Morning Post* friends first garrulously and maliciously "patriotic," screaming her way with incalculable mischiefs through the storm and finally discovering that the Germans were the real aristocrats and organising our national capitulation on that understanding. He knew from talk he had heard that the navy was weak in mines and torpedoes, unprovided with the great monitors obviously needed for a war with Germany; torn by doctrinaire feuds; nevertheless the sea power was our only defence. In the whole country we might muster a military miscellany of perhaps three hundred thousand men. And he had no faith in their equipment, in their direction. General French, the one man who had his entire confidence, had been forced to resign through some lawyer's misunderstanding about the Irish difficulty. He did not believe any plans existed for such a war as Germany might force upon us, any calculation, any foresight of the thing at all.

Why had we no foresight? Why had we this wilful blindness to disagreeable possibilities? Why did we lie so open to the unexpected crisis? Just what he said of himself he said also of his country. It was curious to remember that. To realise how closely Dower House could play the microcosm to the whole Empire. . . .

It became relevant to the trend of his thoughts that his son had through his mother a strong strain of the dark Irish in his composition.

How we had wasted Ireland! The rich values that lay in Ireland, the gallantry and gifts, the possible friendliness, all these things were being left to the Ulster politicians and the Tory women to poison and spoil, just as we left India to the traditions of the chattering army women and the repressive instincts of our mandarins. We were too lazy, we were too negligent. We passed our indolent days leaving everything to somebody else. Was this the incurable British, just as it was the incurable Britling, quality?

Was the whole prosperity of the British, the far-flung empire, the securities, the busy order, just their good luck? It was a question he had asked a hundred times of his national as of his personal self. No doubt luck had favoured him. He was prosperous, and he was still only at the livelier end of middle age. But was there not also a personal factor, a meritorious factor? Luck had favoured the British with a well-placed island, a hardening climate, accessible minerals, but then too was there not also a national virtue? Once he had believed in that, in a certain gallantry, a noble levity, an underlying sound sense. The last ten years of politics had made him doubt that profoundly. He clung to it still but without confidence. In the night that dear persuasion left him altogether. . . . As for himself he had a certain brightness and liveliness of mind, but the year of his fellowship had been a soft year, he had got on to *The Times* through something very like a misapprehension, and it was the chances of a dinner and a duchess that had given him the opportunity of the Kahn show. He'd dropped into good things that suited him. That at any rate was the essence of it. And these lucky chances had been no incentive to further effort. Because things had gone easily and rapidly with him he had developed indolence into a philosophy. Here he was just over forty, and explaining to the world, explaining all through the weekend to this American—until even God could endure it no longer and the smash stopped him—how excellent was the backwardness of Essex and English go-as-you-please, and how through good temper it made in some mysterious way for all that was desirable. A fat English doctrine. *Punch* has preached it for forty years.

But this wasn't what he had always been. He thought of the strenuous intentions of his youth, before he had got into this turmoil of amorous experiences, while he was still out there with the clean star of youth. As Hugh was. . . .

In those days he had had no amiable doctrine of compromise. He had truckled to no "domesticated God," but talked of the "pitiless truth"; he had tolerated no easy-going pseudo-aristocratic social system, but dreamt of such a democracy "mewing its mighty youth" as the world had never seen. He had thought that his brains were to do their share in building up this great national *imago*, winged, divine, out of the clumsy, crawling, snobbish, comfort-loving caterpillar of Victorian England. With such dreams his life had started, and the light of them, perhaps, had helped him to his rapid success. And then his wife had died, and he had married again and become somehow more interested in his income, and then the rather expensive first of the eight experiences had drained off so much of his imaginative energy, and the second had drained off so much, and there had been quarrels and feuds, and the way had been lost, and the days had passed. He hadn't failed. Indeed he counted as a success among his generation. He alone, in the night-watches, could gauge the quality of that success. He was widely known, reputably known; he prospered. Much had come, oh! by a mysterious luck, but everything was doomed by his invincible defects. Beneath that hollow, enviable show there ached waste. Waste, waste, waste—his heart, his imagination, his wife, his son, his country—his automobile. . . .

Then there flashed into his mind a last straw of disagreeable realisation.

He hadn't as yet insured his automobile! He had meant to do so. The papers were on his writing-desk.

§ 7

On these black nights, when the personal Mr. Britling would lie awake thinking how unsatisfactorily Mr. Britling was going on, and when the impersonal Mr. Britling would be thinking how unsatisfactorily his universe was going on, the whole mental process had a likeness to some complex piece of orchestral music wherein the organ deplored the melancholy destinies of the race while the piccolo lamented the secret trouble of Mrs. Harrowdean; the big drum thundered at the Irish politicians, and all the violins bewailed the intellectual laxity of the university system. Meanwhile the trumpets prophesied wars and disasters, the cymbals ever and again inserted a clashing jar about the fatal delay in the automobile insurance, while the triangle broke into a plangent solo on the topic of a certain rotten gate-post he always forgot in the daytime, and how in consequence the cows from the glebe-farm got into the garden and ate Mrs. Britling's carnations.

Time after time he had promised to see to that gate-post. . . .

The organ *motif* battled its way to complete predominance. The lesser themes were drowned or absorbed. Mr. Britling returned from the *rôle* of an incompetent automobilist to the role of a soul naked in space and time wrestling with giant questions. These cosmic solicitudes, it may be, are the last penalty of irreligion. Was Huxley right, and was all humanity, even as Mr. Britling, a careless, fitful thing, playing a tragically hopeless game, thinking too slightly, moving too quickly, against a relentless antagonist?

Or is the whole thing just witless, accidentally cruel perhaps, but not malignant? Or is it wise, and merely refusing to pamper us? Is there somewhere in the immensities some responsive kindliness, some faint hope of toleration and assistance, something sensibly on our side against death and mechanical cruelty? If so, it certainly refuses to pamper us. . . . But if the whole thing is cruel, perhaps also it is witless and will-less? One cannot imagine the ruler of everything a devil—that would be silly. So if at the worst it is inanimate then anyhow we have our poor wills and our poor wits to pit against it. And manifestly then, the good of life, the significance of any life that is not mere receptivity, lies in the disciplined and clarified will and the sharpened and tempered mind. And what for the last twenty years—for all his lectures and writings—had he been doing to marshal the will and harden the mind which were his weapons against the Dark? He was ready enough to blame others—dons, politicians, public apathy, what was he himself doing?

What was he doing now?

Lying in bed!

His son was drifting to ruin, his country was going to the devil, the house was a hospital of people wounded by his carelessness, the country roads choked with his smashed (and uninsured) automobiles, the cows were probably lined up along the borders and munching Edith's carnations at this very moment, his pocketbook and bureau were stuffed with venomous insults about her—and he was just lying in bed!

Suddenly Mr. Britling threw back his bedclothes and felt for the matches on his bedside table.

Indeed this was by no means the first time that his brain had become a whirring torment in his skull. Previous experiences had led to the most careful provision for exactly such states. Over the end of the bed hung a light, warm pyjama suit of llama-wool, and at the feet of it were two tall boots of the same material that buckled to the middle of his calf. So protected, Mr. Britling proceeded to make himself tea. A Primus stove stood ready inside the fender of his fireplace, and on it was a brightly polished brass kettle filled with water; a little table carried a tea-caddy, a teapot, a lemon and a glass. Mr. Britling lit the stove and then strolled to his desk. He was going to write certain "Plain Words about Ireland." He lit his study lamp and meditated beside it until a sound of water boiling called him to his tea-making.

He returned to his desk stirring the lemon in his glass of tea. He would write the plain common sense of this Irish situation. He would put things so plainly that this squabbling folly would *have* to cease. It should be done austerely, with a sort of ironical directness. There should be no abuse, no bitterness, only a deep passion of sanity.

What is the good of grieving over a smashed automobile?

He sipped his tea and made a few notes on his writing-pad. His face in the light of his shaded reading-lamp had lost its distraught expression, his hand fingered his familiar fountain pen. . . .

§ 8

The next morning Mr. Britling came into Mr. Direck's room. He was pink from his morning bath, he was wearing a cheerful green-and-blue silk dressing-gown, he had shaved already, he showed no trace of his nocturnal vigil. In the bathroom he had whistled like a bird. "Had a good night?" he said. "That's famous. So did I. And the wrist and arm even didn't ache enough to keep you awake?"

"I thought I heard you talking and walking about," said Mr. Direck.

"I got up for a little bit and worked. I often do that. I hope I didn't disturb you. Just for an hour or so. It's so delightfully quiet in the night. . . ."

He went to the window and blinked at the garden outside. His two younger sons appeared on their bicycles returning from some early expedition. He waved a hand of greeting. It was one of those summer mornings when attenuated mist seems to fill the very air with sunshine dust.

"This is the sunniest morning bedroom in the house," he said. "It's south-east."

The sunlight slashed into the masses of the blue cedar outside with a score of golden spears.

"The Dayspring from on High," he said. . . . "I thought of rather a useful pamphlet in the night.

"I've been thinking about your luggage at that hotel," he went on, turning to his guest again. "You'll have to write and get it packed up and sent down here——

"No," he said, "we won't let you go until you can hit out with that arm and fell a man. Listen!"

Mr. Direck could not distinguish any definite sound.

"The smell of frying rashers, I mean," said Mr. Britling. "It's the clarion of the morn in every proper English home. . . .

"You'd like a rasher, coffee?

"It's good to work in the night, and it's good to wake in the morning," said Mr. Britling, rubbing his hands together. "I suppose I wrote nearly two thousand words. So quiet one is, so concentrated. And as soon as I have had my breakfast I shall go on with it again."

CHAPTER THE FIFTH

THE COMING OF THE DAY

§ 1

IT was quite characteristic of the state of mind of England in the summer of 1914 that Mr. Britling should be mightily concerned about the conflict in Ireland, and almost deliberately negligent of the possibility of a war with Germany.

The armament of Germany, the hostility of Germany, the consistent assertion of Germany, the world-wide clash of British and German interests, had been facts in the consciousness of Englishmen for more than a quarter of a century. A whole generation had been born and brought up in the threat of this German war. A threat that goes on for too long ceases to have the effect of a threat, and this overhanging possibility had become a fixed and scarcely disturbing feature of the British situation. It kept the navy sedulous and Colonel Rendezvous uneasy; it stimulated a small and not very influential section of the press to a series of reminders that bored Mr. Britling acutely, it was the excuse for an agitation that made national service ridiculous, and quite subconsciously it affected his attitude to a hundred things. For example, it was a factor in his very keen indignation at the Tory levity in Ireland, in his disgust with many things that irritated or estranged Indian feeling. It bored him; there it was, a danger, and there was no denying it, and yet he believed firmly that it was a mine that would never be fired, an avalanche that would never fall. It was a nuisance, a stupidity, that kept Europe drilling and wasted enormous sums on unavoidable preparations; it hung up everything like a noisy argument in a drawing-room, but that human weakness and folly would ever let the mine actually explode he did not believe. He had been in France in 1911, he had seen how close things had come then to a conflict, and the fact that they had not come to a conflict had enormously strengthened his natural disposition to believe that at bottom Germany was sane and her militarism a bluff.

But the Irish difficulty was a different thing. There, he felt, was need for the liveliest exertions. A few obstinate people in influential positions were manifestly pushing things to an outrageous point. . . .

He wrote through the morning—and as the morning progressed the judicial calm of his opening intentions warmed to a certain regrettable vigour of phrasing about our politicians, about our political ladies, and our hand-to-mouth press. . . .

He came down to lunch in a frayed, exhausted condition, and was much afflicted by a series of questions from Herr Heinrich. For it was an incurable characteristic of Herr Heinrich that he asked questions; the greater part of his conversation took the form of question and answer, and his thirst for information was as marked as his belief that German should not simply be spoken but spoken "out loud." He invariably prefaced his inquiries with the word "Please," and he insisted upon ascribing an omniscience to his employer which was extremely irksome to justify after a strenuous morning of enthusiastic literary effort. He now took the opportunity of a lull in the solicitudes and congratulations that had followed Mr. Direck's appearance—and Mr. Direck was so little shattered by his misadventure that with the assistance of the kindly Teddy he had got up and dressed and come down to lunch—to put the matter that had been occupying his mind all the morning, even to the detriment of the lessons of the Masters Britling.

"Please!" he said, going a deeper shade of pink and partly turning to Mr. Britling.

A look of resignation came into Mr. Britling's eyes. "Yes?" he said.

"I do not think it will be wise to take my ticket for the Esperanto Conference at Boulogne. Because I think it is probable to be war between Austria and Serbia, and that Russia may make war on Austria."

"That may happen. But I think it improbable."

"If Russia makes war on Austria, Germany will make war on Russia, will she not?"

"Not if she is wise," said Mr. Britling, "because that would bring in France."

"That is why I ask. If Germany goes to war with France I should have to go to Germany to do my service. It will be a great inconvenience to me."

"I don't imagine Germany will do anything so frantic as to attack Russia. That would not only bring in France but ourselves."

"England?"

"Of course. We can't afford to see France go under. The thing is as plain as daylight. So plain that it cannot possibly happen. . . . Cannot. . . . Unless Germany wants a universal war."

"Thank you," said Herr Heinrich, looking obedient rather than reassured.

"I suppose now," said Mr. Direck after a pause, "that there isn't any strong party in Germany that wants a war. That young Crown Prince, for example."

"They keep him in order," said Mr. Britling a little irritably. "They keep him in order. . . .

"I used to be an alarmist about Germany," said Mr. Britling, "but I have come to feel more and more confidence in the sound common sense of the mass of the German population, and in the Emperor too if it comes to that. He is—if Herr Heinrich will permit me to agree with his own German comic papers— sometimes a little theatrical, sometimes a little egotistical, but in his operatic, boldly coloured way he means peace. I am convinced he means peace. . . ."

§ 2

After lunch Mr. Britling had a brilliant idea for the ease and comfort of Mr. Direck.

It seemed as though Mr. Direck would be unable to write any letters until his wrist had mended. Teddy tried him with a typewriter, but Mr. Direck was very awkward with his left hand, and then Mr. Britling suddenly remembered a little peculiarity he had which it was possible that Mr. Direck might share unconsciously, and that was his gift of looking-glass writing with his left hand. Mr. Britling had found out quite by chance in his schoolboy days that while his right hand had been laboriously learning to write, his left hand, all unsuspected, had been picking up the same lesson, and that by taking a pencil in his left hand and writing from right to left, without watching what he was writing, and then examining the scrawl in a mirror, he could reproduce his own handwriting in exact reverse. About three people out of five have this often quite unsuspected ability. He demonstrated his gift, and then Miss Cecily Corner, who had dropped in in a casual sort of way to ask about Mr. Direck, tried it, and then Mr. Direck tried it. And they could all do it. And then Teddy brought a sheet of copying carbon, and so Mr. Direck, by using the carbon reversed under his paper, was restored to the world of correspondence again.

They sat round a little table under the cedar-trees amusing themselves with these experiments, and after that Cecily and Mr. Britling and the two small boys entertained themselves by drawing pigs with their eyes shut, and then Mr. Britling and Teddy played hard at Badminton until it was time for tea. And Cecily sat by Mr. Direck and took an interest in his accident, and he told her about summer holidays in the Adirondacks and how he loved to travel. She said she would love to travel. He said that so soon as he was better he would go on to Paris and then into Germany. He was extraordinarily curious about this Germany and its tremendous militarism. He'd far rather see it than Italy, which was, he thought, just all art and ancient history. His turn was for modern problems. Though of course he didn't intend to leave out Italy while he was at it. And then their talk was scattered, and there was great excitement because Herr Heinrich had lost his squirrel.

He appeared coming out of the house into the sunshine, and so distraught that he had forgotten the protection of his hat. He was very pink and deeply moved.

"But what shall I do without him?" he cried. "He has gone!"

The squirrel, Mr. Direck gathered, had been bought by Mrs. Britling for the boys some month or so ago; it had been christened "Bill" and adored and then neglected until Herr Heinrich took it over. It had filled a place in his ample heart that the none too demonstrative affection of the Britling household had left empty. He abandoned his pursuit of philology almost entirely for the cherishing and adoration of this busy, nimble little creature. He carried it off to his own room, where it ran loose and took the greatest liberties with him and his apartment. It was an extraordinarily bold and savage little beast even for a squirrel, but Herr Heinrich had set his heart and his very large and patient will upon the establishment of sentimental relations. He believed that ultimately Bill would let himself be stroked, that he would make Bill love him and understand him, and that his would be the only hand that Bill would ever suffer to touch him. In the meanwhile even the untamed Bill was wonderful to watch. One could watch him for ever. His front paws were like hands, like a musician's hands, very long and narrow. "He would be a musician if he could only make his fingers go apart, because when I play my violin he listens. He is attentive."

The entire household became interested in Herr Heinrich's attacks upon Bill's affection. They watched his fingers with particular interest because it was upon those that Bill vented his failures to respond to the stroking advances.

"Today I have stroked him once and he has bitten me three times," Herr Heinrich reported. "Soon I will stroke him three times and he shall not bite me at all. . . . Also yesterday he climbed up me and sat on my shoulder, and suddenly bit my ear. It was not hard he bit, but sudden.

"He does not mean to bite," said Herr Heinrich. "Because when he has bit me he is sorry. He is ashamed.

"You can see he is ashamed."

Assisted by the two small boys, Herr Heinrich presently got a huge bough of oak and brought it into his room, converting the entire apartment into the likeness of an aviary. "For this," said Herr Heinrich, looking grave and diplomatic through his glasses, "Billy will be very grateful. And it will give him confidence with me. It will make him feel we are in the forest together."

Mrs. Britling came to consult her husband in the matter.

"It is not right that the bedroom should be filled with trees. All sorts of dust and litter came in with it."

"If it amuses him," said Mr. Britling.

"But it makes work for the servants."

"Do they complain?"

"No."

"Things will adjust themselves. And it is amusing that he should do such a thing. . . ."

And now Billy had disappeared, and Herr Heinrich was on the verge of tears. It was so ungrateful of Billy. Without a word.

"They leave my window open." he complained to Mr. Direck. "Often I have askit them not to. And of course he did not understand. He has out climbit by the ivy. Anything may have happened to him. Anything. He is not used to going out alone. He is too young.

"Perhaps if I call——"

And suddenly he had gone off round the house crying: "Beelee! Beelee! Here is an almond for you! An almond, Beelee!"

"Makes me want to get up and help," said Mr. Direck. "It's a tragedy."

Everybody else was helping. Even the gardener and his boy knocked off work and explored the upper recesses of various possible trees.

"He is too young," said Herr Heinrich, drifting back. . . . And then presently: "If he heard my voice I am sure he would show himself. But he does not show himself."

It was clear he feared the worst. . . .

At supper Billy was the sole topic of conversation, and condolence was in the air. The impression that on the whole he had displayed rather a brutal character was combated by Herr Heinrich, who held that a certain brusqueness was Billy's only fault, and told anecdotes, almost sacred anecdotes, of the little creature's tenderer, nobler side. "When I feed him always he says, 'Thank you,' " said Herr Heinrich. "He never fails." He betrayed darker thoughts. "When I went round by the barn there was a cat that sat and looked at me out of a laurel bush," he said. "I do not like cats."

Mr. Lawrence Carmine, who had dropped in, was suddenly reminded of that lugubrious old ballad, "The Mistletoe Bough," and recited large worn fragments of it impressively. It tells how a beautiful girl hid away in a chest during a Christmas game of hide-and-seek, and how she was found, a dried vestige, years afterwards. It took a very powerful hold upon Herr Heinrich's imagination. "Let us now," he said, "make an examination of every box and cupboard and drawer. Marking each as we go. . . ."

When Mr. Britling went to bed that night, after a long gossip with Carmine about the Brahma Samaj and modern developments of Indian thought generally, the squirrel was still undiscovered.

The worthy modern thinker undressed slowly, blew out his candle and got into bed. Still meditating deeply upon the God of the Tagores, he thrust his right hand under his pillow according to his usual practice, and encountered something soft and warm and active. He shot out of bed convulsively, lit his candle, and lifted his pillow discreetly.

He discovered the missing Billy looking crumpled and annoyed.

For some moments there was a lively struggle before Billy was gripped. He chattered furiously and bit Mr. Britling twice. Then Mr. Britling was out in the passage with the wriggling lump of warm fur in his hand, and paddling along in the darkness to the door of Herr Heinrich. He opened it softly.

A startled white figure sat up in bed sharply.

"Billy," said Mr. Britling by way of explanation, dropped his capture on the carpet, and shut the door on the touching reunion.

§ 3

A day was to come when Mr. Britling was to go over the history of that sunny July with incredulous minuteness, trying to trace the real succession of events that led from the startling crime at Sarajevo to Europe's last swift rush into war. In a sense it was untraceable; in a sense it was so obvious that he was amazed the whole world had not watched the coming of disaster. The plain fact of the case was that there was no direct connection; the Sarajevo murders were dropped for two whole weeks out of the general consciousness, they went out of the papers, they ceaased to be discussed; then they were picked up again and used as an excuse for war. Germany, armed so as to be a threat to all the world, weary at last of her mighty vigil, watching the course of events, decided that her moment had come, and snatched the dead archduke out of his grave again to serve her tremendous ambition.

It may well have seemed to the belligerent German patriot that all her possible foes were confused, divided within themselves, at an extremity of distraction and impotence. The British Isles seemed slipping steadily into civil war. Threat was met by counter-threat, violent fool competed with violent fool for the admiration of the world, the National Volunteers armed against the Ulster men; everything moved on with a kind of mechanical precision from parade and meeting towards the fatal gun-running of Howth and the first bloodshed in Dublin streets. That wretched affray, far more than any other single thing, must have stiffened Germany in the course she had chosen. There can be no doubt of it; the mischief-makers of Ireland set the final confirmation upon the European war. In England itself there was a summer fever of strikes; Liverpool was choked by a dockers' strike, the East Anglian agricultural labourers were in revolt, and the building trade throughout the country was on the verge of a lock-out. Russia seemed to be in the crisis of a social revolution. From Baku to St. Petersburg there were insurrectionary movements in the towns, and on the 23rd—the very day of the Austrian ultimatum—Cossacks were storming barbed-wire entanglements in the streets of the capital. The London Stock Exchange was in a state of panic disorganisation because of a vast mysterious selling of securities from abroad. And France, France it seemed was lost to all other considerations in the enthralling confrontations and denunciations of the Caillaux murder trial, the trial of the wife of her ex-Prime Minister for the murder of a blackmailing journalist. It was a case full of the vulgarest sexual violence. Before so piquant a spectacle France it seemed could have no time nor attention for the revelation of M. Humbert, the Report of the Army Committee, proclaiming that the artillery was short of ammunition, that her infantry had boots "thirty years old" and not enough of those. . . .

Such were the appearances of things. Can it be wondered if it seemed to the German mind that the moment for the triumphant assertion of the German predominance in the world had come? A day or so before the Dublin shooting, the murder of Sarajevo had been dragged again into the foreground of the world's affairs by an ultimatum from Austria to Serbia of the extremist violence. From the hour when the ultimatum was discharged the way to Armageddon lay wide and unavoidable before the feet of Europe. After the Dublin conflict there was no turning back. For a week Europe was occupied by proceedings that were little more than the recital of a formula. Austria could not withdraw her unqualified threats without admitting error and defeat, Russia could not desert Serbia without disgrace, Germany stood behind Austria, France was bound to Russia by a long confederacy of mutual support, and it was impossible for England to witness the destruction of France or the further strengthening of a loud and threatening rival. It may be that Germany counted on Russia giving way to her, it may be she counted on the indecisions and feeble perplexities of England, both these possibilities were in the reckoning, but chiefly she counted on war. She counted on war, and since no other nation in all the world had ever been so fully prepared in every way for war, she also counted on victory.

One writes "Germany." That is how one writes of nations, as though they had single brains and single purposes. But indeed while Mr. Britling lay awake and thought of his son and Lady Frensham and his smashed automobile and Mrs. Harrowdean's trick of abusive letter-writing and of God and evil and a thousand perplexities, a multitude of other brains must also have been busy, lying also in beds or sitting in studies or watching in guard-rooms or chatting belatedly in cafes or smoking-rooms or pacing the bridges of battleships or walking along in city or country, upon this huge possibility the crime of Sarajevo had just opened, and of the state of the world in relation to such possibilities. Few women, one guesses, heeded what was happening, and of the men, the men whose deicision to launch that implacable threat turned the destinies of the world to war, there is no reason to believe that a single one of them had anything approaching the imaginative power needed to understand fully what it was they were doing. We have looked for an hour or so into the seething pot of Mr. Britling's brain and marked its multiple strands, its inconsistencies, its irrational transitions. It was but a specimen. Nearly every brain of the select few that counted in this cardinal determination of the world's destinies had its streak of personal motive, its absurd and petty impulses and deflections. One man decided to say *this*, because if he said *that* he would contradict something he had said and printed four or five days ago; another took a certain line because so he saw his best opportunity of putting a rival into a perplexity. It would be strange if one could reach out now and recover the states of mind of two such beings as the German Kaiser and his eldest son as Europe stumbled towards her fate through the long days and warm close nights of that July. Here was the occasion for which so much of their lives had been but the large pretentious preparation, coming right into their hands to use or forego, here was the opportunity that would put them into the very forefront of history for ever; this journalist emperor with the paralysed arm, this common-fibred, sly, lascivious son. It is impossible that they did not dream of glory over all the world, of triumphant processions, of a world-throne that would outshine Cæsar's, of a god-like elevation, of acting Divus Cæsar while yet alive. And being what they were they must have imagined spectators, and the young man, who was after all a young man of particularly poor quality, imagined no doubt certain women onlookers, certain humiliated and astonished friends, and thought of the clothes he would wear and the gestures he would make. The nickname his English cousins had given this heir to all the glories was the "White Rabbit." He was the backbone of the war party at court. And presently he stole bric-a-brac. That will help posterity to the proper values of things in 1914. And the Teutonic generals and admirals and strategists with their patient and perfect plans, who were so confident of victory, each within a busy skull must have enated anticipatory dreams of his personal success and marshalled his willing and unwilling admirers. Readers of histories and memoirs as most of this class of men are, they must have composed little eulogistic descriptions of the part themselves were to play in the opening drama, imagined pleasing vindications and interesting documents. Some of them perhaps saw difficulties, but few foresaw failure. For all this set of brains the thing came as a choice to take or reject; they could make war or prevent it. And they chose war.

It is doubtful if any one outside the directing intelligence of Germany and Austria saw anything so plain. The initiative was with Germany. The Russian brains and the French brains and the British brains, the few that were really coming round to look at this problem squarely, had a far less simple set of problems and profounder uncertainties. To Mr. Britling's mind the Round Table Conference at Buckingham Palace was typical of the disunion and indecision that lasted up to the very outbreak of hostilities. The solemn violence of Sir Edward Carson was intensely antipathetic to Mr. Britling, and in his retrospective inquiries he pictured to himself that dark figure with its dropping underlip, seated, heavy and obstinate, at that discussion, still implacable though the King had but just departed after a little speech that was packed with veiled intimations of imminent danger. . . .

Mr. Britling had no mercy in his mind for the treason of obstinate egotism and for persistence in a mistaken course. His own temperamental weaknesses lay in such different directions. He was always ready to leave one trail for another; he was always open to conviction, trusting to the essentials of his character for an ultimate consistency. He hated Carson in those days as a

Scotch terrier might hate a bloodhound, as something at once more effective and impressive, and exasperatingly, infinitely, less intelligent.

§ 4

Thus—a vivid fact as yet only in a few hundred skulls or so—the vast catastrophe of the Great War gathered behind the idle, dispersed, and confused spectacle of an indifferent world, very much as the storms and rains of late September gather behind the glow and lassitudes of August, and with scarcely more of set human intention. For the greater part of mankind the European international situation was at most something in the papers, no more important than the political disturbances in South Africa, where the Herzogites were curiously uneasy, or the possible trouble between Turkey and Greece. The things that really interested people in England during the last months of peace were boxing and the summer sales. A brilliant young Frenchman, Carpentier, who had knocked out Bombardier Wells, came over again to defeat Gunboat Smith, and did so to the infinite delight of France and the whole Latin world, amidst the generous applause of Anglo-Saxondom. And there was also a British triumph over the Americans at polo, and a lively and cultured newspaper discussion about a proper motto for the arms of the London County Council. The trial of Madame Caillaux filled the papers with animated reports and vivid pictures; Gregori Rasputin was stabbed and became the subject of much lively gossip about the Russian Court; and Ulivi, the Italian imposter who claimed he could explode mines be means of an "ultra-red" ray, was exposed and fled with a lady, very amusingly. For a few days all the work at Woolwich

Arsenal was held up because a certain Mr. Entwhistle, having refused to erect a machine on a concrete bed laid down by non-unionists, was rather uncivilly dismissed, and the Irish trouble pounded along its tiresome mischievous way. People gave a divided attention to these various topics, and went about their individual businesses.

And at Dower House they went about their businesses. Mr Direck's arm healed rapidly; Cecily Corner and he talked of their objects in life and Utopias and the books of Mr. Britling, and he got down from a London bookseller Baedeker's guides for Holland and Belgium, South Germany, and Italy; Herr Heinrich after some doubt sent in his application form and his preliminary deposit for the Esperanto Conference at Boulogne, and Billy consented to be stroked three times but continued to bite with great vigour and promptitude. And the trouble abouth Hugh, Mr. Britling's eldest son, resolved itself into nothing of any vital importance, and settled itself very easily.

§ 5

After Hugh had cleared things up and gone back to London, Mr. Britling was inclined to think that such a thing as apprehension was a sin against the general fairness and integrity of life.

Of all things in the world Hugh was the one that could most easily rouse Mr. Britling's unhappy aptitude for distressing imaginations. Hugh was nearer by far to his heart and nerves than any other creature. In the last few years Mr. Britling, by the light of a variety of emotional excursions in other directions, had been discovering this. Whatever Mr. Britling discovered he talked about; he had evolved from his realisation of this tenderness, which was without an effort so much tenderer than all the subtle and tremendous feelings he had attempted in his— excursions, the theory that he had expounded to Mr. Direck that it is only through our children that we are able to achieve disinterested love, real love. But that left unexplained the far more intimate emotional hold of Hugh than of his very jolly little stepbrothers. That was a fact into which Mr. Britling rather sedulously wouldn't look. . . .

Mr. Britling was probably much franker and more open-eyed with himself and the universe than a great number of intelligent people, and yet there was quite a number of aspects of his relations with his wife, with people about him, with his country and God and the nature of things, upon which he turned his back with an attentive persistence. But a back too resolutely turned may be as indicative as a pointing finger, and in this retrogressive way, and tacitly even so far as his formal thoughts, his unspoken comments, went, Mr. Britling knew that he loved his son because he had lavished the most hope and the most imagination upon him, because he was the one living continuation of that dear life with Mary, so lovingly stormy at the time, so fine now in memory, that had really possessed the whole heart of Mr. Britling. The boy had been the joy and marvel of the young parents; it was incredible to them that there had ever been a creature so delicate and sweet, and they brought considerable imagination and humour to the detailed study of his minute personality and to the forecasting of his future. Mr. Britling's mind blossomed with wonderful schemes for his education. all that mental growth no doubt contributed greatly to Mr. Britling's peculiar affection, and with it there interwove still tenderer and subtler elements, for the boy had a score of Mary's traits. But there were other things still more conspicuously ignored. One silent factor in the slow widening of the breach between Edith and Mr. Britling was her cool estimate of her stepson. She was steadfastly kind to this shock-headed, untidy little dreamer, he was extremely well cared for in her hands, she liked him and she was amused by him—it is difficult to imagine what more Mr. Britling could have expected—but it was as plain as daylight that she felt that this was not the child she would have cared to have borne. It was quite preposterous and perfectly natural that this should seem to Mr. Britling to be unfair to Hugh.

Edith's home was more prosperous than Mary's; she brought her own money to it; the bringing up of her children was a far more efficient business than Mary's instinctive proceedings. Hugh had very nearly died in his first year of life; some summer infection had snatched at him; that had tied him to his father's heart by a knot of fear; but no infection had ever come near Edith's own nursery. And it was Hugh that Mr. Britling had seen, small and green-faced and pitiful under an anæsthetic for some necessary operation to his adenoids. His younger children had never stabbed to Mr. Britling's heart with any such pitifulness; they were not so thin-skinned as their elder brother, not so assailable by the little animosities of dust and germ. And out of such things as this evolved a shapeless cloud of championship for Hugh. Jealousies and suspicions are latent in every human relationship. We go about the affairs of life pretending magnificently that they are not so, pretending to the generosities we desire. And in all step-relationships jealousy and suspicion are not merely latent, they stir.

It was Mr. Britling's case for Hugh that he was something exceptional, something exceptionally good, and that the peculiar need there was to take care of him was due to a delicacy of nerve and fibre that was ultimately a virtue. The boy was quick,

quick to hear, quick to move, very accurate in his swift way, he talked unusually soon, he began to sketch at an early age with an incurable roughness and a remarkable expressiveness. That he was sometimes ungainly, often untidy, that he would become so mentally preoccupied as to be uncivil to people about him, that he caught any malaise that was going, was all a part of that. The sense of Mrs. Britling's unexpressed criticisms, the implied contrasts with the very jolly, very uninspired younger family, kept up a nervous desire in Mr. Britling for evidences and manifestations of Hugh's quality. Not always with happy results; it caused much mutual irritation, but not enough to prevent the growth of a real response on Hugh's part to his father's solicitude. The youngster knew and felt that his father was his father just as certainly as he felt that Mrs. Britling was not his mother. To his father he brought his successes and to his father he appealed.

But he brought his successes more readily than he brought his troubles. So far as he himself was concerned he was disposed to take a humorous view of the things that went wrong and didn't come off with him, but as a "Tremendous Set-Down for the Proud Parent" they resisted humorous treatment. . . .

Now the trouble that he had been hesitating to bring before his father was concerned with that very grave interest of the young, his Object in Life. It had nothing to do with those erotic disturbances that had distressed his father's imagination. Whatever was going on below the surface of Hugh's smiling or thoughtful presence in that respect had still to come to the surface and find expression. But he was bothered very much by divergent strands in his own intellectual composition. Two sets of interests pulled at him, one—it will seem a dry interest to many readers, but for Hugh it glittered and fascinated—was crystallography and molecular physics; the other was caricature. Both aptitudes sprang no doubt from the same exceptional sensitiveness to form. As a schoolboy he exercised both very happily, but now he was getting to the age of specialisation, and he was fluctuating very much between science and art. After a spell of scientific study he would come upon a fatigue period and find nothing in life but absurdities and a lark that one could represent very amusingly; after a bout of funny drawings his mind went back to his light and crystals and films like a Magdalen repenting in a church. After his public school he had refused Cambridge and gone to University College, London, to work under the great and in-inspiring Professor Cardinal; simultaneously Cardinal had been arranging to go to Cambridge, and Hugh had scarcely embarked upon his London work when Cardinal was succeeded by the dull, conscientious and depressing Pelkingham, at whose touch crystals became as puddings, bubble films like cotton sheets, transparency vanished from the world, and X-rays dwarfed and died. And Hugh degenerated immediately into a scoffing trifler who wished to give up science for art.

He gave up science for art after grave consultation with his father, and the real trouble that had been fretting him, it seemed, was that now he repented and wanted to follow Cardinal to Cambridge, and—a year lost—go on with science again. He felt it was a discredible fluctuation; he knew it would be a considerable expense; and so he took two weeks before he could screw himself up to broaching the matter.

"So *that* is all!" said Mr. Britling, immensely relieved.

"My dear Parent, you didn't think I had backed a bill or forged a cheque?"

"I thought you might have married a chorus girl or something of that sort," said Mr. Britling.

"Or bought a large cream-coloured motor-car for her on the instalment system, which she'd smashed up. No, that sort of thing comes later. . . . I'll just put myself down on the waiting-list of one of those bits of delight in the Cambridge tobacco-shops— and go on with my studies for a year or two. . . ."

§ 6

Though Mr. Britling's anxiety about his son was dispelled, his mind remained curiously apprehensive throughout July. He had a feeling that things were not going well with the world, a feeling he tried in vain to dispel by various distractions. Perhaps some subtler subconscious analysis of the situation was working out probabilities that his conscious self would not face. And when presently he bicycled off to Mrs. Harrowdean for flattery, amusement, and comfort generally, he found her by no means the exalting confirmation of everything he wished to believe about himself and the universe, that had been her delightful rôle in the early stages of their romantic friendship. She maintained her hostility to Edith; she seemed bent on making things impossible. And yet there were one or two phases of the old sustaining intimacies.

On the afternoon of his arrival they walked across her absurd little park to the summer-house with the view, and they discussed the Irish pamphlet which was now nearly finished.

"Of course," she said, "it will be a wonderful pamphlet."

There was a reservation in her voice that made him wait.

"But I suppose all sorts of people could write an Irish pamphlet. Nobody but you could write 'The Silent Places.' Oh, *why* don't you finish that great beautiful thing, and leave all this world of reality and newspapers, all these Crude, Vulgar,

Quarelsome, Jarring things to other people? You have the magic gift, you might be a poet, you can take us out of all these horrid things that are, away to Beautyland, and you are just content to be a critic and a disputer. It's your surroundings. It's your sordid realities. It's that Practicality at your elbow. You ought never to *see* a newspaper. You ought never to have an American come within ten miles of you. You ought to live on bowls of milk drunk in valleys of asphodel."

Mr. Britling, who liked this sort of thing in a way, and yet at the same time felt ridiculously distended and altogether preposterous while it was going on, answered feebly and self-consciously.

"There was your letter in *The Nation* the other day," she said. "Why do you get drawn into arguments? I wanted to rush into *The Nation* and pick you up and wipe the anger off you, and carry you out of it all—into some quiet beautiful place."

"But one *has* to answer these people," said Mr. Britling, rolling along by the side of her like the full moon beside Venus, and quite artlessly falling in with the tone of her.

She repeated lines from "The Silent Places" from memory. She threw quite wonderful emotion into her voice. She made the words glow. And he had only shown he the thing once. . . .

Was he indeed burying a marvellous gift under the dust of current affairs? When at last in the warm evening light they strolled back from the summer-house to dinner he had definitely promised her that he would take up and finish "The Silent Places." . . . And think over the Irish pamphlet again before he published it. . . .

Pyecrafts was like a crystal casket of finer soil withdrawn from the tarred highways of the earth. . . .

And yet the very next day this angel enemy of controversies broke out in the most abominable way about Edith, and he had to tell her more plainly than he had done hitherto that he could not tolerate that sort of thing. He wouldn't have Edith guyed. He wouldn't have Edith made to seem base. And at that there was much trouble between them, and tears and talk of Oliver. . . .

Mr. Britling found himself unable to get on either with "The Silent Places" or the pamphlet, and he was very unhappy. . . .

Afterwards she repented very touchingly, and said that if only he would love her she would swallow a thousand Ediths. He waived a certain disrespect in the idea of her swallowing Edith, and they had a beautiful reconciliation and talked of exalted things, and in the evening he worked quite well upon "The Silent Places" and thought of half-a-dozen quite wonderful lines, and in the course of the next day he returned to Dower House and Mr. Direck and considerable piles of correspondence and the completion of the Irish pamphlet.

But he was restless. He was more restless in his house than he had ever been. He could not understand it. Everything about him was just as it had always been, and yet it was unsatisfactory, and it seemed more unstable than anything had ever seemed before. He was bored by the solemn development of the Irish dispute; he was irritated by the smouldering threat of the Balkans; he was irritated by the suffragettes and by a string of irrational little strikes; by the general absence of any main plot as it were to hold all these wranglings and trivialities together. . . . At the Dower House the most unpleasant thoughts would come to him. He even had doubts whether in "The Silent Places" he had been plagiarising, more or less unconsciously, from Henry James's "Great Good Place." . . .

On the 21st of July Gladys came back repaired and looking none the worse for her misadventure. Next day he drove her very carefully over to Pyecrafts, hoping to drug his uneasiness with the pretence of a grand passion and the praises of "The Silent Places," that beautiful work of art that was so free from any taint of application, and alas! he found Mrs. Harrowdean in an evil mood. He had been away from her for ten days—ten whole days. No doubt Edith had manœuvred to keep him. She hadn't! *Hadn't* she? How was he, poor simple soul! to tell that she hadn't? That was the prelude to a stormy afternoon.

The burthen of Mrs. Harrowdean was that she was wasting her life, that she was wasting the poor, good, patient Oliver's life, that for the sake of friendship she was braving the worst imputations and that he treated her cavalierly, came when he wished to do so, stayed away heartlessly, never thought she needed *little* treats, *little* attentions, *little* presents. Did he think she could settle down to her poor work, such as it was, in neglect and loneliness? He forgot women were dear little tender things, and had to be made happy and *kept* happy. Oliver might not be clever and attractive, but he did at least in his clumsy way understand and try to do his duty. . . .

Towards the end of the second hour of such complaints the spirit of Mr. Britling rose in revolt. He lifted up his voice against her, he charged his voice with indignant sorrow and declared that he had come over to Pyecrafts with no thought in his mind but sweet and loving thoughts, that he had but waited for Gladys to be ready before he came, that he had brought over the manuscript of "The Silent Places" with him to polish and finish up, that "for days and days" he had been longing to do this in the atmosphere of the dear old summer-house with its distant view of the dear old sea, and that now all that was impossible, that

Mrs. Harrowdean had made it impossible, and that indeed she was rapidly making everything impossible. . . .

And having delivered himself of this judgment Mr. Britling, a little surprised at the rapid vigour of his anger, once he had let it loose, came suddenly to an end of his words, made a renunciatory gesture with his arms, and as if struck with the idea, rushed out of her room and out of the house to where Gladys stood waiting. He got into her and started her up, and after some trouble with the gear due to the violence of his emotion, he turned her round and departed with her—crushing the corner of a small bed of snapdragon as he turned—and drove her with a sulky sedulousness back to the Dower House and newspapers and correspondence and irritations, and that gnawing and irrational sense of a hollow and aimless quality in the world that he had hoped Mrs. Harrowdean would assuage. And the farther he went from Mrs. Harrowdean the harsher and unjuster it seemed to him that he had been to her.

But he went on because he did not see how he could very well go back.

§ 7

Mr. Direck's damaged wrist healed sooner than he desired. From the first he had protested that it was the sort of thing that one can carry about in a sling, that he was quite capable of travelling about and taking care of himself in hotels, that he was only staying on at Matching's Easy because he just loved to stay on and wallow in Mrs. Britling's kindness and Mr. Britling's company. While as a matter of fact he wallowed as much as he could in the freshness and friendliness of Miss Cecily Corner, and for more than a third of this period Mr. Britling was away from home altogether.

Mr. Direck, it should be clear by this time, was a man of more than European simplicity and directness, and his intentions towards the young lady were as simple and direct and altogether honest as such intentions can be. It is the American conception of gallantry more than any other people's, to let the lady call the tune in these affairs; the man's place is to be protective, propitiatory, accommodating and clever, and the lady's to be difficult but delightful until he catches her and houses her splendidly and gives her a surprising lot of pocket-money, and goes about his business; and upon these assumptions Mr. Direck went to work. But quite early it was manifest to him that Cecily did not recognise his assumptions. She was embarrassed when he got down one or two little presents of chocolates and flowers for her from London—the Britling boys were much more appreciative—she wouldn't let him contrive costly little expeditions for her, and she protested against compliments and declared she would stay away when he paid them. And she was not contented by his general sentiments about life, but asked the most direct questions about his occupation and his activities. His chief occupation was being the well-provided heir of a capable lawyer, and his activities in the light of her inquiries struck him as being light and a trifle amateurish, qualities he had never felt as any drawback about them before. So that he had to rely rather upon aspirations and the possibility, under proper inspiration, of a more actively serviceable life in future.

"There's a feeling in the States," he said, "that we've had rather a tendency to overdo work, and that there is scope for a leisure class to develop the refinement and the wider meanings of life."

"But a leisure class doesn't mean a class that does nothing," said Cecily. "It only means a class that isn't busy in business."

"You're too hard on me," said Mr. Direck with that quiet smile of his.

And then by way of putting her on the defensive he asked her what she thought a man in his position ought to do.

"*Something,*" she said, and in the expansion of this vague demand they touched on a number of things. She said that she was a Socialist, and there was still in Mr. Direck's composition a streak of the old-fashioned American prejudice against the word. He associated Socialists with Anarchists and deported aliens. It was manifest too that she was deeply read in the essays and dissertations of Mr. Britling. She thought everybody, man or woman, ought to be chiefly engaged in doing something definite for the world at large. ("There's my secretaryship of the Massachusetts Modern Thought Society, anyhow," said Mr. Direck.) And she herself wanted to be doing something— it was just because she did not know what it was she ought to be doing that she was reading so extensively and voraciously. She wanted to lose herself in something. Deep in the being of Mr. Direck was the conviction that what she ought to be doing was making love in a rapturously egotistical manner, and enjoying every scrap of her own delightful self and her own delightful vitality—while she had it, but for the purposes of their conversation he did not care to put it any more definitely than to say that he thought we owed it to ourselves to develop our personalities. Upon which she joined issue with great vigour.

"That is just what Mr. Britling says about you in his 'American Impressions,' " she said. "He says that America overdoes the development of personalities altogether, that, whatever else is wrong about America, is most clearly wrong. I read that this morning, and directly I read it I thought, 'Yes, that's exactly it! Mr. Direck is overdoing the development of personalities.' "

"Me!"

"Yes. I like talking to you and I don't like talking to you. And I see now it is because you keep on talking of my Personality and your Personality. That makes me uncomfortable. It's like having some one following me about with a limelight. And in a sort of way I do like it. I like it and I'm flattered by it, and then I go off and dislike it, dislike the effect of it. I find myself trying to be what you have told me I am—sort of acting myself. I want to glance at looking-glasses to see if I am keeping it up. It's just exactly what Mr. Britling says in his book about American women. They act themselves, he says; they get a kind of story and explanation about themselves and they are always trying to make it perfectly plain and clear to every one. Well, when you do that you can't think nicely of other things."

"We like a clear light on people," said Mr. Direck.

"We don't. I suppose we're shadier," said Cecily.

"You're certainly much more in half-tones," said Mr. Direck. "And I confess it's the half-tones get hold of me. But still you haven't told me, Miss Cissie, what you think I ought to do with myself. Here I am, you see, very much at your disposal. What sort of business do you think it's my duty to go in for?"

"That's for some one with more experience than I have, to tell you. You should ask Mr. Britling."

"I'd rather have it from you."

"I don't even know for myself," she said.

"So why shouldn't we start to find out together?" he asked.

It was her tantalising habit to ignore all such tentatives.

"One can't help the feeling that one is in the world for something more than oneself," she said.

§ 8

Soon Mr. Direck could measure the time that was left to him at the Dower House no longer by days but by hours. His luggage was mostly packed, his tickets to Rotterdam, Cologne, Munich, Dresden, Vienna, were all in order. And things were still very indefinite between him and Cecily. But God has not made Americans cleanshaven and firm-featured for nothing, and he determined that matters must be brought to some sort of definition before he embarked upon travels that were rapidly losing their attractiveness in this concentration of his attention. . . .

A considerable nervousness betrayed itself in his voice and manner when at last he carried out his determination.

"There's just a lil' thing," he said to her, taking advantage of a moment when they were together after lunch, "that I'd value now more than anything else in the world."

She answered by a lifted eyebrow and a glance that had not so much inquiry in it as she intended.

"If we could just take a lil' walk together for a bit. Round by Claverings park and all that. See the deer again and the old trees. Sort of scenery I'd like to remember when I'm away from it."

He was a little short of breath, and there was a quite disproportionate gravity about her moment for consideration.

"Yes," she said with a cheerful acquiescence that came a couple of bars too late. "Let's. It will be jolly."

"These fine English afternoons are wonderful afternoons," he remarked after a moment or so of silence. "Not quite the splendid blaze we get in our summer, but—sort of glowing."

"It's been very fine all the time you've been here," she said. . . .

After which exchanges they went along the lane, into the road by the park fencing, and so to the little gate that lets one into the park, without another word.

The idea took hold of Mr. Direck's mind that until they got through the park gate it would be quite out of order to say anything. The lane and the road and the stile and the gate were all so much preliminary stuff to be got through before one could get to business. But after the little white gate the way was clear, the park opened out and one could get ahead without bothering about the steering. And Mr. Direck had, he felt, been diplomatically involved in lanes and byways long enough.

"Well," he said as he rejoined her after very carefully closing the gate.

"What I really wanted was an opportunity of just mentioning something that happenes to be of interest to you—if it does happen to interest you. . . . I suppose I'd better put the thing as simply as possible. . . . Practically. . . . I'm just right over the head and all in love with you. . . . I thought I'd like to tell you. . . ."

Immense silences.

"Of course I won't pretend there haven't been others," Mr. Direck suddenly resumed. "There have. One particularly. But I can assure you I've never felt the depth and height or anything like the sort of Quiet Clear Conviction. . . And now I'm just telling you these things, Miss Corner, I don't know whether it will interest you if I tell you that you're really and truly the very first love I ever had as well as my last. I've had sent over—I got it only yesterday—this lil' photograph of a miniature portrait of one of my ancestor's relations—a Corner just as you are. It's here. . . ."

He had considerable difficulties with his pockets and papers. Cecily, mute and flushed and inconvenienced by a preposterous and unaccountable impulse to weep, took the picture he handed her.

"When I was a lil' fellow of fifteen," said Mr. Direck in the tone of one producing a melancholy but conclusive piece of evidence, "I *worshipped* that miniature. It seemed to me—the loveliest person. . . . And—it's just you. . . ."

He too was preposterously moved.

It seemed a long time before Cecily had anything to say, and then what she had to say she said in a softened, indistinct voice. "You're very kind," she said, and kept hold of the little photograph.

They had halted for the photograph. Now they walked on again.

"I thought I'd like to tell you," said Mr. Direck and became tremendously silent.

Cecily found him incredibly difficult to answer. She tried to make herself light and offhand, and to be very frank with him.

"Of course," she said, "I knew—I felt somehow—you meant to say something of this sort to me—when you asked me to come with you——"

"Well?" he said.

"And I've been trying to make my poor brain think of something to say to you."

She paused and contemplated her difficulties. . . .

"Couldn't you perhaps say something of the same kind—such as I've been trying to say?" said Mr. Direck presently, with a note of earnest helpfulness. "I'd be very glad if you could."

"Not exactly," said Cecily, more careful than ever.

"Meaning?"

"I think you know that you are the best of friends. I think you are, oh—a Perfect Dear."

"Well—that's all right—so far."

"That *is* as far."

"You don't know whether you love me? That's what you mean to say."

"No. . . . I feel somehow it isn't that. . . . Yet. . . ."

"There's nobody else by any chance?"

"No." Cecily weighed things. "You needn't trouble about that."

"Only . . . only you don't know."

Cecily made a movement of assent.

"It's no good pretending I haven't thought about you," she said.

"Well, anyhow I've done my best to give you the idea," said Mr. Direck. "I seem now to have been doing that pretty nearly all the time."

"Only what should we do?"

Mr. Direck felt this question was singularly artless. "Why!—we'd marry," he said. "And all that sort of thing."

"Letty has married—and all that sort of thing," said Cecily, fixing her eye on him very firmly because she was colouring brightly. "And it doesn't leave Letty very much—forrarder."

"Well now, they have a good time, don't they? I'd have thought they have a lovely time!"

"They've had a lovely time. And Teddy is the dearest husband. And they have a sweet little house and a most amusing baby. And they play hockey every Sunday. And Teddy does his work. And every week is like every other week. It is just heavenly. Just always the same heavenly. Every Sunday there is a fresh week of heavenly beginning. And this, you see, isn't heaven; it is earth. And they don't know it, but they are getting bored. I have been watching them, and they are getting dreadfully bored. It's heartbreaking to watch, because they are almost my dearest people. Teddy used to be making perpetual jokes about the house and the baby and his work and Letty, and now—he's made all the possible jokes. It's only now and then he gets a fresh one. It's like spring flowers and then—summer. And Letty sits about and doesn't sing. They want something new to happen. . . . And there's Mr. and Mrs. Britling. They love each other. Much more than Mrs. Britling dreams, or Mr. Britling for the matter of that. Once upon a time things were heavenly for them too, I suppose. Until suddenly it began to happen to them that nothing new ever happened. . . ."

"Well," said Mr. Direck, "people can travel."

"But that isn't *real* happening," said Cecily.

"It keeps one interested."

"But real happening is doing something."

"You come back to that," said Mr. Direck. "I never met any one before who'd quite got that spirit as you have it. I wouldn't alter it. It's part of you. It's part of this place. It's what Mr. Britling always seems to be saying and never quite knowing he's said it. It's just as though all the things that are going on weren't the things that ought to be going on—but something else quite different. Somehow one falls into it. It's as if your daily life didn't matter, as if politics didn't matter, as if the King and the social round and business and all those things weren't anything really, and as though you felt there was something else—out of sight—round the corner—that you ought to be getting at. Well, I admit that's got hold of me too. And it's all mixed up with my idea of you. I don't see that there's really a contradiction in it at all. I'm in love with you, all my heart's in love with you, what's the good of being shy about it? I'd just die for your littlest wish right here now, it's just as though I'd got love in my veins instead of blood, but that's not taking me away from that other thing. It's bringing me round to that other thing. I feel as if without you I wasn't up to anything at all, but *with* you——We'd not go settling down in a cottage or just touring about with a Baedeker Guide or anything of that kind. Not for long anyhow. We'd naturally settle down side by side and *do*. . . ."

"But what should we do?" asked Cecily.

There came a hiatus in their talk.

Mr. Direck took a deep breath.

"You see that old felled tree there. I was sitting on it the day before yesterday and thinking of you. Will you come there and sit with me on it? When you sit on it you get a view, oh! a perfectly lovely English view, just a bit of the house and those clumps of trees and the valley away there with the lily-pond. I'd love to have you in my memory of it. . . ."

They sat down, and Mr. Direck opened his case. He was shy and clumsy about opening it, because he had been thinking dreadfully hard about it, and he hated to seem heavy or profound or anything but artless and spontaneous to Cecily. And he felt even when he did open his case that the effect of it was platitudinous and disappointing. Yet when he had thought it out it had seemed very profound and altogether living.

"You see one doesn't want to use terms that have been used in a thousand different senses in any way that isn't a perfectly unambiguous sense, and at the same time one doesn't want to seem to be canting about things or pitching anything a note or two higher than it ought legitimately to go, but it seems to me that this sort of something that Mr. Britling is always asking for in his essays and writings and things, and what you are looking for just as much and which seems so important to you that even love itself is a secondary kind of thing until you can square the two together, is nothing more or less than Religion—I don't mean this Religion, or that Religion but just Religion itself, a Big, Solemn, Comprehensive Idea that holds you and me and all the world together in one great, grand universal scheme. And though it isn't quite the sort of idea of loving-making that's been popular—well, in places like Carrierville—for some time, it's the right idea; it's got to be followed out if we don't want love-making to be a sort of idle, troublesome game of treats and flatteries that is sure as anything to lead right away to disappointments and foolishness and unfaithfulness, and—just Hell. What you are driving at, according to my interpretation, is that marriage has got to be a religious marriage or else you are splitting up life, that religion and love are most of life and all the power there is in it, and that they can't afford to be harnessed in two different directions. . . . I never had these ideas until I came here and met you, but they come up now in my mind as though they had always been there. . . . And that's why you don't want to marry in a hurry. And that's why I'm glad almost that you don't want to marry in a hurry."

He considered. "That's why I'll have to go on to Germany, and just let both of us turn things over in our minds."

"Yes," said Cecily weighing his speech. "I think that is it. I think that I do want a religious marriage, and that what is wrong with Teddy and Letty is that they aren't religious. They pretend they are religious, somewhere out of sight and round the corner. . . . Only——"

He considered her gravely.

"What *is* Religion?" she asked.

Here again there was a considerable pause.

"Very nearly two-thirds of the papers read before our Massachusetts society since my connection with it have dealt with that very question," Mr. Direck began. "And one of our most influential members was able to secure the services of a very able and highly trained young woman from Michigan University to make a digest of all these representative utterances. We are having it printed in a thoroughly artistic manner, as the club book for our autumn season. The drift of her results is that religion isn't the same thing as religions. That most religions are old and that religion is always new. . . . Well, putting it simply, religion is the perpetual rediscovery of that Great Thing Out There. . . . What the Great Thing is goes by all sorts of names, but if you know it's there and if you remember it's there, you've got religion. . . . That's about how she figured it out. . . . I shall send you the book as soon as a copy comes over to me. . . . I can't profess to put it as clearly as she puts it. She's got a real analytical mind. But it's one of the most suggestive lil' books I've ever seen. It just takes hold of you and *makes* you think."

He paused and regarded the ground before him—thoughtfully.

"Life," said Cecily, "has either got to be religious or else it goes to pieces. . . . Perhaps anyhow it goes to pieces. . . ."

Mr. Direck endorsed these observations by a slow nodding of the head.

He allowed a certain interval to elapse. Then a vaguely apprehended purpose that had been for a time forgotten in these higher interests came back to him. He took it up with a breathless sense of temerity.

"Well," he said, "then you don't hate me?"

She smiled.

"You don't dislike me or despise me?"

She was still reassuring.

"You don't think I'm just a slow American sort of portent?"

"No."

"You think, on the whole, I might even—some day——?"

She tried to meet his eyes with a pleasant frankness, and perhaps she was franker than she meant to be.

"Look here," said Mr. Direck, with a little quiver of emotion softening his mouth. "I'll ask you something. We've got to wait. Until you feel clearer. Still. . . . Could you bring yourself——? If just once—I could kiss you. . . .

"I'm going away to Germany," he went on to her silence. "But I shan't be giving so much attention to Germany as I supposed I should when I planned it out. But somehow—if I felt—that I'd kissed you. . . ."

With a delusive effect of calmness the young lady looked first over her left shoulder and then over her right and surveyed the park about them. Then she stood up. "We can go that way home," she said with a movement of her head, "through the little covert."

Mr. Direck stood up too.

"If I was a poet or a bird," said Mr. Direck, "I should sing. But being just a plain American citizen all I can do is just to talk about all I'd do if I wasn't. . . ."

And when they had reached the little covert, with its pathway of soft moss and its sheltering screen of interlacing branches, he broke the silence by saying, "Well, what's wrong with right here and now?" and Cecily stood up to him as straight as a spear, with gifts in her clear eyes. He took her soft cool face between his trembling hands and kissed her sweet half-parted lips. When he kissed her she shivered and he held her tighter and would have kissed her again. But she broke away from him, and he did not press her. And muter than

174

ever, pondering deeply and secretly trembling in the queerest way, these two outwardly sedate young people returned to the Dower House. . . .

And after tea the taxicab from the junction came for him and he vanished, and was last seen as a waving hat receding along the top of the dog-rose hedge that ran beyond the hockey-field towards the village.

"He will see Germany long before I shall," said Herr Heinrich with a gust of nostalgia. "I wish almost I had not agreed to go to Boulogne."

And for some days Miss Cecily Corner was a very grave and dignified young woman indeed. Pondering. . . .

§ 9

After the departure of Mr. Direck things international began to move forward with great rapidity. It was exactly as if his American deliberation had hitherto kept things waiting. Before his postcard from Rotterdam reached the Dower House, Austria had sent an ultimatum to Serbia, and before Cecily had got the letter he wrote her from Cologne, a letter in that curiously unformed handwriting the stenographer and the typewriter are making an American characteristic, Russia was mobilising, and the vast prospect of a European war had opened like the rolling up of a curtain on which the interests of the former week had been but a trivial embroidery. So insistent was this reality that revealed itself that even the shooting of the Dublin people after the gun-running of Howth was dwarfed to unimportance. The mind of Mr. Britling came round from its restless wanderings to a more and more intent contemplation of the hurrying storm-clouds that swept out of nothingness to blacken all his sky. He watched it, he watched amazed and incredulous, he watched this contradiction of all his reiterated confessions of faith in German sanity and pacifism, he watched it with all that was impersonal in his being, and meanwhile his personal life ran in a continually deeper and narrower channel as his intelligence was withdrawn from it.

Never had the double refraction of his mind been more clearly defined. On the one hand the Britling of the disinterested intelligence saw the habitual peace of the world vanish as the daylight vanishes when a shutter falls over the window of a cell; and on the other the Britling of the private life saw all the pleasant comfort of his relations with Mrs. Harrowdean disappearing in a perplexing irrational quarrel. He did not want to lose Mrs. Harrowdean; he contemplated their breach with a profound and profoundly selfish dismay. It seemed the wanton termination of an arrangement of which he was only beginning to perceive the extreme and irreplaceable satisfactoriness.

It wasn't that he was in love with her. He knew, almost as clearly as though he had told himself as much, that he had not. But then, on the other hand, it was equally manifest in its subdued and ignored way that as a matter of fact she was hardly more in love with him. What constituted the satisfactoriness of the whole affair was its essential unlovingness and friendly want of emotion. It left their minds free to play with all the terms and methods of love without distress. She could summon tears and delights as one summons servants, and he could act his part as lover with no sense of lost control. They supplied in each other's lives a long-felt want—if only, that is, she could control her curious aptitude for jealousy and the sexual impulse to vex. There, he felt, she broke the convention of their relations and brought in serious realities, and this little rift it was that had widened to a now considerable breach. He knew that in every sane moment she dreaded and wished to heal that breach as much as he did. But the deep simplicities of the instincts they had tacitly agreed to bridge over washed the piers of their reconciliation away.

And unless they could restore the bridge things would end, and Mr. Britling felt that the ending of things would involve for him the most extraordinary exasperation. She would go to Oliver for comfort; she would marry Oliver; and he knew her well enough to be sure that she would thrust her matrimonial happiness with Oliver unsparingly upon his attention; while he, on the other hand, being provided with no corresponding Olivette, would be left, a sort of emotional celibate, with his slack times and his afternoons and his general need for flattery and amusement dreadfully upon his own hands. He would be tormented by jealousy. In which case—and here he came to verities—his work would suffer. It wouldn't grip him while all these vague demands she satisfied fermented unassuaged.

And, after the fashion of our still too adolescent world, Mr. Britling and Mrs. Harrowdean proceeded to negotiate these extremely unromantic matters in the phrases of that simple, honest, and youthful passionateness which is still the only language available, and at times Mr. Britling came very near persuading himself that he had something of the passionate love for her that he had once had for his Mary, and that the possible loss of her had nothing to do with the convenience of Pyecrafts or any discretion in the world. Though indeed the only thing in the whole plexus of emotional possibility that still kept anything of its youthful freshness in his mind was the very strong objection indeed he felt to handing her over to anybody else in the world. And in addition he had just a touch of fatherly feeling that a younger man would not have had, and it made him very anxious to prevent her making a fool of herself by marrying a man out of spite. He felt that since an obstinate lover is apt to be an exacting husband, in the end the heavy predominance of Oliver might wring much sincerer tears from her than she had ever shed for himself. That generosity was but the bright edge to a jealousy mainly possessive.

It was Mr. Britling who reopened the correspondence by writing a little apology for the corner of the small snapdragon bed, and this evoked an admirably touching reply. He replied quite naturally with assurances and declarations. But before she got his second letter her mood had changed. She decided that if he had really and truly been lovingly sorry, instead of just writing her a note he would have rushed over to her in a wild, dramatic state of mind, and begged forgiveness on his knees. She wrote therefore a second letter to this effect, crossing his second one, and, her literary gift getting the better of her, she expanded her thesis into a general denunciation of his habitual offhandedness with her, to an abandonment of all hope of ever being happy with him, to a decision to end the matter once for all, and after a decent interval of dignified regrets to summon Oliver to the reward of his patience and goodness. The European situation was now at a pitch to get upon Mr. Britling's nerves, and he replied with a letter intended to be conciliatory, but which degenerated into earnest reproaches for her "unreasonableness." Meanwhile she had received his second and tenderly eloquent letter; it moved her deeply, and having now cleared her mind of much that had kept it simmering uncomfortably, she replied with a sweetly loving epistle. From this point their correspondence had a kind of double quality, being intermittently angry and loving; her third letter was tender, and it was tenderly answered in his fourth; but in the interim she had received his third and answered it with considerable acerbity, to which his fifth was a retort, just missing her generous and conclusive fifth. She replied to his fifth on a Saturday evening—it was that eventful Saturday, Saturday the 1st of August, 1914—by a telegram. Oliver was abroad in Holland, engaged in a much-needed emotional rest, and she wired to Mr. Britling: "Have wired for Oliver, he will come to me, do not trouble to answer this."

She was astonished to get no reply for two days. She got no reply for two days because remarkable things were happening to the telegraph-wires of England just then, and her message, in the hands of a boy scout on a bicycle, reached Mr. Britling's house only on Monday afternoon. He was then at Claverings discussing the invasion of Belgium that made Britain's participation in the war inevitable, and he did not open the little red-brown envelope until about half past six. He failed to mark the date and hours upon it, but he perceived that it was essentially a challenge. He was expected, he saw, to go over at once with his renovated Gladys and end this unfortunate clash for ever in one striking and passionate scene. His mind was now so full of the war that he found this the most colourless and unattractive of obligations. But he felt bound by the mysterious code of honour of the illicit love-affair to play his part. He postponed his departure until after supper—there was no reason why he should be afraid of motoring by moonlight if he went carefully—because Hugh came in with Cissie demanding a game of hockey. Hockey offered a nervous refreshment, a scampering forgetfulness of the tremendous disaster of this war he had always believed impossible, that nothing else could do, and he was very glad of the irruption. . . .

§ 10

For days the broader side of Mr. Britling's mind, as distinguished from its egotistical edge, had been reflecting more and more vividly and coherently the spectacle of civilisation casting aside the thousand dispersed activities of peace, clutching its weapons and setting its teeth, for a supreme struggle against militarist imperialism. From the point of view of Matching's Easy that colossal crystallising of accumulated antagonisms was for a time no more than a confusion of head-lines and a rearrangement of columns in the white windows of the newspapers through which those who lived in the securities of England looked out upon the world. It was a display in the sphere of thought and print immeasurably remote from the real green turf on which one walked, from the voice and the church-bells of Mr. Dimple that sounded their ample caresses in one's ears, from the clashing of the stags who were beginning to knock the velvet from their horns in the park, or the clatter of the butcher's cart and the respectful greeting of the butcher's boy down the lane. It was the spectacle of the world less real even to most imaginations than the world of novels or plays. People talked of these things always with an underlying feeling that they romanced and intellectualised.

On Thursday, July 23rd, the Austro-Hungarian minister at Belgrade presented his impossible ultimatum to the Serbian Government, and demanded a reply within forty-eight hours. With the wisdom of retrospect we know now clearly enough what that meant. The Sarajevo crime was to be resuscitated and made an excuse for war. But nine hundred and ninety-nine Europeans out of a thousand had still no suspicion of what was happening to them. The ultimatum figured prominently in the morning papers that came to Matching's Easy on Friday, but it by no means dominated the rest of the news; Sir Edward Carson's rejection of the government proposals for Ulster was given the pride of place, and almost equally conspicuous with the Serbian news were the Caillaux trial and the storming of the St. Petersburg barricades by Cossacks. Herr Heinrich's questions at lunch-time received reassuring replies.

On Saturday Sir Edward Carson was still in the central limelight, Russia had intervened and demanded more time for Serbia, and *The Daily Chronicle* declared the day a critical one for Europe. Dublin with bayonet charges and bullets thrust Serbia into a corner on Monday. No shots had yet been fired in the East, and the mischief in Ireland that Germany had counted on was well ahead. Sir Edward Grey was said to be working hard for peace.

"It's the cry of wolf," said Mr. Britling to Herr Heinrich.

"But at last there did come a wolf," said Herr Heinrich. "I wish I had not sent my first moneys to that Conference upon Esperanto. I feel sure it will be put off."

"See!" said Teddy very cheerfully to Herr Heinrich on Tuesday, and held up the paper, in which "The Bloodshed in Dublin" had squeezed the "War-Cloud Lifting" into a quite subordinate position.

"What did we tell you?" said Mrs. Britling. "Nobody wants a European war."

But Wednesday's paper vindicated his fears. Germany had commanded Russia not to mobilise.

"Of course Russia will mobilise," said Herr Heinrich.

"Or else for ever after hold her peace," said Teddy.

"And then Germany will mobilise," said Herr Heinrich, "and all my holiday will vanish. I shall have to go and mobilise too. I shall have to fight. I have my papers."

"I never thought of you as a soldier before," said Teddy.

"I have deferred my service until I have done my thesis," said Herr Heinrich. "Now all that will be—Piff! And my thesis three-quarters finished."

"That is serious," said Teddy.

"*Verdammte Dummheit!*" said Herr Heinrich. "Why do they do such things?"

On Thursday, the 30th of July, Caillaux, Carson, strikes, and all the common topics of life had been swept out of the front page of the paper altogether; the stock exchanges were in a state of wild perturbation, and food prices were leaping fantastically. Austria was bombarding Belgrade, contrary to the rules of war hitherto accepted; Russia was mobilising; Mr. Asquith was, he declared, not relaxing his efforts "to do everything possible to circumscribe the area of possible conflict," and the Vienna Conference of Peace Societies was postponed. "I do not see why a conflict between Russia and Austria should involve Western Europe," said Mr. Britling. "Our concern is only for Belgium and France."

But Herr Heinrich knew better. "No," he said. "It is the war. It has come. I have heard it talked about in Germany many times. But I have never believed that it was obliged to come. Ach! It considers no one. So long as Esperanto is disregarded, all these things must be."

Friday brought photographs of the mobilisation in Vienna, and the news that Belgrade was burning. Young men in straw hats very like English or French or Belgian young men in straw hats were shown parading the streets of Vienna, carrying flags and banners portentously, blowing trumpets or waving hats and shouting. Saturday saw all Europe mobilising, and Herr Heinrich upon Teddy's bicycle in wild pursuit of evening papers at the junction. Mobilisation and the emotions of Herr Heinrich now became the central facts of the Dower House situation. The two younger Britlings mobilised with great vigour upon the play-room floor. The elder had one hundred and ninety toy soldiers with a considerable equipment of guns and wagons; the younger had a force of a hundred and twenty-three, not counting three railway porters (with trucks complete), a policeman, five civilians and two ladies. Also they made a number of British and German flags out of paper. But as neither would allow his troops to be any existing foreign army, they agreed to be Redland and Blueland, according to the colour of their prevailing uniforms. Meanwhile Herr Heinrich confessed almost promiscuously the complication of his distresses by a hitherto unsuspected emotional interest in the daughter of the village publican. She was a placid receptive young woman named Maud Hickson on whom the young man had, it seemed, imposed the more poetical name of Marguerite.

"Often we have spoken together, oh yes, often," he assured Mrs. Britling. "And now it must all end. She loves flowers, she loves birds. She is most sweet and innocent. I have taught her many words in German and several times I have tried to draw her in pencil, and now I must go away and never see her any more."

His implicit appeal to the whole literature of Teutonic romanticism disarmed Mrs. Britling's objection that he had no business whatever to know the young woman at all.

"Also," cried Herr Heinrich, facing another aspect of his distresses, "how am I to pack my things? Since I have been here I have bought many things, many books, and two pairs of white flannel trousers and some shirts and a tin instrument that I cannot work, for developing privately Kodak films. All this must go into my little portmanteau. And it will not go into my little portmanteau!

"And there is Billy! Who will now go on with the education of Billy?"

The hands of fate paused not for Herr Heinrich's embarrassments and distresses. He fretted from his room downstairs and back to his room, he went out upon mysterious and futile errands towards the village inn, he prowled about the garden. His head and face grew pinker and pinker; his eyes were flushed and distressed. Everybody sought to say and do kind and reassuring things to him.

"Ach!" he said to Teddy; "you are a civilian. You live in a free country. It is not your war. You can be amused at it. . . ."

But then Teddy was amused at everything.

Something but very dimly apprehended at Matching's Easy, something methodical and compelling away in London, seemed to be fumbling and feeling after Herr Heinrich, and Herr Heinrich it appeared was responding. Sunday's post brought the decision.

"I have to go," he said. "I must go right up to London today. To an address in Bloomsbury. Then they will tell me how to go to Germany. I must pack and I must get the taxicab from the junction and I must go. Why are there no trains on the branch line on Sundays for me to go by it?"

At lunch he talked politics. "I am entirely opposed to the war," he said. "I am entirely opposed to any war."

"Then why go?" asked Mr. Britling. "Stay here with us. We all like you. Stay here and do not answer your mobilisation summons."

"But then I shall lose all my country. I shall lose my papers. I shall be outcast. I must go."

"I suppose a man should go with his own country," Mr. Britling reflected.

"If there was only one language in all the world, none of such things would happen," Herr Heinrich declared. "There would be no English, no Germans, no Russians."

"Just Esperantists," said Teddy.

"Or Idoists," said Herr Heinrich. "I am not convinced of which. In some ways Ido is much better."

"Perhaps there would have to be a war between Ido and Esperanto to settle it," said Teddy.

"Who shall we play skat with when you have gone?" asked Mrs. Britling.

"All this morning," said Herr Heinrich expanding in the warmth of sympathy, "I have been trying to pack and I have been unable to pack. My mind is too greatly disordered. I have been told not to bring much luggage. Mrs. Britling, please."

Mrs. Britling became attentive.

"If I could leave much of my luggage, my clothes, some of them, and particularly my violin, it would be much more to my convenience. I do not care to be mobilised with my violin. There may be much crowding. Then I would but just take my rucksack. . . ."

"If you will leave your things packed up."

"And afterwards they could be sent."

But he did not leave them packed up. The taxi-cab to order which he had gone to the junction in the morning on Teddy's complaisant machine, came presently to carry him off, and the whole family and the first contingent of the usual hockey-players gathered about it to see him off. The elder boy of the two juniors put a distended rucksack upon the seat. Herr Heinrich then shook hands with every one.

"Write and tell us how you get on," cried Mrs. Britling.

"But if England also makes war!"

"Write to Reynold's—let me give you his address; he is my agent in New York," said Mr. Britling, and wrote it down.

"We'll come to the village corner with you, Herr Heinrich," cried the boys.

"No," said Herr Heinrich, sitting down in the automobile, "I will part with you altogether. It is too much. . . ."

"*Auf wiedersehen!*" cried Mr. Britling. "Remember, whatever happens, there will be peace at last!"

"Then why not at the beginning?" Herr Heinrich demanded with a reasonable exasperation, and repeated his maturer verdict on the whole European situation: "*Verdammte Bummelei!*"

"Go," said Mr. Britling to the taxi-driver.

"*Auf wiedersehen*, Herr Heinrich!"

"*Auf wiedersehen!*"

"Goodbye, Herr Heinrich!"

"Good luck, Herr Heinrich!"

The taxi started with a whir, and Herr Heinrich passed out of the gates and along the same hungry road that has so recently consumed Mr. Direck. "Give him a last send-off," cried Teddy. "One, Two, Three! *Auf wiedersehen!*"

The voices, gruff and shrill, sounded raggedly together. The dog-rose hedge cut off the sight of the little face. Then the pink head bobbed up again. He was standing up and waving the panama hat. Careless of sunstroke. . . .

Then Herr Heinrich had gone altogether. . . .

"Well," said Mr. Britling, turning away.

"I do hope they won't hurt him," said a visitor.

"Oh, they won't put a youngster like that in the fighting line," said Mr. Britling. "He's had no training yet. And he has to wear glasses. How can he shoot? They'll make a clerk of him."

"He hasn't packed at all," said Mrs. Britling to her husband. "Just come up for an instant and peep at his room. It's—touching."

It was touching.

It was more than touching: in its minute absurd way it was symbolical and prophetic, it was the miniature of one small life uprooted.

The door stood wide open, as he had left it open, careless of all the little jealousies and privacies of occupation and ownership. Even the windows were wide open as though he had needed air; he who had always so sedulously shut his windows since first he came to England. Across the empty fireplace stretched the great bough of oak he had brought in for Billy, but now its twigs and leaves had wilted, and many had broken off and fallen on the floor. Billy's cage stood empty upon a little table in the corner of the room. Instead of packing, the young man had evidently paced up and down in a state of emotional elaboration; the bed was disordered as though he had several times flung himself upon it, and his books had been thrown about the room despairfully. He had made some commencements of packing in a borrowed cardboard box. The violin lay as if it lay in state upon the chest of drawers, the drawers were all partially open, and in the middle of the floor sprawled a pitiful shirt of blue, dropped there, the most flattened and broken-hearted of garments. The fireplace contained an unsuccessful pencil sketch of a girl's face, torn across. . . .

Husband and wife regarded the abandoned room in silence for a time, and when Mr. Britling spoke he lowered his voice.

"I don't see Billy," he said.

"Perhaps he has gone out of the window," said Mrs. Britling also in a hushed undertone. . . .

"Well," said Mr. Britling abruptly and loudly, turning away from this first intimation of coming desolations, "let us go down to our hockey! He had to go, you know. And Billy will probably come back again when he begins to feel hungry. . . ."

§ 11

Monday was a public holiday, the First Monday in August, and the day consecrated by long-established custom to the Matching's Easy Flower-Show in Claverings Park. The day was to live in Mr. Britling's memory with a harsh brightness like the brightness of that sunshine one sees at times at the edge of a thunder-storm. There were tents with the exhibits, and a tent for "Popular Refreshments," there was a gorgeous gold and yellow steam roundabout with motor-cars and horses, and another in green and silver with wonderfully undulating ostriches and lions, and each had an organ that went by steam; there were cocoanut shies and many ingenious prize-giving shooting and dart-throwing and ring-throwing stalls, each displaying a marvellous array of crockery, clocks, metal ornaments, and suchlike rewards. There was a race of gas-balloons, each with a postcard attached to it begging the finder to say where it descended, and you could get a balloon for a shilling and have a chance of winning various impressive and embarrassing prizes if your balloon went far enough—fish-carvers, a silver-handled walking-stick, a bog-oak gramophone-record cabinet, and things like that. And by a special gate one could go for sixpence into the Claverings gardens, and the sixpence would be doubled by Lady Homartyn and devoted next winter to the Matching's

Easy coal club. And Mr. Britling went through all the shows with his boys, and finally left them with a shilling each and his blessing, and paid his sixpence for the gardens and made his way, as he had promised, to have tea with Lady Homartyn.

The morning papers had arrived late, and he had been reading them and rereading them and musing over them intermittently until his family had insisted upon his coming out to the festivities. They said that if for no other reason he must come to witness Aunt Wilshire's extraordinary skill at the cocoanut shy. She could beat everybody. Well, one must not miss a thing like that. The headlines proclaimed, "The Great Powers at War; France Invaded by Germany; Germany Invaded by Russia; 100,000 Germans March into Luxemburg; Can England Abstain? Fifty Million Loan to be Issued." And Germany had not only violated the Treaty of London but she had seized a British ship in the Kiel Canal. . . . The roundabouts were very busy and windily melodious and the shooting-gallery kept popping and jingling as people shot and broke bottles, and the voices of the young men and women inviting the crowd to try their luck at this and that rang loud and clear. Teddy and Letty and Cissie and Hugh were developing a quite disconcerting skill at the dart-throwing, and were bent upon compiling a complete tea-set for the Teddy cottage out of their winnings. There were a score of automobiles and a number of traps and gigs about the entrance to the portion of the park that had been railed off for the festival, the small Britling boys had met some nursery visitors from Claverings House and were busy displaying skill and calm upon the roundabout ostriches, and less that four hundred miles away with a front that reached from Nancy to Liège more than a million and a quarter of grey-clad men, the greatest and best-equipped host the world had ever seen, were pouring westward to take Paris, grip and paralyse France, seize the Channel ports, invade England and make the German Empire the master-state of the earth. Their equipment was a marvel of foresight and scientific organisation, from the motor-kitchens that rumbled in their wake to the telescopic sights of the sharpshooters, the innumerable machine-guns of the infantry, the supply of entrenching material, the preparations already made in the invaded country. . . .

"Let's try at the other place for the sugar-basin!" said Teddy hurrying past. "Don't get *two* sugar-basins," said Cissie breathless in pursuit. "Hugh is trying for a sugar-basin at the other place."

Then Mr. Britling hears a bellicose note.

"Let's have a go at the bottles," said a cheerful young farmer. "Ought to keep up our shooting, these warlike times. . . ."

Mr. Britling ran against Hickson from the village inn, and learned that he was disturbed about his son being called up as a reservist. "Just when he was settling down here. It seems a pity they couldn't leave him for a bit.

" 'Tis a noosence," said Hickson, "but anyhow, they give first prize to his radishes. He'll be glad to hear they give first prize to his radishes. Do you think, sir, there's very much probability of this war? It do seem to be beginning like."

"It looks more like beginning that it has ever done," said Mr. Britling. "It's a foolish business."

"I suppose if they start in on us we got to hit back at them," said Mr. Hickson. "Postman—he's got his papers too. . . ."

Mr. Britling make his way through the drifting throng towards the wicket that led into the gardens. . . .

He was swung round suddenly by a loud bang.

It was the gun proclaiming the start of the balloon-race.

He stood for some moments watching the scene. The balloon start had gathered a little crowd of people, village girls in white gloves and cheerful hats, young men in bright ties and ready-made Sunday suits, fathers and mothers, boy scouts, children, clerks in straw hats, bicyclists, and miscellaneous folk. Over their heads rose Mr. Chesthunt, the factotum of the estate. He was standing on a table and handing the balloons up into the air one by one. They floated up from his hand like many-coloured grapes, some rising and falling, some soaring steadily upward, some spinning and eddying, drifting eastward before the gentle breeze, a string of bubbles against the sky and the big trees that bounded the park. Farther away to the right were the striped canvas tents of the flower-show, still farther off the roundabouts churned out their music, the shooting-galleries popped, and the swing boats creaked through the air. Cut off from these things by a line of fencing lay the open park in which the deer grouped themselves under the great trees and regarded the festival mistrustfully. Teddy and Hugh appeared breaking away from the balloon-race cluster, and hurrying back to their dart-throwing. A man outside a little tent stood apart was putting up a brave-looking notice, "Unstinted Teas One Shilling." The Teddy perambulator was moored against the coconut shy, and Aunt Wilshire was still displaying her terrible prowess at the cocoanuts. Already she had won twenty-seven. Strange children had been impressed by her to carry them, and formed her retinue. A wonderful old lady was Aunt Wilshire. . . .

Then across all the sunshine of this artless festival there appeared, as if it were writing showing through a picture, "France Invaded by Germany; Germany Invaded by Russia."

Mr. Britling turned again towards the wicket, with its collectors of tribute, that led into the gardens.

§ 12

The Claverings gardens, and particularly the great rockery, the lily-pond, and the herbaceous borders, were unusually populous with unaccustomed visitors and shy young couples. Mr. Britling had to go to the house for instructions, and guided by the under-butler found Lady Homartyn hiding in the walled Dutch garden behind the dairy. She had been giving away the prizes of the flower-show, and she was resting in a deck-chair while a spinster relation presided over the tea. Mrs. Britling had fled the outer festival earlier, and was sitting by the tea-things. Lady Meade and two or three visitors had motored out from Hartleytree to assist, and Manning had come in with his tremendous confirmation of all that the morning papers had foreshadowed.

"Have you any news?" asked Mr. Britling.

"It's *war!*" said Mrs. Britling.

"They are in Luxemburg," said Manning. "That can only mean that they are coming through Belgium."

"Then I was wrong," said Mr. Britling, "and the world is altogether mad. And so there is nothing else for us to do but win. . . . Why could they not leave Belgium alone?"

"It's been in all their plans for the last twenty years," said Manning.

"But it brings us in for certain."

"I believe they have reckoned on that."

"Well!" Mr. Britling took his tea and sat down, and for a time he said nothing.

"It is three against three," said one of the visitors, trying to count the Powers engaged.

"Italy," said Manning, "will almost certainly refuse to fight. In fact Italy is friendly to us. She is bound to be. This is, to begin with, an Austrian war. And Japan will fight for us. . . ."

"I think," said old Lady Meade, "that this is the suicide of Germany. They cannot possibly fight against Russia and France and ourselves. Why have they ever begun it?"

"It may be a longer and more difficult war than people suppose," said Manning. "The Germans reckon they are going to win."

"Against us all?"

"Against us all. They are tremendously prepared."

"It is impossible that Germany should win," said Mr. Britling breaking his silence. "Against her Germany has something more than armies; all reason, all instinct—the three greatest peoples in the world."

"At present very badly supplied with war material."

"That may delay things; it may make the task harder; but it will not alter the end. Of course we are going to win. Nothing else is thinkable. I have never believed they meant it. But I see now they meant it. This insolent arming and marching, this forty years of national blustering; sooner or later it had to topple over into action. . . ."

He paused and found they were listening, and he was carried on by his own thoughts into further speech.

"This isn't the sort of war," he said, "that is settled by counting guns and rifles. Something that has oppressed us all has become intolerable and has to be ended. And it will be ended. I don't know what soldiers and politicians think of our prospects, but I do know what ordinary reasonable men think of the business. I know that all we millions of reasonable civilised onlookers are prepared to spend our last shillings and give all our lives now, rather than see Germany unbeaten. I know that the same thing is felt in America, and that given half a chance, given just one extra shake of that foolish mailed fist in the face of America, and America also will be in this war by our side. Italy will come in. She is bound to come in. France will fight like one man. I'm quite prepared to believe that the Germans have countless rifles and guns; have got the most perfect maps, spies, plans you can imagine. I'm quite prepared to hear that thay have got a thousand tremendous surprises in equipment up their sleeves. I'm quite prepared for sweeping victories for them and appalling disasters for us. Those are the first things. What I do know is that the Germans understand nothing of the spirit of man; that they do not dream for a moment of the devil of resentment this war will arouse. Didn't we all trust them not to let off their guns? Wasn't that the essence of our liberal and pacific faith? And here they are in the heart of Europe letting off their guns?"

"And such a lot of guns," said Manning.

"Then you think it will be a long war, Mr. Britling?" said Lady Meade.

"Long or short, it will end in the downfall of Germany. But I do not believe it will be long. I do not agree with Manning. Even now I cannot believe that a whole great people can be possessed by war madness. I think the war is the work of the German armaments party and of the Court party. They have forced this war on Germany. Well—they must win and go on winning. So long as they win, Germany will hold together, so long as their armies are not clearly defeated nor their navy destroyed. But once check them and stay them and beat them, then I believe that suddenly the spirit of Germany will change even as it changed after Jena. . . ."

"Willie Nixon," said one of the visitors, "who came back from Hamburg yesterday, says they are convinced they will have taken Paris and St. Petersburg and one or two other little places and practically settled everything for us by about Christmas."

"And London?"

"I forgot if he said London. But I suppose a London more or less hardly matters. They don't think we shall dare come in, but if we do they will Zeppelin the fleet and walk through our army—if you can call it an army."

Manning nodded confirmation.

"They do not understand," said Mr. Britling.

"Sir George Padish told me the same sort of thing," said Lady Homartyn. "He was in Berlin in June."

"Of course the efficiency of their preparations is almost incredible," said another of Lady Meade's party. "They have thought out and got ready for everything—literally everything."

§ 13

Mr. Britling had been a little surprised by the speech he had made. He hadn't realised before he began to talk how angry and scornful he was at this final coming into action of the Teutonic militarism that had so long menaced his world. He had always said it would never really fight—and here it was fighting! He was furious with the indignation of an apologist betrayed. He had only realised the strength and passion of his own belligerent opinions as he had heard them, and as he walked back with his wife through the village to the Dower House, he was still in the swirl of this self-discovery; he was darkly silent, devising fiercely denunciatory phrases against Krupp and Kaiser. "Krupp and Kaiser," he grasped that obvious, convenient alliteration. "It is all that is bad in mediævalism allied to all that is bad in modernity," he told himself.

"The world," he said, startling Mrs. Britling with his sudden speech, "will be intolerable to live in, it will be unendurable for a decent human being, unless we win this war.

"We must smash or be smashed. . . ."

His brain was so busy with such stuff that for a time he stared at Mrs. Harrowdean's belated telegram without grasping the meaning of a word of it. He realised slowly that it was incumbent upon him to go over to her, but he postponed his departure very readily in order to play hockey. Besides which it would be a full moon, and he felt that summer moonlight was far better than sunset and dinner-time for the declarations he was expected to make. And then he went on phrase-making again about Germany until he had actually bullied off at hockey.

Suddenly in the midst of the game he had an amazing thought. It came to him like a physical twinge.

"What the devil are we doing at this hockey?" he asked abruptly of Teddy, who was coming up to bully after a goal. "We ought to be drilling or shooting against those infernal Germans."

Teddy looked at him questioningly.

"Oh, come on!" said Mr. Britling with a gust of impatience, and snapped the sticks together.

§ 14

Mr. Britling started for his moonlight ride about half past nine that night. He announced that he could neither rest nor work, the war had thrown him into a fever; the driving of the automobile was just the distraction he needed; he might not, he added casually, return for a day or so. When he felt he could work again he would come back. He filled up his petrol tank by the light of an electric torch, and sat in his car in the garage and studied his map of the district. His thoughts wandered from the road to Pyecrafts to the coast, and to the possible route of a raider. Suppose the enemy anticipated a declaration of war! Here he might come, and here.... He roused himself from these speculations to the business in hand.

The evening seemed as light as day, a cool moonshine filled the world. The road was silver that flushed to pink at the approach of Mr. Britling's headlight, the dark turf at the wayside and the bushes on the bank became for a moment an acid green as the glare passed. The full moon was climbing up the sky, and so bright that scarcely a star was visible in the blue-grey of the heavens. Houses gleamed white a mile away, and ever and again a moth would flutter and hang in the light of the lamps, and then vanish again in the night.

Gladys was in excellent condition for a run, and so was Mr. Britling. He went neither fast nor slow, and with a quite unfamiliar confidence. Life, which had seemed all day a congested confusion darkened by threats, became cool, mysterious and aloof and with a quality of dignified reassurance.

He steered along the narrow road by the black dog-rose hedge, and so into the highroad towards the village. The village was alight at several windows but almost deserted. Out beyond, a coruscation of lights burned like a group of topaz and rubies set in the silver shield of the night. The festivities of the flower-show were still in full progress, and the reduction of the entrance fee after seven had drawn in every lingering outsider. The roundabouts churned out their relentless music, and the bottle-shooting galleries popped and crashed. The well-patronised ostriches and motor-cars flickered round in a pulsing rhythm; black, black, black, before the naphtha flares.

Mr. Britling pulled up at the side of the road, and sat for a little while watching the silhouettes move hither and thither from shadow to shadow across the bright spaces.

"On the very brink of war—on the brink of Armageddon," he whispered at last. "Do they understand? Do any of us understand?"

He slipped in his gear to starting, and was presently running quietly with his engine purring almost inaudibly along the level road to Hertleytree. The sounds behind him grew smaller and smaller, and died away leaving an immense unruffled quiet under the moon. There seemed no motion but his own, no sound but the neat, subdued, mechanical rhythm in front of his feet. Presently he ran out into the main road, and heedless of the lane that turned away towards Pyecrafts, drove on smoothly towards the east and the sea. Never before had he driven by night. He had expected a fumbling and tedious journey; he found he had come into an undreamt-of silvery splendour of motion. For it seemed as though even the automobile was running on moonlight that night. . . . Pyecrafts could wait. Indeed the later he got to Pyecrafts the more moving and romantic the little comedy of reconciliation would be. And he was in no hurry for that comedy. He felt he wanted to apprehend this vast summer calm about him, that alone of all the things of the day seemed to convey anything whatever of the majestic tragedy that was happening to mankind. As one slipped through this still vigil one could imagine for the first time the millions away there marching, the wide river-valleys, the villages, cities, mountain ranges, ports and seas inaudibly busy.

"Even now," he said, "the battleships may be fighting."

He listened, but the sound was only the low intermittent drumming of his cylinders as he ran with his throttle nearly closed, down a stretch of gentle hill.

He felt that he must see the sea. He would follow the road beyond the Rodwell villages, and then turn up to the crest of Eastonbury Hill. And thither he went and saw in the gap of the low hills beyond a V-shaped level of moonlit water that glittered and yet lay still. He stopped his car by the roadside, and sat for a long time looking at this and musing. And once it seemed to him three little shapes like short black needles passed in line ahead across the molten silver.

But that may have been just the straining of the eyes. . . .

All sorts of talk had come to Mr. Britling's ears about the navies of England and France and Germany; there had been public disputes of experts, much whispering and discussion in private. We had the heavier vessels, the bigger guns, but it was not certain that we had the pre-eminence in science and invention. Were they relying as we were relying on Dreadnoughts, or had they their secrets and surprises for us? Tonight, perhaps, the great ships were steaming to conflict. . . .

Tonight all over the world ships must be in flight and ships pursuing; ten thousand towns must be ringing with the immediate excitement of war. . . .

Only a year ago Mr. Britling had been lunching on a battleship and looking over its intricate machinery. It had seemed to him then that there could be no better human stuff in the world that the quiet, sunburned, disciplined men and officers he had met. . . . And our little army, too, must be gathering tonight, the little army that had been chastened and reborn in South Africa, that he was convinced was individually more gallant and self-reliant and capable than any other army in the world. He would have sneered or protested if he had heard another Englishman say that, but in his heart he held the dear belief. . . .

And what other aviators in the world could fly as the Frenchmen and Englishmen he had met once or twice at Eastchurch and Salisbury could fly? These are things of race and national quality. Let the German cling to his gas-bags. "We shall beat them in the air," he whispered, "We shall beat them on the seas. Surely we shall beat them on the seas. If we have men enough and guns enough we shall beat them on land. . . . Yet——For years they have been preparing. . . ."

There was little room in the heart of Mr. Britling that night for any love but the love of England. He loved England now as a nation of men. There could be no easy victory. Good for us with our too easy natures that there could be no easy victory. But victory we must have now—or perish. . . .

He roused himself with a sigh, restarted his engine, and went on to find some turning-place. He still had a colourless impression that the journey's end was Pyecrafts.

"We must all do the thing we can," he thought, and for a time the course of his automobile along a winding down-hill road held his attention so that he could not get beyond it. He turned about and ran up over the hill again and down long slopes inland, running very softly and smoothly with his lights devouring the road ahead and sweeping the banks and hedges beside him, and as he came down a little hill through a village he heard a confused clatter and jingle of traffic ahead, and saw the danger triangle that warns of crossroads. He slowed down and then pulled up, abruptly.

Riding across the gap between the cottages was a string of horsemen, and then a grey cart, and then a team drawing a heavy object—a gun, and then more horsemen, and then a second gun. It was all a dim brown procession in the moonlight. A mounted officer came up beside him and looked at him and then went back to the crossroads, but as yet England was not troubling about spies. Four more guns passed, and then a string of carts and more mounted men, sitting stiffly. Nobody was singing or shouting; scarcely a word was audible, and through all the column there was an effect of quiet efficient haste. And so they passed, and rumbled and jingled and clattered out of the scene, leaving Mr. Britling in his car in the dreaming village. He restarted his engine once more, and went his way thoughtfully.

He went so thoughtfully that presently he missed the road to Pyecrafts—if ever he had been on the road to Pyecrafts at all—altogether. He found himself upon a highway running across a flattish plain, and presently discovered by the sight of the Great Bear, faint but traceable in the blue overhead, that he was going due north. Well, presently he would turn south and west; that in good time; now he wanted to feel; he wanted to think. How could he best help England in the vast struggle for which the empty silence and beauty of this night seemed to be waiting? But indeed he was not thinking at all, but feeling, feeling wonder, as he had never felt it since his youth had passed from him. This war might end nearly everything in the world as he had known the world; that idea struggled slowly through the moonlight into consciousness, and won its way to dominance in his mind.

The character of the road changed; the hedges fell away, and pine-trees and pine woods took the place of the black squat shapes of the hawthorn and oak and apple. The houses grew rarer and the world emptier and emptier, until he could have believed that he was the only man awake and out-of-doors in all the slumbering land. . . .

For a time a little thing caught hold of his dreaming mind. Continually as he ran on, black, silent birds rose startled out of the dust of the road before him, and fluttered noiselessly beyond his double wedge of light. What sort of bird could they be? Were they nightjars? Were they different kinds of birds snatching at the quiet of the night for a dustbath in the sand? This independent thread of inquiry ran through the texture of his mind and died away. . . .

And at one place there was a great bolting of rabbits across the road, almost under his wheels. . . .

The phrases he had used that afternoon at Claverings came back presently into his head. They were, he felt assured, the phrases that had to be said now. This war could be seen as the noblest of wars, as the crowning struggle of mankind against national dominance and national aggression; or else it was a mere struggle of nationalities and pure destruction and catastrophe. Its enormous significances, he felt, must not be lost in any petty bickering about the minor issues of the conflict. But were these enormous significances being stated clearly enough? Were they being understood by the mass of liberal and pacific thinkers? He drove more and more slowly as these questions crowded upon his attention until at last he came to a stop altogether. . . . "Certain things must be said clearly," he whispered. "Certain things—The meaning of England. . . . The deep and long-unspoken desire for kindliness and fairness. . . . Now is the time for speaking. It must be put as straight now as her gun-fire, as honestly as the steering of her ships."

Phrases and paragraphs began to shape themselves in his mind as he sat with one arm on his steering-wheel.

Suddenly he roused himself, turned over the map in the map-case beside him, and tried to find his position. . . .

So far as he could judge he had strayed right into Suffolk. . . .

About one o'clock in the morning he found himself in Newmarket. Newmarket too was a moonlit emptiness, but as he hesitated at the crossroads he became aware of a policeman standing quite stiff and still at the corner by the church.

"Matching's Easy?" he cried.

"That road, sir, until you come to Market Saffron, and then to the left. . . ."

Mr. Britling had a definite purpose now in his mind, and he drove faster, but still very carefully and surely. He was already within a mile or so of Market Saffron before he remembered that he had made a kind of appointment with himself at Pyecrafts. He stared at two conflicting purposes. He turned over certain possibilities.

At the Market Saffron crossroads he slowed down, and for a moment he hung undecided.

"Oliver," he said, and as he spoke he threw over his steering-wheel towards the homeward way. . . . He finished his sentence when he had negotiated the corner safely. "Oliver must have her. . . ."

And then, perhaps fifty yards farther along and this time almost indignantly: "She ought to have married him long ago. . . ."

He put his automobile in the garage, and then went round under the black shadow of his cedars to the front door. He had no key, and for a long time he failed to rouse his wife by flinging pebbles and gravel at her half-open window. But at last he heard her stirring and called out to her.

He explained he had returned because he wanted to write. He wanted indeed to write quite urgently. He went straight up to his room, lit his reading-lamp, made himself some tea, and changed into his nocturnal suit.

Daylight found him still writing very earnestly at his pamphlet. The title he had chosen was: "And Now War Ends."

§ 15

In this fashion it was that the great war began in Europe and came to one man in Matching's Easy, as it came to countless intelligent men in countless pleasant homes that had scarcely heeded its coming through all the years of its relentless preparation. The familiar scenery of life was drawn aside, and War stood unveiled. "I am the Fact," said War, "and I stand astride the path of life. I am the threat of death and extinction that has always walked beside life, since life began. There can be nothing else and nothing more in human life until you have reckoned with me."

BOOK II

MATCHING'S EASY AT WAR

CHAPTER THE FIRST

ONLOOKERS

§ 1

O N that eventful night of the first shots and the first deaths Mr. Britling did not sleep until daylight had come. He sat writing at this pamphlet of his, which was to hail the last explosion and the ending of war. For a couple of hours he wrote with energy, and then his energy flagged. There came intervals when he sat still and did not write. He yawned and yawned again and rubbed his eyes. The day had come and the birds were noisy when he undressed slowly, dropping his clothes anyhow upon the floor, and got into bed. . . .

He woke to find his morning tea beside him and the housemaid going out of the room. He knew that something stupendous had happened to the world, but for a few moments he could not remember what it was. Then he remembered that France was invaded by Germany and Germany by Russia, and that almost certainly England was going to war. It seemed a harsh and terrible fact in the morning light, a demand for stresses, a certainty of destruction; it appeared now robbed of all the dark and dignified beauty of the night. He remembered just the same feeling of unpleasant, anxious expectation as he now felt when the Boer War had begun fifteen years ago, before the first news came. The first news of the Boer War had been the wrecking of a British armoured train near Kimberley. What similar story might not the overdue paper presently tell?

Suppose, for instance, that some important division of our Fleet had been surprised and overwhelmed. . . .

Suppose the Germans were already crumpling up the French armies between Verdun and Belfort, very swiftly and dreadfully. . . .

Suppose after all that the Cabinet was hesitating, and that there would be no war for some weeks, but only a wrangle about Belgian neutrality. While the Germans smashed France. . . .

Or, on the other hand, there might be some amazing, prompt success on our part. Our army and navy people were narrow, but in their narrow way he believed they were extraordinarily good. . . .

What would the Irish do? . . .

His thoughts were no more than a thorny jungle of unaswerable questions through which he struggled in unprogressive circles.

He got out of bed and dressed in a slow, distraught manner. When he reached his braces he discontinued dressing for a time; he opened the atlas at Northern France, and stood musing over the Belgian border. Then he turned to Whitaker's Almanack to browse upon the statistics of the great European armies. He was roused from this by the breakfast-gong.

At breakfast there was no talk of anything but war. Hugh was as excited as a cat in thundery weather, and the small boys wanted information about flags. The Russian and the Serbian flag were in dispute, and the flag page of Webster's Dictionary had to be consulted. Newspapers and letters were both abnormally late, and Mr. Britling, tiring of supplying trivial information to his offspring, smoked cigarettes in the garden. He had an idea of intercepting the postman. His eyes and ears informed him of the approach of Mrs. Faber's automobile. It was an old, resolute-looking machine painted red, and driven by a trusted gardener; there was no mistaking it.

Mrs. Faber was in it, and she stopped it outside the gate and made signals. Mrs. Britling, attracted by the catastrophic sounds of Mrs. Faber's vehicle, came out by the front door, and she and her husband both converged upon the caller.

§ 2

"I won't come in," cried Mrs. Faber, "but I thought I'd tell you. I've been getting food."

"Food?"

"Provisions. There's going to be a run on provisions. Look at my flitch of bacon!"

"But——"

"Faber says we have to lay in what we can. This war—it's going to stop everything. We can't tell what will happen. I've got the children to consider, so here I am. I was at Hickson's before nine. . . ."

The little lady was very flushed and bright-eyed. Her fair hair was disordered, her hat a trifle askew. She had an air of enjoying unwonted excitements. "All the gold's being hoarded too," she said, with a crow of delight in her voice. "Faber says that probably our cheques won't be worth *that* in a few days. He's rushed off to London to get gold at his clubs—while he can. I had to insist on Hickson taking a cheque. 'Never,' I said, 'will I deal with you again—never—unless you do. . . .' Even then he looked at me almost as if he thought he wouldn't."

"It's Famine!" she said, turning to Mr. Britling. "I've laid hands on all I can. I've got the children to consider."

"But why is it famine?" asked Mr. Britling.

"Oh! it *is!*" she said.

"But why?"

209

"Faber understands," she said. "Of course it's Famine. . . .

"And would you believe me," she went on, going back to Mrs. Britling, "that man Hickson stood behind his counter—where I've dealt with him for *years*, and refused absolutely to let me have more than a dozen tins of sardines. *Refused!* Point-blank!

"I was there before nine, and even then Hickson's shop was crowded—*crowded*, my dear!"

"What have you got?" said Mr. Britling with an inquiring movement towards the automobile.

She had got quite a lot. She had two sides of bacon, a case of sugar, bags of rice, eggs, a lot of flour.

"What are all these little packets?" said Mr. Britling.

Mrs. Faber looked slightly abashed.

"Cerebos salt," she said. "One gets carried away a little. I just got hold of it and carried it out to the car. I thought we might have to salt things later."

"And the jars are pickles?" said Mr. Britling.

"Yes. But look at all my flour! That's what will go first. . . ."

The lady was a little flurried by Mr. Britling's too detailed examination of her haul. "What good is blacking?" he asked. She would not hear him. She felt he was trying to spoil her morning. She declared she must get on back to her home. "Don't say I didn't warn you," she said. "I've got no end of things to do. There's peas! I want to show cook how to bottle our peas. For this year—it's lucky, we've got no end of peas. I came by here just for the sake of telling you." And with that she presently departed—obviously ruffled by Mrs. Britling's lethargy and Mr. Britling's scepticism.

Mr. Britling watched her go off with a slowly rising indignation.

"And that," he said "is how England is going to war! Scrambling for food—at the very beginning."

"I suppose she is anxious for the children," said Mrs. Britling.

"Blacking!"

"After all," said Mrs. Britling, "if other people are doing that sort of thing——"

"That's the idea of all panics. We've got not to do it. . . . The country hasn't even declared war yet! Hallo, here we are! Better late than never."

The head of the postman, bearing newspapers and letters, appeared gliding along the top of the hedge as he cycled down the road towards the Dower House corner.

§ 3

England was not yet at war, but all the stars were marching to that end. It was as if an event so vast must needs take its time to happen. No doubt was left upon Mr. Britling's mind, though a whole-page advertisement in *The Daily News*, in enormous type and of mysterious origin, implored Great Britain not to play into the hands of Russia, Russia the Terrible, that bugbear of the sentimental Radicals. The news was wide and sweeping, and rather inaccurate. The Germans were said to be in Belgium and Holland, and they had seized English ships in the Kiel Canal. A moratorium had been proclaimed, and the reports of a food panic showed Mrs. Faber to be merely one example of a large class of excitable people.

Mr. Britling found the food panic disconcerting. It did not harmonise with his leading *motif* of the free people of the world rising against the intolerable burthen of militarism. It spoiled his picture. . . .

Mrs. Britling shared the paper with Mr. Britling; they stood by the bed of begonias near the cedar-tree and read, and the air was full of the cheerful activities of the lawn-mower that was being drawn by a carefully booted horse across the hockey-field.

Presently Hugh came flitting out of the house to hear what had happened. "one can't work, somehow, with all these big things going on," he apologised. He secured *The Daily News* while his father and mother read *The Times*. The voices of the younger boys came from the shade of the trees; they had brought all their toy soldiers out-of-doors, and were making entrenched camps in the garden.

"The financial situation is an extraordinary one," said Mr. Britling, concentrating his attention. . . . "All sorts of staggering things may happen. In a social and economic system that has grown just anyhow. . . . Never been planned. . . . In a world full of Mrs. Fabers. . . ."

"Moratorium?" said Hugh over his *Daily News*. "In relation to debts and so on? Modern side you sent me to, Daddy. I live at hand to mouth in etymology. Morse and crematorium—do we burn our bills instead of paying them?"

"Moratorium," reflected Mr. Britling; "moratorium. What nonsense you talk! It's something that delays, of course. Nothing to do with death. Just a temporary stoppage of payments. . . . Of course there's bound to be a tremendous change in values. . . ."

§ 4

"There's bound to be a tremendous change in values."

On that text Mr. Britling's mind enlarged very rapidly. It produced a wonderful crop of possibilities before he got back to his study. He sat down to his desk, but he did not immediately take up his work. He had discovered something so revolutionary in his personal affairs that even the war issue remained for a time in suspense.

Tucked away at the back of Mr. Britling's consciousness was something that had not always been there, something warm and comforting that made life and his general thoughts about life much easier and pleasanter than they would otherwise have been, the sense of a neatly arranged investment list, a shrewdly and geographically distributed system of holdings in national loans, municipal investments, railway debentures, that had amounted altogether to rather over five-and-twenty thousand pounds; his and Mrs. Britling's, a joint accumulation. It was, so to speak, his economic viscera. It sustained him, and kept him going and comfortable. When all was well he did not feel its existence; he had merely a pleasant sense of general well-being. Where here or there a security got a little disarranged he felt a vague discomfort. Now he became aware of grave disorders. It was as if he discovered he had been accidentally eating toadstools, and didn't quite know whether they weren't a highly poisonous sort. But an analogy may be carried too far. . . .

At any rate, when Mr. Britling got back to his writing-desk he was much too disturbed to resume "And Now War Ends."

"There's bound to be a tremendous change in values!"

He had never felt quite so sure as most people about the stability of the modern financial system. He did not, he felt, understand the working of this moratorium, or the peculiar advantage of prolonging the bank holidays. It meant, he supposed, a stoppage of payment all round, and a cutting off of the supply of ready money. And Hickson the grocer, according to Mrs. Faber, was already looking askance at cheques.

Even if the bank did reopen, Mr. Britling was aware that his current balance was low; at the utmost it amounted to twenty or thirty pounds. He had been expecting cheques from his English and American publishers, and the usual *Times* cheque. Suppose these payments were intercepted!

All these people might, so far as he could understand, stop payment under this moratorium! That hadn't at first occurred to him. But, of course, quite probably they might refuse to pay his account when it fell due.

And suppose *The Times* felt his peculiar vein of thoughtfulness unnecessary in these stirring days!

And then if the bank really did lock up his deposit account, and his securities became unsaleable!

Mr. Britling felt like an oyster that is invited to leave its shell. . . .

He sat back from his desk contemplating these things. His imagination made a weak attempt to picture a world in which credit had vanished and money is of doubtful value. He supposed a large number of people would just go on buying and selling at or near the old prices by force of habit.

His mind and conscience made a valiant attempt to pick up "And Now War Ends" and go on with it, but before five minutes were out he was back at the thoughts of food panic and bankruptcy. . . .

§ 5

The conflict of interests at Mr. Britling's desk became unendurable. He felt he must settle the personal question first. He wandered out upon the lawn and smoked cigarettes.

His first conception of a great convergent movement of the nations to make a world peace and an end to militant Germany was being obscured by this second, entirely incompatible, vision of a world confused and disorganised. Mrs. Fabers in great multitudes hoarding provisions, riotous crowds attacking shops, moratorium, shut banks and waiting queues. Was it possible for the whole system to break down through a shock to its confidence? Without any sense of incongruity the dignified pacification of the planet had given place in his mind to these more intimate possibilities. He heard a rustle behind him, and turned to face his wife.

"Do you think," she sasked, "that there is any chance of a shortage of food?"

"If all the Mrs. Fabers in the world run and grab——"

"Then every one must grab. I haven't much in the way of stores in the house."

"H'm," said Mr. Britling, and reflected. . . . "I don't think we must buy stores now."

"But if we are short."

"It's the chances of war," said Mr. Britling.

He reflected. "Those who join a panic make a panic. After all, there is just as much food in the world as there was last month. And short of burning it the only way of getting rid of it is to eat it. And the harvests are good. Why begin a scramble at a groaning board?"

"But people *are* scrambling! It would be awkward—with the children and everything—if we ran short."

"We shan't. And anyhow, you mustn't begin hoarding even if it means hardship."

"Yes. But you won't like it if suddenly there's no sugar for your tea."

Mr. Britling ignored this personal application.

"What is far more serious than a food shortage is the possibility of a money panic."

He paced the lawn with her and talked. He said that even now very few people realised the flimsiness of the credit system by which the modern world was sustained. It was a huge growth of confidence, due very largely to the uninquiring indolence of—everybody. It was sound so long as mankind did, on the whole, believe in it; give only a sufficient loss of faith and it might suffer any sort of collapse. It might vanish altogether—as the credit system vanished at the breaking up of Italy by the Goths—and leave us nothing but tangible things, real property, possession nine points of the law, and that sort of thing. Did she remember that last novel of Gissing's?— "Veranilda," it was called. It was a picture of the world when there was no wealth at all except what one could carry hidden or guarded about with one. That sort of thing came to the Roman Empire slowly, in the course of lifetimes, but nowadays we lived in a rapider world with flimsier institutions. Nobody knew the strength or the weakness of credit; nobody knew whether even the present shock might not send it smashing down. . . . And then all the little life we had lived so far would roll away. . . .

Mrs. Britling, he noted, glanced ever and again at her sunlit house—there were new sun-blinds, and she had been happy in her choice of a colour—and listened with a sceptical expression to this disquisition.

"A few days ago," said Mr. Britling, trying to make things concrete for her, "you and I together were worth five-and-twenty thousand pounds. Now we don't know what we are worth; whether we have lost a thousand or ten thousand. . . .

He examined his sovereign purse and announced he had six pounds. "What have you?"

She had about eighteen pounds in the house.

"We may have to get along with that for an indefinite time."

"But the bank will open again presently," she said. "And people about here trust us."

"Suppose they don't?"

She did not trouble about the hypothesis. "And our investments will recover. They always do recover."

"Everything may recover," he admitted. "But also nothing may recover. All this life of ours which has seemed so settled and secure—isn't secure. I have felt that we were fixed here and rooted—for all our lives. Suppose presently things sweep us out of it? It's a possibility we may have to face. I feel this morning as if two enormous gates had opened in our lives, like the gates that give upon an arena, gates giving on a darkness— through which anything might come. Even death. Suppose suddenly we were to see one of those great Zeppelins in the air, or hear the thunder of guns away towards the coast. And if a messenger came upon a bicycle telling us to leave everything and go inland. . . ."

"I see no reason why one should go out to meet things like that."

"But there is no reason why one should not envisage them. . . .

"The curious thing," said Mr. Britling, pursuing his examination of the matter, "is that, looking at these things as one does now, as things quite possible, they are not nearly so terrifying and devastating to the mind as they would have seemed—last week. I believe I should load you all into Gladys and start off westward with a kind of exhilaration. . . ."

She looked at him as if she would speak, and said nothing. She suspected him of hating his home and affecting to care for it out of politeness to her. . . .

"Perhaps mankind tries too much to settle down. Perhaps these stirrings up have to occur to save us from our disposition to stuffy comfort. There's the magic call of the unknown experience, of dangers and hardships. One wants to go. But unless some push comes one does not go. There is a spell that keeps one to the lair and the old familiar ways. Now I am afraid—and at the same time I feel that the spell is broken. The magic prison is suddenly all doors. You may call this ruin, bankruptcy, invasion, flight; they are doors out of habit and routine. . . . I have been doing nothing for so long, except idle things and discursive things."

"I thought that you managed to be happy here. You have done a lot of work."

"Writing is recording, not living. But now I feel suddenly that we are living intensely. It is as if the whole quality of life was changing. There are such times. There are times when the spirit of life changes altogether. The old world knew that better than we do. It made a distinction between weekdays and Sabbaths, and between feasts and fasts and days of devotion. That is just what has happened now, Weekday rules must be put aside. Before—oh! three days ago, competition was fair, it was fair and tolerable to get the best food one could and hold on to one's own. But that isn't right now. War makes a Sabbath, and we shut the shops. The banks are shut, and the world still feels as though Sunday was keeping on. . . ."

He saw his own way clear.

"The scale has altered. It does not matter now in the least if we are ruined. It does not matter in the least if we have to live upon potatoes and run into debt for our rent. These now are the most incidental of things. A week ago they would have been of the first importance. Here we are face to face with the greatest catastrophe and the greatest opportunity in history. We have to plunge through catastrophe to opportunity. There is nothing to be done now in the whole world except to get the best out of this tremendous fusing up of all the settled things of life."

He had got what he wanted. He left her standing upon the lawn and hurried back to his desk. . . .

§ 6

When Mr. Britling, after a strenuous morning among high ideals, descended for lunch, he found Mr. Lawrence Carmine had come over to join him at that meal. Mr. Carmine was standing in the hall with his legs very wide apart reading *The Times* for the fourth time. "I can do no work," he said, turning round. "I can't fix my mind. I suppose we are going to war. I'd got so used to the war with Germany that I never imagined it would happen. Gods! what a bore it will be. . . . And Maxse and all those scaremongers cock-a-hoop and 'I told you so.' Damn these Germans!"

He looked despondent and worried. He followed Mr. Britling towards the dining-room with his hands deep in his pockets.

"It's going to be a tremendous thing," he said, after he had greeted Mrs. Britling and Hugh and Aunt Wilshire and Teddy, and seated himself at Mr. Britling's hospitable board. "It's going to upset everything. We don't begin to imagine all the mischief it is going to do."

Mr. Britling was full of the heady draught of liberal optimism he had been brewing upstairs. "I am not sorry I have lived to see this war," he said. "It may be a tremendous catastrophe in one sense, but in another it is a huge step forward in human life. It is the end of forty years of evil suspense. It is crisis and solution."

"I wish I could see it like that," said Mr. Carmine.

"It is like a thaw—everything has been in a frozen confusion since that Jew-German Treaty of Berlin. And since 1871."

"Why not since Schleswig-Holstein?" said Mr. Carmine.

"Why not? Or since the Treaty of Vienna?"

"Or since—— One might go back."

"To the Roman Empire," said Hugh.

"To the first conquest of all," said Teddy. . . .

"I couldn't work this morning," said Hugh. "I have been reading in the Encyclopædia about races and religions in the Balkans. . . . It's very mixed."

"So long as it could only be dealt with piecemeal," said Mr. Britling. "And that is just where the tremendous opportunity of this war comes in. Now everything becomes fluid. We can redraw the map of the world. A week ago we were all quarrelling bitterly about things too little for human impatience. Now suddenly we face an epoch. This is an epoch. The world is plastic for men to do what they will with it. This is the end and the beginning of an age. This is something far greater than the French Revolution or the Reformation. . . . And we live in it. . . ."

He paused impressively.

"I wonder what will happen to Albania?" said Hugh, but his comment was disregarded.

"War makes men bitter and narrow," said Mr. Carmine.

"War narrowly conceived," said Mr. Britling. "But this is an indignant and generous war."

They speculated about the possible intervention of the United States. Mr. Britling thought that the attack on Belgium demanded the intervention of every civilised power, that all the best instincts of America would be for intervention. "The more," he said, "the quicker."

"It would be strange if the last power left out to mediate were to be China," said Mr. Carmine. "The one people in the world who really believe in peace. . . . I wish I had your confidence, Britling."

For a time they contemplated a sort of Grand Inquest on Germany and militarism, presided over by the Wisdom of the East. Militarism was, as it were, to be buried as a suicide at four crossroads, with a stake through its body to prevent any untimely resuscitation.

§ 7

Mr. Britling was in a phase of imaginative release. Such a release was one of the first effects of the war upon many educated minds. Things that had seemed solid for ever were visibly in flux; things that had seemed stone were alive. Every boundary, every government, was seen for the provisional thing it was. He talked of his World Congress meeting year by year, until it ceased to be a speculation and became a mere intelligent anticipation; he talked of the "manifest necessity" of a Supreme Court for the world. He beheld that vision at The Hague, but Mr. Carmine preferred Delhi or Samarkand or Alexandria or Nankin. "Let us get away from the delusion of Europe anyhow," said Mr. Carmine. . . .

As Mr. Britling had sat at his desk that morning and surveyed the stupendous vistas of possibility that war was opening, the catastrophe had taken on a more and more beneficial quality. "I suppose that it is only through such crises as these that the world can reconstruct itself," he said. And, on the whole, that afternoon he was disposed to hope that the great military machine would not smash itself too easily. "We want the nations to feel the need of one another," he said. "Too brief a campaign might lead to a squabble for plunder. The Englishman has to learn his dependence on the Irishman, the Russian has to be taught the value of education and the friendship of the Pole. . . . Europe will now have to look to Asia, and recognise that Indians and Chinamen are also 'white.' . . . But these lessons require time and stresses if they are to be learned properly. . . ."

They discussed the possible duration of the war.

Mr. Carmine thought it would be a long struggle; Mr. Britling thought that the Russians would be in Berlin by the next May. He was afraid they might get there before the end of the year. He thought that the Germans would beat out their strength upon the French and Belgian lines, and never be free to turn upon the Russian at all. He was sure they had underrated the strength and energy of the French and of ourselves. "The Russians meanwhile," he said, "will come on, slowly, steadily, inevitably. . . ."

§ 8

That day of vast anticipations drew out into the afternoon. It was a day—obsessed. It was the precursor of a relentless series of doomed and fettered days. There was a sense of enormous occurrences going on just out of sound and sight—behind the mask of Essex peacefulness. From this there was no escape. It made all other interests fitful. Games of Badminton were begun and abruptly truncated by the arrival of the evening papers; conversations started upon any topic whatever returned to the war by the third and fourth remark. . . .

After lunch Mr. Britling and Mr. Carmine went on talking. Nothing else was possible. They repeated things they had already said. They went into things more thoroughly. They sat still for a time, and then suddenly broke out with some new consideration. . . .

It had been their custom to play skat with Herr Heinrich, who had shown them the game very explicitly and thoroughly. But there was no longer any Herr Heinrich—and somehow German games were already out of fashion. The two philosophers admitted that they had already considered skat to be complicated without subtlety, and that its chief delight for them had been the pink earnestness of Herr Heinrich, his inability to grasp their complete but tacit comprehension of its innocent strategy, and his invariable ill success in bringing off the coups that flashed before his imagination.

He would survey the destructive counter-stroke with unconcealed surprise. He would verify his first impression by craning towards it and adjusting his glasses on his nose. He had a characteristic way of doing this with one stiff finger on either side of his sturdy nose.

"It is very fortunate for you that you have played that card," he would say, growing pinker and pinker with hasty cerebration. "Or else—yes"—a glance at his own cards—"it would have been altogether bad for you. I had taken only a very small risk. . . . Now I must——"

He would reconsider his hand.

"*Zo!*" he would say, dashing down a card. . . .

Well, he had gone and skat had gone. A countless multitude of such links were snapping that day between hundreds of thousands of English and German homes.

§ 9

The imminence of war produced a peculiar exaltation in Aunt Wilshire. She developed a point of view that was entirely her own.

It was Mr. Britling's habit, a habit he had set himself to acquire after much irritating experience, to disregard Aunt Wilshire. She was not, strictly speaking, his aunt; she was one of those distant cousins we find already woven into our lives when we attain to years of responsibility. She had been a presence in his father's household when Mr. Britling was a boy. Then she had been called "Jane," or "Cousin Jane," or "Your cousin Wilshire." It had been a kindly freak of Mr. Britling's to promote her to Auntly rank.

She eked out a small inheritance by staying with relatives. Mr. Britling's earlier memories presented her as a slender young woman of thirty, with a nose upon which small boys were forbidden to comment. Yet she commented upon it herself, and called his attention to its marked resemblance to that of the great Duke of Wellington. "He was, I am told," said Cousin Wilshire to the attentive youth, "a great friend of your great-grandmother's. At any rate, they were contemporaries. Since then this nose has been in the family. He would have been the last to draw a veil over it, but other times, other manners. 'Publish,' he said, 'and be damned.'"

She had a knack of exasperating Mr. Britling's father, a knack which to a less marked degree she also possessed in relation to the son. But Mr. Britling senior never acquired the art of disregarding her. Her method—if one may call the natural expression of a personality a method—was an invincibly superior knowledge, a firm and ill-concealed belief that all statements made in her hearing were wrong and most of them absurd, and a manner calm, assured, restrained. She may have been born with it: it is on record that at the age of ten she was pronounced a singularly trying child. She may have been born with the air of thinking the doctor a muff and knowing how to manage all this business better. Mr. Britling had known her only in her ripeness. As a boy, he had enjoyed her confidences—about other people and the general neglect of her advice. He grew up rather to like her—most people rather liked her—and to attach a certain importance to her unattainable approval. She was sometimes kind, she was frequently absurd. . . .

With very little children she was quite wise and jolly. . . .

So she circulated about a number of houses which at any rate always welcomed her coming. In the opening days of each visit she performed marvels of tact, and set a watch upon her lips. Then the demons of controversy and dignity would get the better of her. She would begin to correct, quietly but firmly, she would begin to disapprove of the tone and quality of her treatment. It was quite common for her visit to terminate in speechless rage both on the side of host and of visitor. The remarkable thing was that this speechless rage never endured. Though she could exasperate she could never offend. Always after an interval during which she was never mentioned, people began to wonder how Cousin Jane was getting on. . . . A tentative correspondence would begin, leading slowly up to a fresh invitation.

She spent more time in Mr. Britling's house than in any other. There was a legend that she had "drawn out" his mind, and that she had "stood up" for him against his father. She had certainly contradicted quite a number of those unfavourable comments that fathers are wont to make about their sons.

Though certainly she contradicted everything. And Mr. Britling hated to think of her knocking about alone in boarding-houses and hydropathic establishments with only the most casual chances for contradiction.

Moreover, he liked to see her casting her eye over the morning paper. She did it with a manner as though she thought the terrestrial globe a great fool, and quite beyond the reach of advice. And as though she understood and was rather amused at the way in which the newspaper people tried to keep back the real facts of the case from her.

And now she was scornfully entertained at the behaviour of everybody in the war crisis.

She confided various secrets of state to the elder of the younger Britlings—preferably when his father was within earshot.

"None of these things they are saying about the war," she said, "really matter in the slightest degree. It is all about a spoiled carpet and nothing else in the world—a madman and a spoiled carpet. If people had paid the slightest attention to common sense none of this war would have happened. The thing was perfectly well known. He was a delicate child, difficult to rear and given to screaming fits. Consequently he was never crossed, allowed to do everything. Nobody but his grandmother had the slightest influence with him. And she prevented him spoiling this carpet as completely as he wished to do. The story is perfectly well known. It was at Windsor—at the age of eight. After that he had but one thought: war with England. . . .

"Everybody seems surprised," she said suddenly at tea to Mr. Carmine. "I at least am not surprised. I am only surprised it did not come sooner. If any one had asked me I could have told them, three years, five years ago."

The day was one of flying rumours, Germany was said to have declared war on Italy, and to have invaded Holland as well as Belgium.

"They'll declare war against the moon next!" said Aunt Wilshire.

"And send a lot of Zeppelins," said the smallest boy. "Herr Heinrich told us they can fly thousands of miles."

"He will go on declaring war until there is nothing left to declare war against. That is exactly what he has always done. Once started he cannot desist. Often he has had to be removed from the dinner-table for fear of injury. *Now*, it is ultimatums."

She was much pleased by a headline in *The Daily Express* that streamed right across the page: "The Mad Dog of Europe." Nothing else, she said, had come so near her feelings about the war.

"Mark my words," said Aunt Wilshire in her most impressive tones. "He is insane. It will be proved to be so. He will end his days in an asylum—as a lunatic. I have felt it myself for years and said so in private. . . . Knowing what I did. . . . To such friends as I could trust not to misunderstand me. . . . Now at least I can speak out.

"With his moustaches turned up!" exclaimed Aunt Wilshire after an interval of accumulation. . . . "They say he has completely lost the use of the joint in his left arm, he carries it stiff like a Punch and Judy—and he wants to conquer Europe. . . . While his grandmother lived there was some one to keep him in order. He stood in Awe of her. He hated her but he did not dare defy her. Even his uncle had some influence. Now, nothing restrains him.

"A double-headed mad dog," said Aunt Wilshire. "Him and his eagles! . . . A man like that ought never to have been allowed to make a war. . . . Not even a little war. . . . If he had been put under restraint when I said so, none of these things would have happened. But, of course, I am nobody. . . . It was not considered worth attending to."

§ 10

One remarkable aspect of the English attitude towards the war was the disposition to treat it as a monstrous joke. It is a disposition traceable in a vast proportion of the British literature of the time. In spite of violence, cruelty, injustice, and the vast destruction and still vaster dangers of the struggle, that disposition held. The English mind refused flatly to see anything magnificent or terrible in the German attack, or to regard the German Emperor or the Crown Prince as anything more than figures of fun. From first to last their conception of the enemy was an overstrenuous, foolish man, red with effort, with protruding eyes and a forced frightfulness of demeanour. That he might be tremendously lethal did not in the least obscure the fact that he was essentially ridiculous. And if as the war went on the joke grew grimmer, still it remained a joke. The German might make a desert of the world; that could not alter the British conviction that he was making a fool of himself.

And this disposition kept coming to the surface throughout the afternoon, now in a casual allusion, now in some deliberate jest. The small boys had discovered the goose-step, and it filled their little souls with amazement and delight. That human beings should consent to those ridiculous paces seemed to them almost incredibly funny. They tried it themselves, and then set out upon a goose-step propaganda. Letty and Cissie had come up to the Dower House for tea and news, and they were enrolled with Teddy and Hugh. The six of them, chuckling and swaying, marched in vast scissor strides across the lawn. "Left," cried Hugh. "Left."

"Toes *out* more," said Mr. Lawrence Carmine.

"Keep stiffer," said the youngest Britling.

"Watch the Zeppelins and look proud," said Hugh. "With the chest out. *Zo!*"

Mrs. Britling was so much amused that she went in for her camera, and took a snap-shot of the detachment. It was a very successful snap-shot, and a year later Mr. Britling was to find a print of it among his papers, and recall the sunshine and the merriment. . . .

§ 11

That night brought the British declaration of war against Germany. To nearly every Englishman that came as a matter of course, and it is one of the most wonderful facts in history that the Germans were surprised by it. When Mr. Britling, as a sample Englishman, had said that there would never be war between Germany and England, he had always meant that it was inconceivable to him that Germany should ever attack Belgium or France. If Germany had been content to fight a merely defensive war upon her western frontier and let Belgium alone, there would scarcely have been such a thing as a war-party in Great Britain. But the attack upon Belgium, the westward thrust, made the whole nation flame unanimously into war. It settled a question that was in open debate up to the very outbreak of the conflict. Up to the last the English had cherished the idea that in Germany, just as in England, the mass of people were kindly, pacific, and detached. That has been the English mistake. Germany was really and truly what Germany had been professing to be for forty years, a War State. With a sigh—and a long-forgotten thrill—England roused herself to fight. Even now she still roused her self sluggishly. It was going to be an immense thing, but just how immense it was going to be no one in England had yet imagined.

Countless men that day whom Fate had marked for death and wounds stared open-mouthed at the news, and smiled with the excitement of the headlines, not dreaming that any of these things would come within three hundred miles of them. What was war to Matching's Easy—to all the Matching's Easies great and small that make up England? The last home that was ever burned by an enemy within a hundred miles of Matching's Easy was burned by the Danes rather more than a thousand years ago. . . . And the last trace of those particular Danes in England was certain horny scraps of indurated skin under the heads of the nails in the door of St. Clement Danes in London. . . .

Now again, England was to fight in a war which was to light fires in England and bring death to English people on English soil. These were inconceivable ideas in August, 1914. Such things must happen before they can be comprehended as possible.

§ 12

This story is essentially the history of the opening and of the realisation of the Great War as it happened to one small group of people in Essex, and more particularly as it happened to one human brain. It came at first to all these people in a spectacular manner, as a thing happening dramatically and internationally, as a show, as something in the newspapers, something in the character of an historical epoch rather than a personal experience; only by slow degrees did it and its consequences invade the common texture of English life. If this story could be represented by sketches or pictures the central figure would be Mr. Britling, now sitting at his desk by day or by night and writing first at his tract "And Now War Ends" and then at other things, now walking about his garden or in Claverings Park or going to and fro in London, in his club reading the ticker or in his hall reading the newspaper, with ideas and impressions continually clustering, expanding, developing more and more abundantly in his mind, arranging themselves, reacting upon one another, building themselves into generalisations and conclusions. . . .

All Mr. Britling's mental existence was soon threaded on the war. His more or less weekly *Times* leaders became dissertations upon the German point of view; his reviews of books and Literary Supplement articles were all oriented more and more exactly to that one supreme fact.

It was rare that he really seemed to be seeing the war; few people saw it; for most of the world it came as an illimitable multitude of incoherent, loud, and confusing impressions. But all the time he was at least doing his utmost to see the war, to simplify it and extract the essence of it until it could be apprehended as something epic and explicable, as a stateable issue. . . .

Most typical picture of all would be Mr. Britling writing in a little circle of orange lamplight, with the blinds of his room open for the sake of the moonlight but the window shut to keep out the moths that beat against it. Outside would be the moon and the high summer sky and the old church-tower dim above the black trees half a mile away, with its clock—which Mr. Britling heard at night but never noted by day—beating its way round the slow semicircle of the nocturnal hours. He had always hated conflict and destruction, and felt that war between civilised states was the quintessential expression of human failure, it was a stupidity that stopped progress and all the free variation of humanity, a thousand times he had declared it impossible, but even now with his country fighting he was still far from realising that this was a thing that could possibly touch him more than intellectually. He did not really believe with his eyes and finger-tips and backbone that murder, destruction, and agony on a scale monstrous beyond precedent were going on in the same world as that which slumbered outside the black ivy and silver shining window-sill that framed his peaceful view.

War had not been a reality of the daily life of England for more than a thousand years. The mental habit of the nation for fifty generations was against its emotional recognition. The English were the spoiled children of peace. They had never been wholly at war for three hundred years, and for over eight hundred years they had not fought for life against a foreign power. Spain and France had threatened in turn, but never even crossed the seas. It is true that England had had her civil dissensions and had made wars and conquests in every part of the globe and established an immense empire, but that last, as Mr. Britling had told Mr. Direck, was "an excursion." She had just sent out younger sons and surplus people, emigrants and expeditionary forces. Her own soil had never seen any successful foreign invasion; her homeland, the bulk of her households, her general life, had gone on untouched by these things. Nineteen people out of twenty, the middle class and most of the lower class, knew no more of the empire than they did of the Argentine Republic or the Italian Renaissance. It did not concern them. War that calls upon every man and threatens every life in the land, war of the whole national being, was a thing altogether outside English experience and the scope of the British imagination. It was still incredible, it was still outside the range of Mr. Britling's thoughts all through the tremendous onrush and check of the German attack in the west that opened the Great War. Through those two months he was, as it were, a more and more excited spectator at a show, a show like a baseball match, a spectator with money on the event, rather than a really participating citizen of a nation thoroughly at war. . . .

§ 13

After the jolt of the food panic and a brief financial scare, the vast inertia of everyday life in England asserted itself. When the public went to the banks for the new paper money, the banks tendered gold—apologetically. The supply of the new notes was very insufficient, and there was plenty of gold. After the first impression that a universal catastrophe had happened there was an effect as if nothing had happened.

Shops reopened after the Bank Holiday, in a tentative spirit that speedily became assurance; people went about their business again, and the war, so far as the mass of British folk were concerned, was for some weeks a fever of the mind and intelligence rather than a physical and personal actuality. There was a keen demand for news, and for a time there was very little news. The press did its best to cope with this immense occasion. Led by *The Daily Express*, all the halfpenny newspapers adopted a new and more resonant sort of headline, the streamer, a band of emphatic type that ran clean across the page and announced victories or disconcerting happenings. They did this every day, whether there was a great battle or the loss of a trawler to announce, and the public mind speedily adapted itself to the new pitch.

There was no invitation from the government and no organisation for any general participation in war. People talked unrestrictedly; every one seemed to be talking; they waved flags and displayed much vague willingness to do something. Any opportunity of service was taken very eagerly. Lord Kitchener was understood to have demanded five hundred thousand men; the War Office arrangements for recruiting, arrangements conceived on a scale altogether too small, were speedily overwhelmed by a rush of willing young men. The flow had to be checked by raising the physical standard far above the national average, and recruiting died down to manageable proportions. There was a quite genuine belief that the war might easily be too exclusively considered; that for the great mass of people it was a disturbing and distracting rather than a vital interest. The phrase "Business as Usual" ran about the world, and the papers abounded in articles in which going on as though there was no war at all was demonstrated to be the truest form of patriotism. "Leave things to Kitchener" was another watchword with a strong appeal to the national quality. "Business as usual during Alterations to the Map of Europe" was the advertisement of one cheerful barber, widely quoted. . . .

Hugh was at home all through August. He had thrown up his rooms in London with his artistic ambitions, and his father was making all the necessary arrangements for him to follow Cardinal to Cambridge. Meanwhile Hugh was taking up his scientific work where he had laid it down. He gave a reluctant couple of hours in the afternoon to the mysteries of Little-go Greek, and for the rest of his time he was either working at mathematics and mathematical physics or experimenting in a small upstairs room that had been carved out of the general space of the barn. It was only at the very end of August that it dawned upon him or Mr. Britling that the war might have more than a spectacular and sympathetic appeal for him. Hitherto contemporary history had happened without his personal intervention. He did not see why it should not continue to happen with the same detachment. The last elections—and a general election is really the only point at which the life of the reasonable Englishman becomes in any way public—had happened four years ago, when he was thirteen.

§ 14

For a time it was believed in Matching's Easy that the German armies had been defeated and very largely destroyed at Liège. It was a mistake not confined to Matching's Easy.

The first raiding attack was certainly repulsed with heavy losses, and so were the more systematic assaults on August the 6th and 7th. After that the news from Liège became uncertain, but it was believed in England that some or all of the forts were still holding out right up to the German entry into Brussels. Meanwhile the French were pushing into their lost provinces, occupying Altkirch, Malhausen and Saarburg; the Russians were invading Bukovina and East Prussia; the *Goeben*, the *Breslau* and the *Panther* had been sunk by the newspapers in an imaginary battle in the Mediterranean, and Togoland was captured by the French and British. Neither the force nor the magnitude of the German attack through Belgium was appreciated by the general mind, and it was possible for Mr. Britling to reiterate his fear that the war would be over too soon, long before the full measure of its possible benefits could be secured. But these apprehensions were unfounded; the lessons the war had in store for Mr. Britling were fare more drastic than anything he was yet able to imagine even in his most exalted moods.

He resisted the intimations of the fall of Brussels and the appearance of the Germans at Dinant. The first real check to his excessive anticipations of victory for the Allies came with the sudden reappearance of Mr. Direck in a state of astonishment and dismay at Matching's Easy. He wired from the Strand office, "Coming to tell you about things," and arrived on the heels of his telegram.

He professed to be calling upon Mr. and Mrs. Britling, and to a certain extent he was; but he had a quick eye for the door or windows; his glance roved irrelevantly as he talked. A faint expectation of Cissie came in with him and hovered about him, as the scent of violets follows the flower.

He was, however, able to say quite a number of things before Mr. Britling's natural tendency to do the telling asserted itself.

"My word," said Mr. Direck, "but this is *some* war. It is going on regardless of every decent consideration. As an American citizen I naturally expected to be treated with some respect, war or no war. That expectation has not yet been realised. . . . Europe is dislocated. . . . You have no idea here yet how completely Europe is dislocated. . . .

"I came to Europe in a perfectly friendly spirit—and I must say I am surprised. Practically I have been thrown out, neck and crop. All my luggage is lost. Away at some one-horse junction near the Dutch frontier that I can't even learn the name of. There's joy in some German home, I guess, over my shirts; they were real good shirts. This tweed suit I have is all the wardrobe I've got in the world. All my money—good American notes— well, they laughed at them. And when I produced English gold they suspected me of being English and put me under arrest . . . I can assure you that the English are most unpopular in Germany at the present time, thoroughly unpopular. . . . Considering that they are getting exactly what they were asking for, these Germans are really remarkably annoyed. . . . Well, I had to get the American consul to advance me money, and I've done more waiting about and irregular fasting and travelling on an empty stomach and viewing the world, so far as it was permitted, from railway sidings—for usually they made us pull the blinds down when anything important was on the track—than any cow that ever came to Chicago. . . . I was handled as freight—low-grade freight. . . . It doesn't bear recalling."

Mr. Direck assumed as grave and gloomy an expression as the facial habits of years would permit.

"I tell you I never knew there was such a thing as war until this happened to me. In America we don't know there is such a thing. It's like pestilence and famine; something in the story-books. We've forgotten it for anything real. There's just a few grandfathers go around talking about it. Judge Holmes and sage old fellows like him. Otherwise it's just a game the kids play at. . . . And then suddenly here's everybody running about in the streets—hating and threatening—and nice old gentlemen with white moustaches and fathers of families scheming and planning to burn houses and kill and hurt and terrify. And nice young women, too, looking for an Englishman to spit at; I tell you I've been within range and very uncomfortable several times. . . . And what one can't believe is that they are really doing these things. There's a little village called Visé near the Dutch frontier; some old chap got fooling there with a fowling-piece; and they've wiped it out. Shot the people by the dozen, put them out in rows three deep and shot them, and burned the place. Short of scalping, Red Indians couldn't have done worse. Respectable German soldiers. . . .

"No one in England really seems to have any suspicion what is going on in Belgium. You hear stories——People tell them in Holland. It takes your breath away. They have set out just to cow those Belgians. They have started in to be deliberately frightful. You do not begin to understand. . . . Well. . . . Outrages. The sort of outrages Americans have never heard of. That one doesn't speak of. . . . Well. . . . Rape. . . . They have been raping women for disciplinary purposes on tables in the marketplace of Liège. Yes, sir. It's a fact. I was told it by a man who had just come out of Belgium. Knew the people, knew the place, knew everything. People over here do not seem to realise that those women are the same sort of women that you might find in Chester or Yarmouth, or in Matching's Easy for the matter of that. They still seem to think that Continental women are a different sort of women—more amenable to that sort of treatment. They seem to think there is some special Providential law against such things happening to English people. And it's within two hundred miles of you—even now. And as far as I can see there's precious little to prevent it coming nearer. . . ."

Mr. Britling thought there were a few little obstacles.

"I've seen the new British army drilling in London, Mr. Britling. I don't know if you have. I saw a whole battalion. And they hadn't got half-a-dozen uniforms, and not a single rifle to the whole battalion.

"You don't begin to realise in England what you are up against. You have no idea what it means to be in a country where everybody, the women, the elderly people, the steady middle-aged men, are taking war as seriously as business. They haven't the slightest compunction. I don't know what Germany was like before the war, I had hardly gotten out of my train before the war began; but Germany today is one big armed camp. It's all crawling with soldiers. And every soldier has his uniform and his boots and his arms and his kit.

"And they're as sure of winning as if they had got London now. They mean to get London. They're cockshure they are going to walk through Belgium, cocksure they will get to Paris by Sedan day, and then they are going to destroy your fleet with Zeppelins and submarines and made a dash across the Channel. They say it's England they are after, in this invasion of Belgium. They'll just down France by the way. They say they've got guns to bombard Dover from Calais. They make a boast of it. They know for certain you can't arm your troops. They know you can't turn out ten thousand rifles a week. They come and talk to any one in the trains, and explain just how your defeat is going to be managed. It's just as though they were talking of rounding up cattle."

Mr. Britling said they would soon be disillusioned.

Mr. Direck, with the confidence of his authentic observations, remarked after a perceptible interval, "I wonder how."

He reverted to the fact that had most struck upon his imagination.

"Grown-up people, ordinary intelligent experienced people taking war seriously, talking of punishing England; it's a revelation. A sort of solemn enthusiasm. High and low. . . .

"And the train-loads of men and the train-loads of guns. . . ."

"Liège," said Mr. Britling.

"Liège was just a scratch on the paint," said Mr. Direck. "A few thousand dead, a few score thousand dead, doesn't matter—not a red cent. to them. There's a man arrived at the Cecil who saw them marching into Brussels. He sat at table with me at lunch yesterday. All day it went on, a vast unending river of men in grey. Endless wagons, endless guns, the whole manhood of a nation and all its stuff, marching. . . .

"I thought war," said Mr. Direck, "was a thing where most people stood about and did the shouting, and a sort of special team did the fighting. Well, Germany isn't fighting like that. . . . I confess it, I'm scared. . . . It's the very biggest thing on record; it's the very limit in wars. . . . I dreamt last night of a grey flood washing everything in front of it. You and me—and Miss Corner—curious thing, isn't it? that she came into it—were scrambling up a hill higher and higher, with that flood pouring after us. Sort of splashing into a foam of faces and helmets and bayonets—and clutching hands—and red stuff. . . . Well, Mr. Britling, I admit I'm a little bit over-wrought about it, but I can assure you you don't begin to realise in England what it is you've butted against. . . ."

§ 15

Cissie did not come up to the Dower House that afternoon, and so Mr. Direck, after some vague and transparent excuses, made his way to the cottage.

Here his report became even more impressive. Teddy sat on the writing-desk beside the typewriter and swung his legs slowly. Letty brooded in the arm-chair. Cissie presided over certain limited crawling operations of the young heir.

"They could have the equal of the whole British army killed three times over and scarcely know it had happened. They're *all* in it. It's a whole country in arms."

Teddy nodded thoughtfully.

"There's our fleet," said Letty.

240

"Well, *that* won't save Paris, will it?"

Mr. Direck didn't, he declared, want to make disagreeable talk, but this was a thing people in England had to face. He felt like one of them himself—"naturally." He'd sort of hurried home to them—it was just like hurrying home—to tell them of the tremendous thing that was going to hit them. He felt like a man in front of a flood, a great grey flood. He couldn't hide what he had been thinking. "Where's our army?" asked Letty suddenly.

"Lost somewhere in France," said Teddy. "Like a needle in a bottle of hay."

"What I keep on worrying at is this," Mr. Direck resumed. "Suppose they did come, suppose somehow they scrambled over, sixty or seventy thousand men perhaps."

"Every man would turn out and take a shot at them," said Letty.

"But there's no rifles!"

"There's shotguns."

"That's exactly what I'm afraid of," said Mr. Direck. "They'd massacre. . . .

"You may be the bravest people on earth," said Mr. Direck, "but if you haven't got arms and the other chaps have—you're just as if you were sheep."

He became gloomily pensive.

He roused himself to describe his experiences at some length, and the extraordinary disturbance of his mind. He related more particularly his attempts to see the sights of Cologne during the stir of mobilisation. After a time his narrative flow lost force, and there was a general feeling that he ought to be left alone with Cissie. Teddy had a letter that must be posted; Letty took the infant to crawl on the mossy stones under the pear-tree. Mr. Direck leaned against the window sill and became silent for some moments after the door had closed on Letty.

"As for you, Cissie," he began at last, "I'm anxious. I'm real anxious. I wish you'd let me throw the mantle of Old Glory over you."

He looked at her earnestly.

"Old Glory?" asked Cissie.

"Well—the Stars and Stripes. I want you to be able to claim American citizenship—in certain eventualities. It wouldn't be so very difficult. All the world over, Cissie, Americans are respected. . . . Nobody dares touch an American citizen. We are—an inviolate people."

He paused. "But how?" asked Cissie.

"It would be perfectly easy—perfectly."

"How?"

"Just marry an American citizen," said Mr. Direck, with his face beaming with ingenuous self-approval. "Then you'd be safe, and I'd not have to worry."

"Because we're in for a stiff war!" cried Cissie, and Direck perceived he had blundered.

"Because we may be invaded!" she said, and Mr. Direck's sense of error deepened.

"I vow——" she began.

"No!" cried Mr. Direck, and held out a hand.

There was a moment of crisis.

"Never will I desert my country—while she is at war," said Cissie, reducing her first fierce intention, and adding as though she regretted her concession, "Anyhow."

"Then it's up to me to end the war, Cissie," said Mr. Direck, trying to get her back to a less spirited attitude.

But Cissie wasn't to be got back so easily. The war was already beckoning to them in the cottage, and drawing them down from the auditorium into the arena.

"This is the rightest war in history," she said. "If I was an American I should be sorry to be one now and to have to stand out of it. I wish I was a man now so that I could do something for all the decency and civilisation these Germans have outraged. I can't understand how any man can be content to keep out of this, and watch Belgium being destroyed. It is like looking on at a murder. It is like watching a dog killing a kitten. . . ."

Mr. Direck's expression was that of a man who is suddenly shown strange lights upon the world.

§ 16

Mr. Britling found Mr. Direck's talk indigestible.

He was parting very reluctantly from his dream of a disastrous collapse of German imperialism, of a tremendous, decisive demonstration of the inherent unsoundness of militarist monarchy, to be followed by a world conference of chastened but hopeful nations, and—the Millennium. He tried now to think that Mr. Direck had observed badly and misconceived what he saw. An American, unused to any sort of military occurrences, might easily mistake tens of thousands for millions, and the excitement of a few commercial travellers for the enthusiasm of a united people. But the newspapers now, with a kindred reluctance, were beginning to qualify, bit by bit, their first representation of the German attack through Belgium as a vast and already partly thwarted parade of incompetence. The Germans, he gathered, were being continually beaten in Belgium; but just as continually they advanced. Each fresh newspaper name he looked up on the map marked an oncoming tide. Alost—Charleroi. Farther east the French were retreating from the Saales Pass. Surely the British, who had now been in France for a fortnight, would presently be manifest, stemming the onrush; somewhere perhaps in Brabant or East Flanders. It gave Mr. Britling an unpleasant night to hear at Claverings that the French were very ill-equipped; had no good modern guns either at Lille or Maubeuge, were short of boots and equipment generally, and rather depressed already at the trend of things. Mr. Britling dismissed this as pessimistic talk, and built his hopes on the still invisible British army, hovering somewhere——

He would sit over the map of Belgium, choosing where he would prefer to have the British hover. . . .

Namur fell. The place names continued to shift southward and westward. The British army or a part of it came to light abruptly at Mons. It had been fighting for thirty-eight hours and defeating enormously superior forces of the enemy. That was reassuring until a day or so later "the Cambrai-Le Cateau line" made Mr. Britling realise that the victorious British had recoiled five-and-twenty miles. . . .

And then came the Sunday of *The Times* telegram, which spoke of a "retreating and a broken army." Mr. Britling did not see this, but Mr. Manning brought over the report of it in a state of profound consternation. Things, he said, seemed to be about as bad as they could be. The English were retreating towards the coast and in much disorder. They were "in the air" and already separated from the French. They had narrowly escaped "a Sedan" under the fortifications of Maubeuge. . . . Mr. Britling was stunned. He went to his study and stared helplessly at maps. It was as if David had flung his pebble—and missed!

But in the afternoon Mr. Manning telephoned to comfort his friend. A reassuring despatch from General French had been published and all was well—practically—and the British had been splendid. They had been fighting continuously for several days round and about Mons; they had been attacked at odds of six to one, and they had repulsed and inflicted enormous losses on the enemy. They had established an incontestable personal superiority over the Germans. The Germans had been mown down in heaps; the British had charged through their cavalry like charging through paper. So at last and very gloriously for the British, British and German had met in battle. After the hard fighting of the 26th about Landrecies, the British had been comparatively unmolested, reinforcements covering double the losses had joined them and the German advance was definitely checked. . . . Mr. Britling's mind swung back to elation. He took down the entire despatch from Mr. Manning's dictation, and ran out with it into the garden where Mrs. Britling, with an unwonted expression of anxiety, was presiding over the teas of the usual casual Sunday gathering. . . . The despatch was read aloud twice over. After that there was hockey and high spirits, and then Mr. Britling went up to his study to answer a letter from Mrs. Harrowdean, the first letter that had come from her since their breach at the outbreak of the war, and which he was now in a better mood to answer than he had been hitherto.

She had written ignoring his silence and absence, or rather treating it as if it were an incident of no particular importance. Apparently she had not called upon the patient and devoted Oliver as she had threatened; at any rate there were no signs of Oliver in her communication. But she reproached Mr. Britling for deserting her, and she clamoured for his presence and for kind and strengthening words. She was, she said, scared by this war.

She was only a little thing, and it was all too dreadful, and there was not a soul in the world to hold her hand, at least no one who understood in the slightest degree how she felt. (But why was not Oliver holding her hand?) She was like a child left alone in the dark. It was perfectly horrible the way that people were being kept in the dark. The stories one heard, "*often from quite trustworthy sources,*" were enough to depress and terrify any one. Battleship after battleship had been sunk by German torpedoes, a thing kept secret from us for no earthly reason, and Prince Louis of Battenberg had been discovered to be a spy and had been sent to the Tower. Haldane too was a spy. Our army in France had been "practically *sold*" by the French. Almost all the French generals were in German pay. The censorship and the press were keeping all this back, but what good was it to keep it back? Such folly not to trust the people! But it was all too dreadful for a poor little soul whose only desire was to live happily. Why didn't he come along to her and make her feel she had protecting arms round her? She couldn't think in the daytime; she couldn't sleep at night. . . .

Then she broke away into the praises of serenity. Never had she thought so much of his beautiful "Silent Places" as she did now. How she longed to take refuge in some such dreamland from violence and treachery and foolish rumours! She was weary of every reality. She wanted to fly away into some secret hiding-place and cultivate her simple garden there—as Voltaire had done. . . . Sometimes at night she was afraid to undress. She imagined the sound of guns, she imagined landings and frightful scouts "in masks" rushing inland on motor bicycles. . . .

It was an ill-timed letter. The nonsense about Prince Louis of Battenberg and Lord Haldane and the torpedoed battleships annoyed Mr. Britling extravagantly. He had just sufficient disposition to believe such tales to find their importunity exasperating. The idea of going over to Pyecrafts to spend his days in comforting a timid little dear obsessed by such fears attracted him not at all. He had already heard enough adverse rumours at Claverings to make him thoroughly uncomfortable. He had been doubting whether after all his "Examination of War" was really much less of a futility than "And Now War Ends"; his mind was full of a sense of incomplete statement and unsubstantial arguments. He was indeed in a state of extreme intellectual worry. He was moreover extraordinarily out of love with Mrs. Harrowdean. Never had any affection in the whole history of Mr. Britling's heart collapsed so swiftly and completely. He was left incredulous of ever having cared for her at all. Probably he hadn't. Probably the whole business had been deliberate illusion from first to last. This "dear little thing" business, he felt, was all very well as a game of petting, but times were serious now, and a woman of her intelligence should do something better than wallow in fears and elaborate a winsome feebleness. A very unnecessary and tiresome feebleness. He came almost to the pitch of writing that to her.

The despatch from General French put him into a kindlier frame of mind. He wrote instead briefly but affectionately. As a gentleman should. "How could you doubt our fleet or our army?" was the gist of his letter. He ignored completely every suggestion of a visit to Pyecrafts that her letter had conveyed. He pretended that it had contained nothing of the sort. . . . And that she passed out of his mind again under the stress of more commanding interests. . . .

Mr. Britling's mood of relief did not last through the week. The defeated Germans continued to advance. Through a week of deepening disillusionment the main tide of battle rolled back steadily towards Paris. Lille was lost without a struggle.

It was lost with mysterious ease. . . . The next name to startle Mr. Britling as he sat with newspaper and atlas following these great events was Compiègne. "Here!" Manifestly the British were still in retreat. Then the Germans were in possession of Laon and Rheims and still pressing south. Maubeuge, surrounded and cut off for some days, had apparently fallen. . . .

It was on Sunday, September the 6th, that the final capitulation of Mr. Britling's facile optimism occurred.

He stood in the sunshine reading *The Observer* which the gardener's boy had just brought from the May Tree. He had spread it open on a garden table under the blue cedar, and father and son were both reading it, each as much as the other would let him. There was fresh news from France, a story of further German advances, fighting at Senlis—"But that is quite close to Paris!"—and the appearance of German forces at Nogent-sur-Seine. "Sur Seine!" cried Mr. Britling. "But where can that be? South of the Marne? Or below Paris perhaps?"

It was not marked upon *The Observer's* map, and Hugh ran into the house for the atlas.

When he returned Mr. Manning was with his father, and they both looked grave.

Hugh opened the map of northern France. "Here it is," he said.

Mr. Britling considered the position.

"Manning says they are at Rouen," he told Hugh. "Our base is to be moved round to La Rochelle. . . ."

He paused before the last distasteful conclusion.

"Practically," he admitted, taking his dose, "they have got Paris. It is almost surrounded now."

He sat down to the map. Mr. Manning and Hugh stood regarding him. He made a last effort to imagine some tremendous strategic reversal, some stone from an unexpected sling that should fell this Goliath in the midst of his triumph.

"Russia," he said, without any genuine hope. . . .

§ 17

And then it was that Mr. Britling accepted the truth.

"One talks," he said, "and then weeks and months later one learns the meaning of the things one has been saying. I was saying a month ago that this is the biggest thing that has happened in history. I said that this was the supreme call upon the will and resources of England. I said there was not a life in all our empire that would not be vitally changed by this war. I said all these things; they came through my mouth; I suppose there was a sort of thought behind them. . . . Only at this moment do I understand what it is that I said. Now—let me say it over as if I had never said it before; this *is* the biggest thing in history, that we *are* all called upon to do our utmost to resist this tremendous attack upon the peace and freedom of the world. Well, doing our utmost does not mean standing about in pleasant gardens waiting for the newspaper. . . . It means the abandonment of ease and security. . . .

"How lazy we English are nowadays! How readily we grasp the comforting delusion that excuses us from exertion. For the last three weeks I have been deliberately believing that a little British army—they say it is scarcely a hundred thousand men— would somehow break this rush of millions. But it has been driven back, as any one not in love with easy dreams might have known it would be driven back—here and then here and then here. It has been fighting night and day. It has made the most splendid fight—and the most ineffectual fight. . . . You see the vast swing of the German flail through Belgium. And meanwhile we have been standing about talking of the use we would make of our victory. . . .

"We have been asleep," he said. "This country has been asleep. . . .

"At the back of our minds," he went on bitterly, "I suppose we thought the French would do the heavy work on land—while we stood by at sea. So far as we thought at all. We're so temperate-minded; we're so full of qualifications and discretions. . . . And so leisurely. . . . Well, France is down. We've got to fight for France now over the ruins of Paris. Because you and I, Manning, didn't grasp the scale of it, because we indulged in generalisations when we ought to have been drilling and working. Because we've been doing 'business as usual' and all the rest of that sort of thing, while Western civilisation has been in its death-agony. If this is to be another '71, on a larger scale and against not merely France but all Europe, if Prussianism is to walk rough-shod over civilisation, if France is to be crushed and Belgium murdered, then life is not worth having. Compared with such an issue as that no other issue, no other interest matters. Yet what are we doing to decide it—you and I? How can it end in anything but a German triumph if you and I, by the million, stand by? . . ."

He paused despairfully and stared at the map.

"What ought we to be doing?" asked Mr. Manning.

"Every man ought to be in training," said Mr. Britling. "Every one ought to be participating. . . . In some way. . . . At any rate we ought not to be taking our ease at Matching's Easy any more. . . ."

§ 18

"It interrupts everything," said Hugh suddenly. "These Prussians are the biggest nuisance the world has ever seen."

He considered. "It's like every one having to run out because the house catches fire. But of course we have to beat them. It has to be done. And every one has to take a share.

"Then we can get on with our work again."

Mr. Britling turned his eyes to his eldest son with a startled expression. He had been speaking—generally. For the moment he had forgotten Hugh.

CHAPTER THE SECOND

TAKING PART

§ 1

THERE were now two chief things in the mind of Mr. Britling. One was a large and valiant thing, a thing of heroic and processional quality, the idea of taking up one's share in the great conflict, of leaving the Dower House and its circle of habits and activities and going out——. From that point he wasn't quite sure where he was to go, nor exactly what he meant to do. His imagination inclined to the figure of a volunteer in an improvised uniform inflicting great damage upon a raiding invader from behind a hedge. The uniform one presumes would have been something in the vein of the costume in which he met Mr. Direck. With a "brassard." Or he thought of himself as working at a telephone or in an office engaged upon any useful quasi-administrative work that called for intelligence rather than training. Still, of course, with a "brassard." A month ago he would have had doubts about the meaning of "brassard"; now it seemed to be the very key-word for national organisation. He had started for London by the early train on Monday morning with the intention of immediate enrolment in any such service that offered; of getting, in fact, into his brassard at once. The morning papers he bought at the station dashed his conviction of the inevitable fall of Paris into hopeful doubts, but did not shake his resolution. The effect of rout and pursuit and retreat and retreat and retreat had disappeared from the news. The German right was being counter-attacked, and seemed in danger of getting pinched between Paris and Verdun with the British on its flank. This relieved his mind, but it did nothing to modify his new realisation of the tremendous gravity of the war. Even if the enemy were held and repulsed a little there was still work for every man in the task of forcing them back upon their own country. This war was an immense thing, it would touch everybody. . . . That meant that every man must give himself. That he had to give himself. He must let nothing stand between him and that clear understanding. It was utterly shameful now to hold back and not to do one's utmost for civilisation, for England, for all the ease and safety one had been given—against these drilled, commanded, obsessed millions.

Mr. Britling was a flame of exalted voluntaryism, of patriotic devotion that day.

But behind all this bravery was the other thing, the second thing in the mind of Mr. Britling, a fear. He was prepared now to spread himself like some valiant turkey gobbler, every feather at its utmost, against the aggressor. He was prepared to go out and flourish bayonets, march and dig to the limit of his power, shoot, die in a ditch if needful, rather than permit German militarism to dominate the world. He had no fear for himself. He was prepared to perish upon the battlefield or cut a valiant figure in the military hospital. But what he perceived very clearly and did his utmost not to perceive was this qualifying and discouraging fact, that the war monster was not nearly so disposed to meet him as he was to meet the war, and that its eyes were fixed on something beside and behind him, that it was already only too evidently stretching out a long and shadowy arm past him towards Teddy—and towards Hugh. . . .

The young are the food of war. . . .

Teddy wasn't Mr. Britling's business anyhow. Teddy must do as he thought proper. Mr. Britling would not even advise upon that. And as for Hugh——

Mr. Britling did his best to brazen it out.

"My eldest boy is barely seventeen," he said. "He's keen to go, and I'd be sorry if he wasn't. He'll get into some cadet corps, of course—he's already done something of that kind at school. Or they'll take him into the Territorials. But before he's nineteen everything will be over, one way or another. I'm afraid, poor chap, he'll feel sold. . . ."

And having thrust Hugh safely into the background of his mind as—juvenile, doing a juvenile share, no sort of man yet, Mr. Britling could give a free rein to his generous imaginations of a national uprising. From the idea of a universal participation in the struggle he passed by an easy transition to an anticipation of all Britain armed and gravely embattled. Across gulfs of obstinate reality. He himself was prepared to say, and accordingly he felt that the great mass of the British must be prepared to say to the government: "Here we are at your disposal. This is not a diplomatist's war nor a War Office war; this is a war of the whole people. We are all willing and ready to lay aside our usual occupations and offer our property and ourselves. Whim and individual action are for peace times. Take us and use us as you think fit. Take all we possess." When he thought of the government in this way, he forgot the governing class he knew. The slack-trousered Raeburn, the prim, attentive Philbert, Lady Frensham at the top of her voice, stern, preposterous Carson, boozy Bandershoot, and artful Taper, wily Asquith, the eloquent yet unsubstantial George, and the immobile Grey, vanished out of his mind; all those representative exponents of the way things are done in Great Britain faded in the glow of his imaginative effort; he forgot the dreary debates, the floundering newspapers, the "bluffs," the intrigues, the sly bargains of the weekend party, the "schoolboy honour" of grown men, the universal weak dishonesty in thinking; he thought simply of a simplified and ideal government that governed. He thought vaguely of something behind and beyond them, England, the ruling genius of the land; something with a dignified assurance and a stable will. He imagined this shadowy ruler miraculously provided with schemes and statistics against this supreme occasion which had for so many years been the most conspicuous probability before the country. His mind, leaping forward to the conception of a great nation reluctantly turning its vast resources to the prosecution of a righteous defensive war, filled in the obvious corollaries of plan and calculation. He thought that somewhere "up there" there must be people who could count and who had counted everything that we might need for such a struggle, and organisers who had schemed and estimated down to practicable and manageable details. . . .

Such lapses from knowledge to faith are perhaps necessary that human heroism may be possible. . . .

His conception of his own share in the great national uprising was a very modest one. He was a writer, a foot-note to reality; he had no trick of command over men, his *rôle* was observation rather than organisation, and he saw himself only as an insignificant individual dropping from his individuality into his place in a great machine, taking a rifle in a trench, guarding a bridge, filling a cartridge—just with a brassard or something like that on—until the great task was done. Sunday night was full of imaginations of order, of the countryside standing up to its task, of roads cleared and resources marshalled, of the petty interests of the private life altogether set aside. And mingling with that it was still possible for Mr. Britling, he was still young enough, to produce such dreams of personal service, of sudden emergencies swiftly and bravely met, of conspicuous daring and exceptional rewards, such dreams as hover in the brains of every imaginative recruit. . . .

The detailed story of Mr. Britling's two days' search for some easy and convenient ladder into the service of his threatened country would be a voluminous one. It would begin with the figure of a neatly brushed patriot, with an intent expression upon his intelligent face, seated in the Londonward train, reading the war news—the first comforting war news for many days—and trying not to look as though his life was torn up by the roots and all his being aflame with devotion; and it would conclude after forty-eight hours of fuss, inquiry, talk, waiting, telephoning, with the same gentleman, a little fagged and with a kind of weary apathy in his eyes, returning by the short cut from the station across Claverings Park to resume his connection with his abandoned roots. The essential process of the interval had been the correction of Mr. Britling's temporary delusion that the government of the British Empire is either intelligent, instructed, or wise.

The great "Business as Usual" phase was already passing away, and London was in the full tide of recruiting enthusiasm. That tide was breaking against the most miserable arrangements for enlistment it is possible to imagine. Overtaxed and not very competent officers, whose one idea of being efficient was to refuse civilian help and be very, very slow and circumspect and very dignified and overbearing, sat in dirty little rooms and snarled at this unheard-of England that pressed at door and window for enrolment. Outside every recruiting office crowds of men and youths waited, leaning against walls, sitting upon the pavements, waiting for long hours, waiting to the end of the day and returning next morning, without shelter, without food, many sick with hunger; men who had hurried up from the country, men who had thrown up jobs of every kind, clerks, shopmen, anxious only to serve England and "teach those damned Germans a lesson." Between them and this object they had discovered a perplexing barrier; an inattention. As Mr. Britling made his way by St. Martin's Church and across Trafalgar Square and marked the weary accumulation of this magnificently patriotic stuff, he had his first inkling of the imaginative insufficiency of the War Office that had been so suddenly called upon to organise victory. He was to be more fully informed when he reached his club.

His impression of the streets through which he passed was an impression of great unrest. There were noticeably fewer omnibuses and less road traffic generally, but there was a quite unusual number of drifting pedestrians. The current on the pavements was irritatingly sluggish. There were more people standing about, and fewer going upon their business. This was particularly the case with the women he saw. Many of them seemed to have drifted in from the suburbs and outskirts of London in a state of vague expectation, unable to stay in their homes.

Everywhere there were the flags of the Allies; in shop-windows, over doors, on the bonnets of automobiles, on people's breasts, and there was a great quantity of recruiting posters on the hoardings and in windows: "Your King and Country Need You" was the chief text, and they still called for "A Hundred Thousand Men" although the demand of Lord Kitchener had risen to half a million. There were also placards calling for men on nearly all the taxicabs. The big windows of the offices of the Norddeutscher-Lloyd in Cockspur Street were boarded up, and plastered thickly with recruiting appeals.

At his club Mr. Britling found much talk and belligerent stir. In the hall Wilkins the author was displaying a dummy rifle of bent iron rod to several interested members. It was to be used for drilling until rifles could be got, and it could be made for eighteenpence. This was the first intimation Mr. Britling got that the want of foresight of the War Office only began with its unpreparedness for recruits. Men were talking very freely in the club; one of the temporary effects of the war in its earlier stages was to produce a partial thaw in the constitutional British shyness; and men who had glowered at Mr. Britling over their lunches and had been glowered at by Mr. Britling in silence for years now started conversations with him.

"What is a man of my sort to do?" asked a clean-shaven barrister.

"Exactly what I have been asking," said Mr. Britling. "They are fixing the upward age for recruits at thirty; it's absurdly low. A man well over forty like myself is quite fit to line a trench or guard a bridge. I'm not so bad a shot. . . ."

"We've been discussing home defence volunteers," said the barrister. "Anyhow we ought to be drilling. But the War Office sets its face as sternly against our doing anything of the sort as though we were going to join the Germans. It's absurd. Even if we older men aren't fit to go abroad, we could at least release troops who could."

"If you had the rifles," said a sharp-featured man in grey to the right of Mr. Britling.

"I suppose they are to be got," said Mr. Britling. The sharp-featured man indicated by appropriate facial action and head-shaking that this was by no means the case.

"Every dead man, many wounded men, most prisoners," he said, "mean each one a rifle lost. We have lost five-and-twenty thousand rifles alone since the war began. Quite apart from arming new troops we have to replace those rifles with the drafts we send out. Do you know what is the maximum weekly output of rifles at the present time in this country?"

Mr. Britling did not know.

"Nine thousand."

Mr. Britling suddenly understood the significance of Wilkins and his dummy gun.

The sharp-featured man added with an air of concluding the matter: "It's the barrels are the trouble. Complicated machinery. We haven't got it and we can't make it in a hurry. And there you are!"

The sharp-featured man had a way of speaking almost as if he was throwing bombs. He threw one now. "Zinc," he said.

"We're not short of zinc?" said the lawyer.

The sharp-featured man nodded, and then became explicit.

Zinc was necessary for cartridges; it had to be refined zinc and very pure, or the shooting went wrong. Well, we had let the refining business drift away from England to Belgium and Germany. There were just one or two British firms still left. . . . Unless we bucked up tremendously we should get caught short of cartridges. . . . At any rate of cartridges so made as to ensure good shooting. "And there you are!" said the sharp-featured man.

But the sharp-featured man did not at that time represent any considerable section of public thought. "I suppose after all we can get rifles from America," said the lawyer. "And as for zinc, if the shortage is known the shortage will be provided for. . . ."

The prevailing topic in the smoking-room upstairs was the inability of the War Office to deal with the flood of recruits that was pouring in, and its hostility to any such volunteering as Mr. Britling had in mind. Quite a number of members wanted to volunteer; there was much talk of their fitness; "I'm fifty-four," said one, "and I could do my twenty-five miles in marching kit far better than half those boys of nineteen." Another was thirty-eight. "I must hold the business together," he said; "but why anyhow shouldn't I learn to shoot and use a bayonet?" The personal pique of the rejected lent force to their criticisms of the recruiting and general organisation. "The War Office has one incurable system," said a big mine-owner. "During peace-time it runs all its home administration with men who will certainly be wanted at the front directly there is a war. Directly war comes, therefore, there is a shift all round, and a new untried man—usually a dugout in an advanced state of decay—is stuck into the job. Chaos follows automatically. The War Office always has done this, and so far as one can see it always will. It seems incapable of realising that another man will be wanted until the first is taken away. Its imagination doesn't even run to that."

Mr. Britling found a kindred spirit in Wilkins.

Wilkins was expounding his tremendous scheme for universal volunteering. Everybody was to be accepted. Everybody was to be assigned and registered and—*badged*.

"A brassard," said Mr. Britling.

"It doesn't matter whether we really produce a fighting force or not," said Wilkins. "Everybody now is enthusiastic—and serious. Everybody is willing to put on some kind of uniform and submit to some sort of orders. And the thing to do is to catch them in the willing stage. Now is the time to get the country lined up and organised, ready to meet the internal stresses that are bound to come later. But there's no disposition whatever to welcome this universal offering. It's just as though this war was a treat to which only the very select friends of the War Office were to be admitted. And I don't admit that the national volunteers would be ineffective—even from a military point of view. There are plenty of fit men of our age, and men of proper age who are better employed at home—armament workers for example, and there are all the boys under the age. They may not be under the age before things are over. . . ."

He was even prepared to plan uniforms.

"A brassard," repeated Mr. Britling, "and perhaps coloured strips on the reverse of a coat."

"Colours for the counties," said Wilkins, "and if there isn't coloured cloth to be got there's—red flannel. Anything is better than leaving the mass of people to mob about. . . ."

A momentary vision danced before Mr. Britling's eyes of red flannel petticoats being torn up in a rapid improvisation of soldiers to resist a sudden invasion. Passing washerwomen suddenly requisitioned. But one must not let oneself be laughed out of good intentions because of ridiculous accessories. The idea at any rate was a sound one. . . .

The vision of what ought to be done shone brightly while Mr. Britling and Mr. Wilkins maintained it. But presently under discouraging reminders that there were no rifles, no instructors, and, above all, the open hostility of the established authorities, it faded again. . . .

Afterwards in other conversations Mr. Britling reverted to more modest ambitions.

"Is there no clerical work, no minor administrative work, a man might be used for?" he asked.

"Any old dugout," said the man with the thin face, "any old doddering Colonel Newcome, is preferred to you in that matter. . . ."

Mr. Britling emerged from his club about half-past three with his mind rather dishevelled and with his private determination to do something promptly for his country's needs blunted by a perplexing "How?" His search for doors and ways where no doors and ways existed went on with a gathering sense of futility.

He had a ridiculous sense of pique at being left out, like a child shut out from a room in which a vitally interesting game is being played.

"After, it is *our* war," he said.

He caught the phrase as it dropped from his lips with a feeling that it said more than he intended. He turned it over and examined it, and the more he did so the more he was convinced of its truth and soundness. . . .

§ 2

By night there was a new strangeness about London. The authorities were trying to suppress the more brilliant illumination of the chief thoroughfares, on account of the possibility of an air-raid. Shopkeepers were being compelled to pull down their blinds, and many of the big standard lights were unlit. Mr. Britling thought these precautions were very fussy and unnecessary, and likely to lead to accidents amidst the traffic. But it gave a Rembrantesque quality to the London scene, turned it into mysterious arrangements of brown shadows and cones and bars of light. At first many people were recalcitrant, and here and there a restaurant or a draper's window still blazed out and broke the gloom. There were also a number of insubordinate automobiles with big headlights. But the police were being unusually firm. . . .

"It will all glitter again in a little time," he told himself.

He heard an old lady who was projecting from an offending automobile at Piccadilly Circus in hot dispute with a police officer. "Zeppelins indeed!" she said. "What nonsense! As if they would *dare* to come here! Who would *let* them, I should like to know?"

Probably a friend of Lady Frensham's, he thought. Still—the idea of Zeppelins over London did seem rather ridiculous to Mr. Britling. He would not have liked to be caught talking of it himself. . . . There never had been Zeppelins over London. They were gas-bags. . . .

§ 3

On Wednesday morning Mr. Britling returned to the Dower House, and he was still a civilian unassigned.

In the hall he found a tall figure in khaki standing and reading *The Times* that usually lay upon the hall table. The figure turned at Mr. Britling's entry, and revealed the aquiline features of Mr. Lawrence Carmine.

It was as if his friend had stolen a march on him.

But Carmine's face showed nothing of the excitement and patriotic satisfaction that would have seemed natural to Mr. Britling. He was white and jaded, as if he had not slept for many nights. "You see," he explained almost apologetically of the three stars upon his sleeve, "I used to be a captain of volunteers." He had been put in charge of a volunteer force which had been re-embodied and entrusted with the care of the bridges, gas-works, factories and railway tunnels, and with a number of other minor but necessary duties round about Easinghampton. "I've just got to shut up my house," said Captain Carmine, "and go into lodgings. I confess I hate it. . . . But anyhow it can't last six months. . . . But it's beastly. . . . Ugh! . . ."

He seemed disposed to expand that "Ugh," and then thought better of it. And presently Mr. Britling took control of the conversation.

His two days in London had filled him with matter, and he was glad to have something more than Hugh and Teddy and Mrs. Britling to talk it upon. What was happening now in Great Britain, he declared, was *adjustment*. It was an attempt on the part of a great unorganised nation, an attempt, instinctive at present rather than intelligent, to readjust its government and particularly its military organisation to the new scale of warfare that Germany had imposed upon the world. For two strenuous decades the British navy had been growing enormously under the pressure of German naval preparations, but the British military establishment had experienced no corresponding expansion. It was true there had been a futile, rather foolishly conducted agitation for universal military service, but there had been no accumulation of material, no preparation of armament-making machinery, no planning and no foundations for any sort of organisation that would have facilitated the rapid expansion of the fighting forces of the country in a time of crisis. Such an idea was absolutely antagonistic to the mental habits of the British military caste. The German method of incorporating all the strength and resources of the country into one national fighting machine was quite strange to the British military mind—still. Even after a month of war. War had become the comprehensive business of the German nation; to the British it was an incidental adventure. In Germany the nation was militarised, in England the army was specialised. The nation for nearly every practical purpose got along without it. Just as political life had also become specialised. . . . Now suddenly we wanted a government to speak for every one, and an army of the whole people. How were we to find them?

Mr. Britling dwelt upon this idea of the specialised character of the British army and navy and government. It seemed to him to be the clue to everything that was jarring in the London spectacle. The army had been a thing aloof, for a special end. It had developed all the characteristics of a caste. It had very high standards along the lines of its specialisation, but it was inadaptable and conservative. Its exclusiveness was not so much a deliberate culture as a consequence of its detached function. It touched the ordinary social body chiefly through three other specialised bodies, the court, the church, and the stage. Apart from that it saw the great unofficial civilian world as something vague, something unsympathetic, something possibly antagonistic, which it comforted itself by snubbing when it dared and tricking when it could, something that projected members of Parliament towards it and was stingy about money. Directly one grasped how apart the army lived from the ordinary life of the community, from industrialism, or from economic necessities, directly one understood that the great mass of Englishmen were simply "outsiders" to the War Office mind, just as they were "outsiders" to the political clique, one began to realise the complete unfitness of either government or War Office for the conduct of so great a national effort as was now needed. These people "up there" did not know anything of the broad mass of English life at all, they did not know how or where things were made; when they wanted things they just went to a shop somewhere and got them. This was the necessary psychology of a small army under a clique government. Nothing else was to be expected. But now—somehow—the nation had to take hold of the government that it had neglected so long. . . .

"You see," said Mr. Britling, repeating a phrase that was becoming more and more essential to his thoughts, "this is *our* war. . . .

"Of course," said Mr. Britling, "these things are not going to be done without a conflict. We aren't going to take hold of our country which we have neglected so long without a lot of internal friction. But in England we can make these readjustments without revolution. It is our strength. . . .

"At present England is confused—but it's a healthy confusion. It's astir. We have more things to defeat than just Germany. . . .

"These hosts of recruits—weary, uncared for, besieging the recruiting-stations. It's symbolical. . . . Our tremendous reserves of will and manhood. Our almost incredible insufficiency of direction. . . .

"Those people up there have no idea of the Will that surges up in England. They are timid little manœuvring people, afraid of property, afraid of newspapers, afraid of trade-unions. They aren't leading us against the Germans; they are just being shoved against the Germans by necessity. . . ."

From this Mr. Britling broke away into a fresh addition to his already large collection of contrasts between England and Germany. Germany was a nation which has been swallowed up and incorporated by an army and an administration; the Prussian military system had assimilated to itself the whole German life. It was a State in a state of repletion, a State that had swallowed all its people. Britain was not a State. It was an unincorporated people. The British army, the British War Office, and the British administration has assimilated nothing; they were little old partial things; the British nation lay outside them, beyond their understanding and tradition; a formless new thing, but a great thing; and now this British nation, this real nation, the "outsiders," had to take up arms. Suddenly all the underlying ideas of that outer, greater English life beyond politics, beyond the services, were challenged, its tolerant good humour, its freedom, and its irresponsibility. It was not simply English life that was threatened; it was all the latitudes of democracy, it was every liberal idea and every liberty. It was civilisation in danger. The unchartered liberal system had been taken by the throat; it had to "make good" or perish. . . .

"I went up to London expecting to be told what to do. There is no one to tell any one what to do. . . . Much less is there any one to compel us what to do. . . .

"There's a War Office like a college during a riot, with its doors and windows barred; there's a government like a cockle-boat in an Atlantic gale. . . .

"One feels the thing ought to have come upon us like the sound of a trumpet. Instead, until now, it has been like a great noise, that we just listened to, in the next house. . . . And now slowly the nation awakes. London is just like a dazed sleeper waking up out of a deep sleep to fire and danger, tumult and cries for help, near at hand. The streets give you exactly that effect. People are looking about and listening. One feels that at any moment, in a pause, in a silence, there may come, from far away, over the houses, faint and little, the boom of guns or the small outcries of little French or Belgian villages in agony. . . ."

Such was the gist of Mr. Britling's discourse.

He did most of the table talk, and all that mattered. Teddy was an assenting voice, Hugh was silent and apparently a little inattentive, Mrs. Britling was thinking of the courses and the servants and the boys, and giving her husband only half an ear, Captain Carmine said little and seemed to be troubled by some disagreeable pre-occupation. Now and then he would endorse or supplement the things Mr. Britling was saying. Thrice he remarked: "People still do not begin to understand." . . .

§ 4

It was only when they sat together in the barn court out of the way of Mrs. Britling and the children that Captain Carmine was able to explain his listless bearing and jaded appearance. He was suffering from a bad nervous shock. He had hardly taken over his command before one of his men had been killed—and killed in a manner that had left a scar upon his mind.

The man had been guarding a tunnel, and he had been knocked down by one train when crossing the line behind another. So it was that the bomb of Sarajevo killed its first victim in Essex. Captain Carmine had found the body. He had found the body in a cloudy moonlight; he had almost fallen over it; and his sensations and emotions had been eminently disagreeable. He had had to drag the body—it was very dreadfully mangled— off the permanent way, the damaged, almost severed head had twisted about very horribly in the uncertain light, and afterwards he had found his sleeves saturated with blood. He had not noted this at the time, and when he had discovered it he had been sick. He had thought the whole thing more horrible and hateful than any nightmare, but he had succeeded in behaving with a sufficient practicality to set an example to his men. Since this had happened he had not had an hour of dreamless sleep.

"One doesn't expect to be called upon like that," said Captain Carmine, "suddenly here in England. . . . When one is smoking after supper. . . ."

Mr. Britling listened to this experience with distressed brows. All his talking and thinking became to him like the open page of a monthly magazine. Across it this bloody smear, this thing of red and black, was dragged. . . .

§ 5

The smear was still bright red in Mr. Britling's thoughts when Teddy came to him.

"I must go," said Teddy, "I can't stop here any longer."

"Go where?"

"Into khaki. I've been thinking of it ever since the war began. Do you remember what you said when we were bullying off at hockey on Bank Holiday—the day before war was declared?"

Mr. Britling had forgotten completely; he made an effort. "What did I say?"

"You said: 'What the devil are we doing at this hockey? We ought to be drilling or shooting against those confounded Germans!' . . . I've never forgotten it. . . . I ought to have done it before. I've been a scoutmaster. In a little while they will want officers. In London, I'm told, there are a lot of officers' training corps putting men through the work as quickly as possible. . . . If I could go. . . ."

"What does Letty think?" said Mr. Britling after a pause. This was right, of course—the only right thing—and yet he was surprised.

"She says if you'd let her try to do my work for a time. . . ."

"She *wants* you to go?"

"Of course she does," said Teddy. "She wouldn't like me to be a shirker. . . . But I can't unless you help."

"I'm quite ready to do that," said Mr. Britling. "But somehow I didn't think it of you. I hadn't somehow thought of *you*——"

"What *did* you think of me?" asked Teddy.

"It's bringing the war home to us. . . . Of course you ought to go—if you want to go."

He reflected. It was odd to find Teddy in this mood, strung up and serious and businesslike. He felt that in the past he had done Teddy injustice; this young man wasn't as trivial as he had thought him. . . .

They fell to discussing ways and means; there might have to be a loan for Teddy's outfit, if he did presently secure a commission. And there were one or two other little matters. . . . Mr. Britling dismissed a ridiculous fancy that he was paying to send Teddy away to something that neither that young man nor Letty understood properly. . . .

The next day Teddy vanished Londonward on his bicycle. He was going to lodge in London in order to be near his training. He was zealous. Never before had Teddy been zealous. Mrs. Teddy came to the Dower House for the correspondence, trying not to look self-conscious and important.

Two Mondays later a very bright-eyed, excited little boy came running to Mr. Britling, who was smoking after lunch in the rose-garden. "Daddy!" squealed the small boy. "Teddy! In khaki!"

The other junior Britling danced in front of the hero, who was walking beside Mrs. Britling and trying not to be too aggressively a soldierly figure. He looked a very man in khaki and more of a boy than ever. Mrs. Teddy came behind, quietly elated.

Mr. Britling had a recurrence of that same disagreeable fancy that these young people didn't know exactly what they were going into. He wished he was in khaki himself; then he fancied this compunction wouldn't trouble him quite so much.

The afternoon with them deepened his conviction that they really didn't in the slightest degree understand. Life had been so good to them hitherto, that even the idea of Teddy's going off to the war seemed a sort of fun to them. It was just a thing he was doing, a serious, seriously amusing, and very creditable thing. It involved his dressing up in these unusual clothes, and receiving salutes in the street. . . . They discussed every possible aspect of his military outlook with the zest of children who recount the merits of a new game. They were putting Teddy through his stages at a tremendous pace. In quite a little time he thought he would be given the chance of a commission.

"They want subalterns badly. Already they've taken nearly a third of our people," he said, and added with the wistfulness of one who glances at inaccessible delights: "one or two may get out to the front quite soon."

He spoke as a young actor might speak of a star part. And with a touch of the quality of one who longs to travel in strange lands. . . . One must be patient. Things come at last. . . .

"If I'm killed she gets eighty pounds a year," Teddy explained among many other particulars.

He smiled—the smile of a confident immortal at this amusing idea.

"He's my little annuity," said Letty, also smiling, "dead or alive."

"We'll miss Teddy in all sorts of ways," said Mr. Britling.

"It's only for the duration of the war," said Teddy. "And Letty's very intelligent. I've done my best to chasten the evil in her."

"If you think you're going to get back your job after the war," said Letty, "you're very much mistaken. I'm going to raise the standard."

"*You!*" said Teddy, regarding her coldly, and proceeded ostentatiously to talk of other things.

§ 6

"Hugh's going to be in khaki too," the elder junior told Teddy. "He's too young to go out in Kitchener's army, but he's joined the Territorials. He went off on Thursday. . . . I wish Gilbert and me was older. . . ."

Mr. Britling had known his son's purpose since the evening of Teddy's announcement.

Hugh had come to his father's study as he was sitting musing at his writing-desk over the important question whether he should continue his "Examination of War" uninterruptedly, or whether he should not put that on one side for a time and set himself to state as clearly as possible the not too generally recognised misfit between the will and strength of Britain on the one hand and her administrative and military organisation on the other. He felt that an enormous amount of human enthusiasm and energy was being refused and wasted; that if things went on as they were going there would continue to be a quite disastrous shortage of gear, and that some broadening change was needed immediately if the swift exemplary victory over Germany that his soul demanded was to be ensured. Suppose he were to write some noisy articles at once, an article, for instance, to be called "The War of the Mechanics" or "The War of Gear," and another on "Without Civil Strength there is no Victory." If he wrote such things would they be noted or would they just vanish indistinguishably into the general mental tumult? Would they be audible and helpful shouts, or just waste of shouting? . . . That at least was what he supposed himself to be thinking; it was, at any rate, the main current of his thinking; but all the same, just outside the circle of his attention a number of other things were dimly apprehended, bobbing up and down in the flood and ready at the slightest chance to swirl into the centre of his thoughts. There was, for instance, Captain Carmine in the moonlight lugging up a railway embankment something horrible, something loose and wet and warm that had very recently been a man. There was Teddy, serious and patriotic— filling a futile penman with incredulous respect. There was the thin-faced man at the club, and a curious satisfaction he had betrayed in the public disarrangement. And there was Hugh. Particularly there was Hugh, silent but watchful. The boy never babbled. He had his mother's gift of deep dark silences. Out of which she was wont to flash, a Black Princess waving a sword. He wandered for a little while among memories. . . . But Hugh didn't come out like that, though it always seemed possible he might— perhaps he didn't come out because he was a son. Revelation to his father wasn't his business. . . . . What was he thinking of it all? What was he going to do? Mr. Britling was acutely anxious that his son should volunteer; he was almost certain that he would volunteer, but there was just a little shadow of doubt whether some extraordinary subtlety of mind mightn't have carried the boy into a pacifist attitude. No! that was impossible. In the face of Belgium. . . . But as greatly—and far more deeply in the warm-flesh of his being—did Mr. Britling desire that no harm, no evil should happen to Hugh. . . .

The door opened, and Hugh came in. . . .

Mr. Britling glanced over his shoulder with an affectation of indifference. "Hal-*lo*!" he said. "What do *you* want?"

Hugh walked awkwardly to the hearth-rug.

"Oh!" he said in an offhand tone; "I suppose I've got to go soldiering for a bit. I just thought—I'd rather like to go off with a man I know tomorrow. . . ."

Mr. Britling's manner remained casual.

"It's the only thing to do now, I'm afraid," he said.

He turned in his chair and regarded his son. "What do you mean to do? O.T.C.?"

"I don't think I should make much of an officer. I hate giving orders to other people. We thought we'd just go together into the Essex Regiment as privates. . . ."

There was a little pause. Both father and son had rehearsed this scene in their minds several times, and now they found that they had no use for a number of sentences that had been most effective in these rehearsals. Mr. Britling scratched his cheek with the end of his pen. "I'm glad you want to go, Hugh," he said.

"I *don't* want to go," said Hugh with his hands deep in his pockets. "I want to go and work with Cardinal. But this job has to be done by every one. Haven't you been saying as much all day? . . . It's like turning out to chase a burglar or suppress a mad dog. It's like necessary sanitation. . . ."

"You aren't attracted by soldiering?"

"Not a bit. I won't pretend it, Daddy. I think the whole business is a bore. Germany seems to me now just like some heavy horrible dirty mass that has fallen across Belgium and France. We've got to shove the stuff back again. That's all. . . ."

He volunteered some further remarks to his father's silence.

"You know I can't get up a bit of tootle about this business," he said, "I think killing people or getting killed is a thoroughly nasty habit. . . . I expect my share will be just drilling and fatigue duties and route marches, and loafing here in England. . . ."

"You can't possibly go out for two years," said Mr. Britling, as if he regretted it.

A slight hesitation appeared in Hugh's eyes. "I suppose not," he said.

"Things ought to be over by then—anyhow," Mr. Britling added, betraying his real feelings.

"So it's really just helping at the farthest end of the shove," Hugh endorsed, but still with that touch of reservation in his manner. . . .

The pause had the effect of closing the theoretical side of the question. "Where do you propose to enlist?" said Mr. Britling, coming down to practical details.

§ 7

The battle of the Marne passed into the battle of the Aisne, and then the long lines of the struggle streamed north-westward until the British were back in Belgium, failing to clutch Menin and then defending Ypres. The elation of September followed the bedazzlement and dismay of August into the chapter of forgotten moods; and Mr. Britling's sense of the magnitude, the weight and duration of this war beyond all wars, increased steadily. The feel of it was less and less a feeling of crisis and more and more a feeling of new conditions. It wasn't as it had seemed at first, the end of one human phase and the beginning of another; it was in itself a phase. It was a new way of living. And still he could find for himself no real point of contact with it all except the point of his pen. Only at his writing-desk, and more particularly at night, were the great presences of the conflict his. Yet he was always desiring some more personal and physical participation.

Hugh came along one day in October in an ill-fitting uniform, looking already coarser in fibre and with a nose scorched red by the autumnal sun. He said the life was rough, but it made him feel extraordinarily well; perhaps man was made to toil until he dropped asleep from exhaustion, to fast for ten or twelve hours and then eat like a wolf. He was acquiring a taste for Woodbine cigarettes, and a heady variety of mineral waters called Monsters. He feared promotion; he felt he could never take the high line with other human beings demanded of a corporal. He was still trying to read a little chemistry and crystallography, but it didn't "go with the life." In the scanty leisure of a recruit in training it was more agreeable to lie about and write doggerel verses and draw caricatures of the men in one's platoon. Invited to choose what he liked by his family, he demanded a large tuck-box such as he used to have at school, only "*much* larger," and a big tin of insect powder. It must be able to kill ticks. . . .

When he had gone, the craving for a personal share in the nation's physical exertions became overpowering in Mr. Britling. He wanted, he felt, to "get his skin into it." He had decided that the volunteer movement was a hopeless one. The War Office, after a stout resistance to any volunteer movement at all, decided to recognise it in such a manner as to make it ridiculous. The volunteers were to have no officers and no uniforms that could be remotely mistaken for those of the regulars, so that in the event of an invasion the Germans would be able to tell what they had to deal with miles away. Wilkins found his conception of a whole nation, all enrolled, all listed and badged according to capacity, his dream of every one falling into place in one great voluntary national effort, treated as the childish dreaming of that most ignorant of all human types, a "novelist." *Punch* was delicately funny about him; he was represented as wearing a preposterous cocked hat of his own design, designing cocked hats for every one. Wilkins was told to "shut up" in a multitude of anonymous letters, and publicly and privately to "leave things to Kitchener." To bellow in loud clear tones "leave things to Kitchener," and to depart for the theatre or the river or an automobile tour, was felt very generally at that time to be the proper conduct for a patriot. There was a very general persuasion that to become a volunteer when one ought to be just modestly doing nothing at all, was in some obscure way a form of disloyalty. . . .

So Mr. Britling was out of conceit with volunteering, and instead he went and was duly sworn, and entrusted with the badge of a special constable. The duties of a special constable were chiefly not to understand what was going on in the military sphere, and to do what he was told in the way of watching and warding conceivably vulnerable points. He had also to be available in the event of civil disorder. Mr. Britling was provided with a truncheon and sent out to guard various culverts, bridges, and fords in the hilly country to the north-westward of Matching's Easy. It was never very clear to him what he would do if he found a motor-car full of armed enemies engaged in undermining a culvert, or treacherously deepening some strategic ford. He supposed he would either engage them in conversation, or hit them with his truncheon, or perhaps do both things simultaneously. But as he really did not believe for a moment that any human being was likely to tamper with the telegraphs, telephones, ways and appliances committed to his care, his uncertainty did not trouble him very much. He prowled the lonely lanes and paths in the darkness, and became better acquainted with a multitude of intriguing little cries and noises that came from the hedges and coverts at night. One night he rescued a young leveret from a stoat, who seemed more than half inclined to give him battle for its prey until he cowed and defeated it with the glare of his electric torch. . . .

As he prowled the countryside under the great hemisphere of Essex sky, or leaned against fences or sat drowsily upon gates or sheltered from wind and rain under ricks or sheds, he had much time for meditation, and his thoughts went down and down below his first surface impressions of the war. He thought no longer of the rights and wrongs of this particular conflict but of the underlying forces in mankind that made war possible; he planned no more ingenious treaties and conventions between the nations, and instead he faced the deeper riddles of essential evil and of conceivable changes in the heart of man. And the rain assailed him and thorns tore him, and the soaked soft meadows bogged and betrayed his wandering feet, and the little underworld of the hedges and ditches hissed and squealed in the darkness and pursued and fled, and devoured or were slain.

And one night in April he was perplexed by a commotion among the pheasants and a barking of distant dogs, and then to his great astonishment he heard noises like a distant firework display and saw something like a phantom yellowish fountain pen in the sky far away to the east lit intermittently by a quivering searchlight and going very swiftly. And after he had rubbed his eyes and looked again, he realised that he was looking at a Zeppelin—a Zeppelin flying Londonward over Essex.

And all that night was wonder. . . .

§ 8

While Mr. Britling was trying to find his duty in the routine of a special constable, Mrs. Britling set to work with great energy to attend various classes and qualify herself for Red Cross work. And early in October came the great drive of the Germans towards Antwerp and the sea, the great drive that was apparently designed to reach Calais, and which swept before it multitudes of Flemish refugees. There was an exodus of all classes from Antwerp into Holland and England, and then a huge process of depopulation in Flanders and the Pas de Calais. This flood came to the eastern and southern parts of England and particularly to London, and there hastily improvised organisations distributed it to a number of local committees, each of which took a share of the refugees, hired and furnished unoccupied houses for the use of the penniless, and assisted those who had means into comfortable quarters. The Matching's Easy committee found itself with accommodation for sixty people, and with a miscellaneous bag of thirty individuals entrusted to its care, who had been part of the load of a little pirate steamboat from Ostend. There were two Flemish peasant families, and the rest were more or less middle-class refugees from Antwerp. They were brought from the station to the Tithe barn at Claverings, and there distributed, under the personal supervision of Lady Homartyn and her agent, among those who were prepared for their entertainment. There was something like competition among the would-be hosts; everybody was glad of the chance of "doing something," and anxious to show these Belgians what England thought of their plucky little country. Mr. Britling was proud to lead off a Mr. Van der Pant, a neat little bearded man in a black tail-coat, a black bowler hat, and a knitted muffler, with a large rucksack and a conspicuously foreign-looking bicycle, to the hospitalities of the Dower House. Mr. Van der Pant had escaped from Antwerp at the eleventh hour; he had caught a severe cold and, it would seem, lost his wife and family in the process; he had much to tell Mr. Britling, and in his zeal to tell it he did not at once discover that though Mr. Britling knew French quite well he did not know it very rapidly.

The dinner that night at the Dower House marked a distinct fresh step in the approach of the Great War to the old habits and securities of Matching's Easy. The war had indeed filled every one's mind to the exclusion of all other topics since its very beginning; it had carried off Herr Heinrich to Germany, Teddy to London, and Hugh to Colchester, it had put a special brassard round Mr. Britling's arm and carried him out into the night, given Mrs. Britling several certificates, and interruoted the frequent visits and gossip of Mr. Lawrence Carmine; but so far it had not established a direct contact between the life of Matching's Easy and the grim business of shot, shell, and bayonet at the front. But now here was the Dower House accomplishing wonderful idioms in Anglo-French, and an animated guest telling them— sometimes one understood clearly and sometimes the meaning was clouded—of men blown to pieces under his eyes, of fragments of human beings lying about in the streets; there was trouble over the expression *omoplate d'une femme*, until one of the youngsters got the dictionary and found out it was the shoulder-blade of a woman; of pools of blood—everywhere— and of flight in the darkness.

Mr. Van der Pant had been in charge of the dynamos at the Antwerp Power Station, he had been keeping the electrified wires in the entanglements "alive," and he had stuck to his post until the German high explosives had shattered his wires and rendered his dynamos useless. He gave vivid little pictures of the noises of the bombardment, of the dead lying casually in the open spaces, of the failure of the German guns to hit the bridge of boats across which the bulk of the defenders and refugees escaped. He produced a little tourist's map of the city of Antwerp, and dotted at it with a pencil-case. "The—what do you call?—*obus*, ah, shells! fell, so and so and so." Across here he had fled on his *bécane*, and along here and here. He had carried off his rifle, and hid it with the rifles of various other Belgians between floor and ceiling of a house in Zeebrugge. He had found the pirate steamer in the harbour, its captain resolved to extract the uttermost fare out of every refugee he took to London. When they were all aboard and started they found there was no food except the hard ration biscuits of some Belgian soldiers. They had portioned this out like shipwrecked people on a raft. . . . The *mer* had been *calme;* thank Heaven! All night they had been pumping. He had helped with the pumps. But Mr. Van der Pant hoped still to get a reckoning with the captain of that ship.

Mr. Van der Pant had had shots at various Zeppelins. When the Zeppelins came to Antwerp everybody turned out on the roofs and shot at them He was contemptuous of Zeppelins. He made derisive gestures to express his opinion of them. They could do nothing unless they came low, and if they came low you could hit them. One which ventured down had been riddled; it had had to drop all its bombs—luckily they fell in an open field—in order to make its lame escape. It was all nonsense to say, as the English papers did, that they took part in the final bombardment. Not a Zeppelin. . . . So he talked, and the Britling family listened and understood as much as they could, and replied and questioned in Anglo-French. Here was a man who but a few days ago had been steering his bicycle in the streets of Antwerp to avoid shell craters, pools of blood, and the torn-off arms and shoulder-blades of women. He had seen houses flaring, set afire by incendiary bombs, and once at a corner he had been knocked off his bicycle by the pouff of a bursting shell. . . . Not only were these things in the same world with us, they were sitting at our table.

He told one grim story of an invalid woman unable to move, lying in bed in her *appartement*, and of how her husband went out on the balcony to look at the Zeppelin. There was a great noise of shooting. Ever and again he would put his head back into the room and tell her things, and then after a time he was silent and looked in no more. She called to him, and called again. Becoming frightened, she raised herself by a great effort and peered through the glass. At first she was too puzzled to understand what had happened. He was hanging over the front of the balcony, with his head twisted oddly. Twisted and shattered. He had been killed by shrapnel fired from the outer fortifications. . . .

These are the things that happen in histories and stories. They do not happen at Matching's Easy. . . .

Mr. Van der Pant did not seem to be angry with the Germans. But he manifestly regarded them as people to be killed. He denounced nothing that they had done; he related. They were just an evil accident that had happened to Belgium and mankind. They had to be destroyed. He gave Mr. Britling an extraordinary persuasion that knives were being sharpened in every cellar in

Brussels and Antwerp against the day of inevitable retreat, of a resolution to exterminate the invader that was far too deep to be vindictive. . . . And the man was most amazingly unconquered. Mr. Britling perceived the label on his habitual dinner wine with a slight embarrassment. "Do you care," he asked, "to drink a German wine? This is Berncasteler from the Moselle." Mr. Van der Pant reflected. "But it is a good wine," he said. "After the peace it will be Belgian. . . . Yes, if we are to be safe in the future from such a war as this, we must have our boundaries right up to the Rhine."

So he sat and talked, flushed and, as it were, elated by the vividness of all that he had undergone. He had no trace of tragic quality, no hint of subjugation. But for his costume and his trimmed beard and his language he might have been a Dubliner or a Cockney.

He was astonishingly cut off from all his belongings. His house in Antwerp was abandoned to the invader; valuables and cherished objects very skilfully buried in the garden; he had no change of clothing except what the rucksack held. His only footwear were the boots he came in. He could not get on any of the slippers in the house, they were all too small for him, until suddenly Mrs. Britling bethought herself of Herr Heinrich's pair, still left unpacked upstairs. She produced them, and they fitted exactly. It seemed only poetical justice, a foretaste of national compensations, to annex them to Belgium forthwith. . . .

Also it became manifest that Mr. Van der Pant was cut off from all his family. And suddenly he became briskly critical of the English way of doing things. His wife and child had preceded him to England, crossing by Ostend and Folkestone a fortnight ago; her parents had come in August; both groups had been seized upon by improvised British organisations and very thoroughly and completely lost. He had written to the Belgian Embassy and they had referred him to a committee in London, and the committee had begun its services by discovering a Madame Van der Pant hitherto unknown to him at Camberwell, and displaying a certain suspicion and hostility when he said she would not do. There had been some futile telegrams. "What," asked Mr. Van der Pant, "ought one to do?"

Mr. Britling temporised by saying he would "make inquiries," and put Mr. Van der Pant off for two days. Then he decided to go up to London with him and "make inquiries on the spot." Mr. Van der Pant did not discover his family, but Mr. Britling discovered the profound truth of a comment of Herr Heinrich's which he had hitherto considered utterly trivial, but which had nevertheless stuck in his memory. "The English," Herr Heinrich had said, "do not understand indexing. It is the root of all good organisation."

Finally, Mr. Van der Pant adopted the irregular course of asking every Belgian he met if they had seen any one from his distict in Antwerp, if they had heard of the name of "Van der Pant," if they had encountered So-and-So or So-and-so. And by obstinacy and good fortune he really got on to the track of Madame Van der Pant; she had been carried off into Kent, and a day later the Dower House was the scene of a happy reunion. Madame was a slender lady, dressed well and plainly, with a Belgian common sense and a Catholic reserve, and André was like a child of wax, delicate and charming and unsubstantial. It seemed incredible that he could ever grow into anything so buoyant and incessant as his father. The Britling boys had to be warned not to damage him. A sitting-room was handed over to the Belgians for their private use, and for a time the two families settled into the Dower House side by side.

Anglo-French became the table language of the household. It hampered Mr. Britling very considerably. And both families set themselves to much unrecorded observation, much unspoken mutual criticism, and the exercise of great patience. It was tiresome for the English to be tied to a language that crippled all spontaneous talk; these linguistic gymnastics were fun to begin with, but soon they became very troublesome; and the Belgians suspected sensibilities in their hosts and a vast unwritten code of etiquette that did not exist; at first they were always waiting, as it were, to be invited or told or included; they seemed always deferentially backing out from intrusions. Moreover, they would not at first reveal what food they liked or what they didn't like, or whether they wanted more or less. . . . But these difficulties were soon smoothed away, they Anglicised quickly and cleverly. André grew bold and cheerful, and lost his first distrust of his rather older English playmates. Every day at lunch he produced a new, carefully prepared piece of English, though for some time he retained a marked preference for "Good morning, saire," and "Thank you very mush," over all other locutions, and fell back upon them on all possible and many impossible occasions. And he could do some sleight-of-hand tricks with remarkable skill and humour, and fold paper with quite astonishing results. Meanwhile Mr. Van der Pant sought temporary employment in England, went for long rides upon his bicycle, exchanged views with Mr. Britling upon a variety of subjects, and became a wonderful player of hockey.

He played hockey with an extraordinary zest and nimbleness. Always he played in the tail-coat, and the knitted muffler was never relinquished; he treated the game entirely as an occasion for quick tricks and personal agility; he bounded about the field like a kitten, he pirouetted suddenly, he leaped into the air and came down in new directions; his fresh-coloured face was alive with delight, the coat-tails and the muffler trailed and swished about breathlessly behind his agility. He never passed to other players; he never realised his appointed place in the game; he sought simply to make himself a leaping screen about the ball as he drove it towards the goal. But André he would not permit to play at all, and Madame played like a lady, like a Madonna, like a saint carrying the instrument of her martyrdom. The game and its enthusiasms flowed round her and receded from her; she remained quite valiant but tolerant, restrained; doing her best to do the extraordinary things required of her, but essentially a being of passive dignities, living chiefly for them; Letty careering by her, keen and swift, was like a creature of a different species. . . .

Mr. Britling cerebrated abundantly about these contrasts.

"What has been blown in among us by these German shells," he said, "is essentially a Catholic family. Blown clean out of its setting. . . . We who are really—Neo-Europeans. . . .

"At first you imagine there is nothing separating us but language. Presently you find that language is the least of our separations. These people are people living upon fundamentally different ideas from ours, ideas far more definite and complete than ours. You imagine that home in Antwerp as something much more rounded off, much more closed in, a cell, a real social unit, a different thing altogether from this place of meeting. Our boys play cheerfully with all comers; little André hasn't learned to play with any outside children at all. We must seem incredibly *open* to these Van der Pants. A house without sides. . . . Last Sunday I could not find out the names of the two girls who came on bicycles and played so well. They came with Kitty Westropp. And Van der Pant wanted to know how they were related to us. Or how was it they came? . . .

"Look at Madame. She's built on a fundamentally different plan from any of our womenkind here. Tennis, the bicycle, coeducation, the two-step, the higher education of women. . . . Say these things over to yourself, and think of her. It's like talking of a nun in riding-breeches. She's a specialised woman, specialising in womanhood, her sphere is the home. Soft, trailing, draping skirts, slow movements, a veiled face; for no Oriental veil could be more effectual than her beautiful Catholic quiet. Catholicism invented the invisible purdah. She is far more akin to that sweet little Indian lady with the wonderful robes whom Carmine brought over with her tall husband last summer, than she is to Letty or Cissie. She, too, undertook to play hockey. And played it very much as Madame Van der Pant played it. . . .

"The more I see of our hockey," said Mr. Britling, "the more wonderful it seems to me as a touchstone of character and culture and breeding. . . ."

Mr. Manning, to whom he was delivering this discourse, switched him on to a new track by asking what he meant by "Neo-European."

"It's a bad phrase," said Mr. Britling. "I'll withdraw it. Let me try and state exactly what I have in mind. I mean something that is coming up in America and here and the Scandinavian countries and Russia, a new culture, an escape from the Levantine religion and the Catholic culture that came to us from the Mediterranean. Let me drop Neo-European; let me say Northern. We are Northerners. The key, the heart, the nucleus and essence of every culture is its conception of the relations of men and women; and this new culture tends to diminish the specialisation of women as women, to let them out from the cell of the home into common citizenship with men. It's a new culture, still in process of development, which will make men more social and co-operative and women bolder, swifter, more responsible and less cloistered. It minimises instead of exaggerating the importance of sex. . . .

"And," said Mr. Britling, in very much the tones in which a preacher might say "Sixthly," "it is just all this Northern tendency that this world struggle is going to release. This war is pounding through Europe, smashing up homes, dispersing and mixing homes, setting Madame Van der Pant playing hockey, and André climbing trees with my young ruffians; it is killing young men by the million, altering the proportions of the sexes for a generation, bringing women into business and office and industry, destroying the accumulated wealth that kept so many of them in refined idleness, flooding the world with strange doubts and novel ideas. . . ."

§ 9

But the conflict of manners and customs that followed the invasion of the English villages by French and Belgian refugees did not always present the immigrants as Catholics and the hosts as "Neo-Europeans." In the case of Mr. Dimple it was the other way round. He met Mr. Britling in Claverings Park and told him his troubles. . . .

"Of course," he said, "we have to do our Utmost for Brave Little Belgium. I would be the last to complain of any little inconvenience one may experience in doing that. Still, I must confess I think you and dear Mrs. Britling are fortunate, exceptionally fortunate, in the Belgians you have got. My guests—it's unfortunate—the man is some sort of journalist and quite—oh! much too much—an Atheist. An open positive one. Not simply Honest Doubt. I'm quite prepared for honest doubt nowadays. You and I have no quarrel over that. But he is aggressive. He makes remarks about miracles, quite derogatory remarks, and not always in French. Sometimes he almost speaks English. And in front of my sister. And he goes out, he says, looking for a Café. He never finds a Café, but he certainly finds every public house within a radius of miles. And he comes back smelling dreadfully of beer. When I drop a Little Hint, he blames the beer. He says it is not good beer—our good Essex beer! He doesn't understand any of our Simple Ways. He's sophisticated. The girls about here wear Belgian flags—and air their little bits of French. And he takes it as an encouragement. Only yesterday there was a scene. It seems he tried to kiss the Hickson girl at the inn—Maudie. . . . And his wife; a great big slow woman—in every way she is—Ample; it's dreadful even to seem to criticise, but I do so *wish* she would not see fit to sit down and nourish her baby in my poor old bachelor drawing-room—often at the most *unseasonable* times. And—so lavishly. . . ."

Mr. Britling attempted consolations.

"But anyhow," said Mr. Dimple, "I'm better off than poor dear Mrs. Bynne. She secured two milliners. She insisted upon them. And their clothes were certainly beautifully made—even my poor old unworldly eye could tell that. And she thought two milliners would be so useful with a large family like hers. They certainly *said* they were milliners. But it seems—I don't know what we shall do about them. . . . My dear Mr. Britling, those young women are anything but milliners—anything but milliners. . . ."

A faint gleam of amusement was only too perceptible through the good man's horror.

"Sirens, my dear Mr. Britling. Sirens. By profession. . . ."

§ 10

October passed into November, and day by day Mr. Britling was forced to apprehend new aspects of the war, to think and rethink the war, to have his first conclusions checked and tested, twisted askew, replaced. His thoughts went far and wide and deeper—until all his earlier writing seemed painfully shallow to him, seemed a mere automatic response of obvious comments to the stimulus of the war's surprise. As his ideas became subtler and profounder, they became more difficult to express; he talked less; he became abstracted and irritable at table. To two people in particular Mr. Britling found his real ideas inexpressible, to Mr. Direck and to Mr. Van der Pant.

Each of these gentlemen brought with him the implication or the intimation of a critical attitude towards England. It was all very well for Mr. Britling himself to be critical of England; that is an Englishman's privilege. To hear Mr. Van der Pant questioning British efficiency or to suspect Mr. Direck of high, thin American superiorities to war, was almost worse than to hear Mrs. Harrowdean saying hostile things about Edith. It roused an even acuter protective emotion.

In the case of Mr. Van der Pant matters were complicated by the difficulty of the language, which made anything but the crudest statements subject to incalculable misconception.

Mr. Van der Pant had not the extreme tactfulness of his so typically Catholic wife; he made it only too plain that he thought the British postal and telegraph service slow and slack, and the management of the Great Eastern branch lines wasteful and inefficient. He said the workmen in the fields and the workmen he saw upon some cottages near the junction worked slowlier and with less interest than he had ever seen any workmen display in all his life before. He marvelled that Mr. Britling lit his house with acetylene and not electric light. He thought fresh eggs were insanely dear, and his opinion of Matching's Easy pig-keeping was uncomplimentary. The roads, he said, were not a means of getting from place to place, they were a *dédale;* he drew derisive maps with his finger on the table-cloth of the lane system about the Dower House. He was astonished that there was no Café in Matching's Easy; he declared that the "public house" to which he went with considerable expectation was no public house at all; it was just a sly place for drinking beer. . . . All these were things Mr. Britling might have remarked himself; from a Belgian refugee he found them intolerable.

He set himself to explain to Mr. Van der Pant firstly that these things did not matter in the slightest degree, the national attention, the national interest ran in other directions; and secondly that they were, as a matter of fact and on the whole, merits slightly disguised. He produced a pleasant theory that England is really not the Englishman's field, it is his breeding-place, his resting-place, a place not for efficiency but good humour. If Mr. Van der Pant were to make inquiries he would find there was scarcely a home in Matching's Easy that had not sent some energetic representative out of England to become one of the English of the world. England was the last place in which English energy was spent. These hedges, these dilatory roads were full of associations. There was a road that turned aside near Market Saffron to avoid Turk's wood; it had been called Turk's wood first in the fourteenth century after a man of that name. He quoted Chesterton's happy verses to justify these winding lanes.

> "The road turned first towards the left,
> Where Perkin's quarry made the cleft;
> The path turned next towards the right,
> Because the mastiff used to bite. . . ."

And again:

> "And I should say they wound about
> To find the town of Roundabout,
> The merry town of Roundabout
> That makes the world go round."

If our easy-going ways hampered a hard efficiency, they did at least develop humour and humanity. Our diplomacy at any rate had not failed us. . . .

He did not believe a word of this stuff. His deep irrational love for England made him say these things. . . . For years he had been getting himself into hot water because he had been writing and hinting just such criticisms as Mr. Van der Pant expressed so bluntly. . . . But he wasn't going to accept foreign help in dissecting his mother. . . .

And another curious effect that Mr. Van der Pant had upon Mr. Britling was to produce an obstinate confidence about the war and the nearness of the German collapse. He would promise Mr. Van der Pant that he should be back in Antwerp before May; that the Germans would be over the Rhine by July. He knew perfectly well that his ignorance of all the military conditions was unqualified, but still he could not restrain himself from this kind of thing so soon as he began to speak Entente Cordiale—Anglo-French, that is to say. Something in his relationship to Mr. Van der Pant obliged him to be acutely and absurdly the protecting Briton. . . . At times he felt like a conscious bankrupt talking off the hour of disclosure. But indeed all that Mr. Britling was trying to say against the difficulties of a strange language and an alien temperament was that the honour of England would never be cleared until Belgium was restored and avenged. . . .

While Mr. Britling was patrolling unimportant roads and entertaining Mr. Van der Pant with discourses upon the nearness of victory and the subtle estimableness of all that was indolent, wasteful and evasive in English life, the war was passing from its first swift phases into a slower, grimmer struggle. The German retreat ended at the Aisne, and the long outflanking manœuvres of both hosts towards the Channel began. The English attempts to assist Belgium in October came too late for the preservation of Antwerp, and after a long and complicated struggle in Flanders the British failed to outflank the German right, lost Ghent, Menin and the Belgian coast, but held Ypres and beat back every attempt of the enemy to reach Dunkirk and Calais. Meanwhile the smaller German colonies and islands were falling to the navy, the Australian battleship *Sydney* smashed the *Emden* at Cocos Island, and the British naval disaster of Coronel was wiped out by the battle of the Falklands. The Russians were victorious upon their left and took Lemberg, and after some vicissitudes of fortune advanced to Przemysl, occupying the larger part of Galicia; but the disaster of Tannenberg had broken their progress in East Prussia, and the Germans were pressing towards Warsaw. Turkey had joined the war, and suffered enormous losses in the

Caucasus. The Dardanelles had been shelled for the first time, and the British were at Basra on the Euphrates.

§ 11

The Christmas of 1914 found England, whose landscape had hitherto been almost as peaceful and soldierless as Massachusetts, already far gone along the path of transformation into a country full of soldiers and munition-makers and military supplies. The soldiers came first, on the well-known and greatly admired British principle of "first catch your hare" and then build your kitchen. Always before, Christmas had been a time of much gaiety and dressing-up and prancing and two-stepping at the Dower House, but this year everything was too uncertain to allow of any gathering of guests. Hugh got leave for the day after Christmas, but Teddy was tied; and Cissie and Letty went off with the baby to take lodgings near him. The Van der Pants had hoped to see an English Christmas at Matching's Easy, but within three weeks of Christmas Day Mr. Van der Pant found a job that he could do in Nottingham, and carried off his family. The two small boys cheered their hearts with paper decorations, but the Christmas Tree was condemned as too German, and it was discovered that Santa Claus had suddenly become Old Father Christmas again. The small boys discovered that the price of lead soldiers had risen, and were unable to buy electric torches, on which they had set their hearts. There was to have been a Christmas party at Claverings, but at the last moment Lady Homartyn had to hurry off to an orphan nephew who had been seriously wounded near Ypres, and the light of Claverings was darkened.

Soon after Christmas there were rumours of an impending descent of the Headquarters staff of the South-Eastern army upon Claverings. Then Mr. Britling found Lady Homartyn back from France, and very indignant because after all the Headquarters were to go to Lady Wensleydale at Lady-holt. It was, she felt, a reflection upon Claverings. Lady Homartyn became still more indignant when presently the new armies, which were gathering now all over England like floods in a low-lying meadow, came pouring into the parishes about Claverings to the extent of a battalion and a Territorial battery. Mr. Britling heard of their advent only a day or two before they arrived; there came a bright young officer with an orderly, billeting; he was much exercised to get, as he expressed it several times, a quart into a pint bottle. He was greatly pleased with the barn. He asked the size of it and did calculations. He could "stick twenty-five men into it—easy." It would go far to solve his problems. He could manage without coming into the house at all. It was a ripping place. "No end."

"But beds," said Mr. Britling.

"Lord! they don't want *beds*," said the young officer. . . .

The whole Britling family, who were lamenting the loss of their Belgians, welcomed the coming of the twenty-five with great enthusiasm. It made them feel that they were doing something useful once more. For three days Mrs. Britling had to feed her new lodgers—the kitchen motors had as usual gone astray—and she did so in a style that made their boastings about their billet almost insufferable to the rest of their battery. The billeting allowance at that time was ninepence a head, and Mr. Britling, ashamed of making a profit out of his country, supplied not only generous firing and lighting, but unlimited cigarettes, cards and games, illustrated newspapers, a cocoa supper with such little surprises as sprats and jam roly-poly, and a number of more incidental comforts. The men arrived fasting under the command of two very sage middle-aged corporals, and responded to Mrs. Britling's hospitalities by a number of good resolutions, many of which they kept. They never made noises after half-past ten, or at least only now and then when a singsong broke out with unusual violence; they got up and went out at five or six in the morning without a sound; they were almost inconveniently helpful with washing-up and tidying round.

In quite a little time Mrs. Britling's mind had adapted itself to the spectacle of half-a-dozen young men in khaki breeches and shirts performing their toilets in and about her scullery, or improvising an unsanctioned game of football between the hockey goals. These men were not the miscellaneous men of the new armies; they were the earlier Territorial type with no heroics about them; they came from the midlands; and their two middle-aged corporals kept them well in hand and ruled them like a band of brothers. But they had a lawless side, that developed in directions that set Mr. Britling theorising. They seemed, for example, to poach by nature, as children play and sing. They possessed a promiscuous white dog. They began to add rabbits to their supper menu, unaccountable rabbits. One night there was a mighty smell of frying fish from the kitchen, and the cook reported trout. "Trout!" said Mr. Britling to one of the corporals; "now where did you chaps get trout?"

The "fisherman," they said, had got them with a hair noose. They produced the fisherman, of whom they were manifestly proud. It was, he explained, a method of fishing he had learned when in New York Harbour. He had been a stoker. He displayed a confidence in Mr. Britling that made that gentleman an accessory after his offence, his very serious offence against pre-war laws and customs. It was plain that the trout were the trout that Mr. Pumshock, the stock-broker and amateur gentleman, had preserved so carefully in the Easy. Hitherto the countryside had been forced to regard Mr. Pumshock's trout with an almost superstitious respect. A year ago young Snooker had done a month for one of those very trout. But now things were different.

"But I don't really fancy fresh-water fish," said the fisherman. "It's just the ketchin' of 'em I like. . . ."

And a few weeks later the trumpeter, an angel-faced freckled child with deep-blue eyes, brought in a dozen partridge eggs which he wanted Mary to cook for him. . . .

The domesticity of the sacred birds, it was clear, was no longer safe in England. . . .

Then again the big guns would go swinging down the road and into Claverings Park, and perform various exercises with commendable smartness and a profound disregard for Lady Homartyn's known objection to any departure from the public footpath. . . .

And one afternoon as Mr. Britling took his constitutional walk, a reverie was set going in his mind by the sight of a neglected-looking pheasant with a white collar. The world of Matching's Easy was getting full now of such elderly birds. Would *that* go on after the war? He imagined his son Hugh as a grandfather, telling the little ones about parks and preserves and game-laws, and footmen and butlers and the marvellous game of golf, and how, suddenly, Mars came tramping through the land in khaki and all these things faded and banished, so that presently it was discovered they were gone. . . .

CHAPTER THE THIRD

MALIGNITY

§ 1

AND while the countryside of England changed steadily from its lax pacific amenity to the likeness of a rather slovenly armed camp, while long-fixed boundaries shifted and dissolved and a great irreparable wasting of the world's resources gathered way, Mr. Britling did his duty as a special constable, gave his eldest son to the Territorials, entertained Belgians, petted his soldiers in the barn, helped Teddy to his commission, contributed to war charities, sold out securities at a loss and subscribed to the War Loan, and thought, thought endlessly about the war.

He could think continuously day by day of nothing else. His mind was as caught as a galley-slave, as unable to escape from tugging at this oar. All his universe was a magnetic field which oriented everything, whether he would have it so or not, to this one polar question.

His thoughts grew firmer and clearer; they went deeper and wider. His first superficial judgments were endorsed and deepened or replaced by others. He thought along the lonely lanes at night; he thought at his desk; he thought in bed; he thought in his bath; he tried over his thoughts in essays and leading articles and reviewed them and corrected them. Now and then came relaxation and lassitude, but never release. The war towered over him like a vigilant teacher, day after day, week after week, regardless of fatigue and impatience, holding a rod in its hand.

§ 2

Certain things had to be forced upon Mr. Britling, because they jarred so greatly with his habits of mind that he would never have accepted them if he could have avoided doing so.

Notably he would not recognise at first the extreme bitterness of this war. He would not believe that the attack upon Britain and Western Europe generally expressed the concentrated emotion of a whole nation. He thought that the Allies were in conflict with a system and not with a national will. He fought against the persuasion that the whole mass of a great civilised nation could be inspired by a genuine and sustained hatred. Hostility was an uncongenial thing to him; he would not recognise that the greater proportion of human beings are more readily hostile than friendly. He did his best to believe—in his "And Now War Ends" he did his best to make other people believe—that this war was the perverse exploit of a small group of people, of limited but powerful influences, an outrage upon the general geniality of mankind. The cruelty, mischief, and futility of war were so obvious to him that he was almost apologetic in asserting them. He believed that war had but to begin and demonstrate its quality among the Western nations in order to unify them all against its repetition. They would exclaim: "But we can't do things like this to one another!" He saw the aggressive imperialism of Germany called to account even by its own people; a struggle, a collapse, a liberal-minded conference of world powers, and a universal resumption of amiability upon a more assured basis of security. He believed—and many people in England believed with him—that a great section of the Germans would welcome triumphant Allies as their liberators from intolerable political obsessions.

The English because of their insularity had been political amateurs for endless generations. It was their supreme vice, it was their supreme virtue, to be easy-going. They had lived in an atmosphere of comedy, and denied in the whole tenor of their lives that life is tragic. Not even the Americans had been more isolated. The Americans had had their Indians, their negroes, their War of Secession. Until the Great War the Channel was as broad as the Atlantic for holding off every vital challenge. Even Ireland was away—a four-hour crossing. And so the English had developed to the fullest extent the virtues and vices of safety and comfort; they had a hatred of science and dramatic behaviour; they could see no reason for exactness or intensity; they disliked proceeding "to extremes." Ultimately everything would turn out all right. But they knew what it is to be carried into conflicts by energetic minorities and the trick of circumstances, and they were ready to understand the case of any other country which has suffered that fate. All their habits inclined them to fight good-temperedly and comfortably, to quarrel with a government and not with a people. It took Mr. Britling at least a couple of months of warfare to understand that the Germans were fighting in an altogether different spirit.

The first intimations of this that struck upon his mind were the news of the behaviour of the Kaiser and the Berlin crowd upon the declaration of war, and the violent treatment of the British subjects seeking to return to their homes. Everywhere such people had been insulted and ill-treated. It was the spontaneous expression of a long-gathered bitterness. While the British ambassador was being howled out of Berlin, the German ambassador to England was taking a farewell stroll, quite unmolested, in St. James's Park. . . . One item that stuck particularly upon Mr. Britling's imagination was the story of the chorus of young women who assembled on the railway platform of the station through which the British ambassador was passing to sing—to his drawn blinds—"Deutschland, Deutschland über Alles." Mr. Britling could imagine those young people, probably dressed more or less uniformly in white, with flushed faces and shining eyes, letting their voices go, full-throated, in the modern German way. . . .

And then came stories of atrocities, stories of the shooting of old men and the butchery of children by the wayside, stories of wounded man bayoneted or burned alive, of massacres of harmless citizens, of looting and filthy outrages. . . .

Mr. Britling did his utmost not to believe these things. They contradicted his habitual world. They produced horrible strains in his mind. They might, he hoped, be misreported so as to seem more violent or less justifiable than they were. They might be the acts of stray criminals, and quite disconnected from the normal operations of the war. Here and there some weak-minded officer may have sought to make himself terrible. . . . And as for the bombardment of cathedrals and the crime of Louvain, well, Mr. Britling was prepared to argue that Gothic architecture is not sacrosanct if military necessity cuts through it. . . . It was only after the war had been going on some months that Mr. Britling's fluttering, unwilling mind was pinned down by official reports and a cloud of witnesses to a definite belief in the grim reality of systematic rape and murder, destruction, dirtiness and abominable compulsions that blackened the first rush of the Prussians into Belgium and Champagne. . . .

They came hating and threatening the lands they outraged. They sought occasions to do frightful deeds. . . . When they could not be frightful in the houses they occupied, then to the best of their ability they were destructive and filthy. The facts took Mr. Britling by the throat. . . .

The first thing that really pierced him with the conviction that there was something essentially different in the English and the German attitude towards the war was the sight of a bale of German comic papers in the study of a friend in London. They were filled with caricatures of the Allies and more particularly of the English, and they displayed a force and quality of passion— an incredible force and quality of passion. Their amazing hate and their amazing filthiness alike overwhelmed Mr. Britling. There was no appearance of national pride or national dignity, but a bellowing patriotism and a limitless desire to hurt and humiliate. They spat. They were red in the face and they spat. He sat with these violent sheets in his hands—*ashamed*.

"But I say!" he said feebly. "It's the sort of thing that might come out of a lunatic asylum. . . ."

One incredible craving was manifest in every one of them. The German caricaturist seemed unable to represent his enemies except in extremely tight trousers or in none; he was equally unable to represent them without thrusting a sword or bayonet, spluttering blood, into the more indelicate parts of their persons. This was the *leit-motif* of the war as the German humorist presented it. "But," said Mr. Britling, "these things can't represent anything like the general state of mind in Germany."

"They do," said his friend.

"But it's blind fury—at the dirt-throwing stage."

"The whole of Germany is in that blind futy," said his friend. "While we are going about astonished and rather incredulous about this war, and still rather inclined to laugh, that's the state of mind of Germany. . . . There's a sort of deliberation in it. They think it gives them strength. They *want* to foam at the mouth. They do their utmost to foam more. They write themselves up. Have you heard of the 'Hymn of Hate'?"

"There was a translation of it in last week's *Spectator*. . . . This is the sort of thing we are trying to fight in good temper and without extravagance. Listen, Britling!

> "*You* will we hate with a lasting hate;
> We will never forego our hate—
> Hate by water and hate by land,
> Hate of the head and hate of the hand,
> Hate of the hammer and hate of the crown,
> Hate of seventy millions, choking down;
> We love as one, we hate as one,
> We have *one* foe, and one alone—
> ENGLAND!"

He read on to the end.

"Well," he said when he had finished reading, "what do you think of it?"

"I want to feel his bumps," said Mr. Britling after a pause. "It's incomprehensible."

"They're singing that up and down Germany. Lissauer, I hear, has been decorated. . . .

"It's—stark malignity," said Mr. Britling. "What have we done?"

"It's colossal. What is to happen to the world if these people prevail?"

"I can't believe it—even with this evidence before me. . . . No! I want to feel their bumps. . . ."

§ 3

"You see," said Mr. Britling, trying to get it into focus, "I have known quite decent Germans. There must be some sort of misunderstanding. . . . I wonder what makes them hate us. There seems to me no reason in it."

"I think it is just thoroughness," said his friend. "They are at war. To be at war is to hate."

"That isn't at all my idea."

"We're not a thorough people. When we think of anything, we also think of its opposite. When we adopt an opinion we also take in a provisional idea that it is probably nearly as wrong as it is right. We are—atmospheric. They are concrete. . . . All this filthy, vile, unjust and cruel stuff is honest genuine war. We pretend war does not hurt. They know better. . . . The Germans are a simple honest people. It is their virtue. Possibly it is their only virtue. . . ."

§ 4

Mr. Britling was only one of a multitude who wanted to feel the bumps of Germany at that time. The effort to understand a people who had suddenly become incredible was indeed one of the most remarkable facts in English intellectual life during the opening phases of the war. The English state of mind was unlimited astonishment. There was an enormous sale of any German books that seemed likely to illuminate the mystery of this amazing concentration of hostility; the works of Bernhardi, Treitschke, Nietzsche, Houston Stewart Chamberlain, became the material of countless articles and interminable discussions. One saw little clerks on the way to the office and workmen going home after their work earnestly reading these remarkable writers. They were asking, just as Mr. Britling was asking, what it was the British Empire had struck against. They were trying to account for this wild storm of hostility that was coming at them out of Central Europe.

It was a natural next stage to this, when after all it became manifest that instead of there being a liberal and reluctant Germany at the back of imperialism and Junkerdom, there was apparently one solid, enthusiastic people, to suppose that the Germans were in some distinctive way evil, that they were racially more envious, arrogant, and aggressive than the rest of mankind. Upon that supposition a great number of English people settled. They concluded that the Germans had a peculiar devil of their own—and had to be treated accordingly. That was the second stage in the process of national apprehension, and it was marked by the first beginnings of a spy hunt, by the first denunciation of naturalised aliens, and by some anti-German rioting among the mixed alien population in the East End. Most of the bakers in the East End of London were Germans, and for some months after the war began they went on with their trade unmolested. Now many of these shops were wrecked. . . . It was only in October that the British gave these first signs of a sense that they were fighting not merely political Germany but the Germans.

But the idea of a peculiar malignity in the German quality as a key to the broad issue of the war was even less satisfactory and less permanent in Mr. Britling's mind than his first crude opposition of militarism and a peaceful humanity as embodied respectively in the Central Powers and the Russo-Western alliance. It led logically to the conclusion that the extermination of the German peoples was the only security for the general amiability of the world, a conclusion that appealed but weakly to his essential kindliness. After all, the Germans he had met and seen were neither cruel nor hate-inspired. He came back to that obstinately. From the harshness and vileness of the printed word and the unclean picture, he fell back upon the flesh and blood, the humanity and sterling worth of—as a sample—young Heinrich.

Who was moreover a thoroughly German young German—a thoroughly Prussian young Prussian.

At times young Heinrich alone stood between Mr. Britling and the belief that Germany and the whole German race was essentially wicked, essentially a canting robber nation. Young Heinrich became a sort of advocate for his people before the tribunal of Mr. Britling's mind. (And on his shoulder sat an absurdly pampered squirrel.) Heinrich's fresh pink sedulous face, very earnest, adjusting his glasses, saying "Please," intervened and insisted upon an arrest of judgment. . . .

Since the young man's departure he had sent two postcards of greeting directly to the "Familie Britling," and one letter through the friendly intervention of Mr. Britling's American publisher. Once also he sent a message through a friend in Norway. The postcards simply recorded stages in the passage of a distraught pacifist across Holland to his enrolment. The letter by way of America came two months later. He had been converted into a combatant with extreme rapidity. He had been trained for three weeks, had spent a fortnight in hospital with a severe cold, and had then gone to Belgium as a transport driver—his father had been a horse-dealer and he was familiar with horses. "If anything happens to me," he wrote, "please send my violin at least very carefully to my mother." It was characteristic that he reported himself as very comfortably quartered in Courtrai with "very nice people." The niceness involved restraints. "Only never," he added, "do we talk about the war. It is better not to do so." He mentioned the violin also in the later communication through Norway. Therein he lamented the lost flesh-pots of Courtrai. He had been in Posen, and now he was in the Carpathians, up to his knees in snow and very "uncomfortable." . . .

And then abruptly all news from him ceased.

Month followed month, and no further letter came.

"Something has happened to him. Perhaps he is a prisoner." . . .

"I hope our little Heinrich hasn't got seriously damaged. . . . He may be wounded. . . ."

"Or perhaps they stop his letters. . . . Very probably they stop his letters."

§ 5

Mr. Britling would sit in his arm-chair and stare at his fire, and recall conflicting memories of Germany—of a pleasant land, of friendly people. He had spent many a jolly holiday there. So recently as 1911 all the Britling family had gone up the Rhine from Rotterdam, had visited a string of great cities and stayed for a cheerful month of sunshine at Neunkirchen in the Odenwald.

The little village perches high among the hills and woods, and at its very centre is the inn and the lindentree and—Adam Meyer. Or at least Adam Meyer *was* there. Whether he is there now, only the spirit of change can tell; if he live to be a hundred no friendly English will ever again come tramping along by the track of the Blaue Dreiecke or the Weisse Streiche to enjoy his hospitality; there are rivers of blood between, and a thousand memories of hate. . . .

It was a village distended with hospitalities. Not only the inn but all the houses about the place of the lindentree, the shoemaker's, the postmistress's, the white house beyond, every house indeed except the pastor's house, were full of Adam Meyer's summer guests. And about it and over it went and soared Adam Meyer, seeing they ate well, seeing they rested well, seeing they had music and did not miss the moonlight—a host who forgot profit in hospitality, an innkeeper with the passion of an artist for his inn.

Music, moonlight, the simple German sentiment, the hearty German voices, the great picnic in a Stuhl Wagen, the orderly round games the boys played with the German children, and the tramps and confidences Hugh had with Kurt and Karl, and at last a crowning jollification, a dance, with some gipsy musicians discovered by Mr. Britling, when the Germans taught the English various entertaining sports with baskets and potatoes and forfeits and the English introduced the Germans to the licence of the two-step. And everybody sang "Britannia, Rule the Waves," and "Deutschland, Deutschland über Alles," and Adam Meyer got on a chair and made a tremendous speech more in dialect than ever, and there was much drinking of beer and sirops in the moonlight under the linden. . . .

Afterwards there had been a periodic sending of postcards and greetings, which indeed only the war had ended.

Right pleasant people those Germans had been, sun and green-leaf lovers, for whom "Frisch Auf" seemed the most natural of national cries. Mr. Britling thought of the individual Germans who had made up the assembly. Of the men's amusingly fierce little hats of green and blue with the inevitable feather thrust perkily into the hatband behind, of the kindly plumpnesses behind their turned-up moustaches, of the blonde, sedentary women, very wise about the comforts of life and very kind to the children, of their earnest pleasure in landscape and Art and Great Writers, of their general frequent desire to sing, of their plasticity under the directing hands of Adam Meyer. He thought of the mellow south German landscape, rolling away broad and fair, of the little clean red-roofed townships, the old castles, the big prosperous farms, the neatly marked pedestrian routes, the hospitable inns, and the artless abundant Aussichtthurms. . . .

He saw all those memories now through a veil of indescribable sadness—as of a world lost, gone down like the cities of Lyonesse beneath deep seas. . . .

Right pleasant people in a sunny land! Yet here pressing relentlessly upon his mind were the murders of Visé, the massacres of Dinant, the massacres of Louvain, murder red-handed and horrible upon an inoffensive people, foully invaded, foully treated; murder done with a sickening cant of righteousness and racial pretension. . . .

The two pictures would not stay steadily in his mind together. When he thought of the broken faith that had poured those slaughtering hosts into the decent peace of Belgium, that had smashed her cities, burned her villages and filled the pretty gorges of the Ardennes with blood and smoke and terror, he was flooded with self-righteous indignation, a self-righteous indignation that was indeed entirely Teutonic in its quality, that for a time drowned out his former friendship and every kindly disposition towards Germany, that inspired him with destructive impulses, and obsessed him with a desire to hear of death and more death and yet death in every German town and home. . . .

§ 6

It will be an incredible thing to the happier reader of a coming age—if ever this poor record of experience reaches a reader in the days to come—to learn how much of the mental life of Mr. Britling was occupied at this time with the mere horror and atrocity of warfare. It is idle and hopeless to speculate now how that future reader will envisage this war; it may take on broad dramatic outlines, it may seem a thing just, logical, necessary, the burning of many barriers, the destruction of many obstacles. Mr. Britling was too near to the dirt and pain and heat for any such broad landscape consolations. Every day some new detail of evil beat into his mind. Perhaps it would be the artless story of a refugee. There was a girl from Alost in the village, for example, who had heard the fusillade that meant the shooting of citizens, the shooting of people she had known, she had seen the still blood-stained wall against which two murdered cousins had died, the streaked sand along which their bodies had been dragged; three German soldiers had been quartered in her house with her and her invalid mother, and had talked freely of the massacres in which they had been employed. One of them was in civil life a young schoolmaster, and he had had, he said, to kill a woman and a baby. The girl had been incredulous. Yes, he had done so! Of course he had done so! His officer had made him do it, had stood over him. He could do nothing but obey. But since then he had been unable to sleep, unable to forget.

"We had to punish the people," he said. "They had fired on us."

And besides, his officer had been drunk. It had been impossible to argue. His officer had an unrelenting character at all times. . . .

Over and over again Mr. Britling would try to imagine that young schoolmaster soldier at Alost. He imagined him with a weak staring face and watery blue eyes behind his glasses, and that memory of murder. . . .

Then again it would be some incident of death and mutilation in Antwerp, that Van der Pant described to him.

The Germans in Belgium were shooting women frequently, not simply for grave spying but for trivial offences. . . . . Then came the battleship raid on Whitby and Scarborough, and the killing among other victims of a number of children on their way to school. This shocked Mr. Britling absurdly, much more than the Belgian crimes had done. They were *English* children. At home! . . . The drowning of a great number of people on a torpedoed ship full of refugees from Flanders filled his mind with pitiful imaginings for days. The Zeppelin raids, with their slow crescendo of blood-stained futility, began before the end of 1914. . . . It was small consolation for Mr. Britling to reflect that English homes and women and children were, after all, undergoing only the same kind of experience that our ships have inflicted scores of times in the past upon innocent people in the villages of Africa and Polynesia. . . .

Each month the war grew bitterer and more cruel. Early in 1915 the Germans began their submarine war, and for a time Mr. Britling's concern was chiefly for the sailors and passengers of the ships destroyed. He noted with horror the increasing indisposition of the German submarines to give any notice to their victims; he did not understand the grim reasons that were turning every submarine attack into a desperate challenge of death. For the Germans under the seas had pitted themselves against a sea power far more resourceful, more steadfast and skilful, sterner and more silent, than their own. It was not for many months that Mr. Britling learned the realities of the submarine blockade. Submarine after submarine went out of the German harbours into the North Sea, never to return. No prisoners were reported, no boasting was published by the British fishers of men; U-boat after U-boat vanished into a chilling mystery. . . . Only later did Mr. Britling begin to hear whispers and form ideas of the noiseless, suffocating grip that sought through the waters for its prey.

The *Falaba* crime, in which the German sailors were reported to have jeered at the drowning victims in the water, was followed by the sinking of the *Lusitania*. At that a wave of real anger swept through the Empire. Hate was begetting hate at last. There were violent riots in Great Britain and in South Africa. Wretched little German hairdressers and bakers and so forth fled for their lives, to pay for the momentary satisfaction of the Kaiser and Herr Ballin. Scores of German homes in England were wrecked and looted; hundreds of Germans maltreated. War is war. Hard upon the *Lusitania* storm came the publication of the Bryce Report, with its relentless array of witnesses, its particulars of countless acts of cruelty and arrogant unreason and uncleanness in Belgium and the occupied territory of France. Came also the gasping torture of "gas," the use of flame jets, and a new exacerbation of the savagery of the actual fighting. For a time it seemed as though the taking of prisoners along the western front would cease. Tales of torture and mutilation, tales of the kind that arise nowhere and out of nothing, and poison men's minds to the most pitiless retaliations, drifted along the opposing fronts. . . .

The realities were evil enough without any rumours. Over various dinner-tables Mr. Britling heard this and that first-hand testimony of harshness and spite. One story that stuck in his memory was of British prisoners on the journey into Germany being put apart at a station from their French companions in misfortune, and forced to "run the gauntlet" back to their train between the fists and bayonets of files of German soldiers. And there were convincing stories of the same prisoners robbed of overcoats in bitter weather, baited with dogs, separated from their countrymen, and thrust among Russians and Poles with whom they could hold no speech. So Lissauer's Hate Song bore its fruit in a thousand cruelties to wounded and defenceless men. The English had cheated great Germany of another easy victory like that of '71. They had to be punished. That was all too plainly the psychological process. At one German station a woman had got out of a train and crossed a platform to spit on the face of a wounded Englishman. . . . And there was no monopoly of such things on either side. At some journalistic gathering Mr. Britling met a little white-faced, resolute lady who had recently been nursing in the north of France. She told of wounded men lying among the coal of coal-sheds, of a shortage of nurses and every sort of material, of an absolute refusal to permit any share in such things to reach the German "swine.". . . "Why have they come here? Let our own boys have it first. Why couldn't they stay in their own country? Let the filth die."

Two soldiers impressed to carry a wounded German officer on a stretcher had given him a "joy ride," pitching him up and down as one tosses a man in a blanket. "He was lucky to get off with that." . . .

"All *our* men aren't angels," said a cheerful young captain back from the front. "If you had heard a little group of our East London boys talking of what they meant to do when they got into Germany, you'd feel anxious. . . ."

"But that was just talk," said Mr. Britling weakly, after a pause. . . .

There were times when Mr. Britling's mind was imprisoned beyond any hope of escape amidst such monstrous realities. . . .

He was ashamed of his one secret consolation. For nearly two years yet Hugh could not go out to it. There would surely be peace before that. . . .

§ 7

Tormenting the thought of Mr. Britling almost more acutely than this growing tale of stupidly inflicted suffering and waste and sheer destruction was the collapse of the British mind from its first fine phase of braced-up effort into a state of bickering futility.

Too long had British life been corrupted by the fictions of loyalty to an uninspiring and alien Court, of national piety in an official Church, of freedom in a politician-rigged State, of justice in an economic system where the advertiser, the sweater and usurer had a hundred advantages over the producer and artisan, to maintain itself now steadily at any high pitch of heroic endeavour. It had bought its comfort with the demoralisation of its servants. It had no completely honest organs; its spirit was clogged by its accumulated insincerities. Brought at last face to face with a bitter hostility and a powerful and unscrupulous enemy, an enemy socialistic, scientific and efficient to an unexampled degree, it seemed indeed to be inspired for a time by an unwonted energy and unanimity. Youth and the common people shone. The sons of every class went out to fight and die, full of a splendid dream of this war. Easy-going vanished from the foreground of the picture. But only to creep back again as the first inspiration passed. Presently the older men, the seasoned politicians, the owners and hucksters, the charming women and the habitual consumers, began to recover from this blaze of moral exaltation. Old habits of mind and procedure reasserted themselves. The war which had begun so dramatically missed its climax; there was neither heroic swift defeat nor heroic swift victory. There was indecision; the most trying test of all for an undisciplined people. There were great spaces of uneventful

313

fatigue. Before the Battle of the Yser had fully developed the dramatic quality had gone out of the war. It had ceased to be either a tragedy or a triumph; for both sides it became a monstrous strain and wasting. It had become a wearisome thrusting against a pressure of evils. . . .

Under that strain the dignity of England broke, and revealed a malignity less focused and intense than the German, but perhaps even more distressing. No paternal government had organised the British spirit for patriotic ends; it became now peevish and impatient, like some ill-trained man who is sick, it directed itself no longer against the enemy alone but fitfully against imagined traitors and shirkers; it wasted its energies in a deepening and spreading net of internal squabbles and accusations. Now it was the wily indolence of the Prime Minister, now it was the German culture of the Lord Chancellor, now the imaginative enterprise of the First Lord of the Admiralty that focused a vindictive campaign. There began a hunt for spies and for suspects of German origin in every quarter except the highest; a denunciation now of "traitors," now of people with imaginations, now of scientific men, now of the personal friends of the Commander-in-Chief, now of this group and then of that group. . . . Every day Mr. Britling read his three or four newspapers with a deepening disappointment.

When he turned from the newspaper to his post, he would find the anonymous letter-writer had been busy. . . .

Perhaps Mr. Britling had remarked that Germans were after all human beings, or that if England had listened to Matthew Arnold in the eighties our officers by this time might have added efficiency to their courage and good temper. Perhaps he had himself put a touch of irritant acid into his comment. Back flared the hate. "Who are *you*, sir? What are *you*, sir? What right have *you*, sir? What claim have *you*, sir?" . . .

§ 8

"Life had a wrangling birth. On the head of every one of us rests the ancestral curse of fifty million murders."

So Mr. Britling's thoughts shaped themselves in words as he prowled one night in March, chill and melancholy, across a rushy meadow under an overcast sky. The death squeal of some little beast caught suddenly in a distant copse had set loose this train of thought. "Life struggling under a birth curse?" he thought. "How nearly I come back at times to the Christian theology! . . . And then, Redemption by the shedding of blood."

"Life, like a rebellious child, struggling out of the control of the hate which made it what it is."

But that was Mr. Britling's idea of Gnosticism, not of orthodox Christianity. He went off for a time into faded reminiscences of theological reading. What had been the Gnostic idea? That the God of the Old Testament was the Devil of the New? But that had been the idea of the Manichæans! . . .

Mr. Britling, between the black hedges, came back presently from his attempts to recall his youthful inquiries into man's ancient speculations, to the enduring riddles that have outlasted a thousand speculations. Has hate been necessary, and is it still necessary, and will it always be necessary? Is all life a war for ever? The rabbit is nimble, lives keenly, is prevented from degenerating into a diseased crawling eater of herbs by the incessant ferret. Without the ferret of war, what would life become? . . . War is murder truly, but is not Peace decay?

It was during these prowling nights in the first winter of the war that Mr. Britling planned a new writing that was to go whole abysses beneath the facile superficiality of "And Now War Ends." It was to be called the "Anatomy of Hate." It was to deal very faithfully with the function of hate as a corrective to inefficiency. So long as men were slack, men must be fierce. This conviction pressed upon him. . . .

In spite of his detestation of war, Mr. Britling found it impossible to maintain that any sort of peace state was better than a state of war. If wars produced destructions and cruelties, peace could produce indolence, perversity, greedy accumulation and selfish indulgences. War is discipline for evil, but peace may be relaxation from good. The poor man may be as wretched in peace-time as in war-time. The gathering forces of an evil peace, the malignity and waste of war, are but obverse and reverse of the medal of ill-adjusted human relationships. Was there no Greater Peace possible; not a mere recuperative pause in killing and destruction, but a phase of noble and creative living, a phase of building, of discovery, of beauty and research? He remembered, as one remembers the dead, dreams he had once dreamt of the great cities, the splendid freedoms, of a coming age, of marvellous enlargements of human faculty, of a coming science that would be light and of art that could be power. . . .

But would that former peace have ever risen to this? . . .

After all, had such visions ever been more than idle dreams? Had the war done more than unmask reality? . . .

He came to a gate and leaned over it.

The darkness drizzled about him; he turned up his collar and watched the dim shapes of trees and hedges gather out of the night to meet the dismal dawn. He was cold and hungry and weary.

He may have drowsed; at least he had a vision, very real and plain, a vision very different from any dream of Utopia.

It seemed to him that suddenly a mine burst under a great ship at sea, that men shouted and women sobbed and cowered, and flares played upon the rain-pitted black waves; and then the picture changed and showed a battle upon land, and searchlights were flickering through the rain and shells flashed luridly, and men darkly seen in silhouette against red flames ran with fixed bayonets and slipped and floundered over the mud, and at last, shouting thinly through the wind, leaped down into the enemy trenches. . . .

And then he was alone again staring over a wet black field towards a dim crest of shapeless trees.

§ 9

Abruptly and shockingly, this malignity of warfare, which had been so far only a festering cluster of reports and stories and rumours and suspicions, stretched out its arm into Essex and struck a barb of grotesque cruelty into the very heart of Mr. Britling. Late one afternoon came a telegram from Filmington-on-Sea, where Aunt Wilshire had been recovering her temper in a boarding-house after a round of visits in Yorkshire and the moorlands. And she had been "very seriously injured" by an overnight German air-raid. It was a raid that had not been even mentioned in the morning's papers. She had asked to see him.

It was, ran the compressed telegraphic phrase, "advisable come at once."

Mrs. Britling helped him pack a bag, and came with him to the station in order to drive the car back to the Dower House;

for the gardener's boy who had hitherto attended to these small duties had now gone off as an unskilled labourer to some munition works at Chelmsford. Mr. Britling sat in the slow train that carried him across country to the junction for Filmington, and failed altogether to realise what had happened to the old lady. He had an absurd feeling that it was characteristic of her to intervene in affairs in this manner. She had always been so tough and unbent an old lady that until he saw her he could not imagine her as being really seriously and pitifully hurt. . . .

But he found her in the hospital very much hurt indeed. She had been smashed in some complicated manner that left the upper part of her body intact, and lying slantingly upon pillows. Over the horror of bandaged broken limbs and tormented flesh below sheets and a counterpane were drawn. Morphia had been injected, he understood, to save her from pain, but presently it might be necessary for her to suffer. She lay up in her bed with an effect of being enthroned, very white and still, her strong profile with its big nose and her straggling hair and a certain dignity gave her the appearance of some very important, very old man, of an aged pope, for instance, rather than of an old woman. She had made no remark after they had set her and dressed her and put her to bed except "send for Hughie Britling, The Dower House, Matching's Easy. He is the best of the bunch." She had repeated the address and this commendation firmly over and over again, in large print as it were, even after they had assured her that a telegram had been despatched.

In the night, they said, she had talked of him.

He was not sure at first that she knew of his presence.

"Here I am, Aunt Wilshire," he said.

She gave no sign.

"Your nephew Hugh."

"Mean and preposterous," she said very distinctly.

But she was not thinking of Mr. Britling. She was talking of something else.

She was saying: "It should not have been known I was here. There are spies everywhere. Everywhere. There is a spy now—or a lump very like a spy. They pretend it is a hot-water bottle. Pretext. . . . Oh, yes! I admit—absurd. But I have been pursued by spies. Endless spies. Endless, endless spies. Their devices are almost incredible. . . . He has never forgiven me. . . .

"All this on account of a carpet. A palace carpet. Over which I had no control. I spoke my mind. He knew I knew of it. I never concealed it. So I was hunted. For years he had meditated revenge. Now he has it. But at what a cost! And they call him Emperor. Emperor!

"His arm is withered; his son—imbecile. He will die—without dignity. . . ."

Her voice weakened, but it was evident she wanted to say something more.

"I'm here," said Mr. Britling. "Your nephew Hughie."

She listened.

"Can you understand me?" he asked.

She became suddenly an earnest, tender human being. "My dear!" she said, and seemed to search for something in her mind and fail to find it.

"You have always understood me," she said.

"You have always been a good boy to me, Hughie," she said, rather vacantly, and added after some moments of still reflection, "*au fond.*"

After that she was silent for some minutes, and took no notice of his whispers.

Then she recollected what had been in her mind. She put out a hand that sought for Mr. Britling's sleeve.

"Hughie!"

"I'm here, Auntie," said Mr. Britling. "I'm here."

"Don't let him get at *your* Hughie. . . . Too good for it, dear. Oh! much—much too good. . . . People let these wars and excitements run away with them. . . . They put too much into them. . . . They aren't—they aren't worth it. Don't let him get at your Hughie."

"No!"

"You understand me, Hughie?"

"Perfectly, Auntie."

"Then don't forget it. Ever."

She had said what she wanted to say. She had made her testament. She closed her eyes. He was amazed to find this grotesque old creature had suddenly become beautiful, in that silvery vein of beauty one sometimes finds in very old men. She was exalted as great artists will sometimes exalt the portraits of the aged. He was moved to kiss her forehead.

Then came a little tug at his sleeve.

"I think that is enough," said the nurse, who had stood forgotten at his elbow.

"But I can come again?"

"Perhaps."

She indicated departure by a movement of her hand.

§ 10

The next day Aunt Wilshire was unconscious of her visitor.

They had altered her position so that she lay now horizontally, staring inflexibly at the ceiling and muttering queer old disconnected things.

The Windsor Castle carpet story was still running through her mind, but mixed up with it now were scraps of the current newspaper controversies about the conduct of the war. And she was still thinking of the dynastic aspects of the war. And of spies. She had something upon her mind about the King's more German aunts.

"As a precaution," she said, "as a precaution. Watch them all. . . . The Princess Christian. . . . Laying foundation-stones. . . . Cement. . . . Guns. Or else why should they always be laying foundation-stones? . . . Always. . . . Why? . . . Hushed up. . . .

"None of these things," she said, "in the newspapers. They ought to be."

And then after an interval, very distinctly, "The Duke of Wellington. My ancestor—in reality. . . . Publish and be damned."

After that she lay still. . . .

The doctors and nurses could hold out only very faint hopes to Mr. Britling's enquiries; they said indeed it was astonishing that she was still alive.

And about seven o'clock that evening she died. . . .

§ 11

Mr. Britling, after he had looked at his dead cousin for the last time, wandered for an hour or so about the silent little watering-place before he returned to his hotel. There was no one to talk to and nothing else to do but to think of her death.

The night was cold and bleak, but full of stars. He had already mastered the local topography, and he knew now exactly where all the bombs that had been showered upon the place had fallen. Here was the corner of blackened walls and roasted beams where three wounded horses had been burned alive in a barn, here the row of houses, some smashed, some almost intact, where a mutilated child had screamed for two hours before she could be rescued from the débris that had pinned her down, and taken to the hospital. Everywhere by the dim light of the shaded street-lamps he could see the black holes and gaps of broken windows; sometimes abundant, sometimes rare and exceptional, among otherwise uninjured dwellings. Many of the victims he had visited in the little cottage hospital where Aunt Wilshire had just died. She was the eleventh dead. Altogether fifty-seven people had been killed or injured in this brilliant German action. They were all civilians, and only twelve were men.

Two Zeppelins had come in from over the sea, and had been fired at by an anti-aircraft gun coming on an automobile from Ipswich. The first intimation the people of the town had had of the raid was the report of this gun. Many had run out to see what was happening. It was doubtful if any one had really seen the Zeppelins, though every one testified to the sound of their engines. Then suddenly the bombs had come streaming down. Only six had made hits upon houses or people; the rest had fallen ruinously and very close together on the local golf-links, and at least half had not exploded at all and did not seem to have been released to explode.

A third at least of the injured people had been in bed when destruction came upon them.

The story was like a page from some fantastic romance of Jules Verne's; the peace of the little old town, the people going to bed, the quiet streets, the quiet starry sky, and then for ten minutes an uproar of guns and shells, a clatter of breaking glass, and then a fire here, a fire there, a child's voice pitched high by pain and terror, scared people going to and fro with lanterns, and the sky empty again, the raiders gone. . . .

Five minutes before, Aunt Wilshire had been sitting in the boarding-house drawing-room playing a great stern "Patience," the Emperor Patience ("Napoleon, my dear!—not that Potsdam creature") that took hours to do. Five minutes later she was a thing of elemental terror and agony, bleeding wounds and shattered bones, plunging about in the darkness amidst a heap of wreckage. And already the German airmen were buzzing away to sea again, proud of themselves, pleased no doubt—like boys who have thrown a stone through a window, beating their way back to thanks and rewards, to iron crosses and the proud embraces of Fraus and Fräuleins. . . .

For the first time it seemed to Mr. Britling he really saw the immediate horror of war, the dense cruel stupidity of the business, plain and close. It was as if he had never perceived anything of the sort before, as if he had been dealing with stories, pictures, shows and representations that he knew to be shams. But that this dear, absurd old creature, this thing of home, this being of familiar humours and familiar irritations, should be torn to pieces, left in torment like a smashed mouse over which an automobile has passed, brought the whole business to a raw and quivering focus. Not a soul among all those who had been rent and torn and tortured in this agony of millions, but was to any one who understood and had been near to it, in some way lovable, in some way laughable, in some way worthy of respect and care. Poor Aunt Wilshire was but the sample thrust in his face of all this mangled multitude, whose green-white lips had sweated in anguish, whose broken bones had thrust raggedly through red, dripping flesh. . . . The detested features of the German Crown Prince jerked into the centre of Mr. Britling's picture. The young man stood in his dapper uniform and grinned under his long nose, carrying himself jauntily, proud of his extreme importance to so many lives. . . .

And for a while Mr. Britling could do nothing but rage.

"Devils they are!" he cried to the stars.

"Devils! Devilish fools rather. Cruel blockheads. Apes with all science in their hands! My God! but *we will teach them a lesson yet!*" . . .

That was the key of his mood for an hour of aimless wandering, wandering that was only checked at last by a sentinel who turned him back towards the town. . . .

He wandered, muttering. He found great comfort in scheming vindictive destruction for countless Germans. He dreamt of swift armoured aeroplanes swooping down upon the flying airship, and sending it reeling earthward, the men screaming. He imagined a shattered Zeppelin staggering earthward in the fields behind the Dower House, and how he would himself run out with a spade and smite the Germans down. "Quarter indeed! Kamerad! Take *that*, you foul murderer!"

In the dim light the sentinel saw the retreating figure of Mr. Britling make an extravagant gesture, and wondered what it might mean. Signalling? What ought an intelligent sentry to do? Let fly at him? Arrest him? . . . Take no notice? . . .

Mr. Britling was at that moment killing Count Zeppelin and beating out his brains. Count Zeppelin was killed that night and the German Emperor was assassinated; a score of lesser victims were offered up to the *manes* of Aunt Wilshire; there were memorable cruelties before the wrath and bitterness of Mr. Britling was appeased. And then suddenly he had had enough of these thoughts; they were thrust aside, they vanished out of his mind.

§ 12

All the while that Mr. Britling had been indulging in these imaginative slaughterings and spending the tears and hate that had gathered in his heart, his reason had been sitting apart and above the storm, like the sun waiting above thunder, like a wise nurse watching and patient above the wild passions of a child. And all the time his reason had been maintaining silently and firmly, without shouting, without speech, that the men who had made this hour were indeed not devils, were no more devils than Mr. Britling was a devil, but sinful men of like nature with himself, hard, stupid, caught in the same web of circumstance. "Kill them in your passion if you will," said reason, "but understand. This thing was done neither by devils nor fools, but by a conspiracy of foolish motives, by the weak acquiescences of the clever, by a crime that was no man's crime but the natural necessary outcome of the ineffectiveness, the blind motives and muddle-headedness of all mankind."

So reason maintained her thesis, like a light above the head of Mr. Britling at which he would not look, while he hewed airmen to quivering rags with a spade that he had sharpened, then stifled German princes with their own poison-gas, given slowly and as painfully as possible. "And what of the towns *our* ships have bombarded?" asked reason unheeded. "What of those Tasmanians *our* people utterly swept away?

"What of French machine-guns in the Atlas?" reason pressed the case. "Of Himalayan villages burning? Of the things we did in China? Especially of the things we did in China. . . ."

Mr. Britling gave no heed to that.

"The Germans in China were worse than we were," he threw out. . . .

He was maddened by the thought of the Zeppelin making off, high and far in the sky, a thing dwindling to nothing among the stars, and the thought of those murderers escaping him. Time after time he stood still and shook his fist at Boötes, slowly sweeping up the sky. . . .

And at last, sick and wretched, he sat down on a seat upon the deserted parade under the stars, close to the soughing of the invisible sea below. . . .

His mind drifted back once more to those ancient heresies of the Gnostics and the Manichæans which saw the God of the World as altogether evil, which sought only to escape by the utmost abstinences and evasions and perversions from the black wickedness of being. For a while his soul sank down into the uncongenial darknesses of these creeds of despair. "I who have loved life," he murmured, and could have believed for a time that he wished he had never had a son. . . .

Is the whole scheme of nature evil? Is life in its essence cruel? Is man stretched quivering upon the table of the eternal vivisector for no end—and without pity?

These were thoughts that Mr. Britling had never faced before the war. They came to him now, and they came only to be rejected by the inherent quality of his mind. For weeks, consciously and subconsciously, his mind had been grappling with this riddle. He had thought of it during his lonely prowlings as a special constable; it had flung itself in monstrous symbols across the dark canvas of his dreams. "Is there indeed a devil of pure cruelty? Does any creature, even the very cruelest of creatures, really apprehend the pain it causes, or inflict it for the sake of the infliction?" He summoned a score of memories, a score of imaginations, to bear their witness before the tribunal of his mind. He forgot cold and loneliness in this speculation. He sat, trying all Being, on this score, under the cold indifferent stars.

He thought of certain instances of boyish cruelty that had horrified him in his own boyhood, and it was clear to him that indeed it was not cruelty, it was curiosity, dense-textured, thick-skinned, so that it could not feel even the anguish of a blinded cat. Those boys who had wrung his childish soul to nigh intolerable misery had not indeed been tormenting so much as observing torment, testing life as wantonly as one breaks thin ice in the early days of winter. In very much cruelty the real motive is surely no worse than that obtuse curiosity; a mere step of understanding, a mere quickening of the nerves and mind, makes it impossible. But that is not true of all or most cruelty. Most cruelty has something else in it, something more than the clumsy plunging into experience of the hobbledehoy; it is vindictive or indignant; it is never tranquil and sensuous; it draws its incentive, however crippled and monstrous the justification may be, from something punitive in man's instinct, something therefore that implies a sense, however misguided, of righteousness and vindication. That factor is present even in spite; when some vile or atrocious thing is done out of envy or malice, that envy and malice has in it always—*always?* Yes, always—a genuine condemnation of the hated thing as an unrighteous thing, as an unjust usurpation, as an inexcusable privilege, as a sinful overconfidence. Those men in the airship?—he was coming to that. He found himself asking himself whether it was possible for a human being to do any cruel act without an excuse—or, at least, without the feeling of excusability. And in the case of these Germans and the outrages they had committed and the retaliations they had provoked, he perceived that always there was the element of a perceptible if inadequate justification. Just as there would be if presently he were to maltreat a fallen German airman. There was anger in their vileness. These Germans were an unsubtle people, a people in the worst and best sense of the words, plain and honest; they were prone to moral indignation; and moral indignation is the mother of most of the cruelty in the world. They perceived the indolence of the English and Russians, they perceived their disregard of science and system, they could not perceive the longer reach of these greater races, and it seemed to them that the mission of Germany was to chastise and correct this laxity. Surely, they had argued, God was not on the side of those who kept an untilled field. So they had butchered these old ladies and slaughtered these children just to show us the consequences:

> "All along of dirtiness, all along of mess,
> All along of doing things rather more or less."

The very justification our English poet has found for a thousand overbearing actions in the East! "Forget not order and the real," that was the underlying message of bomb and gas and submarine. After all, what right had we English *not* to have a gun or an aeroplane fit to bring down that Zeppelin ignominiously and conclusively? Had we not undertaken Empire? Were we not the leaders of great nations? Had we indeed much right to complain if our imperial pose was flouted? "There, at least," said Mr. Britling's reason, "is one of the lines of thought that brought that unseen cruelty out of the night high over the houses of Filmington-on-Sea. That, in a sense, is the cause of this killing. Cruel it is and abominable, yes, but is it altogether cruel? Hasn't it, after all, a sort of stupid rightness?—isn't it a stupid reaction to an indolence at least equally stupid?"

What was this rightness that lurked below cruelty? What was the inspiration of this pressure of spite, this anger that was aroused by ineffective gentleness and kindliness? Was it indeed an altogether evil thing; was it not rather an impulse, blind as yet, but in its ultimate quality *as good as mercy*, greater perhaps in its ultimate values than mercy?

This idea had been gathering in Mr. Britling's mind for many weeks; it had been growing and taking shape as he wrote, making experimental beginnings for his essay, "The Anatomy of Hate." Is there not, he now asked himself plainly, a creative and corrective impulse behind all hate? Is not this malignity indeed only the ape-like precursor of the great disciplines of a creative state?

The invincible hopefulness of his sanguine temperament had now got Mr. Britling well out of the pessimistic pit again. Already he had been on the verge of his phrase while wandering across the rushy fields towards Market Saffron; now it came to him again like a legitimate monarch returning from exile.

"When hate shall have become creative energy. . . .

"Hate which passes into creative power; gentleness which is indolence and the herald of euthanasia. . . .

"Pity is but a passing grace; for mankind will not always be pitiful."

But meanwhile, meanwhile. . . . How long were men so to mingle wrong with right, to be energetic without mercy and kindly without energy? . . .

For a time Mr. Britling sat on the lonely parade under the stars and in the sound of the sea, brooding upon these ideas.

His mind could make no further steps. It had worked for its spell. His rage had ebbed away now altogether. His despair was no longer infinite. But the world was dark and dreadful still. It seemed none the less dark because at the end there was a gleam of light. It was a gleam of light far beyond the limits of his own life, far beyond the life of his son. It had no balm for these sufferings. Between it and himself stretched the weary generations still to come, generations of bickering and accusation, greed and faint-heartedness, the half-truth and the hasty blow. And all those years would be full of pitiful things, such pitiful things as the blackened ruins in the town behind, the little grey-faced corpses, the lives torn and wasted, the hopes extinguished and the gladness gone. . . .

He was no longer thinking of the Germans as diabolical. They were human; they had a case. It was a stupid case, but our case, too, was a stupid case. How stupid were all our cases! What was it we missed? Something, he felt, very close to us, and very elusive. Something that would resolve a hundred tangled oppositions. . . .

His mind hung at that. Back upon his consciousness came crowding the horrors and desolations that had been his daily food now for three-quarters of a year. He groaned aloud. He struggled against that renewed envelopment of his spirit. "Oh, blood-stained fools!" he cried, "oh, pitiful, tormented fools!

"Even that vile airship was a ship of fools!

"We are all fools still. Striving apes, irritated beyond measure by our own striving, easily moved to anger."

Some train of subconscious suggestion brought a long-forgotten speech back into Mr. Britling's mind, a speech that is full of that light which still seeks so mysteriously and indefatigably to break through the darkness and thickness of the human mind.

He whispered the words. No unfamiliar words could have had the same effect of comfort and conviction.

He whispered it of those men whom he still imagined flying far away there eastward, through the clear freezing air beneath the stars, those muffled sailors and engineers who had caused so much pain and agony in this little town.

"Father, forgive them, for they know not what they do."

CHAPTER THE FOURTH

IN THE WEB OF THE INEFFECTIVE

§ 1

HUGH's letters were becoming a very important influence upon Mr. Britling's thought. Hugh had always been something of a letter-writer, and now what was perhaps an inherited desire to set things down was manifest. He had been accustomed to decorate his letters from school with absurd little sketches—sometimes his letters had been all sketches—and now he broke from drawing to writing and back to drawing in a way that pleased his father mightily. The father loved this queer trick of caricature; he did not possess it himself, and so it seemed to him the most wonderful of all Hugh's little equipment of gifts. Mr. Britling used to carry these letters about until their edges got grimy; he would show them to any one he felt capable of appreciating their youthful freshness; he would quote them as final and conclusive evidence to establish this or that. He did not dream how many thousands of mothers and fathers were treasuring such documents. He thought other sons were dull young men by comparison with Hugh.

The earlier letters told much of the charms of discipline and the open air. "All the bother about what one has to do with oneself is over," wrote Hugh. "One has disposed of oneself. That has the effect of a great relief. Instead of telling oneself that one ought to get up in the morning, a bugle tells you that. . . . And there's no nonsense about it, no chance of lying and arguing about it with oneself. . . . I begin to see the sense of men going into monasteries and putting themselves under rules. One is carried along in a sort of moral automobile instead of trudging the road. . . ."

And he was also sounding new physical experiences.

"Never before," he declared, "have I known what fatigue is. It's a miraculous thing. One drops down in one's clothes on any hard old thing and sleeps. . . ."

And in his early letters he was greatly exercised by the elementary science of drill and discipline, and the discussion of whether these things were necessary. He began by assuming that their importance was overrated. He went on to discover that they constituted the very essentials of all good soldiering. "In a crisis," he concluded, "there is no telling what will get hold of a man, his higher instincts or his lower. He may show courage of a very splendid sort—or a hasty discretion. A habit is much more trustworthy than an instinct. So discipline sets up a habit of steady and courageous bearing. If you keep your head you are at liberty to be splendid. If you lose it, the habit will carry you through."

The young man was also very profound upon the effects of the suggestion of various exercises upon the mind.

"It is surprising how bloodthirsty one feels in a bayonet charge. We have to shout; we are encouraged to shout. The effect is to paralyse one's higher centres. One ceases to question—anything. One becomes a 'bayoneteer.' As I go bounding forward I imagine fat men, succulent men ahead, and I am filled with the desire to do them in neatly. This sort of thing——"

A sketch of slaughter followed, with a large and valiant Hugh leaving a train of fallen behind him.

"Not like this. This is how I used to draw it in my innocent childhood, but it is incorrect. More than one German on the bayonet at a time is an encumbrance. And it would be swank—a thing we detest in the army."

The second sketch showed the same brave hero with half-a-dozen of the enemy skewered like cat's meat.

"As for the widows and children, I disregard 'em."

§ 2

But presently Hugh began to be bored.

"Route marching again," he wrote. "For no earthly reason than that they can do nothing else with us. We are getting no decent musketry training because there are no rifles. We are wasting half our time. If you multiply half a week by the number of men in the army you will see we waste centuries weekly.... If most of these men here had just been enrolled and left to go about their business while we trained officers and instructors and got equipment for them, and if they had then been put through their paces as rapidly as possible, it would have been infinitely better for the country.... In a sort of way we are keeping raw; in a sort of way we are getting stale.... I get irritated by this. I feel we are not being properly done by.

"Half our men are educated men, reasonably educated, but we are always being treated as though we were too stupid for words. . . .

"No good grousing, I suppose, but after Statesminster and a glimpse of old Cardinal's way of doing things, one gets a kind of toothache in the mind at the sight of everything being done twice as slowly and half as well as it need be."

He went off at a tangent to describe the men in his platoon. "The best man in our lot is an ex-grocer's assistant, but in order to save us from vain generalisations it happens that the worst man—a moon-faced creature, almost incapable of lacing up his boots without help and objurgation—is also an ex-grocer's assistant. Our most offensive member is a little cad with a snub nose, who had read Kipling and imagines he is the nearest thing that ever has been to Private Ortheris. He goes about looking for the other two of the Soldiers Three; it is rather like an unpopular politician trying to form a ministry. And he is conscientiously foul-mouthed. He feels losing a chance of saying 'bloody' as acutely as a snob feels dropping an H. He goes back sometimes and says the sentence over again and puts the 'bloody' in. I used to swear a little out of the range of your parental ear, but Ortheris has cured me. When he is about I am mincing in my speech. I perceive now that cursing is a way of chewing one's own dirt. In a platoon there is no elbow-room for indifference; you must either love or hate. I have a feeling that my first taste of battle will not be with Germans, but with Private Ortheris. . . ."

And one letter was just a picture, a parody of the well-known picture of the bivouac below and the soldier's dream of return to his beloved above. But Master Hugh in the dream was embracing an enormous retort, while a convenient galvanometer registered his emotion and little tripods danced around him.

§ 3

Then came a letter which plunged abruptly into criticism.

"My dear Parent, this is a swearing letter. I must let go to somebody. And somehow none of the other chaps are convenient. I don't know if I ought to be put against a wall and shot for it, but I hereby declare that all the officers of this battalion over and above the rank of captain are a constellation of incapables—and several of the captains are herewith included. Some of them are men of a pleasant disposition and carefully aborted mental powers, and some are men of an unpleasant disposition and no mental powers at all. And I believe—a little enlightenment by your recent letter to *The Times*—that they are a fair sample of the entire 'army' class which has got to win this war. Usually they are indolent, but when they are thoroughly roused they are fussy. The time they should spend in enlarging their minds and increasing their military efficiency they devote to keeping fit. They are, roughly speaking, fit—for nothing. They cannot move us thirty miles without getting half of us left about, without losing touch with food and shelter and starving us for thirty-six hours or so in the process, and they cannot count beyond the fingers of one hand, not having learned to use the nose for arithmetical operations. . . . I conclude this war is going to be a sort of Battle of Inkerman on a large scale. We chaps in the ranks will have to do the job. Leading is 'off.' . . .

"All of this, my dear Parent, is just a blow off. I have been needlessly starved, and fagged to death and exasperated. We have moved five-and-twenty miles across country in fifty-seven hours. And without food for about eighteen hours. I have been with my Captain, who has been billeting us here in Cheasingholt. Oh, he is a MUFF! Oh God! oh God of

335

Heaven! what a MUFF! He is afraid of printed matter, but he controls himself heroically. He prides himself upon having no 'sense of locality, confound it!' Prides himself! He went about this village, which is a little dispersed, at a slight trot, and wouldn't avail himself of the one-inch map I happened to have. He judged the capacity of each room with his eye and wouldn't let me measure, even with God's own paces. Not with the legs I inherit. 'We'll put five fellahs hea!' he said. 'What d'you want to measure the room for? We haven't come to lay down carpets.' Then, having assigned men by *coup d'œil*, so as to congest half the village miserably, he found the other half unoccupied and had to begin all over again. 'If you measured the floor space first, sir,' I said, 'and made a list of the houses——' 'That isn't the way I'm going to do it,' he said, fixing me with a pitiless eye. . . .

"That isn't the way they are going to do it, Daddy! The sort of thing that is done over here in the green army will be done over there in the dry. They won't be in time; they'll lose their guns where now they lose our kitchens. I'm a mute soldier; I've got to do what I'm told; still, I begin to understand the Battle of Neuve Chapelle.

"They say the relations of men and officers in the new army are beautiful. Some day I may learn to love my officer—but not just yet. Not till I've forgotten the operations leading up to the occupation of Cheasingholt. . . . He muffs his real job without a blush, and yet he would rather be shot than do his bootlaces up crisscross. What I say about officers applies only and solely to him really. . . . How well I understand now the shooting of officers by their men. . . . But indeed, fatigue and exasperation apart, this shift has been done atrociously. . . ."

The young man returned to these criticisms in a later letter.

"You will think I am always carping, but it does seem to me that nearly everything is being done here in the most wasteful way possible. We waste time, we waste labour, we waste material, oh Lord! how we waste our country's money. These aren't, I can assure you, the opinions of a conceited young man. It's nothing to be conceited about. . . . We're bored to death by standing about this infernal little village. There is nothing to do—except trail after a small number of slatternly young women we despise and hate. I *don't*, Daddy. And I don't drink. Why have I inherited no vices? We had a fight here yesterday—sheer boredom. Ortheris has a swollen lip, and another private has a bad black eye. There is to be a return match. I perceive the chief horror of warfare is boredom. . . .

"Our feeding here is typical of the whole system. It is a system invented not with any idea of getting the best results—that does not enter into the War Office philosophy—but to have a rule for everything, and avoid arguments. There is rather too generous an allowance of bread and stuff per man, and there is a very fierce but not very efficient system of weighing and checking. A rather too generous allowance is, of course, a direct incentive to waste or stealing—as any one but our silly old duffer of a War Office would know. The checking is for quantity, which any fool can understand, rather than for quality. The test for the quality of army meat is the smell. If it doesn't smell bad, it is good. . . .

"Then the raw material is handed over to a cook. He is a common soldier who has been made into a cook by a simple ceremony. He is told, 'You are a cook.' He does his best to be. Usually he roasts or bakes to begin with, guessing when the joint is done, afterwards he hacks up what is left of his joints and makes a stew for next day. A stew is hacked meat boiled up in a big pot. It has much fat floating on the top. After you have eaten your fill you want to sit about quiet. The men are fed usually in a large tent or barn. We have a barn. It is not a clean barn, and just to make it more like a picnic there are insufficient plates, knives and forks. (I tell you, no army people can count beyond eight or ten.) The corporals after their morning's work have to carve. When they have done carving they tell me they feel they have had enough dinner. They sit about looking pale, and wander off afterwards to the village pub. (I shall probably become a corporal soon.) In these islands before the war began there was a surplus of women over men of about a million. (See the publications of the Fabian Society, now so popular among the young.) None of these women have been trusted by the government with the difficult task of cooking and giving out food to our soldiers. No man of the ordinary soldier class ever cooks anything until he is a soldier. . . . All food left over after the stew or otherwise rendered uneatable by the cook is thrown away. We throw away pail-loads. *We bury meat.* . . .

"Also we get three pairs of socks. We work pretty hard. We don't know how to darn socks. When the heels wear through, come blisters. Bad blisters disable a man. Of the million of surplus women (see above) the government has not had the intelligence to get any to darn our socks. So a certain percentage of us go lame. And so on. And so on.

"You will think all this is awful grousing, but the point I want to make—I hereby to ease my feelings make it now in a fair round hand—is that all this business could be done far better and far cheaper if it wasn't left to these absolutely inexperienced and extremely exclusive military gentlemen. They think they are leading England and showing us all how; instead of which they are just keeping us back. Why in thunder are they doing everything? Not one of them, when he is at home, is allowed to order the dinner or poke his nose into his own kitchen or check the household books. . . . The ordinary British colonel is a helpless old gentleman; he ought to have a nurse. . . . This is not merely the trivial grievance of my insulted stomach, it is a serious matter for the country. Sooner or later the country may want the food that is being wasted in all these capers. In the aggregate it must amount to a daily destruction of tons of stuff of all sorts. Tons. . . . Suppose the war lasts longer than we reckon!"

From this point Hugh's letter jumped to a general discussion of the military mind.

"Our officers are beastly good chaps, nearly all of them. That's where the perplexity of the whole thing comes in. If only they weren't such good chaps! If only they were like the Prussian officers to their men, then we'd just take on a revolution as well as the war, and make everything tidy at once. But they are decent, they are charming. . . . Only they do not think hard, and they do not understand that doing a job properly means doing it as directly and thought-outly as you possibly can. They won't worry about things. If their tempers were worse perhaps their work might be better. They won't use maps or time-tables or books of reference. When we move to a new place they pick up what they can about it by hearsay; not one of our lot has the gumption to possess a contoured map, or a Michelin guide. They have hearsay minds. They are fussy and petty and wasteful—and, in the way of getting things done, pretentious. By their code they're paragons of honour. Courage—they're all right about that; no end of it; honesty, truthfulness, and so on—high. They have a kind of horsy standard of smartness and pluck, too, that isn't bad, and they have a fine horror of whiskers and being unbuttoned. But the mistake they make is to class thinking with whiskers, as a sort of fussy sidegrowth. Instead of classing it with buttoned-upness. They hate economy. And preparation. . . .

"They won't see that inefficiency is a sort of dishonesty. If a man doesn't steal sixpence, they think it a light matter if he wastes half a crown. Here follows wisdom! *From the point of view of a nation at war, sixpence is just a fifth part of half a crown. . . .*

"When I began this letter I was boiling with indignation, complicated, I suspect, by this morning's 'stew'; now I have written thus far I feel I'm an ungenerous grumbler. . . . It is remarkable, my dear Parent, that I let off these things to you. I like writing to you. I couldn't possibly say the things I can write. Heinrich had a confidential friend at Breslau to whom he used to write about his Soul. I never had one of these Teutonic friendships. And I haven't got a Soul. But I have to write. One must write to some one—and in this place there is nothing else to do. And now the old lady downstairs is turning down the gas; she always does at half-past ten. She didn't ought. She gets—ninepence each. Excuse the pencil. . . ."

That letter ended abruptly. The next two were brief and cheerful. Then suddenly came a new note.

"We've got rifles! We're real armed soldiers at last. Every blessed man has got a rifle. And they come from Japan! They are of a sort of light wood that is like new oak and art furniture, and makes one feel that one belongs to the First Garden Suburb Regiment; but I believe much can be done with linseed-oil. And they are real rifles, they go bang. We are a little light-headed about them. Only our training and discipline prevent our letting fly at incautious spectators on the sky-line. I saw a man yesterday about half a mile off. I was possessed by the idea that

I could get him—right in the middle. . . . Ortheris, the little beast, has got a motor-bicycle, which he calls his 'b——y oto'— no one knows why—and only death or dishonourable conduct will save me, I gather, from becoming a corporal in the course of the next month. . . ."

§ 4

A subsequent letter threw fresh light on the career of the young man with the "oto." Before the rifle and the "oto," and in spite of his fights with some person or persons unknown, Ortheris found trouble. Hugh told the story with the unblushing *savoir-faire* of the very young.

"By-the-by, Ortheris, following the indications of his creator and succumbing to the universal boredom before the rifles came, forgot Lord Kitchener's advice and attempted 'seduktion.' With painful results which he insists upon confiding to the entire platoon. He has been severely smacked and scratched by the proposed victim, and warned off the premises (licenced premises) by her father and mother—both formidable persons. They did more than warn him off the premises. They had displayed neither a proper horror of Don Juan nor a proper respect for the King's uniform. Mother, we realise, got hold of him and cuffed him severely. 'What the 'ell's a chap to do?' cried Ortheris. 'You can't go 'itting a woman back.' Father had set a dog on him. A less ingenuous character would be silent about such passages—I should be too egotistical and humiliated altogether—but that is not his quality. He tells us in tones of naïve wonder. He talks about it and talks about it. 'I don't care what the old woman did,' he says, 'not—reely. What 'urts me about it is that I jest made a sort of mistake 'ow *she'd* tike it. You see, I sort of feel I've 'urt and insulted '*er*. And reely I didn't mean to. Swap me, I didn't mean to. Gawd 'elp me. I wouldn't 'ave 'ad it 'appen as it 'as 'appened, not for worlds. And now I can't get round to 'er, or anyfing, not to explain. . . . You chaps may laugh, but you don't know what there is *in* it. . . . I tell you it worries me something frightful. You think I'm just a little cad who took liberties he didn't ought to. (Note of anger drowning uncharitable grunts of assent.) 'Ow the 'ell is 'e to know *when* 'e didn't ought to? . . . . I *swear* she liked me. . . .'

"This sort of thing goes on for hours—in the darkness.

" 'I'd got regular sort of fond of 'er.'

"And the extraordinary thing is it makes me begin to get regular fond of Ortheris.

"I think it is because the affair has surprised him right out of acting Ortheris and Tommy Atkins for a bit, into his proper self. He's frightfully like some sort of mongrel with a lot of wire-haired terrier and a touch of Airedale in it. A mongrel you like in spite of the flavour of all the horrid things he's been nosing into. And he's as hard as nails and, my dear daddy! he can't box for nuts."

§ 5

Mr. Britling, with an understanding much quickened by Hugh's letters, went about Essex in his automobile, and on one or two journeys into Berkshire and Buckinghamshire, and marked the steady conversion of the old pacific countryside into an armed camp. He was disposed to minimise Hugh's criticisms. He found in them something of the harshness of youth, which is far too keen-edged to be tolerant with half performance and our poor human evasion of perfection's overstrain. "Our poor human evasion of perfection's overstrain"; this phrase was Mr. Britling's. To Mr. Britling, looking less closely and more broadly, the new army was a pride and a marvel.

He liked to come into some quiet village and note the clusters of sturdy khaki-clad youngsters going about their business, the tethered horses, the air of subdued bustle, the occasional glimpses of guns and ammunition trains. Wherever one went now there were soldiers and still more soldiers. There was a steady flow of men into Flanders, and presently to Gallipoli, but it seemed to have no effect upon the multitude in training at home. He was pleasantly excited by the evident increase in the proportion of military material upon the railways; he liked the promise and mystery of the long lines of trucks bearing tarpaulin-covered wagons and carts and guns that he would pass on his way to Liverpool Street station. He could apprehend defeat in the silence of the night, but when he saw the men, when he went about the land, then it was impossible to believe in any end but victory. . . .

But through the spring and summer there was no victory. The "great offensive" of May was checked and abandoned after a series of ineffective and very costly attacks between Ypres and Soissons. The Germans had developed a highly scientific defensive in which machine-guns replaced rifles and a maximum of punishment was inflicted upon an assaulting force with a minimum of human loss. The War Office had never thought much of machine-guns before, but now it thought a good deal. Moreover, the energies of Britain were being turned more and more towards the Dardanelles.

The idea of an attack upon the Dardanelles had a traditional attractiveness for the British mind. Old men had been brought up from childhood with "forcing the Dardanelles" as a familiar phrase; it had none of the flighty novelty and vulgarity about it that made an "aerial offensive" seem so unwarrantable a proceeding. Forcing the Dardanelles was historically British. It made no break with tradition. Soon after Turkey entered the war British submarines appeared in the Sea of Marmora, and in February a systematic bombardment of the Dardanelles began; this was continued intermittently for a month, the defenders profiting by their experiences and by spells of bad weather to strengthen their works. This first phase of the attack culminated in the loss of the *Irresistible, Ocean*, and *Bouvet*, when on the 17th of March the attacking fleet closed in upon the Narrows. After an interlude of six weeks to allow of further preparations on the part of the defenders, who were now thoroughly alive to what was coming, the Allied armies gathered upon the scene, and a difficult and costly landing was achieved at two points upon the peninsula of Gallipoli. With that began a slow and bloody siege of the defences of the Dardanelles, clambering up to the surprise landing of a fresh British army in Suvla Bay in August, and its failure in the battle of Anafarta, through incompetent commanders and a general sloppiness of leading, to cut off and capture Maidos and the Narrows defences. . . . Meanwhile the Russian hosts, which had reached their high-water mark in the capture of Przemysl, were being forced back first in the south and then in the north. The Germans recaptured Lemberg, entered Warsaw, and pressed on to take Brest Litowsk. The Russian lines rolled back with an impressive effect of defeat, and the Germans thrust towards Riga and Petrograd, reaching Vilna about the middle of September. . . .

Day after day Mr. Britling traced the swaying fortunes of the conflict, with impatience, with perplexity, but with no loss of confidence in the ultimate success of Britain. The country was still swarming with troops, and still under summer sunshine. A second hay-harvest redeemed the scantiness of the first, the wheat-crops were wonderful, and the great fig-tree at the corner of the Dower House had never borne so bountifully nor such excellent juicy figs. . . .

And one day in early June while those figs were still only a hope, Teddy appeared at the Dower House with Letty, to say goodbye before going to the front. He was going out in a draft to fill up various gaps and losses; he did not know where. Essex was doing well but bloodily over there. Mrs. Britling had tea set out upon the lawn under the blue cedar, and Mr. Britling found himself at a loss for appropriate sayings, and talked in his confusion almost as though Teddy's departure was of no significance at all. He was still haunted by that odd sense of responsibility for Teddy. Teddy was not nearly so animated as he had been in his pre-khaki days; there was a quiet exaltation in his manner rather than a lively excitement. He knew now what he was in for. He knew now that war was not a lark, that for him it was to be the gravest experience he had ever had or was likely to have. There were no more jokes about Letty's pension, and a general avoidance of the topics of high explosives and asphyxiating gas. . . .

Mr. and Mrs. Britling took the young people to the gate.

"Good luck!" cried Mr. Britling as they receded.

Teddy replied with a wave of the hand.

Mr. Britling stood watching them for some moments as they walked towards the little cottage which was to be the scene of their private parting.

"I don't like his going," he said. "I hope it will be all right with him. . . . Teddy's so grave nowadays. It's a mean thing, I know, it has none of the Roman touch, but I am glad that this can't happen with Hugh——" He computed. "Not for a year and three months, even if they march him into it upon his very birthday. . . .

"It may all be over by then. . . ."

§ 6

In that computation he reckoned without Hugh.

Within a month Hugh was also saying "Goodbye."

"But how's this?" protested Mr. Britling, who had already guessed the answer. "You're not nineteen."

"I'm nineteen enough for this job," said Hugh. "In fact, I enlisted as nineteen."

Mr. Britling said nothing for a little while. Then he spoke with a catch in his breath. "I don't blame you," he said. "It was— the right spirit."

Drill and responsibilities of non-commissioned rank had imposed a novel manliness upon the bearing of Corporal Britling. "I always classified a little above my age at Statesminster," he said as though that cleared up everything.

He looked at a rosebud as though it interested him. Then he remarked rather casually:

"I thought," he said, "that if I was to go to war I'd better do the thing properly. It seemed—sort of half and half—not to be eligible for the trenches. . . . I ought to have told you. . . ."

"Yes," Mr. Britling decided.

"I was shy about it at first. . . . I thought perhaps the war would be over before it was necessary to discuss anything. . . . Didn't want to go into it."

"Exactly," said Mr. Britling as though that was a complete explanation.

"It's been a good year for your roses," said Hugh.

346

§ 7

Hugh was to stay the night. He spent what seemed to him and every one a long, shy, inexpressive evening. Only the small boys were really natural and animated. They were much impressed and excited by his departure, and wanted to ask a hundred questions about the life in the trenches. Many of them Hugh had to promise to answer when he got there. Then he would see just exactly how things were. Mrs. Britling was motherly and intelligent about his outfit. "Will you want winter things?" she asked. . . .

But when he was alone with his father after every one had gone to bed they found themselves able to talk.

"This sort of thing seems more to us than it would be to a French family," Hugh remarked, standing on the hearth-rug.

"Yes," agreed Mr. Britling. "Their minds would be better prepared. . . . They'd have their appropriate things to say. They have been educated by the tradition of service—and '71."

Then he spoke—almost resentfully.

"The older men ought to go before you boys. Who is to carry on if a lot of you get killed?"

Hugh reflected. "In the stiffest battle that ever can be the odds are against getting killed," he said.

"I suppose they are."

"One in three or four in the very hottest corners."

Mr. Britling expressed no satisfaction.

"Every one is going through something of this sort."

"All the decent people, at any rate," said Mr. Britling. . . .

"It will be an extraordinary experience. Somehow it seems out of proportion——"

"With what?"

"With life generally. As one has known it."

347

"It isn't in proportion," Mr. Britling admitted.

"Incommensurables," said Hugh.

He considered his phrasing. "It's not," he said, "as though one was going into another part of the same world, or turning up another side of the world one was used to. It is just as if one had been living in a room and one had been asked to step outside. . . . It makes me think of a queer little thing that happened when I was in London last winter. I got into Queer Company. I don't think I told you. I went to have supper with some students in Chelsea. I hadn't been to the place before, but they seemed all right—just people like me—and everybody. And after supper they took me on to some people *they* didn't know very well; people who had to do with some School of Dramatic Art. There were two or three young actresses there and a singer and people of that sort, sitting about smoking cigarettes, and we began talking plays and books and picture-shows and all that stuff; and suddenly there was a knocking at the door and some one went out and found a policeman with a warrant on the landing. They took off our host's son. . . . It had to do with a murder. . . ."

Hugh paused. "It was the Bedford Mansions mystery. I don't suppose you remember about it or read about it at the time. He'd killed a man. . . . It doesn't matter about the particulars anyhow, but what I mean is the effect. The effect of a comfortable well-lit orderly room and the sense of harmless people—and then the door opening and the policeman and the cold draught flowing in. *Murder!* A girl who seemed to know the people well explained to me in whispers what was happening. It was like the opening of a trap-door going down into some pit you have always known was there, but never really believed in."

"I know," said Mr. Britling. "I know."

"That's just how I feel about this war business. There's no real death over here. It's laid out and boxed up. And accidents are all padded about. If one got a toss from a horse here, you'd be in bed and comfortable in no time. . . . And there; it's like another planet. It's outside. . . . I'm going outside. . . . Instead of there being no death anywhere, it is death everywhere, outside there. We shall be using our utmost wits to kill each other. A kind of reverse to this world."

Mr. Britling nodded.

"I've never seen a dead body yet. In Dower-Houseland there aren't dead bodies."

"We've kept things from you—horrid things of that sort."

"I'm not complaining," said Hugh. . . . "But—Master Hugh— the Master Hugh you kept things from—will never come back."

He went on quickly as his father raised distressed eyes to him. "I mean that anyhow *this* Hugh will never come back. Another one may. But I shall have been outside, and it will all be different. . . ."

He paused. Never had Mr. Britling been so little disposed to take up the discourse.

"Like a man," he said, seeking an image and doing no more than imitate his son's, "who goes out of a busy lighted room through a trap-door into a blizzard, to mend the roof. . . ."

For some moments neither father nor son said anything more. They had a queer sense of insurmountable insufficiency. Neither was saying what he had wanted to say to the other, but it was not clear to them now what they had to say to one another. . . .

"It's wonderful," said Mr. Britling.

Hugh could only manage: "The world has turned right over. . . ."

"The job has to be done," said Mr. Britling.

"The job has to be done," said Hugh.

The pause lengthened.

"You'll be getting up early tomorrow," said Mr. Britling. . . .

§ 8

When Mr. Britling was alone in his own room all the thoughts and feelings that had been held up downstairs began to run more and more rapidly and abundantly through his mind.

He had a feeling—every now and again in the last few years he had had the same feeling—as though he were only just beginning to discover Hugh. This perpetual rediscovery of one's children is the experience of every observant parent. He had always considered Hugh as a youth, and now a man stood over him and talked, as one man to another. And this man, this very new man, mint new and clean and clear, filled Mr. Britling with surprise and admiration.

It was as if he perceived the beauty of youth for the first time in Hugh's slender, well-balanced, khaki-clad body. There was infinite delicacy in his clear complexion, his clear eyes; the delicately pencilled eyebrow that was so exactly like his mother's. And this thing of brightness and bravery talked as gravely and as wisely as any weather-worn, shop-soiled, old fellow. . . .

The boy was wise.

Hugh thought for himself; he thought round and through his position, not egotistically but with a quality of responsibility. He wasn't just hero-worshipping and imitating, just spinning some self-centred romance. If he was a fair sample of his generation, then it was a better generation than Mr. Britling's had been. . . .

At that Mr. Britling's mind went off at a tangent to the grievance of the rejected volunteer. It was acutely shameful to him that all these fine lads should be going off to death and wounds while the men of forty and over lay snug at home. How stupid it was to fix things like that! Here were the fathers, who had done their work, shot their bolts, returned some value for the costs of their education, unable to get training, unable to be of any service, shamefully safe, doing April fool work as special constables; while their young innocents, untried, all their gathering possibilities of service unbroached, went down into the deadly trenches. . . . The war would leave the world a world of cripples and old men and children. . . .

He felt himself as a cowardly brute, fat, wheezy, out of training, sheltering behind this dear one branch of Mary's life.

He writhed with impotent humiliation. . . .

How stupidly the world is managed.

He began to fret and rage. He could not lie in peace in his bed; he got up and prowled about his room, blundering against chairs and tables in the darkness. . . . We were too stupid to do the most obvious things; we were sending all these boys into hardship and pitiless danger; we were sending them ill-equipped, insufficiently supported, we were sending our children through the fires to Moloch, because essentially we English were a world of indolent, pampered, sham good-humoured, old and middle-aged men. (So he distributed the intolerable load of self-accusation.) Why was he doing nothing to change things, to get them better? What was the good of an assumed modesty, an effort at tolerance for and confidence in these boozy old lawyers, these ranting platform men, these stiff-witted officers and hide-bound officials? They were butchering the youth of England. Old men sat out of danger contriving death for the lads in the trenches. That was the reality of the thing. "My son!" he cried sharply in the darkness. His sense of our national deficiencies became tormentingly, fantastically acute. It was as if all his cherished delusions had fallen from the scheme of things. . . . What was the good of making believe that up there they were planning some great counter-stroke that would end in victory? It was as plain as daylight that they had neither the power of imagination nor the collective intelligence even to conceive of a counter-stroke. Any dull mass may resist, but only imagination can strike. Imagination! To the end we should not strike. We might strike through the air. We might strike across the sea. We might strike hard at Gallipoli instead of dribbling inadequate armies thither as our fathers dribbled men at the Redan. . . . But the old men would sit at their tables, replete and sleepy, and shake their cunning old heads. The press would chatter and make odd ambiguous sounds like a ship-load of monkeys in a storm. The political harridans would get the wrong men appointed, would attack every possible leader with scandal and abuse and falsehood. . . .

The spirit and honour and drama had gone out of this war.

Our only hope now was exhaustion. Our only strategy was to barter blood for blood—trusting that our tank would prove the deeper. . . .

While into this tank stepped Hugh, young and smiling. . . .

The war became a nightmare vision.

§ 9

In the morning Mr. Britling's face was white from his overnight brainstorm, and Hugh's was fresh from wholesome sleep. They walked about the lawn, and Mr. Britling talked hopefully of the general outlook until it was time for them to start to the station. . . .

The little old station-master grasped the situation at once, and presided over their last hand-clasp.

"Good luck, Hugh!" cried Mr. Britling.

"Good luck!" cried the little old station-master.

"It's not easy aparting," he said to Mr. Britling as the train slipped down the line. "There's been many a parting hea' since this here old war began. Many. And some as won't come back again neether."

§ 10

For some days Mr. Britling could think of nothing but Hugh, and always with a dull pain at his heart. He felt as he had felt long ago while he had waited downstairs and Hugh upstairs had been under the knife of a surgeon. But this time the operation went on and still went on. At the worst his boy had but one chance in five of death or serious injury, but for a time he could think of nothing but that one chance. He felt it pressing upon his mind, pressing him down. . . .

Then instead of breaking under that pressure, he was released by the trick of the sanguine temperament. His mind turned over, abruptly, to the four chances out of five. It was like a dislocated joint slipping back into place. It was as sudden as that. He found he had adapted himself to the prospect of Hugh in mortal danger. It had become a fact established, a usual thing. He could bear with it and go about his affairs.

He went up to London, and met other men at the club in the same emotional predicament. He realised that it was neither very wonderful nor exceptionally tragic now to have a son at the front.

"My boy is in Gallipoli," said one. "It's tough work there."

"My lad's in Flanders," said Mr. Britling. "Nothing would satisfy him but the front. He's three months short of eighteen. He misstated his age."

And they went on to talk newspaper just as if the world was where it had always been.

But until a postcard came from Hugh Mr. Britling watched the postman like a love-sick girl.

Hugh wrote more frequently than his father had dared to hope, pencilled letters for the most part. It was as if he were beginning to feel an inherited need for talk, and was a little at a loss for a sympathetic ear. Park, his schoolmate, who had enlisted with him, wasn't, it seemed, a theoriser. "Park becomes a martinet," Hugh wrote. "Also he is a sergeant now, and this makes rather a gulf between us." Mr. Britling had the greatest difficulty in writing back. There were many grave deep things he wanted to say, and never did. Instead he gave elaborate details of the small affairs of the Dower House. Once or twice, with a half-unconscious imitation of his boy's style, he took a shot at the theological and philosophical hares that Hugh had started. But the exemplary letters that he composed of nights from a Father to a Son at War were never written down. It was just as well, for there are many things of that sort that are good to think and bad to say. . . .

Hugh was not very explicit about his position or daily duties. What he wrote now had to pass through the hands of a Censor, and any sort of definite information might cause the suppression of his letter. Mr. Britling conceived him for the most part as quartered some way behind the front, but in a flat, desolated country and within hearing of great guns. He assisted his imagination with the illustrated papers. Sometimes he put him farther back into pleasant old towns after the fashion of Beauvais, and imagined loitering groups in the front of cafés; sometimes he filled in the obvious suggestions of the phrase that all the Pas de Calais was now one vast British camp. Then he crowded the picture with tethered horses and tents and grey-painted wagons, and Hugh in the foreground—bare-armed, with a bucket. . . .

Hugh's letters divided themselves pretty fairly between two main topics; the first was the interest of the art of war, the second the reaction against warfare. "After one has got over the emotion of it," he wrote, "and when one's mind has just accepted and forgotten (as it does) the horrors and waste of it all, then I begin to perceive that war is absolutely the best game in the world. That is the real strength of war, I submit. Not as you put it in that early pamphlet of yours; ambition, cruelty, and all those things. Those things give an excuse for war, they rush timid and base people into war, but the essential matter is the hold of the thing itself upon an active imagination. It's such a big game. Instead of being fenced into a field and tied down to one set of tools as you are in almost every other game, you have all the world to play with, and you may use whatever you can use. You can use every scrap of imagination and invention that is in you. And it's wonderful. . . . But real soldiers aren't cruel. And war isn't cruel in its essence. Only in its consequences. Over here one gets hold of scraps of talk that light up things. Most of the barbarities were done—it is quite clear—by an excited civilian sort of men, men in a kind of inflamed state. The great part of the German army in the early stage of the war was really an army of demented civilians. Trained civilians no doubt, but civilians in soul. They were nice orderly clean law-abiding men suddenly torn up by the roots and flung into quite shocking conditions. They felt they were rushing at death, and that decency was at an end. They thought every Belgian had a gun behind the hedge and a knife in his trouser leg. They saw villages burning and dead people, and men smashed to bits. They lived in a kind of nightmare. They didn't know what they were doing. They did horrible things just as one does them sometimes in dreams. . . ."

He flung out his conclusion with just his mother's leaping consecutiveness. "Conscript soldiers are the ruin of war. . . . Half the Germans and a lot of the French ought never to have been brought within ten miles of a battle-field.

"What makes all this so plain are the diaries the French and English have been finding on the dead. You know at the early stage of the war every German soldier was expected to keep a diary. He was ordered to do it. The idea was to keep him interested in the war. Consequently, from the dead and wounded our people have got thousands. . . . It helps one to realise that the Germans aren't really soldiers at all. Not as our men are. They are obedient, law-abiding, intelligent people, who have been shoved into this. They have to see the war as something romantic and melodramatic, or as something moral, or as tragic fate. They have to bellow songs about 'Deutschland,' or drag in 'Gott.' They don't take to the game as our men take to the game. . . .

"I confess I'm taking to the game. I wish at times I had gone into the O.T.C. with Teddy, and got a better hold of it. I was too high-browed about this war business. I dream now of getting a commission. . . .

"That diary-hunting strategy is just the sort of thing that makes this war intellectually fascinating. Everything is being thought out and then tried over that can possibly make victory.

The Germans go in for psychology much more than we do, just as they go in for war more than we do, but they don't seem to be really clever about it. So they set out to make all their men understand the war, while our chaps are singing 'Tipperary.' But what the men put down aren't the beautiful things they ought to put down; most of them shove down lists of their meals, some of the diaries are all just lists of things eaten, and a lot of them have written the most damning stuff about outrages and looting. Which the French are translating and publishing. The Germans would give anything now to get back these silly diaries. And now they have made an order that no one shall go into battle with any written papers at all. . . . Our people got so keen on documenting and the value of chance writings, that one of the principal things to do after a German attack had failed had been to hook in the documentary dead, and find out what they had on them. . . . It's a curious sport, this body-fishing. You have a sort of triple hook on a rope, and you throw it and drag. They do the same. The other day one body near Hooghe was hooked by both sides, and they had a tug of war. With a sharpshooter or so cutting in whenever our men got too excited. Several men were hit. The Irish—it was an Irish regiment—got him—or at least they got the better part of him. . . .

"Now that I am a sergeant, Parks talks to me again about all these things, and we have a first lieutenant too keen to resist such technical details. They are purely technical details. You must take them as that. One does not think of the dead body as a man recently deceased, who had perhaps a wife and business connections and a weakness for oysters or pale brandy. Or as something that laughed and cried and didn't like getting hurt. That would spoil everything. One thinks of him merely as a uniform with marks upon it that will tell us what kind of stuff we have against us, and possibly with papers that will give us a hint of how far he and his lot are getting sick of the whole affair. . . .

"There's a kind of hardening not only of the body but of the mind through all this life out here. One is living on a different level. You know just before I came away—you talked of Dower-House-land—and outside. This is outside. It's different. Our men here are kind enough still to little things—kittens or birds or flowers. Behind the front, for example, everywhere there are Tommy gardens. Some are quite bright little patches. But it's just nonsense to suppose we are tender to the wounded up here—and, putting it plainly, there isn't a scrap of pity left for the enemy. Not a scrap. Not a trace of such feeling. They were tender about the wounded in the early days—men tell me—and reverent about the dead. It's all gone now. There have been atrocities, gas, unforgettable things. Everything is harder. Our people are inclined now to laugh at a man who gets hit, and to be annoyed at a man with a troublesome wound. The other day, they say, there was a big dead German outside the Essex trenches. He became a nuisance, and he was dragged in and taken behind the line and buried. After he was buried, a kindly soul was putting a board over him with 'Somebody's Fritz' on it, when a shell burst close by. It blew the man with the board a dozen yards and wounded him, and it restored Fritz to the open air. He was lifted clean out. He flew head over heels like a windmill. This was regarded as a tremendous joke against the men who had been at the pains of burying him. For a time nobody else would touch Fritz, who was now some yards behind his original grave. Then as he got worse and worse he was buried again by some devoted sanitarians, and this time the inscription was 'Somebody's Fritz. R.I.P.' And as luck would have it, he was spun up again. In pieces. The trench howled with laughter and cries of 'Good old Fritz!' 'This isn't the Resurrection, Fritz.' . . .

"Another thing that appeals to the sunny humour of the trenches as a really delicious practical joke is the trick of the fuses. We have two kinds of fuse, a slow-burning fuse such as is used for hand-grenades and suchlike things, a sort of yard-a-minute fuse, and a rapid fuse that goes a hundred yards a second—for firing mines and so on. The latter is carefully distinguished from the former by a conspicuous red thread. Also, as you know, it is the habit of the enemy and ourselves when the trenches are near enough, to enliven each other by the casting of homely but effective hand-grenades made out of tins. When a grenade drops in a British trench somebody seizes it instantly and throws it back. To hoist the German with his own petard is particularly sweet to the British mind. When a grenade drops into a German trench everybody runs. (At least that is what I am told happens by the men from our trenches; though possibly each side has its exceptions.) If the bomb explodes, it explodes. If it doesn't, Hans and Fritz presently come creeping back to see what has happened. Sometimes the fuse hasn't caught properly, it has been thrown by a nervous man; or it hasn't burned properly. Then Hans or Fritz puts in a new fuse and sends it back with loving care. To hoist the Briton with his own petard is particularly sweet to the German mind. . . . But here it is that military genius comes in. Some gifted spirit on our side procured (probably by larceny) a length of mine fuse, the rapid sort, and spent a laborious day removing the red thread and making it into the likeness of its slow brother. Then bits of it were attached to tin-bombs and shied—unlit of course—into the German trenches. A long but happy pause followed. I can see the chaps holding themselves in. Hans and Fritz were understood to be creeping back, to be examining the unlit fuse, to be applying a light thereunto, in order to restore it to its maker after their custom. . . .

"A loud bang in the German trenches indicated the moment of lighting, and the exit of Hans and Fritz to worlds less humorous.

"The genius in the British trenches went on with the preparation of the next surprise bomb—against the arrival of Kurt and Karl. . . .

"Hans, Fritz, Kurt, Karl, Michael and Wilhelm; it went for quite a long time before they grew suspicious. . . .

"You once wrote that all fighting ought to be done nowadays by metal soldiers. I perceive, my dear Daddy, that all real fighting is. . . ."

§ 11

Not all Hugh's letters were concerned with these grim technicalities. It was not always that news and gossip came along; it was rare that a young man with a commission would condescend to talk shop to two young men without one; there were few newspapers and fewer maps, and even in France and within sound of guns, Hugh could presently find warfare almost as much a bore as it had been at times in England. But his criticism of military methods died away. "Things are done better out here," he remarked, and "We're nearer reality here. I begin to respect my Captain. Who is developing a sense of locality. Happily for our prospects." And in another place he speculated in an oddly characteristic manner whether he was getting used to the army way, whether he was beginning to see the sense of the army way, or whether it really was that that army way braced up nearer and nearer to efficiency as it got nearer to the enemy. "And here one hasn't the haunting feeling that war is after all an hallucination. It's already common sense and the business of life. . . .

"In England I always had a sneaking idea that I had 'dressed up' in my uniform. . . .

"I never dreamt before I came here how much war is a business of waiting about and going through duties and exercises that were only too obviously a means of preventing our discovering just how much waiting about we were doing. I suppose there is no great harm in describing the place I am in here; it's a kind of scenery that is somehow all of a piece with the life we lead day by day. It is a village that has been only partly smashed up; it has never been fought through, indeed the Germans were never within two miles of it, but it was shelled intermittently for months before we made our advance. Almost all the houses are still standing, but there is not a window left with a square foot of glass in the place. One or two houses have been burned out, and one or two are just as though they had been kicked to pieces by a lunatic giant. We sleep in batches of four or five on the floors of the rooms; there are very few inhabitants about, but the village inn still goes on. It has one poor weary billiard-table, very small with very big balls, and the cues are without tops; it is The Amusement of the place. Ortheris does miracles at it. When he leaves the army he says he's going to be a marker, 'a b——y marker.' The country about us is flat—featureless—desolate. How I long for hills, even for Essex mud hills. Then the road runs on towards the front, a brick road frightfully worn, lined with poplars. Just at the end of the village mechanical transport ends and there is a kind of depot from which all the stuff goes up by mules or men or bicycles to the trenches. It is the only movement in the place, and I have spent hours watching men shift grub or ammunition or lending them a hand. All day one hears guns, a kind of thud at the stomach, and now and then one sees an aeroplane, very high and small. Just beyond this point there is a group of poplars which have been punished by a German shell. They are broken off and splintered in the most astonishing way; all split and ravelled out like the end of a cane that has been broken and twisted to get the ends apart. The choice of one's leisure is to watch the A.S.C. or play football, twenty a side, or sit about indoors, or stand in the doorway, or walk down to the Estaminet and wait five or six deep for the billiard-table. Ultimately one sits. And so you get these unconscionable letters."

"Unconscionable!" said Mr. Britling. "Of course—he will grow out of that sort of thing."

"And he'll write some day, sure enough. He'll write."

He went on reading the letter.

"We read, of course. But there never could be a library here big enough to keep us going. We can do with all sorts of books, but I don't think the ordinary sensational novel is quite the catch it was for a lot of them in peace-time. Some break towards serious reading in the oddest fashion. Old Park, for example, says he wants books you can chew; he is reading a cheap edition of 'The Origin of Species.' He used to regard Florence Warden and William le Queux as the supreme delights of print. I wish you could send him Metchnikoff's 'Nature of Man' or Pearson's 'Ethic of Free-thought.' I feel I am building up his tender mind. Not for me though, Daddy. Nothing of that sort for me. These things take people differently. What I want here is literary opium. I want something about fauns and nymphs in broad low glades. I would like to read

Spenser's 'Faerie Queen.' I don't think I have read it, and yet I have a very distinct impression of knights and dragons and sorcerers and wicked magic ladies moving through a sort of Pre-Raphaelite tapestry scenery—only with a light on them. I could do with some Hewlett of the 'Forest Lovers' kind. Or with Joseph Conrad in his Kew Palm-house mood. And there is a book, I once looked into at a man's rooms in London; I don't know the title, but it was by Richard Garnett, and it was all about gods who were in reduced circumstances but amidst sunny picturesque scenery. Scenery without steel or poles or wire. A thing after the manner of Heine's 'Florentine Nights.' Any book about Greek gods would be welcome, anything about temples of ivory-coloured stone and purple seas, red caps, chests of jewels, and lizards in the sun. I wish there was another 'Thais.' The men here are getting a kind of newspaper sheet of literature scraps called *The Times* Broadsheets. Snippets, but mostly from good stuff. They're small enough to stir the appetite, but not to satisfy it. Rather an irritant—and one wants no irritant. . . . I used to imagine reading was meant to be a stimulant. Out here it has to be an anodyne. . . .

"Have you heard of a book called 'Tom Cringle's Log'?

"War is an exciting game—that I never wanted to play. It excites once in a couple of months. And the rest of it is dirt and muddle and boredom, and smashed houses and spoiled roads and muddy scenery and boredom, and the lumbering along of supplies and the lumbering back of the wounded and weary— and boredom, and continual vague guessing of how it will end and boredom and boredom and boredom, and thinking of the work you were going to do and the travel you were going to have, and the waste of life and the waste of days and boredom, and splintered poplars and stink, everywhere stink and dirt and boredom. . . . And all because these accursed Prussians were too stupid to understand what a boredom they were getting ready when they pranced and stuck their chests out and earned the praises of Mr. Thomas Carlyle. . . . *Gott strafe Deutschland*. . . . So send me some books, books of dreams, books about China and the willow-pattern plate and the golden age and fairyland. And send them soon and address them very carefully. . . ."

§ 12

Teddy's misadventure happened while figs were still ripening on Mr. Britling's big tree. It was Cissie brought the news to Mr. Britling. She came up to the Dower House with a white, scared face.

"I've come up for the letters," she said. "There's bad news of Teddy, and Letty's rather in a state."

"He's not——?" Mr. Britling left the word unsaid.

"He's wounded and missing," said Cissie.

"A prisoner!" said Mr. Britling.

"And wounded. *How*, we don't know."

She added: "Letty has gone to telegraph."

"Telegraph to whom?"

"To the War Office, to know what sort of wound he has. They tell nothing. It's disgraceful."

"It doesn't say *severely?*"

"It says just nothing. Wounded and missing! Surely they ought to give us particulars."

Mr. Britling thought. His first thought was that now news might come at any time that Hugh was wounded and missing. Then he set himself to persuade Cissie that the absence of "seriously" meant that Teddy was only quite bearably wounded, and that if he was also "missing" it might be difficult for the War Office to ascertain at once just exactly what she wanted to know. But Cissie said merely that "Letty was in an awful state," and after Mr. Britling had given her a few instructions for his typing, he went down to the cottage to repeat these mitigatory considerations to Letty. He found her much whiter than her sister, and in a state of cold indignation with the War Office. It was clear she thought that organisation ought to have taken better care of Teddy. She had a curious effect of feeling that something was being kept back from her. It was manifest too that she was disposed to regard Mr. Britling as biased in favour of the authorities.

"At any rate," she said, "they could have answered my telegram promptly. I sent it at eight. Two hours of scornful silence."

This fierce, strained, unjust Letty was a new aspect to Mr. Britling. Her treatment of his proffered consolations made him feel slightly henpecked.

"And just fancy!" she said. "They have no means of knowing if he has arrived safely on the German side. How can they know he is a prisoner without knowing that?"

"But the word is 'missing.' "

"That *means* a prisoner," said Letty uncivilly. . . .

§ 13

Mr. Britling returned to the Dower House perplexed and profoundly disturbed. He had a distressful sense that things were far more serious with Teddy than he had tried to persuade Letty they were; that "wounded and missing" meant indeed a man abandoned to very sinister probabilities. He was distressed for Teddy, and still more acutely distressed for Mrs. Teddy, whose every note and gesture betrayed suppositions even more sinister than his own. And that preposterous sense of liability, because he had helped Teddy to get his commission, was more distressful than it had ever been. He was surprised that Letty had not assailed him with railing accusations.

And this event had wiped off at one sweep all the protective scab of habituation that had gathered over the wound of Hugh's departure. He was back face to face with the one evil chance in five. . . .

In the hall there was lying a letter from Hugh that had come by the second post. It was a relief even to see it. . . .

Hugh had had his first spell in the trenches.

Before his departure he had promised his half-brothers a long and circumstantial account of what the trenches were really like. Here he redeemed his promise. He had evidently written with the idea that the letter would be handed over to them.

"Tell the bruddykinses I'm glad they're going to Brinsmead school. Later on, I suppose, they will go on to Statesminster. I suppose that you don't care to send them so far in these troubled times. . . .

"And now about those trenches—as I promised. The great thing to grasp is that they are narrow. They are a sort of negative wall. They are more like giant cracks in the ground than anything else. . . . But perhaps I had better begin by telling how we got there. We started about one in the morning ladened up with everything you can possibly imagine on a soldier, and in addition I had a kettle—filled with water—most of the chaps had bundles of firewood, and some had extra bread. We marched out of our quarters along the road for a mile or more, and then we took the fields, and presently came to a crest and dropped into a sort of maze of zigzag trenches going up to the front trench. These trenches, you know, are much deeper than one's height; you don't see anything. It's like walking along a mud-walled passage. You just trudge along them in single file. Every now and then some one stumbles into a soak-away for rain-water or swears at a soft place, or somebody blunders into the man in front of him. This seems to go on for hours and hours. It certainly went on for an hour; so I suppose we did two or three miles of it. At one place we crossed a dip in the ground and a ditch, and the trench was built up with sand-bags up to the ditch and there was a plank. Overhead there were stars, and now and then a sort of blaze thing they send up lit up the edge of the trench and gave one a glimpse of a treetop or a factory roof far away. Then for a time it was more difficult to go on because you were blinded. Suddenly just when you were believing that this sort of trudge was going on for ever, we were in the support trenches behind the firing-line, and found the men we were relieving ready to come back.

"And the firing-line itself? Just the same sort of ditch with a parapet of sand-bags, but with dugouts, queer big holes helped out with sleepers from a nearby railway track, opening into it from behind. Dugouts vary a good deal. Many are rather like the cubby-house we made at the end of the orchard last summer; only the walls are thick enough to stand a high-explosive shell. The best dugout in our company's bit of front was quite a dressy affair with some woodwork and a door got from the ruins of a house twenty or thirty yards behind us. It had a stove in it too, and a chimbley, and pans to keep water in. It was the best dugout for miles. This house had a well, and there was a special trench ran back to that, and all day long there was a coming and going for water. There had once been a pump over the well, but a shell had smashed that. . . .

367

"And now you expect me to tell of Germans and the fight and shelling and all sorts of things. *I haven't seen a live German*; I haven't been within two hundred yards of a shell burst, there has been no attack and I haven't got the V.C. I have made myself muddy beyond describing; I've been working all the time, but I've not fired a shot or fought a ha'porth. We were busy all the time—just at work, repairing the parapet, which had to be done gingerly because of snipers, bringing our food in from the rear in big carriers, getting water, pushing our trench out from an angle slanting-ways forward. Getting meals, clearing up and so on takes a lot of time. We make tea in big kettles in the big dugout, which two whole companies use for their cooking, and carry them with a pole through the handles to our platoons. We wash up and wash and shave. Dinner preparation (and consumption) takes two or three hours. Tea too uses up time. It's like camping out and picnicking in the park. This first time (and next too) we have been mixed with some Sussex men who have been here longer and know the business. . . . It works out that we do most of the fatigue. Afterwards we shall go up alone to a pitch of our own. . . .

"But all the time you want to know about the Germans. They are a quarter of a mile away at this part, or nearly a quarter of a mile. When you snatch a peep at them it is like a low parti-coloured stone wall—only the stones are sand-bags. The Germans have them black and white, so that you cannot tell which are loopholes and which are black bags. Our people haven't been so clever—and the War Office love of uniformity has given us only white bags. No doubt it looks neater. But it makes our loopholes plain. For a time black sand-bags were refused. The Germans sniped at us, but not very much. Only one of our lot was hit, by a chance shot that came through the sand-bag at the top of the parapet. He just had a cut in the neck which didn't prevent his walking back. They shelled the trenches half a mile to the left of us though, and it looked pretty hot. The sand-bags flew about. But the men lie low, and it looks worse than it is. The weather was fine and pleasant, as General French always says. And after three days and nights of cramped existence and petty chores, one in the foremost trench and two a little way back, and then two days in support, we came back—and here we are again waiting for our second Go.

"The night-time is perhaps a little more nervy than the day. You get your head up and look about, and see the flat dim country with its ruined houses and its lumps of stuff that are dead bodies and its long vague lines of sand-bags, and the search-lights going like white windmill arms and an occasional flare or star shell. And you have a nasty feeling of people creeping and creeping all night between the trenches. . . .

"Some of us went out to strengthen a place in the parapet that was only one sand-bag thick, where a man had been hit during the day. We made it four bags thick right up to the top. All the while you were doing it, you dreaded to find yourself in the white glare of a search-light, and you had a feeling that something would hit you suddenly from behind. I had to make up my mind not to look round, or I should have kept on looking round. . . . Also our chaps kept shooting over us, within a foot of one's head. Just to persuade the Germans that we were not out of the trench. . . .

"Nothing happened to us. We got back all right. It was silly to have left that parapet only one bag thick. There's the truth, and all of my first time in the trenches.

"And the Germans?

"I tell you there was no actual fighting at all. I never saw the head of one.

"But now see what a good bruddykins I am. I have seen a fight, a real exciting fight, and I have kept it to the last to tell you about. . . . It was a fight in the air. And the British won. It began with a German machine appearing, very minute and high, sailing towards our lines a long way to the left. We could tell it was a German because of the black cross; they decorate every aeroplane with a black Iron Cross on its wings and tail; that our officer could see with his glasses. (He let me look.) Suddenly whack, whack, whack came a line of little puffs of smoke behind it, and then one in front of it, which meant that our anti-aircraft guns were having a go at it. Then, as suddenly, Archibald stopped, and we could see the British machine buzzing across the path of the German. It was just like two birds circling in the air. Or wasps. They buzzed like wasps. There was a little crackling—like brushing you hair in frosty weather. They were shooting at each other. Then our lieutenant called out, 'Hit, by Jove!' and handed the glasses to Park and instantly wanted them back. He says he saw bits of the machine flying off.

"When he said that you could fancy you saw it too, up there in the blue.

"Anyhow the little machine cocked itself up on end. Rather slowly. . . . Then down it came like dropping a knife. . . .

"It made you say 'Ooooo!' to see that dive. It came down, seemed to get a little bit under control, and then dive down again. You could hear the engine roar louder and louder as it came down. I never saw anything fall so fast. We saw it hit the ground among a lot of smashed-up buildings on the crest behind us. It went right over and flew to pieces, all to smithereens. . . .

"It hurt your nose to see it hit the ground. . . .

"Somehow—I was sort of overcome by the thought of the men in that dive. I was trying to imagine how they felt it. From the moment when they realised they were going.

"What on earth must it have seemed like at last?

"They fell seven thousand feet, the men say; some say nine thousand feet. A mile and a half!

"But all the chaps were cheering. . . . And there was our machine hanging in the sky. You wanted to reach up and pat it on the back. It went up higher and away towards the German lines, as though it was looking for another German. It seemed to go now quite slowly. It was an English machine, though for a time we weren't sure; our machines are done in tri-colour just as though they were French. But everybody says it was English. It was one of our crack fighting-machines, and from first to last it has put down seven Germans. . . . And that's really all the fighting there was. There has been fighting here; a month ago. There are perhaps a dozen dead Germans lying out still in front of the lines. Little twisted figures, like overthrown scarecrows, about a hundred yards away. But that is all.

"No, the trenches have disappointed me. They are a scene of tiresome domesticity. They aren't a patch on our quarters in the rear. There isn't the traffic. I've not found a single excuse for firing my rifle. I don't believe I shall ever fire my rifle at an enemy—ever. . . .

"You've seen Rendezvous' fresh promotion, I suppose? He's one of the men the young officers talk about. Everybody believes in him. Do you remember how Manning used to hide from him? . . ."

§ 14

Mr. Britling read this through, and then his thoughts went back to Teddy's disappearance and then returned to Hugh. The youngster was right in the front now, and one had to steel oneself to the possibilities of the case. Somehow Mr. Britling had not expected to find Hugh so speedily in the firing-line, though he would have been puzzled to find a reason why this should not have happened. But he found he had to begin the lesson of stoicism all over again.

He read the letter twice, and then he searched for some indication of its date. He suspected that letters were sometimes held back. . . .

Four days later this suspicion was confirmed by the arrival of another letter from Hugh in which he told of his second spell in the trenches. This time things had been much more lively. They had been heavily shelled and there had been a German attack. And this time he was writing to his father, and wrote more freely. He had scribbled in pencil.

"Things are much livelier here than they were. Our guns are getting to work. They are firing in spells of an hour or so, three or four times a day, and just when they seem to be leaving off they begin again. The Germans suddenly got the range of our trenches the day before yesterday, and began to pound us with high explosive. . . . Well, it's trying. You never seem quite to know when the next bang is coming, and that keeps your nerves hung up; it seems to tighten your muscles and tire you. We've done nothing but lie low all day, and I feel as weary as if I had marched twenty miles. Then 'whop,' one's near you, and there is a flash and everything flies. It's a mad sort of smash-about. One came much too close to be pleasant; as near as the old oil-jars are from the barn court door. It bowled me clean over and sent a lot of gravel over me. When I got up there was twenty yards of trench smashed into a mere hole, and men lying about, and some of them groaning and one three-quarters buried. We had to turn to and get them out as well as we could. . . .

"I felt stunned and insensitive; it was well to have something to do. . . .

"Our guns behind felt for the German guns. It was the damnedest racket. Like giant lunatics smashing about amidst colossal pots and pans. They fired different sorts of shells; stink shells as well as Jack Johnsons, and though we didn't get much of that at our corner there was a sting of chlorine in the air all through the afternoon. Most of the stink shells fell short. We hadn't masks, but we rigged up a sort of protection with our handkershiefs. And it didn't amount to very much. It was rather like the chemistry room after Heinrich and the kids had been mixing things. Most of the time I was busy helping with the men who had got hurt. Suddenly there came a lull. Then some one said the Germans were coming, and I had a glimpse of them.

"You don't look at anything steadily while the guns are going. When a big gun goes off or a shell bursts anywhere near you, you seem neither to see nor hear for a moment. You keep on being intermittently stunned. One sees in a kind of flicker in between the impacts. . . .

"Well there they were. This time I saw them. They were coming out and running a little way and dropping, and our shell was bursting among them and behind them. A lot of it was going too far. I watched what our men were doing, and poured out a lot of cartridges ready to my hand and began to blaze away. Half the German attack never came out of their trench. If they really intended business against us, which I doubt, they were half-hearted in carrying it out. They didn't show for five minutes, and they left two or three score men on the ground. Whenever we saw a man wriggle we were told to fire at him; it might be an unwounded man trying to crawl back. For a time our guns gave them beans. Then it was practically over, but about sunset their guns got back at us again, and the artillery fight went on until it was moonlight. The chaps in our third company caught it rather badly, and then our guns seemed to find something and get the upper hand. . . .

"In the night some of our men went out to repair the wire entanglements, and one man crawled half-way to the enemy trenches to listen. But I had done my bit for the day, and I was supposed to sleep in the dugout. I was far too excited to sleep. All my nerves were jumping about, and my mind was like a lot of flying fragments flying about very fast. . . .

"They shelled us again next day and our tea dixy was hit; so that we didn't get any tea. . . .

"I slept thirty hours after I got back here. And now I am slowly digesting these experiences. Most of our fellows are. My mind and nerves have been rather bumped and bruised by the shelling, but not so much as you might think. I feel as though I'd presently not think very much of it. Some of out men have got the stun of it a lot more than I have. It gets at the older men more. Everybody says that. The men of over thirty-five don't recover from a shelling for weeks. They go about—sort of hesitatingly. . . .

"Life is very primitive here—which doesn't mean that one is getting down to anything fundamental, but only going back to something immediate and simple. It's fetching and carrying and getting water and getting food and going up to the firing-line and coming back. One goes on for weeks, and then one day one finds oneself crying out, 'What is all this for? When is it to end?' I seemed to have something ahead of me before this war began, education, science, work, discoveries; all sorts of things, but it is hard to feel that there is anything ahead of us here. . . .

"Somehow the last spell in the fire trench has shaken up my mind a lot. I was getting used to the war before, but now I've got back to my original amazement at the whole business. I find myself wondering what we are really up to, why the war began, why we were caught into this amazing routine. It looks, it feels orderly, methodical, purposeful. Our officers give us orders and get their orders, and the men back there get their orders. Everybody is getting orders. Back, I suppose, to Lord Kitchener. It goes on for weeks with the effect of being quite sane and intended and the right thing, and then, then suddenly it comes whacking into one's head, 'But this—this is utterly *mad!*' This going to and fro and to and fro and to and fro; this monotony which breaks ever and again into violence—violence that never gets anywhere—is exactly the life that a lunatic leads. Melancholia and mania. . . . It's just a collective obsession—by war. The world is really quite mad. I happen to be having just one gleam of sanity, that won't last after I have finished this letter. I suppose when an individual man goes mad and gets out of the window because he imagines the door is magically impossible, and dances about in the street without his trousers, jabbing at passers-by with a toasting fork, he has just the same sombre sense of unavoidable necessity that we have, all of us, when we go off with our packs into the trenches. . . .

"It's only by an effort that I can recall how life felt in the spring of 1914. Do you remember Heinrich and his attempt to make a table chart of the roses, so that we could sit outside the barn and read the names of all the roses in the barn court? Like the mountain charts they have on tables in Switzerland. What an inconceivable thing that is now! For all I know I shot Heinrich the other night. For all I know he is one of the lumps that we counted after the attack went back.

"It's a queer thing, Daddy, but I have a sort of *seditious* feeling in writing things like this. One gets to feel that it is wrong to think. It's the effect of discipline. Of being part of a machine. Still, I doubt if I ought to think. If one really looks into things in this spirit, where is it going to take us? Ortheris—his real name by-the-by is Arthur Jewell—hasn't any of these troubles. 'The b——y Germans butted into Belgium,' he says. 'We've got to 'oof 'em out again. That's all abart it. Least-ways it's all *I* know. . . . I don't know nothing about Serbia, I don't know nothing about anything, except that the Germans got to stop this sort of Gime for Everlasting, Amen.' . . .

"Sometimes I think he's righter than I am. Sometimes I think he is only madder."

§ 15

These letters weighed heavily upon Mr. Britling's mind. He perceived that this precociously wise, subtle youngster of his was now close up to the line of injury and death, going to and fro from it, in a perpetual fluctuating danger. At any time now in the day or night the evil thing might wing its way to him. If Mr. Britling could have prayed, he would have prayed for Hugh. He began and never finished some ineffectual prayers.

He tried to persuade himself of a Roman stoicism; that he would be sternly proud, sternly satisfied, if this last sacrifice for his country was demanded from him. He perceived he was merely humbugging himself. . . .

This war had no longer the simple greatness that would make any such stern happiness possible. . . .

The disaster to Teddy and Mrs. Teddy hit him hard. He winced at the thought of Mrs. Teddy's white face; the unspoken accusation in her eyes. He felt he could never bring himself to say his one excuse to her: "I did not keep Hugh back. If I had done that, then you might have the right to blame."

If he had overcome every other difficulty in the way to an heroic pose there was still Hugh's unconquerable lucidity of outlook. War *was* a madness. . . .

But what else was to be done? What else could be done? We could not give in to Germany. If a lunatic struggles, sane men must struggle too. . . .

Mr. Britling had ceased to write about the war at all. All his later writings about it had been abandoned unfinished. He could not imagine them counting, affecting any one, producing any effect. Indeed he was writing now very intermittently. His contributions to *The Times* had fallen away. He was perpetually thinking now about the war, about life and death, about the religious problems that had seemed so remote in the days of the peace; but none of his thinking would become clear and definite enough for writing. All the clear stars of his mind were hidden by the stormy clouds of excitement that the daily newspaper perpetually renewed and by the daily developments of life. And just as his professional income shrank before his mental confusion and impotence, the private income that came from his and his wife's investments became uncertain. She had had two thousand pounds in the Constantinople loan, seven hundred in debentures of the Ottoman railway; he had held similar sums in two Hungarian and one Bulgarian loan. There seemed no limit set to the possibilities of shrinkage of capital and income. Income tax had leaped to colossal dimensions, the cost of most things had risen, and the tangle of life was now increased by the need for retrenchments and economies. He decided that Gladys, his facetiously named automobile, was a luxury, and sold her for a couple of hundred pounds. He lost his gardener, who had gone to higher-priced work with a miller, and he had great trouble to replace him, so that the garden became disagreeably unkempt and unsatisfactory. He had to give up his frequent trips to London. He was obliged to defer Statesminster for the boys. For a time at any rate they must go as day boys to Brinsmead. At every point he met this uncongenial consideration of ways and means. For years now he had gone easy, lived with a certain self-indulgence. It was extraordinarily vexatious to have one's greater troubles for one's country and one's son and one's faith crossed and complicated by these little troubles of the extra sixpence and the untimely bill.

What worried his mind perhaps more than anything else was his gradual loss of touch with the essential issues of the war. At first the militarism, the aggression of Germany, had seemed so bad that he could not see the action of Britain and her allies as anything but entirely righteous. He had seen the war plainly and simply in the phrase: "Now this militarism must end." He had seen Germany as a system, as imperialism and junkerism, as a callous materialist aggression, as the spirit that makes war, and the Allies as the protest of humanity against all these evil things.

Insensibly, in spite of himself, this first version of the war was giving place to another. The tawdry, rhetorical German Emperor, who had been the great antagonist at the outset, the last upholder of Cæsarism, God's anointed with the withered arm and the mailed fist, had receded from the foreground of the picture; that truer Germany which is thought and system, which is the will to do things thoroughly, the Germany of Ostwald and the once rejected Hindenburg, was coming to the fore. It made no apology for the errors and crimes that had been imposed upon it by its Hohenzollern leadership, but it fought now to save itself from the destruction and division that would be its inevitable lot if it accepted defeat too easily; fought to hold out, fought for a second chance, with discipline, with skill and patience, with a steadfast will, It fought with science, it fought with economy, with machines and thought against all too human antagonists. It necessitated an implacable hostility, but also it commanded respect. Against it fought three great peoples with as fine a will; but they had neither the unity, the habitual discipline, nor the science of Germany, and it was the latter defect that became more and more the distressful matter of Mr. Britling's thoughts. France after her initial experiences, after her first reeling month, had risen from the very verge of defeat to a steely splendour of resolution, but England and Russia, those twin slack giants, still wasted force, were careless, negligent, uncertain. Everywhere up and down the scale, from the stupidity of the uniform sand-bags and Hugh's young Officer who would not use a map, to the general conception and direction of the war, Mr. Britling's inflamed and oversensitised intelligence perceived the same bad qualities for which he had so often railed upon his countrymen in the days of the peace, that impatience, that indolence, that wastefulness and inconclusiveness, that failure to grip issues and do obviously necessary things. The same lax qualities that had brought England so close to the supreme imbecility of a civil war in Ireland in July, 1914, were now muddling and prolonging the war, and postponing, it might be for ever, the victory that had seemed so certain only a year ago. The politician still intrigued, the ineffectives still directed. Against brains used to the utmost their fight was a stupid thrusting forth of men and men and yet more men, men badly trained, under-equipped, stupidly led. A press clamour for invention and scientific initiative was stifled under a committee of elderly celebrities and eminent dufferdon; from the outset, the Ministry of Munitions seemed under the influence of the "business man." . . .

It is true that righteousness should triumph over the tyrant and the robber, but have carelessness and incapacity any right to triumph over capacity and foresight? Men were coming now to dark questionings between this intricate choice. And, indeed, was our cause all righteousness?

There surely is the worst doubt of all for a man whose son is facing death.

Where we indeed standing against tyranny for freedom?

There came drifting to Mr. Britling's ears a confusion of voices, voices that told of reaction, of the schemes of employers to best the trade-unions, of greedy shippers and greedy house-landlords reaping their harvest, of waste and treason in the very households of the Ministry, of religious cant and intolerance at large, of self-advertisement written in letters of blood, of forestalling and jobbery, of irrational and exasperating oppressions in India and Egypt. . . It came with a shock to him. too, that Hugh should see so little else than madness in the war, and have so pitiless a realisation of its essential futility. The boy forced his father to see—what indeed all along he had been seeing more and more clearly. The war, even by the standards of adventure and conquest, had long since become a monstrous absurdity. Some way there must be out of this bloody entanglement that was yielding victory to neither side, that was yielding nothing but waste and death beyond all precedent. The vast majority of people everywhere must be desiring peace, willing to buy peace at any reasonable price, and in all the world it seemed there was insufficient capacity to end the daily butchery and achieve the peace that was so universally desired, the peace that would be anything better than a breathing space for further warfare. . . . Every day came the papers with the balanced story of battles, losses, destruction, ships sunk, towns smashed. And never a decision, never a sign of decision.

One Saturday afternoon Mr. Britling found himself with Mrs. Britling at Claverings. Lady Homartyn was in mourning for her two nephews, the Glassington boys, who had both been killed, one in Flanders, the other in Gallipoli. Raeburn was there too, despondent and tired-looking. There were three young men in khaki, one with the red of a staff officer; there were two or three women whom Mr. Britling had not met before, and Miss Sharsper, the novelist, fresh from nursing experience among the convalescents in the south of France. But he was disgusted to find that the gathering was dominated by his old antagonist, Lady Frensham, unsubdued, unaltered, rampant over them all, arrogant, impudent, insulting. She was in mourning, she had the most splendid black furs Mr. Britling had ever seen; her large triumphant profile came out of them like the head of a vulture out of its ruff; her elder brother was a wounded prisoner in Germany, her second was dead; it would seem that hers were the only sacrifices the war had yet extorted from any one. She spoke as though it gave her the sole right to criticise the war or claim compensation for the war.

Her incurable propensity to split the country, to make mischievous accusations against classes and districts and public servants, was having full play. She did her best to provoke Mr. Britling into a dispute, and throw some sort of imputation upon his patriotism as distinguished from her own noisy and intolerant conceptions of "loyalty."

She tried him first with conscription. She threw out insults at the shirkers and the "funk classes." All the middle-class people clung on to their wretched little businesses, made any sort of excuse. . . .

Mr. Britling was stung to defend them. "A business," he said acidly, "isn't like land, which waits and grows rich for its owner. And these people can't leave ferrety little agents behind them when they go off to serve. Tens of thousands of middle-class men have ruined themselves and flung away every prospect they had in the world to go to this war."

"And scores of thousands haven't!" said Lady Frensham. "They are the men I'm thinking of. . . ."

Mr. Britling ran through a little list of aristocratic stay-at-homes that began with a duke.

"And not a soul speaks to him in consequence," she said.

She shifted her attack to the Labour people. They would rather see the country defeated than submit to a little discipline.

"Because they have no faith in the house of lawyers or the house of landlords," said Mr. Britling. "Who can blame them?"

She proceeded to tell everybody what she would do with strikers. She would give them "short shrift." She would give them a taste of the Prussian way—homœopathic treatment. "But of course old vote-catching Asquith daren't—he daren't!" Mr. Britling opened his mouth and said nothing; he was silenced. The men in khaki listened respectfully but ambiguously; one of the younger ladies it seemed was entirely of Lady Frensham's way of thinking, and anxious to show it. The good lady having now got her hands upon the Cabinet proceeded to deal faithfully with its two-and-twenty members.

Winston Churchill had overridden Lord Fisher upon the question of Gallipoli, and incurred terrible responsibilities. Lord Haldane—she called him "Tubby Haldane"—was a convicted traitor. "The man's a German out and out. Oh! what if he hasn't a drop of German blood in his veins? He's a German by choice—which is worse."

"I thought he had a certain capacity for organisation," said Mr. Britling.

"We don't want his organisation, and we don't want *him*," said Lady Frensham.

Mr. Britling pleaded for particulars of the late Lord Chancellor's treasons. There were no particulars. It was just an idea the good lady had got into her head, that had got into a number of accessible heads. There was only one strong man in all the country now, Lady Frensham insisted. That was Sir Edward Carson.

Mr. Britling jumped in his chair.

"But has he ever done anything?" he cried, "except embitter Ireland?"

Lady Frensham did not hear that question. She pursued her glorious theme. Lloyd George, who had once been worthy only of the gallows, was now the sole minister fit to put beside her hero. He had won her heart by his condemnation of the working man. He was the one man who was not afraid to speak out, to tell them they drank, to tell them they shirked and loafed, to tell them plainly that if defeat came to this country the blame would fall upon *them!*

"*No!*" cried Mr. Britling.

"Yes," said Lady Frensham. "Upon them and those who have flattered and misled them. . . ."

And so on. . . .

It presently became necessary for Lady Homartyn to rescue Mr. Britling from the great lady's patriotic tramplings. He found himself drifting into the autumnal garden—the show of dahlias had never been so wonderful—in the company of Raeburn and the staff-officer and a small woman who was presently discovered to be remarkably well informed. They were all despondent. "I think all this promiscuous blaming of people is quite the worse—and most ominous—thing about us just now," said Mr. Britling after the restful pause that followed their departure from the presence of Lady Frensham.

"It goes on everywhere," said the staff-officer.

"Is it really—honest?" said Mr. Britling.

Raeburn, after reflection, decided to answer. "As far as it is stupid, yes. There's a lot of blame coming; there's bound to be a day of reckoning, and I suppose we've all got an instinctive disposition to find a scapegoat for our common sins. The Tory press is pretty rotten, and there's a strong element of mere personal spite—in the Churchill attacks for example. Personal jealousy probably. Our 'old families' seem to have got vulgar-spirited imperceptibly—in a generation or so. They quarrel and shirk and lay blame exactly as bad servants do—and things are still far too much in their hands. Things are getting muffed, there can be no doubt about that—not fatally, but still rather seriously. And the government—it was human before the war, and we've added no archangels. There's muddle. There's mutual suspicion. You never know what newspaper office Lloyd George won't be in touch with next. He's honest and patriotic and energetic, but he's mortally afraid of old women and class intrigues. He doesn't know where to get his backing. He's got all a labour member's terror of the dagger at his back. There's a lack of nerve, too, in getting rid of prominent officers—who have friends."

The Staff-officer nodded.

"Northcliffe seems to me to have a case," said Mr. Britling. "Every one abuses him."

"I'd stop his *Daily Mail*," said Raeburn, "I'd leave *The Times*, but I'd stop *The Daily Mail* on the score of its placards alone. It overdoes Northcliffe. It translates him into the shrieks and yells of underlings. The plain fact is that Northcliffe is scared out of his wits by German efficiency—and in war-time when a man is scared out of his wits, whether he is honest or not, you put his head in a bag or hold a pistol to it to calm him. . . What is the good of all this clamouring for a change of government? We haven't change of government. It's like telling a tramp to get a change of linen. Our men, all our public men, are second-rate men, with the habits of advocates. There is nothing masterful in their minds. How can you expect the system to produce anything else? But they are doing as well as they can, and there is no way of putting in any one else now, and there you are."

"Meanwhile," said Mr. Britling, "our boys—get killed."

"They'd get killed all the more if you had—let us say— Carson and Lloyd George and Northcliffe and Lady Frensham, with, I suppose, Austin Harrison and Horatio Bottomley thrown in—as a Strong Silent Government. . . . I'd rather have Northcliffe as dictator than that. . . We can't suddenly go back on the past and alter our type. We didn't listen to Matthew Arnold. We've never thoroughly turned out and cleaned up our higher schools. We've resisted instruction. We've preferred to maintain our national luxuries of a bench of bishops and party politics. And compulsory Greek and the university sneer. And Lady Frensham. And all that sort of thing. And here we are! . . . Well, damn it, we're in for it now; we've got to plough through with it—with what we have—as what we are."

The young staff-officer nodded. He thought that was "about it."

"You've got no sons," said Mr. Britling.

"I'm not even married," said Raeburn, as though he thanked God.

The little well-informed lady remarked abruptly that she had two sons; one was just home wounded from Suvla Bay. What her son told her made her feel very grave. She said that the public was still quite in the dark about the battle of Anafarta. If had been a hideous muddle, and we had been badly beaten. The staff work had been awful. Nothing joined up, nothing was on the spot and in time. The water-supply, for example, had gone wrong; the men had been mad with thirst. One regiment which she named had not been supported by another; when at last the first came back the two battalions fought in the trenches regardless of the enemy. There had been no leading, no correlation, no plan. Some of the guns, she declared, had been left behind in Egypt. Some of the train was untraceable to this day. It was mislaid somewhere in the Levant. At the beginning Sir Ian Hamilton had not even been present. He had failed to get there in time. It had been the reckless throwing away of an army. And so hopeful an army! Her son declared it meant the complete failure of the Dardanelles project. . .

"And when one hears how near we came to victory!" she cried, and left it at that.

"Three times this year," said Raeburn, "we have missed victories because of the badness of our staff work. It's no good picking out scapegoats. It's a question of national habit. It's because the sort of man we turn out from our public schools has never learned how to catch trains, get to an office on the minute, pack a knapsack properly, or do anything smartly and quickly—anything whatever that he can possibly get done for him. You can't expect men who are habitually easy-going to keep bucked up to a high pitch of efficiency for any length of time. All their training is against it. All their tradition. They hate being prigs. An Englishman will be any sort of stupid failure rather than appear a prig. That's why we've lost three good fights that we ought to have won—and thousands and thousands of men— and material and time, precious beyond reckoning. We've lost a year. We've dashed the spirit of our people."

"My boy in Flanders," said Mr. Britling, "says about the same thing. He says our officers have never learned to count beyond ten, and that they are scared at the sight of a map. . . ."

"And the war goes on," said the little woman.

"How long, oh Lord! how long?" cried Mr. Britling.

"I'd give them another year," said the staff-officer. "Just going as we are going. Then something *must* give way. There will be no money anywhere. There'll be no more men. . . . I suppose they'll feel that shortage first anyhow. Russia alone has over twenty millions."

"That's about the size of it," said Raeburn. . . .

"Do you think, sir, there'll be civil war?" asked the young staff-officer abruptly after a pause.

There was a little interval before any one answered this surprising question.

"After the peace, I mean," said the young officer.

"There'll be just the devil to pay," said Raeburn.

"One thing after another in the country is being pulled up by its roots," reflected Mr. Britling.

"We've never produced a plan for the war, and it isn't likely we shall have one for the peace," said Raeburn, and added: "and Lady Frensham's little lot will be doing their level best to sit on the safety-valve. . . . They'll rake up Ireland and Ulster from the very start. But I doubt if Ulster will save 'em.

"We shall squabble. What else do we ever do?"

No one seemed able to see more than that. A silence fell on the little party.

"Well, thank heaven for these dahlias," said Raeburn, affecting the philosopher.

The young staff-officer regarded the dahlias without enthusiasm. . . .

§ 16

Mr. Britling sat one September afternoon with Captain Lawrence Carmine in the sunshine of the barn court, and smoked with him and sometimes talked and sometimes sat still.

"When it began I did not believe that this war could be like other wars," he said. "I did not dream it. I thought that we had grown wiser at last. It seemed to me like the dawn of a great clearing up. I thought the common sense of mankind would break out like a flame, an indignant flame, and consume all this obsolete foolery of empires and banners and militarism directly it made its attack upon human happiness. A score of things that I see now were preposterous, I thought must happen— naturally. I thought America would declare herself against the Belgian outrage; that she would not tolerate the smashing of the great sister republic—if only for the memory of Lafayette. Well—I gather America is chiefly concerned about our making cotton contraband. I thought the Balkan States were capable of a reasonable give and take; of a common care for their common freedom. I see now three German royalties trading in peasants, and no men in their lands to gainsay them. I saw this war, as so many Frenchmen have seen it, as something that might legitimately command a splendid enthusiasm of indignation. . . . It was all a dream, the dream of a prosperous comfortable man who had never come to the cutting edge of life. Everywhere cunning, everywhere small feuds and hatreds, distrusts, dishonesties, timidities, feebleness of purpose, dwarfish imaginations, swarm over the great and simple issues. . . . It is a war now like any other of the mobbing, many-aimed cataclysms that have shattered empires and devastated the world; it is a war without point, a war that has lost its soul, it has become mere incoherent fighting and destruction, a demonstration in vast and tragic forms of the stupidity and ineffectiveness of our species. . . ."

He stopped, and there was a little interval of silence.

Captain Carmine tossed the fag end of his cigar very neatly into a tub of hydrangeas. "Three thousand years ago in China," he said, "there were men as sad as we are, for the same cause."

"Three thousand years ahead perhaps," said Mr. Britling, "there will still be men with the same sadness. . . . And yet— and yet. . . . No. Just now I have no elasticity. It is not in my nature to despair, but things are pressing me down. I don't recover as I used to recover. I tell myself still that though the way is long and hard the spirit of hope, the spirit of creation, the generosities and gallantries in the heart of man, must end in victory. But I say that over as one repeats a worn-out prayer. The light is out of the sky for me. Sometimes I doubt if it will ever come back. Let younger men take heart and go on with the world. If I could die for the right thing now—instead of just having to live on in this world of ineffective struggle—I would be glad to die now, Carmine. . . ."

§ 17

In these days also Mr. Direck was very unhappy.

For Cissie, at any rate, had not lost touch with the essential issues of the war. She was as clear as ever that German militarism and the German attack on Belgium and France was the primary subject of the war. And she dismissed all secondary issues. She continued to demand why America did not fight. "We fight for Belgium. Won't you fight for the Dutch and Norwegian ships? Won't you even fight for your own ships that the Germans are sinking?"

Mr. Direck attempted explanations that were ill received.

"You were ready enough to fight the Spaniards when they blew up the *Maine*, But the Germans can sink the *Lusitania!* That's—as you say—a different proposition."

His mind was shot by an extraordinary suspicion that she thought the *Lusitania* an American vessel. But Mr. Direck was learning his Cissie, and he did not dare to challenge her on this score.

"You haven't got hold of the American proposition," he said. "We're thinking beyond wars."

"That's what we have been trying to do," said Cissie. "Do you think we came into it for the fun of the thing?"

"Haven't I shown in a hundred ways that I sympathise?"

"Oh—sympathy! . . ."

He fared little better at Mr. Britling's hands. Mr. Britling talked darkly, but pointed all the time only too plainly at America. "There's two sorts of liberalism," said Mr. Britling, "that pretend to be the same thing; there's the liberalism of great aims and the liberalism of defective moral energy. . . ."

§ 18

It was not until Teddy had been missing for three weeks that Hugh wrote about him. The two Essex battalions on the Flanders front were apparently wide apart, and it was only from home that Hugh learned what had happened.

"You can't imagine how things narrow down when one is close up against them. One does not know what is happening even within a few miles of us, until we get the newspapers. Then, with a little reading between the lines and some bold guessing, we fit our little bit of experience with a general shape. Of course I've wondered at times about Teddy. But oddly enough I've never thought of him very much as being out here. It's queer, I know, but I haven't. I can't imagine why. . . .

"I don't know about 'missing.' We've had nothing going on here that has led to any missing. All our men have been accounted for. But every few miles along the front conditions alter. His lot may have been closer up to the enemy, and there may have been a rush and a fight for a bit of trench either way. In some parts the German trenches are not thirty yards away, and there is mining, bomb-throwing, and perpetual creeping up and give and take. Here we've been getting a bit forward. But I'll tell you about that presently. And, anyhow, I don't understand about 'missing.' There's very few prisoners taken now. But don't tell Letty that. I try to imagine old Teddy in it. . . .

"Missing's a queer thing. It isn't tragic—or pitiful. Or partly reassuring like 'prisoner.' It just sends one speculating and speculating. I can't find any one who knows where the 14th Essex are. Things move about here so mysteriously that for all I know we may find them in the next trench next time we go up. But there *is* a chance for Teddy. It's worth while bucking Letty all you can. And at the same time there's odds against him. There plainly and unfeelingly is how things stand in my mind. I think chiefly of Letty. I'm glad Cissie is with her, and I'm glad she's got the boy. Keep her busy. She was frightfully fond of him. I've seen all sorts of things between them, and I know that. . . . I'll try and write to her soon, and I'll find something hopeful to tell her.

"Meanwhile I've got something to tell you. I've been through a fight, a big fight, and I haven't got a scratch. I've taken two prisoners with my lily hand. Men were shot close to me. I didn't mind that a bit. It was as exciting as one of those bitter fights we used to have round the hockey-goal. I didn't mind anything till afterwards. Then when I was in the trench in the evening I trod on something slippery—pah! And after it was all over one of my chums got it—sort of unfairly. And I kept on thinking of those two things so much that all the early part is just dreamlike. It's more like something I've read in a book, or seen in *The Illustrated London News* than actually been through. One had been thinking so often, how will it feel? how shall I behave? that when it came it had an effect of being flat and ordinary.

"They say we hadn't got enough guns in the spring or enough ammunition. That's all right now—anyhow. They started in plastering the Germans overnight, and right on until it was just daylight. I never heard such a row, and their trenches—we could stand up and look at them without getting a single shot at us—were flying about like the crater of a volcano. We were not in our firing trench. We had gone back into some new trenches at the rear—I think to get out of the way of the counter-fire. But this morning they weren't doing very much. For once our guns were on top. There was a feeling of anticipation—very like waiting for an examination paper to be given out; then we were at it. Getting out of a trench to attack gives you an odd feeling of being just hatched. Suddenly the world is big. I don't remember our gun-fire stopping. And then you rush. 'Come on! Come on!' say the officers. Everybody gives a sort of howl and rushes. When you see men dropping, you rush the faster. The only thing that checks you at all is the wire twisted about everywhere. You don't want to trip over that. The frightening thing is the exposure. After being in the trenches so long you feel naked. You run like a scared child for the German trench ahead. I can't understand the iron nerve of a man who can expose his back by turning to run away. And there's a thirsty feeling with one's bayonet. But they didn't wait. They dropped rifles and ran. But we ran so fast after them that we caught one or two in the second trench. I got down into that, heard a voice behind me, and found my two prisoners lying artful in a dugout. They held up their hands as I turned. If they hadn't I doubt if I should have done anything to them. I didn't feel like it. I felt *friendly*.

"Not all the Germans ran. Three or four stuck to their machine-guns until they got bayoneted. Both the trenches were frightfully smashed about, and in the first one there were little knots and groups of dead. We got to work at once shying the sand-bags over from the old front of the trench to the parados. Our guns had never stopped all the time; they were now plastering the third-line trenches. And almost at once the German shells began dropping into us. Of course they had the range to an inch. One didn't have any time to feel and think; one just set oneself with all one's energy to turn the trench over. . . .

393

"I don't remember that I helped or cared for a wounded man all the time, or felt anything about the dead except to step over them and not on them. I was just possessed by the idea that we had to get the trench into a sheltering state before they tried to come back. And then stick there. I just wanted to win, and there was nothing else in my mind. . . .

"They did try to come back, but not very much. . . .

"Then when I began to feel sure of having got hold of the trench for good, I began to realise just how tired I was and how high the sun had got. I began to look about me, and found most of the other men working just as hard as I had been doing. 'We've done it!' I said, and that was the first word I'd spoken since I told my two Germans to come out of it, and stuck a man with a wounded leg to watch them. 'It's a bit of All Right,' said Ortheris, knocking off also, and lighting a half-consumed cigarette. He had been wearing it behind his ear, I believe, ever since the charge. Against this occasion. He'd kept close up to me all the time, I realised. And then old Park turned up very cheerful with a weak bayonet jab in his forearm that he wanted me to rebandage. It was good to see him practically all right too.

" 'I took two prisoners,' I said, and everybody I spoke to I told that. I was fearfully proud of it.

"I thought that if I could take two prisoners in my first charge I was going to be some soldier.

"I had stood it all admirably. I didn't feel a bit shaken. I was as tough as anything. I'd seen death and killing, and it was all just hockey.

"And then that confounded Ortheris must needs go and get killed.

"The shell knocked me over, and didn't hurt me a bit. I was a little stunned, and some dirt was thrown over me, and when I got up on my knees I saw Jewell lying about six yards off—and his legs were all smashed about. Ugh! Pulped!

"He looked amazed. 'Bloody,' he said, 'bloody.' He fixed his eyes on me, and suddenly grinned. You know we'd once had two fights about his saying 'bloody,' I think I told you at the time, a fight and a return match, he couldn't box for nuts, but he stood up like a Briton, and it appealed now to his sense of humour that I should be standing there too dazed to protest at the old offence. 'I thought *you* was done in,' he said. 'I'm in a mess—a bloody mess, ain't I? Like a stuck pig. Bloody—right enough. Bloody! I didn't know I 'ad it *in* me.'

"He looked at me and grinned with a sort of pale satisfaction in keeping up to the last—dying good Ortheris to the finish. I just stood up helpless in front of him, still rather dazed.

"He said something about having a thundering thirst on him.

"I really don't believe he felt any pain. He would have done if he had lived.

"And then while I was fumbling with my water-bottle, he collapsed. He forgot all about Ortheris. Suddenly he said something that cut me all to ribbons. His face puckered up just like the face of a fretful child which refuses to go to bed. 'I didn't want to be aut of it,' he said petulantly. 'And I'm done!' And then—then he just looked discontented and miserable and died—right off. Turned his head a little way over. As if he was impatient at everything. Fainted—and fluttered out.

"For a time I kept trying to get him to drink. . . .

"I couldn't believe he was dead. . . .

"And suddenly it was all different. I began to cry. Like a baby. I kept on with the water-bottle at his teeth long after I was convinced he was dead. I didn't want him to be *aut* of it! God

395

knows how I didn't. I wanted my dear little Cockney cad back. Oh! most frightfully I wanted him back.

"I shook him. I was like a scared child. I blubbered and howled things. . . . It's all different since he died.

"My dear, dear Father, I am grieving and grieving—and it's altogether nonsense. And it's all mixed up in my mind with the mess I trod on. And it gets worse and worse. So that I don't seem to feel anything really, even for Teddy.

"It's been just the last straw of all this hellish foolery. . . .

"If ever there was a bigger lie, my dear Daddy, than any other, it is that man is a reasonable creature. . . .

"War is just foolery—lunatic foolery—hell's foolery. . . .

"But, anyhow, your son is sound and well—if sorrowful and angry. We were relieved that night. And there are rumours that very soon we are to have a holiday and a refit. We lost rather heavily. We have been praised. But all along, Essex has done well. I can't reckon to get back yet, but there are such things as leave for eight-and-forty hours or so in England. . . .

"I shall be glad of that sort of turning round. . . .

"I'm tired. Oh! I'm tired. . . .

"I wanted to write all about Jewell to his mother or his sweetheart or some one; I wanted to wallow in his praises, to say all the things I really find now that I thought about him, but I haven't even had that satisfaction. He was a Poor Law child; he was raised in one of those awful places between Sutton and Banstead in Surrey. I've told you of all the sweet-hearting he had. 'Soldiers Three' was his Bible; he was always singing 'Tipperary,' and he never got the tune right nor learned more than three lines of it. He laced all his talk with 'b——y'; it was his jewel, his ruby. But he had the pluck of a robin or a squirrel; I never knew him scared or anything but cheerful. Misfortunes, humiliations, only made him chatty. And he'd starve to have something to give away.

"Well, well, this is the way of war, Daddy. This is what war is. Damn the Kaiser! Damn all fools.... Give my love to the Mother and the bruddykins and every one...."

§ 19

It was just a day or so over three weeks after this last letter from Hugh that Mr. Direck reappeared at Matching's Easy. He had had a trip to Holland—a trip that was as much a flight from Cissie's reproaches as a mission of inquiry. He had intended to go on into Belgium, where he had already been doing useful relief work under Mr. Hoover, but the confusion of his own feelings had checked him and brought him back.

Mr. Direck's mind was in a perplexity only too common during the stresses of that tragic year. He was entangled in a paradox; like a large majority of Americans at that time his feelings were quite definite pro-Ally, and like so many in that majority he had a very clear conviction that it would be wrong and impossible for the United States to take part in the war. His sympathies were intensely with the Dower House and its dependent cottage; he would have wept with generous emotion to see the Stars and Stripes interwoven with the three other great banners of red, white and blue that led the world against German imperialism and militarism, but for all that his mind would not march to that tune. Against all these impulses fought something very fundamental in Mr. Direck's composition, a preconception of America that had grown almost insensibly in his mind, the idea of America as a polity aloof from the Old World system, as a fresh start for humanity, as something altogether too fine and precious to be dragged into even the noblest of European conflicts. America was to be the beginning of the fusion of mankind, neither German nor British nor French nor in any way national. She was to be the great experiment in peace and reasonableness. She had to hold civilisation and social order out of this fray, to be a refuge for all those finer things that die under stress and turmoil; it was her task to maintain the standards of life and the claims of humanitarianism in the conquered province and the prisoners' compound, she had to be the healer and arbitrator, the remonstrance and not the smiting hand. Surely there were enough smiting hands.

But this idea of an America judicial, remonstrating, and aloof, led him to a conclusion that scandalised him. If America will not, and should not use force in the ends of justice, he argued, then America has no right to make and export munitions of war. She must not trade in what she disavows. He had a quite exaggerated idea of the amount of munitions that America was sending to the Allies, he was inclined to believe that they were entirely dependent upon their transatlantic supplies, and so he found himself persuaded that the victory of the Allies and the honour of America were incompatible things. And—in spite of his ethical aloofness— he loved the Allies. He wanted them to win, and he wanted America to abandon a course that he believed was vitally necessary to their victory. It was an intellectual dilemma. He hid this self-contradiction from Matching's Easy with much the same feelings that a curate might hide a poisoned dagger at a tea-party. . . .

It was entirely against his habits of mind to hide anything—more particularly an entanglement with a difficult

398

proposition—but he perceived quite clearly that neither Cecily nor Mr. Britling was really to be trusted to listen calmly to what, under happier circumstances, might be a profoundly interesting moral complication. Yet it was not in his nature to conceal; it was in his nature to state.

And Cecily made things much more difficult. She was pitiless with him. She kept him aloof. "How can I let you make love to me," she said, "when our Englishmen are all going to the war, when Teddy is a prisoner and Hugh is in the trenches. If I were a man——!"

She couldn't be induced to see any case for America. England was fighting for freedom, and America ought to be beside her. "All the world ought to unite against this German wickedness," she said.

"I'm doing all I can to help in Belgium," he protested. "Aren't I working? We've fed four million people."

He had backbone, and he would not let her, he was resolved, bully him into a falsehood about his country. America was aloof. She was right to be aloof. . . . At the same time, Cecily's reproaches were unendurable. And he could feel he was drifting apart from her. . . .

He couldn't make America go to war.

In the quiet of his London hotel he thought it all out. He sat at a writing-table making notes of a perfectly lucid statement of the reasonable, balanced liberal American opinion. An instinct of caution determined him to test it first on Mr. Britling.

But Mr. Britling realised his worst expectations. He was beyond listening.

"I've not heard from my boy for more than three weeks," said Mr. Britling in the place of any salutation. "This morning makes three-and-twenty days without a letter."

It seemed to Mr. Direck that Mr. Britling had suddenly grown ten years older. His face was more deeply lined; the colour and texture of his complexion had gone grey. He moved restlessly and badly; his nerves were manifestly unstrung.

"It's intolerable that one should be subjected to this ghastly suspense. The boy isn't three hundred miles away."

Mr. Direck made obvious inquiries.

"Always before he's written—generally once a fortnight."

They talked of Hugh for a time, but Mr. Britling was fitful and irritable and quite prepared to hold Mr. Direck accountable for the laxity of the War Office, the treachery of Bulgaria, the ambiguity of Roumania or any other barb that chanced to be sticking into his sensibilities. They lunched precariously. Then they went into the study to smoke.

There Mr. Direck was unfortunate enough to notice a copy of that innocent American publication *The New Republic*, lying close to two or three numbers of *The Fatherland*, a pro-German periodical which at that time inflicted itself upon English writers with the utmost determination. Mr. Direck remarked that *The New Republic* was an interesting effort on the part of "*la Jeunesse Américaine.*" Mr. Britling regarded the interesting effort with a jaded, unloving eye.

"You Americans," he said, "are the most extraordinary people in the world."

"Our conditions are exceptional," said Mr. Direck.

"You think they are," said Mr. Britling, and paused, and then began to deliver his soul about America in a discourse of accumulating bitterness. At first he reasoned and explained, but as he went on he lost self-control; he became dogmatic, he became denunciatory, he became abusive. He identified Mr. Direck more and more with his subject; he thrust the uncivil

"You" more and more directly at him. He let his cigar go out, and flung it impatiently into the fire. As though America was responsible for its going out. . . .

Like many Britons Mr. Britling had that touch of patriotic feeling towards America which takes the form of impatient criticism. No one in Britain ever calls an American a foreigner. To see faults in Germany or Spain is to tap boundless fountains of charity; but the faults of America rankle in an English mind almost as much as the faults of England. Mr. Britling could explain away the faults of England readily enough; our Hanoverian monarchy, our Established Church and its deadening effect on education, our imperial obligations and the strain they made upon our supplies of administrative talent were all very serviceable for that purpose. But there in America was the old race, without Crown or Church or international embarrassment, and it was still falling short of splendour. His speech to Mr. Direck had the rancour of a family quarrel. Let me only give a few sentences that were to stick in Mr. Direck's memory.

"You think you are out of it for good and all. So did we think. We were as smug as you are when France went down in '71. . . . Yours is only one further degree of insularity. You think this vacuous aloofness of yours is some sort of moral superiority. So did we, so did we. . . .

"It won't last you ten years if we go down. . . .

"Do you think that our disaster will leave the Atlantic for you? Do you fancy there is any Freedom of the Seas possible beyond such freedom as we maintain, except the freedom to attack you? For forty years the British fleet has guarded all America from European attack. Your Monroe Doctrine skulks behind it now. . . .

"I'm sick of this high thin talk of yours about the war. . . . You are a nation of ungenerous onlookers—watching us throttle or be throttled. You gamble on our winning. And we shall win; we shall win. And you will profit. And when we have won a victory only one shade less terrible than defeat, then you think you will come in and tinker with our peace. Bleed us a little more to please your hyphenated patriots. . . ."

He came to his last shaft. "You talk of your New Ideals of Peace. You say that you are too proud to fight. But your business men in New York give the show away. There's a little printed card now in half the offices in New York that tells of the real pacificism of America. They're busy, you know. Trade's real good. And so as not to interrupt it they stick up this card: 'Nix on the war!' Think of it!—'Nix on the war!' Here is the whole fate of mankind at stake, and America's contribution is a little grumbling when the Germans sank the *Lusitania*, and no end of grumbling when we hold up a ship or two and some fool of a harbour-master makes an overcharge. Otherwise—'Nix on the war!' . . .

"Well, let it be Nix on the war! Don't come here and talk to me! You who were searching registers a year ago to find your Essex kin. Let it be Nix! Explanations! What do I want with explanations? And"—he mocked his guest's accent and his guest's mode of thought—"dif'cult prap'sitions."

He got up and stood irresolute. He knew he was being preposterously unfair to America, and outrageously uncivil to a trusting guest; he knew he had no business now to end the talk in this violent fashion. But it was an enormous relief. And to mend matters——

No! He was glad he'd said these things. . . .

He swung a shoulder to Mr. Direck, and walked out of the room. . . .

Mr. Direck heard him cross the hall and slam the door of the little parlour. . . .

Mr. Direck had been stirred deeply by the tragic indignation of this explosion, and the ring of torment in Mr. Britling's voice. He had stood up also, but he did not follow his host.

"It's his boy," said Mr. Direck at last, confidentially to the writing-desk. "How can one argue with him? It's just hell for him. . . ."

§ 20

Mr. Direck took his leave of Mrs. Britling, and went very slowly towards the little cottage. But he did not go to the cottage. He felt he would only find another soul in torment there.

"What's the good of hanging round talking?" said Mr. Direck.

He stopped at the stile in the lane, and sat thinking deeply. "Only one thing will convince her," he said.

He held out his fingers. "First this," he whispered, "and then that. Yes."

He went on as far as the bend from which one sees the cottage, and stood for a little time regarding it.

He returned still more sorrowfully to the junction, and with every step he took it seemed to him that he would rather see Cecily angry and insulting than not see her at all.

At the post-office he stopped and wrote a letter-card.

"Dear Cissie," he wrote. "I came down today to see you—and thought better of it. I'm going right off to find out about Teddy. Somehow I'll get that settled. I'll fly around and do that somehow if I have to go up to the German front to do it. And when I've got that settled I've got something else in my mind—well, it will wipe out all this little trouble

403

that's got so big between us about neutrality. And I love you dearly, Cissie."

That was all the card would hold.

§ 21

And then as if it were something that every one in the Dower House had been waiting for, came the message that Hugh had been killed.

The telegram was brought up by a girl in a pinafore instead of the boy of the old dispensation, for boys now were doing the work of youths, and youths the work of the men who had gone to the war.

Mr. Britling was standing at the front door; he had been surveying the late October foliage, touched by the warm light of the afternoon, when the messenger appeared. He opened the telegram, hoping as he had hoped when he opened any telegram since Hugh had gone to the front that it would not contain the exact words he read; that it would say wounded, that at the worst it would say "missing," that perhaps it might even tell of some pleasant surprise, a brief return to home such as the last letter had foreshadowed. He read the final, unqualified statement, the terse regrets. He stood quite still for a moment or so, staring at the words. . . .

It was a mile and a quarter from the post-office to the Dower House, and it was always his custom to give telegraph-messengers who came to his house twopence, and he wanted very much to get rid of the telegraph girl, who stood expectantly before him holding her red bicycle. He felt now very sick and strained; he had a conviction that if he did not by an effort maintain his bearing cool and dry he would howl aloud. He felt in his pocket for money; there were some coppers and a shilling. He pulled it all out together and stared at it.

He had an absurd conviction that this ought to be a sixpenny telegram. The thing worried him. He wanted to give the brat sixpence, and he had only threepence and a shilling, and he didn't know what to do and his brain couldn't think. It would be a shocking thing to give her a shilling, and he couldn't somehow give just coppers for so important a thing as Hugh's death. Then all this problem vanished and he handed the child the shilling. She stared at him, inquiring, incredulous. "Is there a reply, sir, please?"

"No," he said, "that's for you. All of it. . . . This is a peculiar sort of telegram. . . . It's news of importance. . . ."

As he said this he met her eyes, and had a sudden persuasion that she knew exactly what it was the telegram had told him, and that she was shocked at this gala-like treatment of such terrible news. He hesitated, feeling that he had to say something else, that he was socially inadequate, and then he decided that at any cost he must get his face away from her staring eyes. She made no movement to turn away. She seemed to be taking him in, recording him, for repetition, greedily, with every fibre of her being.

He stepped past her into the garden, and instantly forgot about her existence. . . .

§ 22

He had been thinking of this possibility for the last few weeks almost continuously, and yet now that it had come to him he felt that he had never thought about it before, that he must go off alone by himself to envisage this monstrous and terrible fact, without distraction or interruption.

He saw his wife coming down the alley between the roses.

He was wrenched by emotions as odd and unaccountable as the emotions of adolescence. He had exactly the same feeling now that he had had when in his boyhood some unpleasant admission had to be made to his parents. He felt he could not go through a scene with her yet, that he could not endure the task of telling her, of being observed. He turned abruptly to his left. He walked away as if he had not seen her, across his lawn towards the little summer-house upon a knoll that commanded the high-road. She called to him, but he did not answer. . . .

He would not look towards her, but for a time all his senses were alert to hear whether she followed him. Safe in the summer-house he could glance back.

It was all right. She was going into the house.

He drew the telegram from his pocket again furtively, almost guiltily, and reread it. He turned it over and read it again. . . .

Killed.

Then his own voice, hoarse and strange to his ears, spoke his thought.

"My God! how unutterably silly. . . . Why did I let him go? Why did I let him go?"

§ 23

Mrs. Britling did not learn of the blow that had struck them until after dinner that night. She was so accustomed to ignore his incomprehensible moods that she did not perceive that there was anything tragic about him until they sat at table together. He seemed heavy and sulky and disposed to avoid her, but that sort of moodiness was nothing very strange to her. She knew that things that seemed to her utterly trivial, the reading of political speeches in *The Times*, little comments on life made in the most casual way, mere movements, could so avert him. She had cultivated a certain disregard of such fitful darknesses. But at the dinner-table she looked up, and was stabbed to the heart to see a haggard white face and eyes of deep despair regarding her ambiguously.

"Hugh!" she said, and then with a chill intimation, "*What is it?*"

They looked at each other. His face softened and winced.

"My Hugh," he whispered, and neither spoke for some seconds.

"*Killed,*" he said, and suddenly stood up whimpering, and fumbled with his pocket.

It seemed he would never find what he sought. It came at last, a crumpled telegram. He threw it down before her, and then thrust his chair back clumsily and went hastily out of the room. She heard him sob. She had not dared to look at his face again.

"*Oh!*" she cried, realising that an impossible task had been thrust upon her.

"But what can I *say* to him?" she said, with the telegram in her hand.

The parlour-maid came into the room.

"Clear the dinner away!" said Mrs. Britling, standing at her place. "Master Hugh is killed. . . ." And then wailing: "Oh! what can I *say?* What can I *say?*"

§ 24

That night Mrs. Britling made the supreme effort of her life to burst the prison of self-consciousness and inhibition in which she was confined. Never before in all her life had she so desired to be spontaneous and unrestrained; never before had she so felt herself hampered by her timidity, her self-criticism, her deeply ingrained habit of never letting herself go. She was rent by reflected distress. It seemed to her that she would be ready to give her life and the whole world to be able to comfort her husband now. And she could conceive no gesture of comfort. She went out of the dining-room into the hall and listened. She went very softly upstairs until she came to the door of her husband's room. There she stood still. She could hear no sound from within. She put out her hand and turned the handle of the door a little way, and then she was startled by the loudness of the sound it made, and at her own boldness. She withdrew her hand, and then with a gesture of despair, with a face of white agony, she flitted along the corridor to her own room.

Her mind was beaten to the ground by this catastrophe, of which to this moment she had never allowed herself to think. She had never allowed herself to think of it. The figure of her husband, like some pitiful beast, wounded and bleeding, filled her mind. She gave scarcely a thought to Hugh. "Oh, what can I *do* for him?" she asked herself, sitting down before her unlit bedroom fire. . . . "What can I say or do?"

She brooded until she shivered, and then she lit her fire. . . .

It was late that night and after an eternity of resolutions and doubts and indecisions that Mrs. Britling went to her husband. He was sitting close up to the fire with his chin upon his hands, waiting for her; he felt that she would come to him, and he was thinking meanwhile of Hugh with a slow unprogressive movement of the mind. He showed by a movement that he heard her enter the room, but he did not turn to look at her. He shrank a little from her approach.

She came and stood beside him. She ventured to touch him very softly, and to stroke his head. "My dear," she said. "My poor dear!"

"It is so dreadful for you," she said, "it is so dreadful for you. I know how you loved him. . . ."

He spread his hands over his face and became very still.

"My poor dear!" she said, still stroking his hair, "my poor dear!"

And then she went on saying "poor dear," saying it presently because there was nothing more had come into her mind. She desired supremely to be his comfort, and in a little while she was acting comfort so poorly that she perceived her own failure. And that increased her failure, and that increased her paralysing sense of failure. . . .

And suddenly her stroking hand ceased. Suddenly the real woman cried out from her.

"I can't *reach* you!" she cried aloud. "I can't reach you. I would do anything. . . . You! You with your heart half broken. . . ."

She turned towards the door. She moved clumsily, she was blinded by her tears.

Mr. Britling uncovered his face. He stood up astonished, and then pity and pitiful understanding came storming across his grief. He made a step and took her in his arms. "My dear," he said, "don't go from me. . . ."

She turned to him weeping, and put her arms about his neck, and he too was weeping.

"My poor wife!" he said, "my dear wife. If it were not for you—I think I could kill myself tonight. Don't cry, my dear. Don't, don't cry. You do not know how you comfort me. You do not know how you help me."

He drew her to him; he put her cheek against his own. . . .

His heart was so sore and wounded that he could not endure that another human being should go wretched. He sat down in his chair and drew her upon his knees, and said everything he could think of to console her and reassure her and make her feel that she was of value to him. He spoke of every pleasant aspect of their lives, of every aspect, except that he never named that dear pale youth who waited now. . . . He could wait a little longer. . . .

At last she went from him.

"Good night," said Mr. Britling, and took her to the door. "It was very dear of you to come and comfort me," he said. . . .

§ 25

He closed the door softly behind her.

The door had hardly shut upon her before he forgot her. Instantly he was alone again, utterly alone. He was alone in an empty world. . . .

Loneliness struck him like a blow. He had dependents, he had cares. He had never a soul to whom he might weep. . . .

For a time he stood beside his open window. He looked at the bed—but no sleep, he knew, would come that night—until the sleep of exhaustion came. He looked at the bureau at which he had so often written. But the writing there was a shrivelled thing. . . .

This room was unendurable. He must go out. He turned to the window, and outside was a troublesome noise of nightjars and a distant roaring of stags, black trees, blacknesses, the sky clear and remote with a great company of stars. . . . The stars seemed attentive. They stirred and yet were still. It was as if they were the eyes of watchers. He would go out to them. . . .

Very softly he went towards the passage door, and still more softly felt his way across the landing and down the staircase. Once or twice he paused to listen.

He let himself out with elaborate precautions. . . .

Across the dark he went, and suddenly his boy was all about him, playing, climbing the cedars, twisting miraculously about the lawn on a bicycle, discoursing gravely upon his future, lying on the grass, breathing very hard and drawing preposterous caricatures. Once again they walked side by side up and down—it was athwart this very spot—talking gravely but rather shyly. . . .

And here they had stood a little awkwardly, before the boy went in to say goodbye to his step-mother and go off with his father to the station. . . .

"I will work tomorrow again," whispered Mr. Britling, "but tonight—tonight. . . . Tonight is yours. . . . Can you hear me, can you hear? Your father . . . who had counted on you. . . ."

§ 26

He went into the far corner of the hockey paddock, and there he moved about for a while and then stood for a long time holding the fence with both hands and staring blankly into the darkness. At last he turned away, and went stumbling and blundering towards the rose-garden. A spray of creeper tore his face and distressed him. He thrust it aside fretfully, and it scratched his hand. He made his way to the seat in the arbour, and sat down and whispered a little to himself, and then became very still with his arm upon the back of the seat and his head upon his arm.

BOOK III

THE TESTAMENT OF
MATCHING'S EASY

CHAPTER THE FIRST

MRS. TEDDY GOES FOR A WALK

§ 1

A LL over England now, where the livery of mourning had been a rare thing to see, women and children went about in the October sunshine in new black clothes. Everywhere one met these fresh griefs, mothers who had lost their sons, women who had lost their men, lives shattered and hopes destroyed. The dyers had a great time turning coloured garments to black. And there was also a growing multitude of crippled and disabled men. It was so in England, much more was it so in France and Russia, in all the countries of the Allies, and in Germany and Austria; away into Asia Minor and Egypt, in India and Japan and Italy there was mourning, the world was filled with loss and mourning and impoverishment and distress.

And still the mysterious powers that required these things of mankind were unappeased and each day added its quota of heart-stabbing messages and called for new mourning, and sent home fresh consignments of broken and tormented men.

Some clung to hopes that became at last almost more terrible than black certainties. . . .

Mrs. Teddy went about the village in a coloured dress bearing herself confidently. Teddy had been listed now as "missing, since reported killed," and she had had two letters from his comrades. They said Teddy had been left behind in the ruins of a farm with one or two other wounded, and that when the Canadians retook the place these wounded had all been found butchered. None had been found alive. Afterwards the

Canadians had had to fall back. Mr. Direck had been at great pains to hunt up wounded men from Teddy's company, and also any likely Canadians both at the base hospital in France and in London, and to get what he could from them. He had made it a service to Cissie. Only one of his witnesses was quite clear about Teddy, but he, alas! was dreadfully clear. There had been only one lieutenant among the men left behind, he said, and obviously that must have been Teddy. "He had been prodded in half-a-dozen places. His head was nearly severed from his body."

Direck came down and told the story to Cissie. "Shall I tell it to her?" he asked.

Cissie thought. "Not yet," she said. . . .

Letty's face changed in those pitiful weeks when she was denying death. She lost her pretty colour, she became white; her mouth grew hard and her eyes had a hard brightness. She never wept, she never gave a sign of sorrow, and she insisted upon talking about Teddy, in a dry offhand voice. Constantly she referred to his final return. "Teddy" she said, "will be surprised at this," or "Teddy will feel sold when he sees how I have altered that."

"Presently we shall see his name in a list of prisoners," she said. "He is a wounded prisoner in Germany."

She adopted that story. She had no justification for it, but she would hear no doubts upon it. She presently began to prepare parcels to send him. "They want almost everything," she told people. "They are treated abominably. He has not been able to write to me yet, but I do not think I ought to wait until he asks me."

Cissie was afraid to interfere with this.

After a time Letty grew impatient at the delay in getting any address and took her first parcel to the post-office.

"Unless you know what prison he is at," said the postmistress.

"Pity!" said Letty. "I don't know that. Must it wait for that? I thought the Germans were so systematic that it didn't matter."

The postmistress made tedious explanations that Letty did not seem to hear. She stared straight in front of her at nothing. Then in a pause in the conversation she picked up her parcel.

"It's tiresome for him to have to wait," she said. "But it can't be long before I know."

She took the parcel back to the cottage.

"After all," she said, "it gives us time to get the better sort of throat lozenges for him—the sort the syndicate shop doesn't keep."

She put the parcel conspicuously upon the dresser in the kitchen where it was most in the way, and set herself to make a jersey for Teddy against the coming of the cold weather.

But one night the white mask fell for a moment from her face.

Cissie and she had been sitting in silence before the fire. She had been knitting—she knitted very badly—and Cissie had been pretending to read, and had been watching her furtively. Cissie eyed the slow, toilsome growth of the slack woolwork for a time, and the touch of angry effort in every stroke of the knitting-needles. Then she was stirred to remonstrance.

"Poor Letty!" she said very softly. "Suppose, after all, he is dead?"

Letty met her with a pitiless stare.

"He is a prisoner," she said. "Isn't that enough? Why do you jab at me by saying that? A wounded prisoner. Isn't that enough despicable trickery for God even to play on Teddy—our Teddy?

417

To the very last moment he shall not be dead. Until the war is over. Until six months after the war. . . .

"I will tell you why, Cissie. . . ."

She leaned across the table and pointed her remarks with her knitting-needles, speaking in a tone of reasonable remonstrance. "You see," she said, "if people like Teddy are to be killed, then all our ideas that life is meant for honesty and sweetness and happiness are wrong, and this world is just a place of devils; just a dirty cruel hell. Getting born would be getting damned. And so one must not give way to that idea, however much it may seem likely that he is dead. . . .

"You see, if he *is* dead, then Cruelty is the Law, and some one must pay me for his death. . . . Some one must pay me. . . . I shall wait for six months after the war, dear, and then I shall go off to Germany and learn my way about there. And I will murder some German. Not just a common German, but a German who belongs to the guilty kind. A sacrifice. It ought for instance, to be comparatively easy to kill some of the children of the Crown Prince or some of the Bavarian princes. I shall prefer German children. I shall sacrifice them to Teddy. It ought not to be difficult to find people who can be made directly responsible, the people who invented the poison-gas, for instance, and kill them, or to kill people who are dear to them. Or necessary to them. . . . Women can do that so much more easily than men. . . .

"That perhaps is the only way in which wars of this kind will ever be brought to an end. By women insisting on killing the kind of people who make them. Rooting them out. By a campaign of pursuit and assassination that will go on for years and years after the war itself is over. . . . Murder is such a little gentle punishment for the crime of war. . . . It would be hardly more than a reproach for what has happened. Falling like snow. Death after death. Flake by flake. This prince. That statesman. The count who writes so fiercely for war. . . . That is what I am going to do. If Teddy is really dead. . . . We women were ready enough a year or so ago to starve and die for the Vote, and that was quite a little thing in comparison with this business. . . . Don't you see what I mean? It's so plain and sensible, Cissie. Whenever a man sits and thinks whether he will make a war or not, then he will think too of women, women with daggers, bombs; of a vengeance that will never tire nor rest; of consecrated patient women ready to start out upon a pilgrimage that will only end with his death. . . . I wouldn't hurt these war-makers. No. In spite of the poison-gas. In spite of trench feet and the men who have been made blind and the wounded who have lain for days, dying slowly in the wet. Women ought not to hurt. But I would kill. Like killing dangerous vermin. It would go on year by year. Balkan kings. German princes, chancellors, they would have schemed for so much—and come to just a rattle in the throat. . . . And if presently other kings and emperors began to prance about and review armies, they too would go. . . .

"Until all the world understood that women would not stand war any more for ever. . . .

"Of course I shall do something of the sort. What else is there to do now for me?"

Letty's eyes were bright and intense, but her voice was soft and subdued. She went on after a pause in the same casual voice. "You see now, Cissie, why I cling to the idea that Teddy is alive. If Teddy is alive, then even if he is wounded he will get some happiness out of it—and all this won't be—just rot. If he is dead, then everything is so desperately silly and cruel from top to bottom——"

She smiled wanly to finish her sentence.

"But, Letty," said Cissie, "there is the boy!"

"I shall leave the boy to you. Compared with Teddy I don't care *that* for the boy. I never did. What is the good of pretending? Some women are made like that."

She surveyed her knitting. "Poor stitches," she said. . . .

"I'm hard stuff, Cissie. I take after mother more than father. Teddy is my darling. All the tenderness of my life is Teddy. If he goes, it goes. . . . I won't crawl about the world like all these other snivelling widows. If they've killed my man I shall kill. Blood for blood and loss for loss. I shall get just as close to the particular Germans who made this war as I can, and I shall kill them and theirs. . . .

"The Women's Association for the Extirpation of the whole breed of War Lords," she threw out. "If I *do* happen to hurt—does it matter?"

She looked at her sister's shocked face and smiled again.

"You think I go about staring at nothing," she remarked. . . . "Not a bit of it! I have been planning all sorts of things. . . . I have been thinking how I could get to Germany. . . . Or one might catch them in Switzerland. . . . I've had all sorts of plans. They can't go guarded for ever. . . .

"Oh, it makes me despise humanity to see how many soldiers and how few assassins there are in the world. . . . After the things we have seen. If people did their duty by the dagger there wouldn't be such a thing as a War Lord in the world. Not one. . . . The Kaiser and his son and his sons' sons would know nothing but fear now for all their lives. Fear would only cease to pursue as the coffin went down into the grave. Fear by sea, fear by land, for the vessel he sailed in, the train he travelled in, fear when he slept for the death in his dreams, fear when he waked for the death in every shadow; fear in every crowd, fear whenever he was alone. Fear would stalk him through the trees, hide in the corner of the staircase; make all his food taste perplexingly, so that he would want to spit it out. . . ."

She sat very still brooding on that idea for a time, and then stood up.

"What nonsense one talks!" she cried, and yawned. "I wonder why poor Teddy doesn't send me a postcard or something to tell me his address. I tell you what I *am* afraid of sometimes about him, Cissie."

"Yes?" said Cissie.

"Loss of memory. Suppose a beastly lump of shell or something whacked him on the head. . . . I had a dream of him looking strange about the eyes and not knowing me. That, you know, really *may* have happened. . . . It would be beastly, of course. . . ."

Cissie's eyes were critical, but she had nothing ready to say.

There were some moments of silence.

"Oh! bed," said Letty. "Though I shall just lie scheming."

§ 2

Cissie lay awake that night thinking about her sister as if she had never thought about her before.

She began to weigh the concentrated impressions of a thousand memories. She and her sister were near in age; they knew each other with an extreme intimacy, and yet it seemed to Cissie that night as though she did not know Letty at all. A year ago she would have been certain she knew everything about her. But the old familiar Letty, with the bright complexion and the wicked eye, with her rebellious schoolgirl insistence upon the beautifulness of "Boof'l young men," and her frank and glowing passion for Teddy, with her delight in humorous mystifications and open-air exercise and all the sunshine and laughter of life, this sister Letty who had been so satisfactory and complete and final, had been thrust aside like a mask. Cissie no longer knew her sister's eyes. Letty's hands had become thin and unfamiliar and a little wrinkled; she was sharp-featured and thin-lipped; her acts, which had once been predictable, were incomprehensible, and Cissie was thrown back upon speculations. In their school-days Letty had had a streak of intense sensibility; she had been easily moved to tears. But never once had she wept or given any sign of weeping since Teddy's name had appeared in the casualty list. . . . What was the strength of this tragic tension? How far would it carry her? Was Letty really capable of becoming a Charlotte Corday? Of carrying out a scheme of far-seeing vengeance, of making her way through long months and years nearer and nearer to revenge?

Were such revenges possible?

Would people presently begin to murder the makers of the Great War? What a strange thing it would be in history if so there came a punishment and end to the folly of kings!

Only a little while ago Cissie's imagination might have been captured by so romantic a dream. She was still but a year or so out of the stage of melodrama. But she was out of it. She was growing up now to a subtler wisdom. People, she was beginning to realise, do not do these simple things. They make vows of devotion and they are not real vows of devotion; they love—quite honestly—and qualify. There are no great revenges but only little mean ones; no lifelong vindications except the unrelenting vengeance of the law. There is no real concentration of people's lives anywhere such as romance demands. There is change, there is forgetfulness. Everywhere there is dispersal. Even to the tragic story of Teddy would come the modifications of time. Even to the wickedness of the German princes would presently be added some conflicting aspects. Could Letty keep things for years in her mind, hard and terrible, as they were now? Surely they would soften; other things would overlay them. . . .

There came a rush of memories of Letty in a dozen schoolgirl adventures, times when she had ventured, and times when she had failed; Letty frightened, Letty vexed, Letty launching out to great enterprises, going high and hard and well for a time, and then failing. She had seen Letty snivelling and dirty; Letty ashamed and humiliated. She knew her Letty to the soul. Poor Letty! Poor dear Letty! With a sudden clearness of vision Cissie realised what was happening in her sister's mind. All this tense scheming of revenges was the imaginative play with which Letty warded off the black alternative to her hope; it was not strength, it was weakness. It was a form of giving way. She could not face starkly the simple fact of Teddy's death. That was too much for her. So she was building up this dream of a mission of judgment against the day when she could resist the facts no longer. She was already persuaded, only she would not be persuaded until her dream was ready. If this state of suspense went on she might establish her dream so firmly that it would at last take complete possession of her mind. And by that time also she would have squared her existence at Matching's Easy with the elaboration of her reverie.

She would go about the place then, fancying herself preparing for this tremendous task she would never really do; she would study German maps; she would read the papers about German statesmen and rulers; perhaps she would even make weak attempts to obtain a situation in Switzerland or in Germany. Perhaps she would buy a knife or a revolver. Perhaps presently she would begin to hover about Windsor or Sandringham when peace was made, and the German cousins came visiting again. . . .

Into Cissie's mind came the image of the thing that might be; Letty, shabby, draggled, and her sharp bright prettiness become haggard, an assassin dreamer, still dependent on Mr. Britling, doing his work rather badly, in a distraught unpunctual fashion.

She must be told, she must be convinced soon, or assuredly she would become an eccentric, a strange character, a Matching's Easy Miss Flite. . . .

§ 3

Cissie could think more clearly of Letty's mind than of her own.

She herself was in a tangle. She had grown to be very fond of Mr. Direck and to have a profound trust and confidence in him, and her fondness seemed able to find no expression at all except a constant girding at his and America's avoidance of war. She had fallen in love with him when he was wearing fancy dress; she was a young woman with a stronger taste for body and colour than she supposed; what indeed she resented about him, though she did not know it, was that he seemed never disposed to carry the spirit of fancy dress into everyday life. To begin with he had touched both her imagination and senses, and she wanted him to go on doing that. Instead of which he seemed lapsing more and more into reiterated assurances of devotion and the flat competent discharge of humanitarian duties. Always nowadays he was trying to persuade her that what he was doing was the right and honourable thing for him to do; what he did not realise, what indeed she did not realise, was the exasperation his rightness and reasonableness produced in her. When he saw he exasperated her he sought very earnestly to be righter and reasonabler and more plainly and demonstrably right and reasonable than ever.

Withal, as she felt and perceived, he was such a good thing, such a very good thing; so kind, so trustworthy with a sort of slow strength, with a careful honesty, a big good childishness, a passion for fairness. And so helpless in her hands. She could lash him and distress him. Yet she could not shake his slowly formed convictions.

When Cissie had dreamt of the lover that fate had in store for her in her old romantic days, he was to be *perfect* always, he and she were always to be absolutely in the right (and, if the story needed it, the world in the wrong). She had never expected to find herself tied by her affections to a man with whom she disagreed, and who went contrary to her standards, very much as if she was lashed on the back of a very nice elephant that would wince to but not obey the goad. . . .

So she nagged him and taunted him, and would hear no word of his case. And he wanted dreadfully to discuss his case. He felt that the point of conscience about the munitions was particularly fine and difficult. He wished she would listen and enter into it more. But she thought with that more rapid English flash which is not so much thinking as feeling. He loved that flash in her in spite of his persuasion of its injustice.

Her thought that he ought to go to the war made him feel like a renegade; her claim that he was somehow still English held him in spite of his reason. In the midst of such perplexities he was glad to find one neutral task wherein he could find himself wholeheartedly with and for Cissie.

He hunted up the evidence of Teddy's fate with a devoted pertinacity.

And in the meanwhile the other riddle resolved itself. He had had a certain idea in his mind for some time. He discovered one day that it was an inspiration. He could keep his conscientious objection about America, and still take a line that would satisfy Cissie. He took it.

When he came down to Matching's Easy at her summons to bear his convincing witness of Teddy's fate, he came in an unwonted costume. It was a costume so wonderful in his imagination that it seemed to cry aloud, to sound like a trumpet as he went through London to Liverpool Street Station; it was a costume like an international event; it was a costume that he felt would blare right away to Berlin. And yet it was a costume so commonplace, so much the usual wear now, that Cissie, meeting him at the station and full of the thought of Letty's trouble, did not remark it, felt indeed rather than observed that he was looking more strong and handsome than he had ever done since he struck upon her imagination in the fantastic wrap that Teddy had found for him in the merry days when there was no death in the world. And Letty too, resistant, incalculable, found no wonder in the wonderful suit.

He bore his testimony. It was the queer halting telling of a patched-together tale. . . .

"I suppose," said Letty, "if I tell you now that I don't believe that that officer was Teddy you will think I am cracked. . . . But I don't."

She sat staring straight before her for a time after saying this. Then suddenly she got up and began taking down her hat and coat from the peg behind the kitchen door. The hanging strap of the coat was twisted and she struggled with it petulantly until she tore it.

"Where are you going?" cried Cissie.

Letty's voice over her shoulder was the harsh voice of a scolding woman.

"I'm going out—anywhere." She turned, coat in hand. "Can't I go out if I like?" she asked. "It's a beautiful day. . . . Mustn't I go out? . . . I suppose you think I ought to take in what you have told me in a moment. Just smile and say '*Indeed!*' . . . Abandoned!— while his men retreated! How jolly! And then not think of it any more. . . . Besides, I must go out. You two want to be left together. You want to canoodle. Do it while you can!"

Then she put on coat and hat, jamming her hat down on her head, and said something that Cissie did not immediately understand.

"*He'll* have his turn in the trenches soon enough. Now that he's made up his mind. . . . He might have done it sooner. . . ."

She turned her back as though she had forgotten them. She stood for a moment as though her feet were wooden, not putting her feet as she usually put her feet. She took slow, wide, unsure steps. She went out—like something that is mortally injured and still walks—into the autumnal sunshine. She left the door wide open behind her.

§ 4

And Cissie, with eyes full of distress for her sister, had still to grasp the fact that Direck was wearing a Canadian uniform. . . .

He stood behind her, ashamed that in such a moment this fact and its neglect by every one could be so vivid in his mind.

427

§ 5

Cissie's estimate of her sister's psychology had been just. The reverie of revenge had not yet taken a grip upon Letty's mind sufficiently strong to meet the challenge of this conclusive evidence of Teddy's death. She walked out into a world of sunshine now almost completely convinced that Teddy was dead, and she knew quite well that her dream of some dramatic and terrible vindication had gone from her. She knew that in truth she could do nothing of that sort. . . .

She walked out with a set face and eyes that seemed unseeing, and yet it was as if some heavy weight had been lifted from her shoulders. It was over; there was no more to hope for and there was nothing more to fear. She would have been shocked to realise that her mind was relieved.

She wanted to be alone. She wanted to be away from every eye. She was like some creature that after a long nightmare incubation is at last born into a clear, bleak day. She had to feel herself; she had to stretch her mind in this cheerless sunshine, this new world, where there was to be no more Teddy and no real revenge nor compensation for Teddy. Teddy was past. . . .

Hitherto she had had an angry sense of being deprived of Teddy—almost as though he were keeping away from her. Now, there was no more Teddy to be deprived of. . . .

She went through the straggling village and across the fields to the hillside that looks away towards Mertonsome and its steeple. And where the hill begins to fall away she threw herself down under the hedge by the path, near by the stile into the lane, and lay still. She did not so much think as remain blank, waiting for the beginning of impressions. . . .

It was as it were a blank stare at the world. . . .

She did not know if it was five minutes or half an hour later that she became aware that some one was looking at her. She turned with a start, and discovered the Reverend Dimple with one foot on the stile, and an expression of perplexity and consternation upon his chubby visage.

Instantly she understood. Already on four different occasions since Teddy's disappearance she had seen the good man coming towards her, always with a manifest decision, always with the same faltering doubt as now. Often in their happy days had she and Teddy discussed him and derided him and rejoiced over him. They had agreed he was as good as Jane Austen's Mr. Collins. He really was very like Mr. Collins, except that he was plumper. And now, it was as if he was transparent to her hard defensive scrutiny. She knew he was impelled by his tradition, by his sense of fitness, by his respect for his calling, to offer her his ministrations and consolations, to say his large flat amiabilities over her and pat her kindly with his hands. And she knew too that he dreaded her. She knew that the dear old humbug knew at the bottom of his heart quite certainly that he was a poor old humbug, and that she was in his secret. And at the bottom of his heart he found himself too honest to force his poor platitudes upon any who would not be glad of them. If she could have been glad of them he would have had no compunction. He was a man divided against himself; failing to carry through his rich pretences, dismayed.

He had been taking his afternoon "constitutional." He had discovered her beyond the stile just in time to pull up. Then had came a fatal, a preposterous hesitation. She stared at him now, with hard, expressionless eyes.

He stared back at her, until his plump pink face was all consternation. He was extraordinarily distressed. It was as if a thousand unspoken things had been said between them.

"No wish," he said, "intrude."

If he had had the certain balm, how gladly would he have given it!

He broke the spell by stepping back into the lane. He made a gesture with his hands, as if he would have wrung them. And then he had fled down the lane—almost at a run.

"Po' girl," he cried. "Po' girl," and left her staring.

Staring—and then she laughed.

This was good. This was the sort of thing one could tell Teddy, when at last he came back and she could tell him anything. And then she realised again; there was no more Teddy, there would be no telling. And suddenly she fell weeping.

"Oh, Teddy, Teddy," she cried through her streaming tears. "How could you leave me? How can I bear it?"

Never a tear had she shed since the news first came, and now she could weep, she could weep her grief out. She abandoned herself unreservedly to this blessed relief. . . .

§ 6

There comes an end to weeping at last, and Letty lay still, in the red light of the sinking sun.

She lay so still that presently a little foraging robin came flirting down to the grass not ten yards away and stopped and looked at her. And then it came a hop or so nearer.

She had been lying in a state of passive abandonment, her swollen wet eyes open, regardless of everything. But those quick movements caught her back to attention. She began to watch the robin, and to note how it glanced sidelong at her and appeared to meditate further approaches. She made an almost imperceptible movement, and straightway the little creature was in a projecting spray of berried hawthorn overhead.

Her tear-washed mind became vaguely friendly. With an unconscious comfort it focused down to the robin. She rolled over, sat up, and imitated his friendly "cheep."

§ 7

Presently she became aware of footsteps rustling through the grass towards her.

She looked over her shoulder and discovered Mr. Britling approaching by the field path. He looked white and tired and listless, even his bristling hair and clipped moustache conveyed his depression; he was dressed in an old tweed knickerbocker suit and carrying a big atlas and some papers. He had an effect of hesitation in his approach. It was as if he wanted to talk to her and doubted her reception for him.

He spoke without any preface. "Direck has told you?" he said, standing over her.

She answered with a sob.

"I was afraid it was so, and yet I did not believe it," said Mr. Britling. "Until now."

He hesitated as if he would go on, and then he knelt down on the grass a little way from her and seated himself. There was an interval of silence.

"At first it hurts like the devil," he said at last, looking away at Mertonsome spire and speaking as if he spoke to no one in particular. "And then it hurts. It goes on hurting. . . . And one can't say much to any one. . . ."

He said no more for a time. But the two of them comforted one another, and knew that they comforted each other. They had a common feeling of fellowship and ease. They had been stricken by the same thing; they understood how it was with each other. It was not like the attempted comfort they got from those who had not loved and dreaded. . . .

She took up a little broken twig and dug small holes in the ground with it.

"It's strange," she said, "but I'm glad I know for sure."

"I can understand that," said Mr. Britling.

"It stops the nightmares. . . . It isn't hopes I've had so much as fears. . . . I wouldn't admit he was dead or hurt. Because—— I couldn't think it without thinking it—horrible. *Now*——"

"It's final," said Mr. Britling.

"It's definite," she said after a pause. "It's like thinking he's asleep—for good."

But that did not satisfy her. There was more than this in her mind. "It does away with the half and half," she said. "He's dead or he is alive. . . ."

She looked up at Mr. Britling as if she measured his understanding.

"You don't still doubt?" he said.

"I'm content now in my mind—in a way. He wasn't anyhow there—unless he was dead. But if I saw Teddy coming over the hedge there to me—— It would be just natural. . . . No, don't stare at me. I know really he is dead. And it is a comfort. It is peace. . . . All the thoughts of him being crushed dreadfully or being mutilated or lying and screaming—or things like that— they've gone. He's out of his spoiled body. He's my unbroken Teddy again. . . . Out of sight somewhere. . . . Unbroken . . . . Sleeping."

She resumed her excavation with the little stick, with the tears running down her face.

Mr. Britling presently went on with the talk. "For me it came all at once, without a doubt or a hope. I hoped until the last that nothing would touch Hugh. And then it was like a black shutter falling—in an instant. . . ."

He considered. "Hugh, too, seems just round the corner at times. But at times, it's a blank place. . . .

"At times," said Mr. Britling, "I feel nothing but astonishment. The whole thing becomes incredible. Just as for weeks after the war began I couldn't believe that a big modern nation could really go to war—seriously—with its whole heart. . . . And they have killed Teddy and Hugh. . . .

"They have killed millions. Millions—who had fathers and mothers and wives and sweethearts. . . ."

§ 8

"Somehow I can't talk about this to Edith. It is ridiculous, I know. But in some way, I can't. . . . It isn't fair to her. If I could, I would. . . . Quite soon after we were married I ceased to talk to her. I mean talking really and simply—as I do to you. And it's never come back. I don't know why. . . . And particularly I can't talk to her of Hugh. . . . Little things, little shadows of criticism, but enough to make it impossible. . . . And I go about thinking about Hugh, and what has happened to him, sometimes . . . as though I was stifling."

Letty compared her case.

"I don't want to talk about Teddy—not a word."

"That's queer. . . . But perhaps—a son is different. Now I come to think of it—I've never talked of Mary. . . . Not to any one ever. I've never thought of that before. But I haven't. I couldn't. No. Losing a lover, that's a thing for oneself. I've been through that, you see. But a son's more outside you. Altogether. And more your own making. It's not losing a thing *in* you; it's losing a hope and a pride. . . . Once when I was a little boy I did a drawing very carefully. It took me a long time. . . . And a big boy tore it up. For no particular reason. Just out of cruelty. . . . That—that was exactly like losing Hugh. . . ."

Letty reflected.

"No," she confessed, "I'm more selfish than that."

"It isn't selfish," said Mr. Britling. "But it's a different thing. It's less intimate, and more personally important."

"I have just thought, 'He's gone. He's gone.' Sometimes, do you know, I have felt quite angry with him. Why need he have gone—so soon?"

Mr. Britling nodded understandingly.

"I'm not angry. I'm not depressed. I'm just bitterly hurt by the ending of something I had hoped to watch—always—all my life," he said. "I don't know how it is between most fathers and sons, but I admired Hugh. I found exquisite things in him. I doubt if other people saw them. He was quiet. He seemed clumsy. But he had an extraordinary fineness. He was a creature of the most delicate and rapid responses. . . . These aren't my fond delusions. It was so. . . . You know, when he was only a few days old, he would start suddenly at any strange sound. He was alive like an æolian harp from the very beginning. . . . And his hair when he was born—he had a lot of hair—was like the down on the breast of a bird. I remember that now very vividly—and how I used to like to pass my hand over it. It was silk, spun silk. Before he was two he could talk—whole sentences. He had the subtlest ear. He loved long words. . . . And then," he said with tears in his voice, "all this beautiful fine structure, this brain, this fresh life as nimble as water—as elastic as a steel spring, it is destroyed. . . ."

"I don't make out he wasn't human. Often and often I have been angry with him, and disappointed in him. There were all sorts of weaknesses in him. We all knew them. And we didn't mind them. We loved him the better. And his odd queer cleverness. . . . And his profound wisdom. And then all this beautiful and delicate fabric, all those clear memories in his dear brain, all his whims, his sudden inventions. . . .

"You know, I have had a letter from his chum Park. He was shot through a loophole. The bullet went through his eye and brow. . . . Think of it!

"An amazement . . . a blow . . . a splattering of blood. Rags of tormented skin and brain stuff. . . . In a moment. What had taken eighteen years—love and care. . . ."

He sat thinking for an interval, and then went on, "The reading and writing alone! I taught him to read myself—because his first governess, you see, wasn't very clever. She was a very good methodical sort, but she had no inspiration. So I got up all sorts of methods for teaching him to read. But it wasn't necessary. He seemed to leap all sorts of difficulties. He leaped to what one was trying to teach him. It was as quick as the movement of some wild animal. . . .

"He came into life as bright and quick as this robin looking for food. . . .

"And he's broken up and thrown away. . . . Like a cartridge-case by the side of a covert. . . ."

He choked and stopped speaking. His elbows were on his knees, and he put his face between his hands and shuddered and became still. His hair was troubled. The end of his stumpy moustache and a little roll of flesh stood out at the side of his hand, and made him somehow twice as pitiful. His big atlas, from which papers projected, seemed forgotten by his side. So he sat for a long time, and neither he nor Letty moved or spoke. But they were in the same shadow. They found great comfort in one another. They had not been so comforted before since their losses came upon them.

§ 9

It was Mr. Britling who broke silence. And when he drew his hands down from his face and spoke, he said one of the most amazing and unexpected things she had ever heard in her life.

"The only possible government in Albania," he said, looking steadfastly before him down the hillside, "is a group of republican cantons after the Swiss pattern. I can see no other solution that is not offensive to God. It does not matter in the least what we owe to Serbia or what we owe to Italy. We have got to set this world on a different footing. We have got to set up the world at last—on justice and reason."

Then, after a pause, "The Treaty of Bucharest was an evil treaty. It must be undone. Whatever this German King of Bulgaria does, that treaty must be undone and the Bulgarians united again into one people. They must have themselves, whatever punishment they deserve, they must have nothing more, whatever reward they win."

She could not believe her ears.

"After this precious blood, after this precious blood, if we leave one plot of wickedness or cruelty in the world——"

And therewith he began to lecture Letty on the importance of international politics—to every one. How he and she and every one must understand, however hard it was to understand.

"No life is safe, no happiness is safe, there is no chance of bettering life until we have made an end to all that causes war. . . .

"We have to put an end to the folly and vanity of kings, and to any people ruling any people but themselves. There is no convenience, there is no justice in any people ruling any people but themselves; the ruling of men by others, who have not their creeds and their languages and their ignorances and prejudices, that is the fundamental folly that has killed Teddy and Hugh—and these millions. To end that folly is as much our duty and business as telling the truth or earning a living. . . ."

"But how can you alter it?"

He held out a finger at her. "Men may alter anything if they have motive enough and faith enough."

He indicated the atlas beside him.

"Here I am planning the real map of the world," he said. "Every sort of district that has a character of its own must have its own rule; and the great republic of the United States of the World must keep the federal peace between them all. That's the plain sense of life; the federal world-republic. Why do we bother ourselves with loyalties to any other government but that? It needs only that sufficient men should say it, and that republic would be here now. Why have we loitered so long—until these tragic punishments come? We have to map the world out into its states, and plan its government and the way of its tolerations."

"And you think it will come?"

"It will come."

437

"And you believe that men will listen to such schemes?" said Letty.

Mr. Britling, with his eyes far away over the hills, seemed to think. "Yes," he said. "Not perhaps today—not steadily. But kings and empires die; great ideas, once they are born, can never die again. In the end this world-republic, this sane government of the world, is as certain as the sunset. Only . . ."

He sighed, and turned over a page of his atlas blindly.

"Only we want it soon. The world is weary of this bloodshed, weary of all this weeping, of this wasting of substance, and this killing of sons and lovers. We want it soon, and to have it soon we must work to bring it about. We must give our lives. What is left of our lives. . . .

"That is what you and I must do, Letty. What else is there left for us to do? . . . I will write of nothing else, I will think of nothing else now but of safety and order. So that all these dear dead—not one of them but will have brought the great days of peace and man's real beginning nearer, and these cruel things that make men whimper like children, that break down bright lives into despair and kill youth at the very moment when it puts out its clean hands to take hold of life—these cruelties, these abominations of confusion, shall cease from the earth for ever."

§ 10

Letty regarded him frowning, and with her chin between her fists. . . .

"But do you really believe," said Letty, "that things can be better than they are?"

"But—*Yes!*" said Mr. Britling.

438

"I don't," said Letty. "The world is cruel. It is just cruel. So it will always be."

"It need not be cruel," said Mr. Britling.

"It is just a place of cruel things. It is all set with knives. It is full of diseases and accidents. As for God—either there is no God or he is an idiot. He is a slobbering idiot. He is like some idiot who pulls off the wings of flies."

"No," said Mr. Britling.

"There is no progress. Nothing gets better. How can *you* believe in God after Hugh? *Do* you believe in God?"

"Yes," said Mr. Britling after a long pause; "I do believe in God."

"Who lets these things happen!" She raised herself on her arm and thrust her argument at him with her hand. "Who kills my Teddy and your Hugh—and millions."

"No," said Mr. Britling.

"But he *must* let these things happen. Or why do they happen?"

"No," said Mr. Britling. "It is the theologians who must answer that. They have been extravagant about God. They have had silly absolute ideas—that he is all-powerful. That he's omni-everything. But the common sense of men knows better. Every real religious thought denies it. After all, the real God of the Christians is Christ, not God Almighty; a poor mocked and wounded God nailed on a cross of matter. . . . Some day he will triumph. . . . But it is not fair to say that he causes all things now. It is not fair to make out a case against him. You have been misled. It is a theologian's folly. God is not absolute; God is finite. . . . A finite God who struggles in his great and comprehensive way as we struggle in our weak and silly way—who is *with* us—that is the essence of all real religion. . . . I agree with you so—— Why!

If I thought there was an omnipotent God who looked down on battles and deaths and all the waste and horror of this war—able to prevent these things—doing them to amuse himself—I would spit in his empty face. . . ."

"Any one would. . . ."

"But it's your teachers and catechisms have set you against God. . . . They want to make out he owns all Nature. And all sorts of silly claims. Like the heralds in the Middle Ages who insisted that Christ was certainly a great gentleman entitled to bear arms. But God is within Nature and necessity. Necessity is a thing beyond God—beyond good and ill, beyond space and time, a mystery everlastingly impenetrable. God is nearer than that. Necessity is the uttermost thing, but God is the innermost thing. Closer he is than breathing and nearer than hands and feet. He is the Other Thing than this world. Greater than Nature or Necessity, for he is a spirit and they are blind, but not controlling them. . . . Not yet. . . ."

"They always told me he was the maker of Heaven and Earth."

"That's the Jew God the Christians took over. It's a Quack God, a Panacea. It's not my God."

Letty considered these strange ideas.

"I never thought of him like that," she said at last. "It makes it all seem different."

"Nor did I. But I do now. . . . I have suddenly found it and seen it plain. I see it so plain that I am amazed that I have not always seen it. . . . It is, you see, so easy to understand that there is a God, and how complex and wonderful and brotherly he is, when one thinks of those dear boys who by the thousand, by the hundred thousand, have laid down their lives. . . . Aye, and there were German boys too who did the same. . . . The cruelties, the injustice, the brute aggression—they saw it differently. They laid down their lives—they laid down their lives. . . . Those dear lives, those lives of hope and sunshine. . . .

"Don't you see that it must be like that, Letty? Don't you see that it must be like that?"

"No," she said, "I've seen things differently from that."

"But it's so plain to me," said Mr. Britling. "If there was nothing else in all the world but our kindness for each other, or the love that made you weep in this kind October sunshine, or the love I bear Hugh—if there was nothing else at all—if everything else was cruelty and mockery and filthiness and bitterness, it would still be certain that there was a God of love and righteousness. If there were no signs of God in all the world but the godliness we have seen in those two boys of ours; if we had no other light but the love we have between us. . . .

"You don't mind if I talk like this?" said Mr. Britling. "It's all I can think of now—this God, this God who struggles, who was in Hugh and Teddy, clear and plain, and how he must become the ruler of the world. . . ."

"This God who struggles," she repeated. "I have never thought of him like that."

"Of course he must be like that," said Mr. Britling. "How can God be a Person; how can he be anything that matters to man, unless he is limited and defined and—human like ourselves. . . . With things outside him and beyond him."

§ 11

Letty walked back slowly through the fields of stubble to her cottage.

She had been talking to Mr. Britling for an hour, and her mind was full of the thought of this changed and simplified man, who talked of God as he might have done of a bird he had seen or of a tree he had sheltered under. And all mixed up with this thought of Mr. Britling was this strange idea of God who was also a limited person, who could come as close as Teddy, whispering love in the darkness. She had a ridiculous feeling that God really struggled like Mr. Britling, and that with only some indefinable inferiority of outlook Mr. Britling loved like God. She loved him for his maps and his dreams and the bareness of his talk to her. It was strange how the straining thought of the dead Teddy had passed now out of her mind. She was possessed by a sense of ending and beginning, as though a page had turned over in her life and everything was new. She had never given religion any thought but contemptuous thought for some years, since indeed her growing intelligence had dismissed it as a scheme of inexcusable restraints and empty pretences, a thing of discords where there were no discords except of its making. She had been a happy Atheist. She had played in the sunshine, a natural creature with the completest confidence in the essential goodness of the world in which she found herself. She had refused all thought of painful and disagreeable things. Until the bloody paw of war had wiped out all her assurance. Teddy, the playmate, was over, the love-game was ended for ever; the fresh happy acceptance of life as life; and in the place of Teddy was the sorrow of life, the pity of life, and this coming of God out of utter remoteness into a conceivable relation to her own existence.

She had left Mr. Britling to his atlas. He lay prone under the hedge with it spread before him. His occupation would have seemed to her only a little while ago the absurdest imaginable.

He was drawing boundaries on his maps very carefully in red ink, with a fountain pen. But now she understood.

She knew that those red-ink lines of Mr. Britling's might in the end prove wiser and stronger than the bargains of the diplomats. . . .

In the last hour he had come very near to her. She found herself full of an unwonted affection for him. She had never troubled her head about her relations with any one except Teddy before. Now suddenly she seemed to be opening out to all the world for kindness. This new idea of a friendly God, who had a struggle of his own, who could be thought of as kindred to Mr. Britling, as kindred to Teddy—had gripped her imagination. He was behind the autumnal sunshine; he was in the little bird that had seemed so confident and friendly. Whatever was kind, whatever was tender; there was God. And a thousand old phrases she had read and heard and given little heed to, that had lain like dry bones in her memory, suddenly were clothed in flesh and became alive. This God—if this was God—then indeed it was not nonsense to say that God was love, that he was a friend and companion. . . . With him it might be possible to face a world in which Teddy and she would never walk side by side again nor plan any more happiness for ever. After all she had been very happy; she had had wonderful happiness. She had had far more happiness, far more love, in her short year or so than most people had in their whole lives. And so in the reaction of her emotions, Letty who had gone out with her head full of murder and revenge, came back through the sunset thinking of pity, of the thousand kindnesses and tendernesses of Teddy that were after all, perhaps, only an intimation of the limitless kindnesses and tendernesses of God. . . . What right had she to a white and bitter grief, self-centred and vindictive, while old Britling could still plan an age of mercy in the earth and a red-gold sunlight that was warm as a smile from Teddy lay on all the world. . . .

She must go into the cottage and kiss Cissie, and put away that parcel out of sight until she could find some poor soldier to whom she could send it. She had been pitiless towards Cissie in her grief. She had, in the egotism of her sorrow, treated Cissie as she might have treated a chair or a table, with no thought that Cissie might be weary, might dream of happiness still to come. Cissie had still to play the lover, and her man was already in khaki. There would be no such year as Letty had had in the days before the war darkened the world. Before Cissie's marrying the peace must come, and the peace was still far away. And Direck too would have to take his chances. . . .

Letty came through the little wood and over the stile that brought her into sight of the cottage. The windows of the cottage as she saw it under the bough of the big walnut-tree were afire from the sun. The crimson rambler over the porch that she and Teddy had planted was still bearing roses. The door was open and people were moving in the porch.

Some one was coming out of the cottage, a stranger, in an unfamiliar costume, and behind him was a man in khaki—but that was Mr. Direck! And behind him again was Cissie.

But the stranger!

He came out of the frame of the porch towards the garden-gate. . . .

Who—who was this stranger?

It was a man in queer-looking foreign clothes, baggy trousers of some soft-looking blue stuff and a blouse, and he had a white-bandaged left arm. He had a hat stuck at the back of his head, and a beard. . . .

He was entirely a stranger, a foreigner. Was she going insane? Of course he was a stranger!

And then he moved a step, he made a queer sideways pace, a caper, on the path, and instantly he ceased to be strange and foreign. He became amazingly, incredibly, familiar by virtue of that step. . . .

No!

Her breath stopped. All Letty's being seemed to stop. And this stranger who was also incredibly familiar, after he had stared at her motionless form for a moment, waved his hat with a gesture—a gesture that crowned and sealed the effect of familiarity. She gave no sign in reply.

No, that familiarity was just a mad freakishness in things.

This strange man came from Belgium perhaps, to tell something about Teddy. . . .

And then she surprised herself by making a groaning noise, an absurd silly noise, just like the noise when one imitated a cow to a child. She said "Mooo-oo."

And she began to run forward, with legs that seemed misfits, waving her hands about, and as she ran she saw more and more certainly that this wounded man in strange clothing was Teddy. She ran faster and still faster, stumbling and nearly falling. If she did not get to him speedily the world would burst.

To hold him, to hold close to him! . . .

"Letty! Letty! Just one arm. . . ."

She was clinging to him and he was holding her. . . .

It was all right. She had always known it was all right. (Hold close to him.) Except just for a little while. But that had been foolishness. Hadn't she always known he was alive? And here he was alive! (Hold close to him.) Only it was so good to be sure—after all her torment; to hold him, to hang about him, to feel the solid man, kissing her, weeping too, weeping together with her. "Teddy my love!"

§ 12

Letty was in the cottage struggling to hear and understand things too complicated for her emotion-crowded mind. There was something that Mr. Direck was trying to explain about a delayed telegram that had come soon after she had gone out. There was much indeed that Mr. Direck was trying to explain. What did any explanation really matter when you had Teddy, with nothing but a strange beard and a bandaged arm between him and yourself? She had an absurd persuasion at first that those two strangenesses would also presently be set aside, so that Teddy would become just exactly what Teddy had always been.

Teddy had been shot through the upper arm. . . .

"My hand has gone, dear little Letty. It's my left hand, luckily. I shall have to wear a hook like some old pirate. . . ."

There was something about his being taken prisoner. "That other officer"—that was Mr. Direck's officer—"had been lying there for days." Teddy had been shot through the upper arm, and stunned by a falling beam. When he came to he was disarmed, with a German standing over him. . . .

Then afterwards he had escaped. In quite a little time he had escaped. He had been in a railway station somewhere in Belgium; locked in a waiting-room with three or four French prisoners, and the junction had been bombed by French and British aeroplanes. Their guard and two of the prisoners had been killed. In the confusion the others had got away into the town. There were trucks of hay on fire, and a store of petrol was

446

in danger. "After that one was bound to escape. One would have been shot if one had been found wandering about."

The bomb had driven some splinters of glass and corrugated iron into Teddy's wrist; it seemed a small place at first; it didn't trouble him for weeks. But then some dirt got into it.

In the narrow cobbled street beyond the station he had happened upon a woman who knew no English, but who took him to a priest, and the priest had hidden him.

Letty did not piece together the whole story at first. She did not want the story very much; she wanted to know about this hand and arm.

There would be queer things in the story when it came to be told. There was an old peasant who had made Teddy work in his fields in spite of his smashed and aching arm, and who had pointed to a passing German when Teddy demurred; there were the people called "they" who had at that time organised the escape of stragglers into Holland. There was the night watch, those long nights in succession before the dash for liberty. But Letty's concern was all with the hand. Inside the sling there was something that hurt the imagination, something bandaged, a stump. She could not think of it. She could not get away from the thought of it.

"But why did you lose your hand?"

It was only a little place at first, and then it got painful. . . .

"But I didn't go into a hospital, because I was afraid they would intern me, and so I wouldn't be able to come home. And I was dying to come home. I was—homesick. No one was ever so homesick. I've thought of this place and the garden, and how one looked out of the window at the passers-by, a thousand times. I seemed always to be seeing them. Old Dimple with his benevolent smile, and Mrs. Wolker at the end cottage, and how she used to fetch her beer and wink when she caught us looking at her, and little Charlie Slobberface sniffing on his way to the pigs and all the rest of them. And you, Letty. Particularly you. And how we used to lean on the window-sill with our shoulders touching, and your cheek just in front of my eyes. . . . And nothing aching at all in one. . . .

"How I thought of that and longed for that! . . .

"And so, you see, I didn't go to the hospital. I kept hoping to get to England first. And I left it too long. . . ."

"Life's come back to me with you!" said Letty. "Until just today I've believed you'd come back. And today—I doubted. . . . I thought it was all over—all the real life, love, and the dear fun of things, and that there was nothing before me, nothing before me but just holding out—and keeping your memory. . . . Poor arm. Poor arm. And being kind to people. And pretending you were alive somewhere. . . . I'll not care about the arm. In a little while. . . . I'm glad you've gone, but I'm gladder you're back and can never go again. . . . And I will be your right hand, dear, and your left hand and all your hands. Both my hands for your dear lost left one. You shall have three hands instead of two. . . ."

§ 13

Letty stood by the window as close as she could to Teddy in a world that seemed wholly made up of unexpected things. She could not heed the others, it was only when Teddy spoke to the others, or when they spoke to Teddy, that they existed for her.

For instance, Teddy was presently talking to Mr. Direck.

They had spoken about the Canadians who had come up and relieved the Essex men after the fight in which Teddy had been captured. And then it was manifest that Mr. Direck was talking of his regiment. "I'm not the only American who has gone Canadian—for the duration of the war."

He had got to his explanation at last.

"I've told a lie," he said triumphantly. "I've shifted my birthplace six hundred miles.

"Mind you, I don't admit a thing that Cissie has ever said about America—not one thing. You don't understand the sort of proposition America is up against. America is the New World, where there are no races and nations any more; she is the Melting-Pot, from which we will cast the better state. I've believed that always—in spite of a thousand little things I believe it now. I go back on nothing. I'm not fighting as an American either. I'm fighting simply as myself.... I'm not going fighting for England, mind you. Don't you fancy that. I don't know I'm so particularly in love with a lot of English ways as to do that. I don't see how any one can be very much in love with your Empire, with its dead-alive Court, its artful politicians, its lords and ladies and snobs, its way with the Irish and its way with India, and everybody shifting responsibility and telling lies about your common people. I'm not going fighting for England. I'm going fighting for Cissie—and justice and Belgium and all that—but more particularly for Cissie. And anyhow I can't look Pa Britling in the face any more. . . . And I want to see those trenches—close. I reckon they're a thing it will be interesting to talk about some day. . . . So I'm going," said Mr. Direck. "But chiefly—it's Cissie. See?"

Cissie had come and stood by the side of him.

She looked from poor broken Teddy to him and back again.

"Up to now," she said, "I've wanted you to go. . . ."

Tears came into her eyes.

"I suppose I must let you go," she said. "Oh! I'd hate you not to go. . . ."

§ 14

"Good God! how old the Master looks!" cried Teddy suddenly.

He was standing at the window, and as Mr. Direck came forward inquiringly he pointed to the figure of Mr. Britling passing along the road towards the Dower House.

"He does look old. I hadn't noticed," said Mr. Direck.

"Why, he's gone grey!" cried Teddy, peering. "He wasn't grey when I left."

They watched the knickerbockered figure of Mr. Britling receding up the hill, atlas and papers in his hands behind his back.

"I must go out to him," said Teddy, disengaging himself from Letty.

"No," she said, arresting him with her hand.

"But he will be glad——"

She stood in her husband's way. She had a vision of Mr. Britling suddenly called out of his dreams of God ruling the United States of the World, to rejoice at Teddy's restoration. . . .

"No," she said; "it will only make him think again of Hugh—and how he died. Don't go out, Teddy. Not now. What does he care for *you?* . . . Let him rest from such things. . . . Leave him to dream over his atlas. . . . He isn't so desolate—if you knew. . . . I will tell you, Teddy—when I can. . . .

"But just now—— No, he will think of Hugh again. . . . Let him go. . . . He has God and his atlas there. . . . They're more than you think."

CHAPTER THE SECOND

MR. BRITLING WRITES UNTIL SUNRISE

§ 1

I T was some weeks later. It was now the middle of November, and Mr. Britling, very warmly wrapped in his thick dressing-gown and his thick llama-wool pyjamas, was sitting at his night desk, and working ever and again at an essay, an essay of preposterous ambitions, for the title of it was "The Better Government of the World."

Latterly he had had much sleepless misery. In the day life was tolerable, but in the night—unless he defended himself by working, the losses and cruelties of the war came and grimaced at him, insufferably. Now he would be haunted by long processions of refugees, now he would think of the dead lying stiff and twisted in a thousand dreadful attitudes. Then again he would be overwhelmed with anticipations of the frightful economic and social dissolution that might lie ahead. . . . At other times he thought of wounds and the deformities of body and spirit produced by injuries. And sometimes he would think of the triumph of evil. Stupid and triumphant persons went about a world that stupidity had desolated, with swaggering gestures, with a smiling consciousness of enhanced importance, with their scornful hatred of all measured and temperate and kindly things turned now to scornful contempt. And mingling with the soil they walked on lay the dead body of Hugh, face downward. At the back of the boy's head, rimmed by blood-stiffened hair—the hair that had once been "as soft as the down of a bird"—was a big red hole. That hole was always pitilessly distinct. They stepped on him—heedlessly. They heeled the scattered stuff of his exquisite brain into the clay. . . .

From all such moods of horror Mr. Britling's circle of lamplight was his sole refuge. His work could conjure up visions, like opium visions, of a world of order and justice. Amidst the gloom of world bankruptcy he stuck to the prospectus of a braver enterprise—reckless of his chances of subscribers. . . .

§ 2

But this night even this circle of lamplight would not hold his mind. Doubt had crept into this last fastness. He pulled the papers towards him, and turned over the portion he had planned.

His purpose in the book he was beginning to write was to reason out the possible methods of government that would give a stabler, saner control to the world. He believed still in democracy, but he was realising more and more that democracy had yet to discover its method. It had to take hold of the consciences of men, it had to equip itself with still unformed organisations. Endless years of patient thinking, of experimenting, of discussion lay before mankind ere this great idea could become reality, and right, the proven right thing, could rule the earth.

Meanwhile the world must still remain a scene of bloodstained melodrama, of deafening noise, contagious follies, vast irrational destructions. One fine life after another went down from study and university and laboratory to be slain and silenced. . . .

Was it conceivable that this mad monster of mankind would ever be caught and held in the thin-spun webs of thought?

Was it, after all, anything but pretension and folly for a man to work out plans for the better government of the world?—was it any better than the ambitious scheming of some fly upon the wheel of the romantic gods?

Man has come, floundering and wounding and suffering, out of the breeding darknesses of Time, that will presently crush and consume him again. Why not flounder with the rest, why not eat, drink, fight, scream, weep and pray, forget Hugh, stop brooding upon Hugh, banish all these priggish dreams of "The Better Government of the World," and turn to the brighter aspects, the funny and adventurous aspects of the war, the Chestertonian jolliness, the *Punch* side of things. Think you because your sons are dead that there will be no more cakes and ale? Let mankind blunder out of the mud and blood as mankind has blundered in. . . .

Let us at any rate keep our precious Sense of Humour. . . .

He pulled his manuscript towards him. For a time he sat decorating the lettering of his title, "The Better Government of the World," with little grinning gnomes' heads and waggish tails. . . .

§ 3

On the top of Mr. Britling's desk, beside the clock, lay a letter, written in clumsy English and with its envelope resealed by a label which testified that it had been "OPENED BY CENSOR."

The friendly go-between in Norway had written to tell Mr. Britling that Herr Heinrich also was dead; he had died a wounded prisoner in Russia some months ago. He had been wounded and captured, after undergoing great hardships, during the great Russian attack upon the passes of the Carpathians in the early spring, and his wound had mortified. He had recovered partially for a time, and then he had been beaten and injured again in some struggle between German and Croatian prisoners, and he had sickened and died. Before he died he had written to his parents, and once again he had asked that the fiddle he had left in Mr. Britling's care should if possible be returned to them. It was manifest that both for him and them now it had become a symbol with many associations.

The substance of this letter invaded the orange circle of the lamp; it would have to be answered, and the potentialities of the answer were running through Mr. Britling's brain to the exclusion of any impersonal composition. He thought of the old parents away there in Pomerania—he believed but he was not quite sure, that Heinrich had been an only son—and of the pleasant spectacled figure that had now become a broken and decaying thing in a prisoner's shallow grave. . . .

Another son had gone—all the world was losing its sons. . . .

He found himself thinking of young Heinrich in the very manner, if with a lesser intensity, in which he thought about his own son, as of hopes senselessly destroyed. His mind took no note of the fact that Heinrich was an enemy, that by the reckoning of a "war of attrition" his death was balance and compensation for the death of Hugh. He went straight to the root fact that they had been gallant and kindly beings, and that the same thing had killed them both. . . .

By no conceivable mental gymnastics could he think of the two as antagonists. Between them there was no imaginable issue. They had both very much the same scientific disposition; with perhaps more dash and inspiration in the quality of Hugh; more docility and method in the case of Karl. Until war had smashed them one against the other. . . .

He recalled his first sight of Heinrich at the junction, and how he had laughed at the sight of his excessive Teutonism. The close-cropped shining fair head surmounted by a yellowish-white corps cap had appeared dodging about among the people upon the platform, and manifestly asking questions. The face had been very pink with the effort of an unaccustomed tongue. The young man had been clad in a suit of white flannel refined by a purple line; his boots were of that greenish-yellow leather that only a German student could esteem "chic"; his rucksack was upon his back, and the precious fiddle in its case was carried very carefully in one hand; this same dead fiddle. The other hand held a stick with a carved knob and a pointed end. He had been too German for belief. "Herr Heinrich!" Mr. Britling had said, and straightway the heels had clashed together for a bow, a bow from the waist, a bow that a heedless old lady much burthened with garden produce had greatly disarranged. From first to last amidst our offhand English ways Herr Heinrich had kept his bow—and always it had been getting disarranged.

That had been his constant effect; a little stiff, a little absurd, and always clean and pink and methodical. The boys had liked him without reserve, Mrs. Britling had liked him; everybody had found him a likeable creature. He never complained of anything except picnics. But he did object to picnics; to the sudden departure of the family to wild surroundings for the consumption of cold, knifeless and forkless meals in the serious middle hours of the day. He protested to Mr. Britling, respectfully but very firmly. It was, he held, implicit in their understanding that he should have a cooked meal in the middle of the day. Otherwise his Magen was perplexed and disordered. In the evening he could not eat with any gravity or profit. . . .

Their disposition towards underfeeding and a certain lack of fine sentiment were the only flaws in the English scheme that Herr Heinrich admitted. He certainly found the English unfeeling. His heart went even less satisfied than his Magen. He was a being of expressive affections; he wanted great friendships, mysterious relationships, love. He tried very bravely to revere and to understand and be occultly understood by Mr. Britling; he sought long walks and deep talks with Hugh and the small boys; he tried to fill his heart with Cissie; he found at last marvels of innocence and sweetness in the Hickson girl. She wore her hair in a pigtail when first he met her, and it made her almost Marguerite. This young man had cried aloud for love, warm and filling, like the Mittagsessen that was implicit in their understanding. And all these Essex people failed to satisfy him; they were silent, they were subtle, they slipped through the fat yet eager fingers of his heart, so that he fell back at last upon himself and his German correspondents and the idealisation of Maud Hickson and the moral education of Billy. Billy. Mr. Britling's memories came back at last to the figure of young Heinrich with the squirrel on his shoulder, that had so often stood in the way of the utter condemnation of Germany. That, seen closely, was the stuff of one brutal Prussian. What quarrel had we with him? . . .

Other memories of Heinrich flitted across Mr. Britling's reverie. Heinrich at hockey, running with extreme swiftness and little skill, tricked and baffled by Letty, dodged by Hugh, going headlong forward and headlong back, and then with a cry flinging himself flat on the ground exhausted. . . . Or again Heinrich very grave and very pink, peering through his glasses at his cards at Skat. . . . Or Heinrich in the boats upon the great pond, or Heinrich swimming, or Heinrich hiding very, very artfully from the boys about the garden on a theory of his own, or Heinrich in strange postures, stalking the deer in Claverings Park. For a time he had had a great ambition to creep quite close to a deer and *touch* it. . . . Or Heinrich indexing. He had a passion for listing and indexing books, music, any loose classifiable thing. His favourite amusement was devising schemes for the indentation of dictionary leaves, so that one could turn instantly to the needed word. He had bought and cut the edges of three dictionaries; each in succession improved upon the other; he had had great hopes of patents and wealth arising therefrom. . . And his room had been a source of strange sounds; his search for music upon the violin. He had hoped when he came to Matching's Easy to join "some string quartet." But Matching's Easy produced no string quartet. He had to fall back upon the pianola, and try to play duets with that. Only the pianola did all the duet itself, and in the hands of a small Britling was apt to betray a facetious moodiness; sudden alternations between extreme haste and extreme lassitude. . . .

Then there came a memory of Heinrich talking very seriously; his glasses magnifying his round blue eyes, talking of his ideas about life, of his beliefs and disbeliefs, of his ambitions and prospects in life.

He confessed two principal ambitions. They varied perhaps in their absolute dimensions, but they were of equal importance in his mind. The first of these was, so soon as he had taken his doctorate in philology, to give himself to the perfecting of an International Language; it was to combine all the virtues of Esperanto and Ido. "And then," said Herr Heinrich, "I do not think there will be any more wars—ever." The second ambition which was important first because Herr Heinrich found much delight in working at it, and secondly because he thought it would give him great wealth and opportunity for propagating the perfect speech, was the elaboration of his system of marginal indentations for dictionaries and alphabetical books of reference of all sorts. It was to be so complete that one would just stand over the book to be consulted, run hand and eye over its edges and open the book—"at the very exact spot." He proposed to follow this business up with a quite Germanic thoroughness. "Presently," he said, "I must study the machinery by which the edges of books are cut. It is possible I may have to invent these also." This was the double-barrelled scheme of Herr Heinrich's career. And along it he was to go, and incidentally develop his large vague heart that was at present so manifestly unsatisfied. . . .

Such was the brief story of Herr Heinrich.

That story was over—just as Hugh's story was over. That first volume would never now have a second and a third. It ended in some hasty grave in Russia. The great scheme for marginal indices would never be patented, the duets with the pianola would never be played again.

Imagination glimpsed a little figure toiling manfully through the slush and snow of the Carpathians; saw it staggering under its first experience of shell-fire; set it amidst attacks and flights and fatigue and hunger and a rush perhaps in the darkness; guessed at the wounding blow. Then came the pitiful pilgrimage of the prisoners into captivity, captivity in a land desolated, impoverished and embittered. Came wounds wrapped in filthy rags, pain and want of occupation, and a poor little bent and broken Heinrich sitting aloof in a crowded compound nursing a mortifying wound. . . .

He used always to sit in a peculiar attitude with his arms crossed on his legs, looking slantingly through his glasses. . . .

So he must have sat, and presently he lay on some rough bedding and suffered, untended, in infinite discomfort; lay motionless and thought at times, it may be, of Matching's Easy and wondered what Hugh and Teddy were doing. Then he became fevered, and the world grew bright-coloured and fantastic and ugly for him. Until one day an infinite weakness laid hold of him, and his pain grew faint and all his thoughts and memories grew faint—and still fainter. . . .

The violin had been brought into Mr. Britling's study that afternoon, and lay upon the farther window-seat. Poor little broken sherd, poor little fragment of a shattered life! It looked in its case like a baby in a coffin.

"I must write a letter to the old father and mother," Mr. Britling thought. "I can't just send the poor little fiddle—without a word. In all this pitiful storm of witless hate—surely there may be one greeting—not hateful.

"From my blackness to yours," said Mr. Britling aloud.

He would have to write it in English. But even if they knew no English some one would be found to translate it to them. He would have to write very plainly.

§ 4

He pushed aside the manuscript of "The Better Government of the World," and began to write rather slowly, shaping his letters roundly and distinctly:

Dear Sir,

I am writing this letter to you to tell you I am sending back the few little things I had kept for your son at his request when the war broke out. I am sending them——

Mr. Britling left that blank for the time until he could arrange the method of sending to the Norwegian intermediary.

Especially I am sending his violin, which he had asked me thrice to convey to you. Either it is a gift from you or it symbolised many things for him that he connected with home and you. I will have it packed with particular care, and I will do all in my power to ensure its safe arrival.

I want to tell you that all the stress and passion of this war has not made us here in Matching's Easy forget our friend your son. He was one of us, he had our affection, he had friends here who are still his friends. We found him honourable and companionable, and we share something of your loss. I have got together for you a few snap-shots I chance to possess in which you will see him in the sunshine, and which will enable you perhaps to picture a little more definitely than you would otherwise do the life he led here. There is one particularly that I have marked. Our family is lunching out-of-doors, and you will see that next to your son is a youngster, a year or so his junior, who is touching glasses with him. I have put a cross over his head. He is my eldest son, he was very dear to me, and he too has been killed in this war. They are, you see, smiling very pleasantly at each other.

While writing this Mr. Britling had been struck by the thought of the photographs, and he had taken them out of the little drawer into which he was accustomed to thrust them. He picked out the ones that showed the young German, but there were others, bright with sunshine, that were now charged with acquired significances; there were two showing the children and Teddy and Hugh and Cissie and Letty doing the goose-step, and there was one of Mr. Van der Pant, smiling at the front door, in Heinrich's abandoned slippers. There were endless pictures of Teddy also. It is the happy instinct of the Kodak to refuse those days that are overcast, and the photographic record of a life is a chain of all its kindlier aspects. In the drawer above these snap-shots there were Hugh's letters and a miscellany of trivial documents touching on his life.

Mr. Britling discontinued writing and turned these papers over and mused. Heinrich's letters and postcards had got in among them, and so had a letter of Teddy's. . . .

The letters reinforced the photographs in their reminder how kind and pleasant a race mankind can be. Until the wild asses of nationalism came kicking and slaying amidst them, until suspicion and jostling greed and malignity poison their minds, until the fools with the high explosives blow that elemental goodness into shrieks of hate and splashes of blood. How kindly men are—up to the very instant of their cruelties! His mind teemed suddenly with little anecdotes and histories of the goodwill of men breaking through the ill-will of war, of the mutual help of sorely wounded Germans and English lying together in the mud and darkness between the trenches, of the fellowship of captors and prisoners, of the Saxons at Christmas fraternising with the English.... Of that he had seen photographs in one of the daily papers....

His mind came back presently from these wanderings to the task before him.

He tried to picture these Heinrich parents. He supposed they were kindly, civilised people. It was manifest the youngster had come to him from a well-ordered and gentle-spirited home. But he imagined them—he could not tell why—as people much older than himself. Perhaps young Heinrich had on some occasion said they were old people—he could not remember. And he had a curious impulse too to write to them in phrases of consolation; as if their loss was more pitiable than his own. He doubted whether they had the consolation of his sanguine temperament, whether they could resort as readily as he could to his faith, whether in Pomerania there was the same consoling possibility of an essay on the Better Government of the World. He did not think this very clearly, but that was what was at the back of his mind. He went on writing.

If you think that these two boys have both perished, not in some noble common cause but one against the other in a struggle of dynasties and boundaries and trade routes and tyrannous ascendancies, then it seems to me that you must feel as I feel that this war is the most tragic and dreadful thing that has ever happened to mankind.

He sat thinking for some minutes after he had written that, and when presently he resumed his writing, a fresh strain of thought was traceable even in his opening sentence.

If you count dead and wounded this is the most dreadful war in history; for you as for me, it has been almost the extremity of personal tragedy. . . . Black sorrow. . . .

But is it the most dreadful war?

I do not think it is. I can write to you and tell you that I do indeed believe that our two sons have died not altogether in vain. Our pain and anguish may not be wasted—may be necessary. Indeed they may be necessary. Here am I bereaved and wretched—and I hope. Never was the fabric of war so black; that I admit. But never was the black fabric of war so threadbare. At a thousand points the light is shining through.

Mr. Britling's pen stopped.

There was perfect stillness in the study bedroom.

"The tinpot style," said Mr. Britling at last in a voice of extreme bitterness.

He fell into an extraordinary quarrel with his style. He forgot about those Pomeranian parents altogether in his exasperation at his own inexpressiveness, at his incomplete control of these rebel words and phrases that came trailing each its own associations and suggestions to hamper his purpose with it. He read over the offending sentence.

"The point is that it is true," he whispered. "It is exactly what I want to say." . . .

Exactly? . . .

His mind stuck on that "exactly." . . . When one has much to say style is troublesome. It is as if one fussed with one's uniform before a battle. . . . But that is just what one ought to do before a battle. . . . One ought to have everything in order. . . .

He took a fresh sheet and made three trial beginnings.

"War is like a black fabric." . . .

"War is a curtain of black fabric across the pathway."

"War is a curtain of dense black fabric across all the hopes and kindliness of mankind. Yet always it has let through some gleams of light, and now—I am not dreaming—it grows threadbare, and here and there and at a thousand points the light is breaking through. We owe it to all these dear youths——"

His pen stopped again.

"I must work on a rough draft," said Mr. Britling.

§ 5

Three hours later Mr. Britling was working by daylight, though his study lamp was still burning, and his letter to old Heinrich was still no better than a collection of material for a letter. But the material was falling roughly into shape, and Mr. Britling's intentions were finding themselves. It was clear to him now that he was no longer writing as his limited personal self to those two personal selves grieving, in the old large high-walled steep-roofed household amidst pinewoods, of which Heinrich had once shown him a picture. He knew them too little for any such personal address. He was writing, he perceived, not as Mr. Britling but as an Englishman—that was all he could be to them—and he was writing to them as Germans; he could apprehend them as nothing more. He was just England bereaved to Germany bereaved. . . .

He was no longer writing to the particular parents of one particular boy, but to all that mass of suffering, regret, bitterness and fatigue that lay behind the veil of the "front."

Slowly, steadily, the manhood of Germany was being wiped out. As he sat there in the stillness he could think that at least two million men of the Central Powers were dead, and an equal number maimed and disabled. Compared with that our British losses, immense and universal as they were by the standard of any previous experience, were still slight; our larger armies had still to suffer, and we had lost irrevocably not very much more than a quarter of a million. But the tragedy gathered against us. We knew enough already to know what must be the reality of the German homes to which those dead men would nevermore return. . . .

If England had still the longer account to pay, the French had paid already nearly to the limits of endurance. They must have lost well over a million of their mankind, and still they bled and bled. Russia too in the East had paid far more than man for man in this vast swapping off of lives. In a little while no Censorship would hold the voice of the peoples. There would be no more talk of honour and annexations, hegemonies and trade routes, but only Europe lamenting for her dead. . . .

The Germany to which he wrote would be a nation of widows and children, rather pinched boys and girls, crippled men, old men, deprived men, men who had lost brothers and cousins and friends and ambitions. No triumph now on land or sea could save Germany from becoming that. France too would be that, Russia, and lastly Britain, each in their degree. Before the war there had been no Germany to which an Englishman could appeal; Germany had been a threat, a menace, a terrible trampling of armed men. It was as little possible then to think of talking to Germany as it would have been to stop the Kaiser in mid-career in his hooting car down the Unter den Linden and demand a quiet talk with him. But the Germany that had watched those rushes with a slightly doubting pride had her eyes now full of tears and blood. She had believed, she had obeyed, and no real victory had come. Still she fought on, bleeding, agonising, wasting her substance and the substance of the whole world, to no conceivable end but exhaustion, so capable she was, so devoted, so proud and utterly foolish. And the mind of Germany, whatever it was before the war, would now be something residual, something left over and sitting beside a reading-lamp as he was sitting beside a reading-lamp, thinking, sorrowing, counting the cost, looking into the dark future. . . .

And to that he wrote, to that dimly apprehended figure outside a circle of the light like his own circle of light—which was the father of Heinrich, which was great Germany, Germany which lived before and which will yet outlive the flapping of the eagles. . . .

Our boys, he wrote, *have died, fighting one against the other. They have been fighting upon an issue so obscure that your German press is still busy discussing what it was. For us it was that Belgium was invaded and France in danger of destruction. Nothing else could have brought the English into the field against you. But why you invaded Belgium and France and whether that might have been averted we do not know to this day. And still this war goes on and still more boys die, and these men who do not fight, these men in the newspaper offices and in the ministries, plan campaigns and strokes and counter-strokes that belong to no conceivable plan at all. Except that now for them there is something more terrible than war. And that is the day of reckoning with their own people.*

What have we been fighting for? What are we fighting for? Do you know? Does any one know? Why am I spending what is left of my substance and you what is left of yours to keep on this war against each other? What have we to gain from hurting one another still further? Why should we be puppets any longer in the hands of crowned fools and witless diplomatists? Even if we were dumb and acquiescent before, does not the blood of our sons now cry out to us that this foolery should cease? We have let these people send our sons to death.

It is you and I who must stop these wars, these massacres of boys.

Massacres of boys! That indeed is the essence of modern war. The killing off of the young. It is the destruction of the human inheritance, it is the spending of all the life and material of the future upon present-day hate and greed. Fools and knaves, politicians, tricksters, and those who trade on the suspicious and thoughtless, generous angers of men, make wars; the indolence and modesty of the mass of men permit them. Are you and I to suffer such things until the whole fabric of our civilisation, that has been so slowly and so laboriously built up, is altogether destroyed?

When I sat down to write to you I had meant only to write to you of your son and mine. But I feel that what can be said in particular of our loss, need not be said: it can be understood without saying. What needs to be said and written about is this, that war must be put an end to and that nobody else but you and me and all of us can do it. We have to do that for the love of our sons and our race and all that is human. War is no longer human; the chemist and the metallurgist have changed all that. My boy was shot through the eye; his brain was blown to pieces by some man who never knew what he had done. Think what that means! . . . It is plain to me, surely it is plain to you and all the world, that war is now a mere putting of the torch to explosives that flare out to universal ruin. There is nothing for one sane man to write to another about in these days but the salvation of mankind from war.

Now I want you to be patient with me and hear me out. There was a time in the earlier part of this war when it was hard to be patient because there hung over us the dread of losses and disaster. Now we need dread no longer. The dreaded thing has happened. Sitting together as we do in spirit beside the mangled bodies of our dead, surely we can be as patient as the hills.

I want to tell you quite plainly and simply that I think that Germany, which is chief and central in this war, is most to blame for this war. Writing to you as an Englishman to a German and with war still being waged, there must be no mistake between us upon this point. I am persuaded that in the decade that ended with your overthrow of France in 1871, Germany turned her face towards evil, and that her refusal to treat France generously and to make friends with any other great power in the world, is the essential cause of this war. Germany triumphed—and she trampled on the loser. She inflicted intolerable indignities. She set herself to prepare for further aggressions; long before this killing began she was making war upon land and sea, launching warships, building strategic railways, setting up a vast establishment of war material, threatening, straining all the world to keep pace with her threats. . . . At last there was no choice before any European nation but submission to the German will, or war. And it was no will to which righteous men could possibly submit. It came as an illiberal and ungracious will. It was the will of Zabern. It is not as if you had set yourselves to be an imperial people and embrace and unify the world. You did not want to unify the world. You wanted to set the foot of an intensely national

468

Germany, a sentimental and illiberal Germany, a Germany that treasured the portraits of your ridiculous Kaiser and his litter of sons, a Germany wearing uniform, reading black letter, and despising every kultur but her own, upon the neck of a divided and humiliated mankind. It was an intolerable prospect. I had rather the whole world died.

Forgive me for writing "you." You are as little responsible for that Germany as I am for—Sir Edward Grey. But this happened over you; you did not do your utmost to prevent it—even as England has happened, and I have let it happen over me. . . .

"It is so dry; so general," whispered Mr. Britling. "And yet—it is this that has killed our sons."

He sat still for a time, and then went on reading a fresh sheet of his manuscript.

When I bring these charges against Germany I have little disposition to claim any righteousness for Britain. There has been small splendour in this war for either Germany or Britain or Russia; we three have chanced to be the biggest of the combatants, but the glory lies with invincible France. It is France and Belgium and Serbia who shine as the heroic lands. They have fought defensively and beyond all expectation, for dear land and freedom. This war for them has been a war of simple, definite issues, to which they have risen with an entire nobility. Englishman and German alike may well envy them that simplicity. I look to you, as an honest man schooled by the fierce lessons of this war, to meet me in my passionate desire to see France, Belgium and Serbia emerge restored from all this blood and struggle, enlarged to the limits of their nationality, vindicated and secure. Russia I will not write about here; let me go on at once to tell you about my own

469

country; remarking only that between England and Russia there are endless parallelisms. We have similar complexities, kindred difficulties. We have for instance an imported dynasty, we have a soul-destroying State Church which cramps and poisons the education of our ruling class, we have a people out of touch with a secretive government, and the same traditional contempt for science. We have our Irelands and Polands. Even our kings bear a curious likeness. . . .

At this point there was a break in the writing, and Mr. Britling made, as it were, a fresh beginning.

Politically the British Empire is a clumsy collection of strange accidents. It is a thing as little to be proud of as the outline of a flint or the shape of a potato. For the mass of English people India and Egypt and all that side of our system mean less than nothing; our trade is something they do not understand, our imperial wealth something they do not share. Britain has been a group of four democracies caught in the net of a vast yet casual imperialism; the common man here is in a state of political perplexity from the cradle to the grave. None the less there is a great people here even as there is a great people in Russia, a people with a soul and character of its own, a people of unconquerable kindliness and with a peculiar genius, which still struggle towards will and expression. We have been beginning that same great experiment that France and America and Switzerland and China are making, the experiment of democracy. It is the newest form of human association, and we are still but half awake to its needs and necessary conditions. For it is idle to pretend that the little city democracies of ancient times were comparable to the great essays in practical republicanism that mankind is making today. This age of the democratic republics that dawns is a new age. It has not yet lasted for a century, not for a paltry hundred years. . . . All new things are weak things; a rat can kill a man child with ease; the greater the destiny, the weaker the immediate self-protection may be. And to me it seems that your complete and perfect imperialism, ruled by Germans for Germans, is in its scope and outlook a more antiquated and smaller and less noble thing than these sprawling emergent giant democracies of the West that struggle so confusedly against it. . . .

But we do not struggle confusedly, with pitiful leaders and infinite waste and endless delay; that it is to our indisciplines and to the dishonesties and tricks our incompleteness provokes, that the prolongation of this war is to be ascribed I readily admit. At the outbreak of this war I had hoped to see militarism felled within a year. . . .

§ 6

From this point onward Mr. Britling's notes became more fragmentary. They had a consecutiveness, but they were discontinuous. His thought had leaped across gaps that his pen had had no time to fill. And he had begun to realise that his letter to the old people in Pomerania was becoming impossible. It had broken away into dissertation.

"Yet there must be dissertations," he said. "Unless such men as we are take these things in hand, always we shall be misgoverned, always the sons will die. . . ."

§ 7

I do not think you Germans realise how steadily you were conquering the world before this war began. Had you given half the energy and intelligence you have spent upon this war to the peaceful conquest of men's minds and spirits, I believe that you would have taken the leadership of the world tranquilly—no man disputing. Your science was five years, your social and economic organisation was a quarter of a century, in front of ours. . . . Never has it so lain in the power of a great people to lead and direct mankind towards the world republic and universal peace. It needed but a certain generosity of the imagination. . . .

But your Junkers, your Imperial court, your foolish vicious Princes; what were such dreams to them? . . . With an envious satisfaction they hurled all the accomplishment of Germany into the fires of war. . . .

§ 8

Your boy, as no doubt you know, dreamt constantly of such a world peace as this that I have foreshadowed; he was more generous than his country. He could envisage war and hostility only as misunderstanding. He thought that a world that could explain itself clearly would surely be at peace. He was scheming always therefore for the perfection and propagation of Esperanto or Ido, or some such universal link. My youngster too was full of a kindred and yet larger dream, the dream of human science, which knows neither king nor country nor race. . . .

These boys, these hopes, this war has killed. . . .

That fragment ended so. Mr. Britling ceased to read for a time. "But has it killed them?" he whispered. . . .

"If you had lived, my dear, you and your England would have talked with a younger Germany—better than I can ever do. . . ."

He turned the pages back, and read here and there with an accumulating discontent.

§ 9

"Dissertations," said Mr. Britling.

Never had it been so plain to him that he was a weak, silly, ill-informed, and hasty-minded writer, and never had he felt so invincible a conviction that the Spirit of God was in him, and that it fell to him to take some part in the establishment of a new order of living upon the earth; it might be the most trivial part by the scale of the task, but for him it was to be now his supreme concern. And it was an almost intolerable grief to him that his services should be, for all his desire, so poor in quality, so weak in conception. Always he seemed to be on the verge of some illuminating and beautiful statement of his cause; always he was finding his writing inadequate, a thin treachery to the impulse of his heart, always he was finding his effort weak and ineffective. In this instance, at the outset he seemed to see with a golden clearness the message of brotherhood, of forgiveness, of a common call. To whom could such a message be better addressed than to those sorrowing parents; from whom could it come with a better effect than from himself? And now he read what he had made of this message. It seemed to his jaded mind a pitifully jaded effort. It had no light, it had no depth. It was like the disquisition of a debating society.

He was distressed by a fancy of an old German couple, spectacled and peering, puzzled by his letter. Perhaps they would be obscurely hurt by his perplexing generalisations. Why, they would ask, should this Englishman preach to them?

He sat back in his chair wearily, with his chin sunk upon his chest. For a time he did not think, and then he read again the sentence in front of his eyes.

"These boys, these hopes, this war has killed."

The words hung for a time in his mind.

"No!" said Mr. Britling stoutly. "They live!"

And suddenly it was borne in upon his mind that he was not alone. There were thousands and tens of thousands of men and women like himself, desiring with all their hearts to say, as he desired to say, the reconciling word. It was not only his hand that thrust against the obstacles. . . . Frenchmen and Russians sat in the same stillness, facing the same perplexities; there were Germans seeking a way through to him. Even as he sat and wrote. And for the first time clearly he felt a Presence of which he had thought very many times in the last few weeks, a Presence so close to him that it was behind his eyes and in his brain and hands. It was no trick of his vision: it was a feeling of immediate reality. And it was Hugh, Hugh that he had thought was dead, it was young Heinrich living also, it was himself, it was those others that sought, it was all these and it was more, it was the Master, the Captain of Mankind, it was God, there present with him, and he knew that it was God. It was as if he had been groping all this time in the darkness, thinking himself alone amidst rocks and pitfalls and pitiless things, and suddenly a hand, a firm strong hand, had touched his own. And a voice within him bade him be of good courage. There was no magic trickery in that moment; he was still weak and weary; a discouraged rhetorician, a good intention ill equipped; but he was no longer lonely and wretched, no longer in the same world with despair. God was beside him and within him and about him. . . . It was the crucial moment of Mr. Britling's life. It was a thing as light as the passing of a cloud on an April morning; it was a thing as great as the first day of creation. For some moments he still sat back with his chin upon his chest and his hands dropping from the arms of his chair. Then he sat up and drew a deep breath. . . .

This had come almost as a matter of course.

For weeks his mind had been playing about this idea. He had talked to Letty of this Finite God, who is the king of man's adventure in space and time. But hitherto God had been for him a thing of the intelligence, a theory, a report, something told about but not realised. . . . Mr. Britling's thinking about God hitherto had been like some one who has found an empty house, very beautiful and pleasant, full of the promise of a fine personality. And then as the discoverer makes his lonely, curious explorations, he hears downstairs, dear and friendly, the voice of the Master coming in. . . .

There was no need to despair because he himself was one of the feeble folk. God was with him indeed, and he was with God. The King was coming to his own. Amidst the darkness and confusions, the nightmare cruelties and the hideous stupidities of the great war, God, the Captain of the World Republic, fought his way to empire. So long as one did one's best and utmost in a cause so mighty, did it matter though the thing one did was little and poor?

"I have thought too much of myself," said Mr. Britling, "and of what I would do by myself. I have forgotten *that which was with me. . . .*"

§ 10

He turned over the rest of the night's writing presently, and read it now as though it was the work of another man.

475

These later notes were fragmentary, and written in a sprawling hand.

"Let us make ourselves watchers and guardians of the order of the world. . . .

"If only for love of our dead. . . .

"Let us pledge ourselves to service. Let us set ourselves with all our minds and with all our hearts to the perfecting and working out of the methods of democracy and the ending for ever of the kings and emperors and priestcrafts and the bands of adventurers, the traders and owners and forestallers who have betrayed mankind into this morass of hate and blood—in which our sons are lost—in which we flounder still. . . ."

How feeble was this squeak of exhortation! It broke into a scolding note.

"Who have betrayed," read Mr. Britling, and judged the phrase.

"Who have fallen with us," he emended. . . .

"One gets so angry and bitter—because one feels alone, I suppose. Because one feels that for them one's reason is no reason. One is enraged by the sense of their silent and regardless contradiction, and one forgets the Power of which one is a part. . . ."

The sheet that bore the sentence he criticised was otherwise blank except that written across it obliquely in a very careful hand were the words "Hugh" and "Hugh Philip Britling." . . .

On the next sheet he had written: "Let us set up the peace of the World Republic amidst these ruins. Let it be our religion, our calling."

There he had stopped.

The last sheet of Mr. Britling's manuscript may be more conveniently given in facsimile than described.

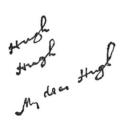

§ 11

He sighed.

He looked at the scattered papers, and thought of the letter they were to have made.

His fatigue spoke first.

"Perhaps after all I'd better just send the fiddle. . . ."

He rested his cheeks between his hands, and remained so for a long time. His eyes stared unseeingly. His thoughts wandered and spread and faded. At length he recalled his mind to that last idea. "Just send the fiddle without a word."

"No. I must write to them plainly.

"About God as I have found Him.

"As He has found me. . . ."

He forgot the Pomeranians for a time. He murmured to himself. He turned over the conviction that had suddenly become clear and absolute in his mind.

"Religion is the first thing and the last thing, and until a man has found God and been found by God, he begins at no beginning, he works to no end. He may have his friendships, his partial loyalties, his scraps of honour. But all these things fall into place and life falls into place only with God. Only with God. God, who fights through men against Blind Force and Night and Non-Existence; who is the end, who is the meaning. He is the only King. . . . Of course I must write about Him. I must tell all my world of Him. And before the coming of the true King, the inevitable King, the King who is present whenever just men forgather, this bloodstained rubbish of the ancient world, these puny kings and tawdry emperors, these wily politicians and artful lawyers, these men who claim and grab and trick and compel, these war-makers and oppressors, will presently shrivel and pass—like paper thrust into a flame. . . ."

Then after a time he said:

"Our sons who have shown us God. . . ."

§ 12

He rubbed his open hands over his eyes and forehead.

The night of effort had tired his brain, and he was no longer thinking actively. He had a little interval of blankness, sitting at his desk with his hands pressed over his eyes. . . .

He got up presently, and stood quite motionless at the window, looking out.

His lamp was still burning, but for some time he had not been writing by the light of his lamp. Insensibly the day had come and abolished his need for that individual circle of yellow light. Colour had returned to the world, clean pearly colour, clear and definite like the glance of a child or the voice of a girl, and a golden wisp of cloud hung in the sky over the tower of the church. There was a mist upon the pond, a soft grey mist not a yard high. A covey of partridges ran and halted and ran again in the dewy grass outside his garden railings. The partridges were very numerous this year because there had been so little shooting. Beyond in the meadow a hare sat up as still as a stone. A horse neighed. . . . Wave after wave of warmth and light came sweeping before the sunrise across the world of Matching's Easy. It was as if there was nothing but morning and sunrise in the world.

From away towards the church came the sound of some early worker whetting a scythe.

THE END.

479